THE RULES OF SEDUCTION

"Hunter is masterful at drawing readers in and creating realistic characters and powerful emotions so that each of her romances both satisfies readers and leaves them anxious for the next book."

—*Booklist*

"Rich in plot and characters, rich in wit and emotion, and rich in satisfaction for any reader."

—*Romance Reviews Today*

"A carefully crafted, riveting romance showcasing Hunter's talent for both great storytelling and unforgettable romance. Her strong hero and equally fascinating heroine make this an irresistible read.... Hunter finds herself in the enviable position of being a writer whose novels every reader will adore."

—*Romantic Times*

LORD OF SIN

"Snappily paced and bone-deep satisfying, Hunter's books are so addictive they should come with a surgeon general's warning. [Hunter] doesn't neglect the absorbing historical details that set her apart from most of her counterparts, engaging the reader's mind even as she deftly captures the heart."

—*Publishers Weekly*

THE ROMANTIC

"Every woman dreams of being the object of some man's secret passion, and readers will be swept away by Hunter's hero and her latest captivating romance."

—*Booklist*

THE SINNER

"Packed with sensuality and foreboding undertones, this book boasts rich historical details and characters possessing unusual depth and vitality, traits that propel it beyond the standard historical romance fare."

—*Publishers Weekly*

"Sensual, intriguing, and absorbing, prolific Hunter scores again."

—*Booklist*

"There are books you finish with a sigh because they are so rich, so tender, so near to the heart that they will stay with you for a long, long time. Madeline Hunter's historical romance, *The Sinner,* is such a book."

—*Oakland Press*

THE CHARMER

"With its rich historical texture, steamy love scenes, and indelible protagonists, this book embodies the best of the genre."

—*Publishers Weekly (starred review)*

"In yet another excellent offering from Hunter, her intriguing characters elicit both fascination and sympathy."

—*Booklist*

THE SAINT

"[An] amusing, witty, and intriguing account of how love helps, not hinders, the achievement of dreams."

—*Booklist*

THE SEDUCER

"Hunter . . . sweeps both her readers and her characters up in the embrace of history. Lush in detail and thrumming with sensuality, this offering will thrill those looking for a tale as rich and satisfying as a multicourse gourmet meal."

—*Publishers Weekly*

"*The Seducer* is a well-crafted novel. . . . Characteristically intense and frankly sexual."

—*Contra Costa Times*

"[An] intriguing and redemptive tale."

—*Booklist*

"Angst and passion battle it out in this very sensual story."

—*Oakland Press*

LORD OF A THOUSAND NIGHTS

"Hunter's fresh, singular voice and firm grasp of history set this lively 14th-century romance apart. An electrifying blend of history, romance, and intrigue, this fast-paced tale is a testament to Hunter's considerable narrative prowess."

—*Publishers Weekly*

"I have enjoyed every novel Ms. Hunter has penned to date, and it's difficult to say, but each one seems better than the one before. *Lord of a Thousand Nights* is no exception; it's a masterpiece of storytelling, one that stands alone as a superb read, and one I very highly recommend."

—*Romance Reviews Today*

THE PROTECTOR

"Hunter is at home with this medieval setting, and her talent for portraying intelligent, compelling characters seems to develop with each book. This feisty tale is likely to win her the broader readership she deserves."

—*Publishers Weekly*

"Madeline Hunter has restored my faith in historicals and in the medieval romance especially. *The Protector* is definitely a wonderful read."

—*All About Romance*

BY DESIGN

"Realistic details that make the reader feel they are truly living in the 13th century enhance a story of love that knows no bounds; not social, political, or economic barriers. Ms. Hunter's knowledge of the period and her ability to create three-dimensional characters who interact with history make her an author medievalists will adore."

—*Romantic Times*

"I'd heard a lot about the previous two books in this trilogy, *By Arrangement* and *By Possession*, but little did that prepare me for the experience that was reading this book. Whether you've already enjoyed Ms. Hunter's books or she is a new-to-you author, this is a wonderful, sensual, masterfully written tale of love overcoming odds, and one I heartily recommend."

—*All About Romance*

"With each of the books in this series, Ms. Hunter's skill shines like a beacon."

—*Rendezvous*

"Ms. Hunter has raised the bar, adding depth and texture to the medieval setting. With well-crafted characters and a delightful love story, *By Design* is well-plotted and well-timed without the contrived plot twists so often used in romances. I highly recommend *By Design* not only to lovers of medieval romance but to all readers."

—*Romance Reviews Today*

BY POSSESSION

"With the release of this new volume, [Madeline Hunter] cements her position as one of the brightest new writers in the genre. Brimming with intelligent writing, historical detail, and passionate, complex protagonists . . . Hunter makes 14th-century England come alive—from the details of its sights, sounds, and smells to the political context of this rebellious and dangerous time, when alliances and treason went hand in hand. For all the historical richness of the story, the romantic aspect is never lost, and the poignancy of the characters' seemingly untenable love is truly touching."

—*Publishers Weekly*

"Madeline Hunter's tale is a pleasant read with scenes that show the writer's brilliance. *By Possession* is rich in description and details that readers of romance will savor."

—*Oakland Press*

"Ms. Hunter skillfully weaves historical details into a captivating love story that resounds with sights, sounds, and more of the Middle Ages. This is another breathtaking romance from a talented storyteller."

—*Romantic Times*

"With elegance and intelligence, Ms. Hunter consolidates her position as one of the best new voices in romantic fiction. I'm waiting on tenterhooks to see what is in store for readers in her next book, *By Design*."

—*Romance Journal*

BY ARRANGEMENT

"Debut author Hunter begins this new series with a thoroughly satisfying launch that leaves the reader eager for the next episode in the lives of her engaging characters."

—*Publishers Weekly*

"Romance author Madeline Hunter makes a dazzling debut into the genre with her medieval *By Arrangement*, a rich historical with unforgettable characters. . . . Layered with intrigue, history, passion, and multidimensional characters, this book has it all. Quite simply, it's one of the best books I've read this year."

—*Oakland Press*

"The first in a marvelous trilogy by a fresh voice in the genre, *By Arrangement* combines historical depth and riveting romance in a manner reminiscent of Roberta Gellis. Ms. Hunter has a true gift for bringing both history and her characters to life, making readers feel a part of the danger and pageantry of the era."

—*Romantic Times*

"*By Arrangement* is richly textured, historically fascinating, and filled with surprises."

—*All About Romance*

"Splendid in every way."

—*Rendezvous*

LESSONS
of
DESIRE

Madeline Hunter

BANTAM BOOKS

LESSONS OF DESIRE
A Bantam Book / October 2007

PUBLISHED BY
Bantam Dell
A Division of Random House, Inc.
New York, New York

ISBN: 978-0-440-24394-6

Printed in the United States of America
Published simultaneously in Canada

www.bantamdell.com

OPM 10 9 8 7 6 5 4 3 2

LESSONS

of

DESIRE

CHAPTER ONE

A man who has committed a crime needs to cover his tracks, even if he made them while wearing the best shoes that money can buy.

In order to cover his, Lord Elliot Rothwell reentered his family's London home amidst the late arrivals to his brother's ball. He acted like a young man who had briefly gone out to take some air on this glorious, breezy May night.

With one step over the threshold he no longer entered but instead greeted. The tall, handsome, youngest brother of the fourth Marquess of Easterbrook—the Rothwell sibling considered the most amiable and normal—bestowed smiles on everyone and very warm ones on certain ladies.

A quarter hour later Elliot slid into a conversation with Lady Falrith as smoothly as he had just slipped back into the ballroom. He resumed a topic aborted two hours earlier, and flattered the lady so adroitly that she forgot that he had excused himself long ago. Within minutes Lady Falrith ceased to care about the passage of time.

While Elliot charmed Lady Falrith he scanned the crush in the ballroom for his brother. Not his brother Hayden, who along with his new wife, Alexia, was hosting this ball. He sought the eye of his other brother, Christian, Marquess of Easterbrook.

Christian's gaze never met his but Elliot's return to the ball was noted. Christian disengaged from a circle of lords on the far side of the room and walked to the door.

Elliot danced a waltz with Lady Falrith before continuing this night's mission. He did so in penance for using the lady, and in silent thanks for her unwitting aid. Lady Falrith's sense of time could be fluid, and her memory very optimistic. By the morning she would believe that Elliot had attended on her all night and was in pursuit of her. Her confidence in her own appeal would prove useful should something untoward develop regarding his activities in the city tonight.

The waltz over, he again excused himself. Unlike Christian, who had walked in isolation and with purpose for the door, Elliot strolled down the ballroom sociably, greeting and chatting until he sidled next to his new sister-in-law, Alexia.

"It is going well, don't you agree?" she asked. Her gaze swept the chamber, seeking empirical confirmation.

"It is a triumph, Alexia." And it was, for her. A triumph of spirit and character, and maybe a triumph of love.

Alexia was not the sort of woman whom society had expected Hayden to marry. She had no family and no fortune. She was so sensible that she had never learned how to dissemble, let alone flirt. Yet here she was hosting a grand ball in the home of a marquess, her dark hair impeccably styled and her headdress and garments the last word in fashion. The penniless orphan had married a man who loved her in a way he had never loved before.

Elliot trusted the marriage would be a good one. Alexia would see to that. History had proven that love was a dangerous emotion for Rothwell men. Sensible, practical Alexia would know how to use the love to keep the danger corralled, however. Elliot suspected that she had already tamed the beast several times.

He joined her in admiring the night's success. In the far corner a small, pale woman held court. One too many plumes flourished in the headdress decorating her blonde hair. All the while she kept one gleaming eye on the male attention being paid to a pretty girl nearby.

"The triumph is yours, Alexia, but I think that my aunt intends to take home the biggest prize this hunting season."

"Your aunt Henrietta is understandably happy about Caroline's first season. Two titles have paid addresses of late. However, she is vexed with me tonight because I did not invite one of those titles to this ball, despite her command to do so."

Elliot had little interest in his aunt's vexations. He did, however, have a strong interest in the guest list.

"I have not seen Miss Blair, Alexia. No black habits. No undressed hair. Did Hayden forbid you to invite her?"

"Not at all. Phaedra is abroad. She embarked over a fortnight ago."

He did not want to appear too curious, but... "Abroad, you say?"

Her violet eyes warmed with humor. She gave him all of her attention, which, considering the subject, he would rather not have.

"Naples first, then a tour of the south. I told her that you say it is unwise to visit Italy in the heat of summer, but she spoke of desiring to investigate the rituals and feasts of that season." She inclined her head confidentially. "I believe that her father's passing affected her more than she admits. Her final meeting with him was an emotional one. It distressed her. I believe she undertook this voyage in order to lift her spirits."

He did not doubt a deathbed parting with a father could be emotional. His own had touched him indelibly. Tonight, however, he was more interested in Miss Blair's whereabouts, and in matters that had been discussed with her father before they made that permanent farewell.

"If you know where she planned to reside in Naples, I will call on her when I go if she is still there."

"She did leave a residence that she hoped to use. She had learned about it from a friend. If she has not returned prior to your own journey, I will be grateful if you call on her. Her independence sometimes leads to carelessness, so I do worry about her."

He doubted Phaedra Blair took well anyone's worrying about her. Alexia was very good to do so anyway.

"Oh, dear," muttered Alexia.

He saw what caused the sigh that followed. Henrietta

aimed for them, her plumes dancing and her dreamy, sparkling eyes displaying glints of determination.

"I think she is after *you*," Alexia whispered. "Float away, or she will bend your ear complaining how Easterbrook permitted me to host a ball without asking for her agreement. She thinks her residence in this house makes her the mistress of it."

Elliot could float with the best of them. He was long gone downstream before his aunt arrived.

After a quick cut to the servants' corridor and a fast nip up the back stairs, Elliot approached Christian's chambers. He entered the sitting room to find his brother lounging in a chair in the corner.

The sharp look Christian shot at him proved Easterbrook's mind was not nearly as relaxed as his body.

"I did not find it," Elliot said, answering the question those dark eyes asked. "If it is in his offices or his home, it is very well hidden."

Christian audibly exhaled. The sound carried his annoyance that this matter had recently interrupted his freedom to spend his days doing whatever it was that he normally did. Elliot had no idea what those activities might be. No one really knew what Christian was about anymore.

"On knowing he was about to die, he may have burned it," Elliot suggested.

"Merris Langton displayed a character that was unlikely to think of sparing others, even when he was at death's door." Christian crooked a finger under the top of his perfectly tied cravat and gave a little yank to loosen it.

Christian appeared splendid tonight, every inch the lord of the realm. His coats and linens announced their superior quality with every thread. His gesture with the cravat hinted at his discomfort with the night's formality, however, as surely as the long queue of his unfashionably long, dark hair indicated his eccentric bent.

Elliot assumed his brother longed to shed the sartorial symbols of civilization and swathe himself in that exotic robe he often wore. One normally found him barefoot in these chambers, not wearing silk hose and pumps. Currently the only hint of his normal dishabille in the house was the unbuttoned frock coat and the liquid manner in which his tall body molded itself to the chair's upholstery.

"You checked for loose floorboards and such?" Christian asked.

"I risked discovery to do so. I was in both buildings too long, and a constable passed by as I left the City offices. It is dark, there was no lamp near the door, however . . ."

His description of his adventure suggested more caution than he had experienced. He believed there were occasions when there was no choice except to break a law, but he had never expected to be so coldly indifferent to doing so when such an occasion arrived for him.

"You have been at this ball all night, should any questions arise," Christian said. "Langton owned a small publishing house that favored radical texts. He was also a man with a taste for blackmail, as we have learned. The pity is that he went and died before I could pay him off. Now Richard Drury's manuscript is God knows where, and its sordid lie about our father may yet see the light of day."

"I will make sure it does not."

"Do you think someone else got to it before you? I am probably not the only person Langton approached."

"I saw no indication that anyone had gone through his belongings yet. Not even his solicitor or executor. He was only buried this afternoon. I do not think it was in either place when he died."

"That is damned inconvenient."

"Inconvenient but not insurmountable. I will find it, and I will destroy it if necessary."

Christian's attention narrowed on him. "You speak with confidence. You know where that damned manuscript is, don't you?"

"I have a good idea. If I am right, we will be done with this soon. It may still cost you."

"Pay. Richard Drury was a member of Parliament and, despite his extreme views, a respected intellectual. If his memoirs include such an accusation against my father, many will believe it."

They will believe it because it fits with what they already think to be true. Elliot did not voice the response, but it had whispered in his head since first hearing that Merris Langton planned to publish Richard Drury's posthumous memoirs. The book would include secrets and gossip that reflected badly on many of the great and powerful, both past and present. The accusation it purportedly contained about their father fit too well what society already assumed about his parents' marriage.

Society had been wrong about most of it, however. His own father had explained that to him at a moment when men do not lie.

You were her favorite. She kept you to herself and I allowed it since you were the youngest. It was a relief to see her remember she was a mother at times. Only now here I am dying and I barely know you. I do not expect love or grief from you, but I'll not go with you thinking I am a monster like she probably told you I am.

"Where do you think the manuscript is? I demand that you keep me informed every step of the way, Elliot. If you are not making progress, I will handle this myself."

It was not clear just how Christian would handle it. That ambiguity had led Elliot to take the charge on himself. His brother might be ruthless in silencing these echoes from the past.

"Although I did not find the manuscript, I did discover financial papers in Langton's office. That press is in trouble. Of more interest were documents regarding the ownership of the press. Richard Drury had been a silent partner from the start. That is no doubt why Langton received those memoirs."

Christian found that interesting. "We will have to approach Langton's solicitor and see who gets it all now."

"The documents indicated that Drury's share was bequeathed to his only child. There is a living partner still to deal with, who probably was complicit in the little blackmail scheme from the start."

"His only child? Hell." Christian pressed his head against the chair's back cushion, closed his eyes, and emitted an exasperated groan. "Not Phaedra Blair. Damnation."

"Yes, Phaedra Blair."

Christian muttered another curse. "How like Mr. Drury, with his radical views and unconventional life, to bequeath a business partnership to a woman, and his illegitimate daughter at that." His lids lowered. "Of course, she may be glad for the money if the press is in trouble. She may even welcome a reason not to publish her father's memoirs. They are no doubt full of private matters regarding her and her mother."

"Possibly." Elliot was not optimistic that negotiations would be so simple. Miss Blair was an unwelcome complication.

She might see in those memoirs and their secrets the making of a strong seller that would save that press. Or worse, she might believe her notions of social justice would be served by revealing the underbelly of polite society.

"Her own book was published by Langton, wasn't it? It is in the library here somewhere. I confess I never read it. I have little interest in mythology and folklore, let alone the syncretist studies on it," Christian said.

"I have heard that the scholarship was more than respectable." Elliot believed in giving the devil her due, as it were. "She inherited her parents' intelligence along with their indifference toward rules of conduct and conformity."

"Under the circumstances, none of her legacies is good news for us." Christian rose to his feet. He buttoned his coat and checked his collar in preparation for returning to the ball. "Best if you did not tell Hayden about any of this. He is very protective of his new wife, and Miss Blair is one of Alexia's friends. If you are obligated to get harsh it would be better if they remained ignorant."

"Miss Blair sailed for Naples two weeks ago. I will deal with her before she and Alexia can have another tête-à-tête."

"Will you be following her?"

"I had intended to travel there this autumn anyway. I want to study the recent excavations at Pompeii for my next book. I will move my journey forward now."

They walked side by side to the staircase. With each step the strains of music grew louder and the gentle roar of voices filled the majestic spaces. As they descended into the gay crush, Elliot noticed Christian's hooded, distracted expression.

"Do not be concerned, Christian. I will make sure that the accusation against Father is never printed."

Christian's fleeting smile did not clear his expression. "I do not doubt your abilities or resolve. That is not what I was contemplating just now."

"Then what?"

"I was thinking about Phaedra Blair, and wondering if any man can, as you put it, deal with her."

Elliot walked in darkness, his way lit by the flame of the small lamp that he carried.

The guests were gone and the servants slept. Hayden and Alexia were probably enjoying the marriage bed in their house on Hill Street. Christian might still be awake but he would not leave his chambers for several days now.

The faint light reflected off the gilt frames in the gallery. The moon shed a bit more through the long windows piercing the other wall. Elliot paused in front of two of the portraits. He had not come down seeking this chamber, but his purpose had everything to do with the man and woman immortalized by these images.

The artist had used similar backgrounds for the two bodies, so it appeared one painting continued the setting and world of the other. It was good to see his parents together like this, two halves of a whole, even if the implied unity was a lie. He could count the number of times he had even seen them both in the same room while they lived.

I'll not go with you thinking I am a monster, like she probably told you I am.

His father had been wrong there. Except for one emotional outpouring his mother had never spoken to him about the estrangement or its reasons. She had rarely spoken at all during those hours he spent with her in the library at Aylesbury.

He had feared his father all on his own, without his mother's help. He had also relished the rare moments of attention from the father who did not seem to remember that he had three, not two, sons.

He continued his walk toward the library, thinking about that long conversation with his father, the only and last one they ever held. He learned important truths that day, about people and passions, about pride and the soul, and about the ways in which a child does not see the world around him very well.

He had left that conversation no longer afraid. After those confidences he felt like his father's son for the first time in his life.

He moved his light along the leather bindings in the library. He sought the corner stacks, and the lowest shelf there. After his mother's death he had brought her private books here, the ones he had watched her read at Aylesbury during her exile.

He did not know why he had moved these books to London. Maybe so a part of her would remain where the family most often collected. It had been an impulse long before that talk with his father, a rebellious act of subterfuge to try to finally end the way she had been so separate from their lives.

No one ever noticed their addition to the hundreds of volumes. Down here in their obscure corner, it did not even matter that their bindings did not match.

He fingered along a group that were not bound at all. Thin and small, these were pamphlets that his mother had owned. He pulled them out, fanned them on the floor, and tipped the lamp over their titles.

He saw the one he wanted. It was a radical essay arguing against marriage, written thirty years ago by a famous bluestocking. The author had gone on to live her beliefs. She had even refused the married state when she found herself with child by her lifelong lover, Richard Drury.

He carried the pamphlet and the lamp to the shelf where Easterbrook stored the recent additions to the library. He slipped out a mythological dissertation still smelling of fresh leather.

He took both texts back to his chamber. He began reading, to prepare himself for dealing with Phaedra Blair.

CHAPTER TWO

"Signora, I do not think I should have to pay for these chambers when I do not even want to be using them."

Phaedra cobbled her objection out of Latin and the few words of the Neapolitan language that she had learned. She hoped her tone would communicate her displeasure regarding Signora Cirillo's bill in ways that her words might fail to accomplish.

She received a long, angry response, rattled off in a tone that was equally eloquent. Signora Cirillo did not care if Phaedra remained in the chambers against her will. Nor did she like the implications of the royal guardsman stationed outside her modest but respectable hostel. She wanted to be paid, and had boldly added a supplement to account for the intrusion of the guard's presence on her other guests.

Tempted sorely to tell this woman to take her bill to the king, Phaedra nonetheless went to her bedchamber and brought back the coins.

It had been a mistake to dally in this city even a week

before heading down to the ruins. If her confinement lasted much longer she would not have the money to buy passage back to England, let alone continue her mission here. This was intended to be a fairly short journey abroad. She had not come as a tourist, after all. She was here for a reason, and had pressing matters to address back home upon her return.

Mollified for another week, Signora Cirillo left. Phaedra returned to her baggage and weighed her situation. She dug into her portmanteau and retrieved a black shawl. She picked at the knot tied at one end, releasing the object snugly stored inside it.

A large gem fell onto her lap, its hues gleaming in the shadowed light of the chamber. Exquisitely carved tiny figures rose in pearly white relief against their dark red background. They depicted a mythological scene of the god Bacchus and his entourage.

This cameo had been the most valuable item bequeathed by her mother, and added to the will in her mother's own handwritten codicil. *To ensure my daughter's future, I leave her my only item of value, my agate cameo, an antiquity from Pompeii.*

Phaedra had never thought twice about that codicil in the six years since her mother's death. She had treasured the cameo as she did all reminders of the unusual and brilliant Artemis Blair. Its value had reassured her about her financial future, that was true, but she hoped she would never have to sell it. Now, however, that beautifully penned sentence raised questions that demanded answers.

She tied the cameo back into its home, tucked it away, and returned to the sitting room. She opened the interior shutters of the long window facing west. The bay appeared very blue in the distance, and the island of Ischia could be glimpsed in the far haze.

A salty scent fluttered in, blowing a few tendrils of her hair. The voice of her guardsman drifted in too. She leaned out her third story window to see with whom he conversed.

She saw a dark-haired head positioned in front of the guardsman's metal helmet and dramatic scabbard. The fashionably cut, romantically breeze-swept hair belonged to a man much taller than the guard. His broad shoulders appeared to be garbed in an expensive frock coat. The boots were the kind seen on the best feet in London. The other man down there was English, and a gentleman from the looks of his garments.

She strained to hear their conversation. The presence of her countryman gave her surprising comfort, even if he only requested directions out of the back streets of the Spanish Quarter.

She debated calling down and begging him for help. She was not even sure that the English people here in Naples knew she had been imprisoned. Of course, she also doubted that they would care if they did know. Those who knew her did not approve of her or want her company. Normally she did not want theirs either, but her inability to penetrate English society here had created problems even before her unexpected incarceration.

It was not going well for the Englishman. The guardsman's gestures made a pantomime of deferential regret. *I have my duty. I would accommodate you if I could, but . . .*

The Englishman moved away. He strolled to the other side of the street and paused. He looked up with a slightly furrowed, perfect brow. His alert, dark eyes scanned the facade of the building.

Phaedra's heart lightened, and not only because he possessed the sort of face that would raise any woman's pulse. She knew this man. That was the famous historian, Lord Elliot Rothwell, down there. Alexia had said he was going to visit Naples this autumn but it appeared he had come sooner.

She leaned out the window and waved. Lord Elliot barely nodded his greetings. She put a finger to her lips and pointed to the guardsman. Then she gestured in her own pantomime, asking him to make his way to the back of the building.

Lord Elliot strolled away like a man studying the architecture along the street. Phaedra closed the shutters and hurried to the other side of her apartment. She opened the window that looked out on the small garden in the back.

It took Lord Elliot some time to get there. Finally she saw him enter at the far end, through the door that gave out onto a fetid alley that separated the properties. His movements lacked any furtive hesitation. He walked toward her, tall and confident, like a man accustomed to doing as he pleased. Even without the angular face that nature had so blessed with beauty, his relaxed carriage and assured demeanor demanded that one be impressed.

She was so happy to see someone from home that she did not mind the critical glint in his dark eyes when he saw her. She had seen a similar flicker above Lord Elliot's slow smile when they met at Alexia's wedding.

It was the reaction of a man who thought her vaguely amusing even though he disapproved of her appearance, her beliefs, her history, her family, her . . . everything.

"Miss Blair, I am relieved to see you in good health and spirits." Another of those slow smiles accompanied the greeting.

"And I am relieved to see you, Lord Elliot."

"Alexia gave me the name of your hostel and asked I look in on you, to make sure you needed nothing."

"That was kind of her. I regret that I cannot receive you properly now that you have called."

"It appears that you cannot receive me at all."

So much for him allowing a few pleasantries first. "No doubt you find my imprisonment surprising, even shocking."

"I am a man rarely shocked and seldom surprised. I will admit some curiosity, however. You have only been in Naples a few weeks. It would take most people at least a year to amass sufficient crimes to deserve such punishment."

Was he enjoying this? Under the circumstances she found his flair for clever conversation inappropriate. "There have been no crimes, just a small misunderstanding."

"Small? Miss Blair, that is a member of the king's guard in front of your door."

"I am not convinced the king put him there. One of the court functionaries has done this to me. He is a loathsome little man with too much power and a small intelligence."

Lord Elliot crossed his arms, which made him look judgmental and powerful. She really hated it when men took that stance with her. It personified all that was wrong with their half of humanity.

"The guard spoke of a duel," Lord Elliot said.

"How was I to know that these men are so possessive that they try to kill each other if women so much as speak with—"

"Swords and daggers. Blood was drawn, the guard said."

"Marsilio is a young artist. A mere boy. Headstrong but very sweet. I had no idea that he had misinterpreted our friendship to the point where he would challenge Pietro simply because I strolled along the bay with him."

"Regrettably for you, Marsilio the headstrong, sweet boy is the king's relative. He came out of that duel almost dead. Fortunately for you, the guard says he will live."

"Oh, thank goodness. Although they do exaggerate here. As I understand it he was not badly hurt, even though any wound would be serious in such a climate. I am most contrite about the whole matter. I said so. I expressed my regrets and apologies in very slow English and also in Latin so I would be understood, but that officious, odious, stupid little man would not listen to me. He even accused me of being a prostitute, which was beyond the pale. I explained that I have never taken a penny from any man."

"Did you protest your virtue and honor, or did you tell the odious, stupid little man that you think women should give themselves freely?"

She did not like the deep, knowing look in his eyes when he spoke his bald insinuation. If she were not in such a ridiculous situation she would let him know that she might be unconventional but that did not give him permission to be rude. Right now, however, diplomacy was required.

"I explained my belief in free love, which is not the same as giving oneself away freely, Lord Elliot. I tried to educate him. I would be glad to do the same for you, should we ever have a more opportune meeting."

"What a tempting offer, Miss Blair. However, I expect the philosophical niceties were lost on your gaoler. Better if you had declared yourself a courtesan. They know all about that here. Radical concepts of free love, on the other hand—well . . ."

His offhand gesture said it all. *What do you expect, woman? You live outside the rules and even your appearance invites misunderstandings.*

She swallowed her instinctive reaction once more. Arguing would only drive him away, and she really wanted him to stay awhile longer. She had not realized how lonely this apartment was, and how sad the isolation had become. Just hearing her own language was a comfort.

"Do you think that they will release me soon?"

Again that offhand gesture, only now it substituted for a shrug. "There is no constitution here. No sense of precedent as in England either. No codified rights. It is an old-fashioned monarchy. You could be released tomorrow, or sent back to England, or brought to trial, or you might remain in those chambers for years at the pleasure of the king."

"Years! That is uncivilized."

"I do not think it will come to that. However, it could

be some months before your odious, stupid little man loses interest." He glanced across the face of the building, then to the garden door. "Miss Blair, I cannot lurk in this garden much longer or I may find myself a guest of the king's guards along with you. I will arrange to have some food delivered to you, and leave a sum for the hire of that apartment, which no doubt you still must pay. I will also ask the British envoy here to have someone check on you periodically."

Good heavens, he was leaving! She might grow old in these few rooms, eventually starving to death when the money ran out.

She was not a woman who depended on men for support or protection. Lord Elliot's side of this conversation had not endeared him to her either. The ambiguity of her future helped her overcome her natural aversion to asking this particular man for assistance, however.

"Lord Elliot," she said, stopping him after he took three steps toward the garden door. "Lord Elliot, my situation and my station do not interest diplomats. I don't suppose you would consider interceding on my behalf. I am sure the odious little man would be impressed by your family connections and your fame as a historian. If you spoke for me, perhaps it would help."

His expression was sympathetic but not encouraging. "I am a younger son. My station is much diminished here, and my fame of little account. Nor does this court have reason to grant me any favors."

"I am sure you will get a better hearing than I ever will. At least you know their language. I saw you conversing with the guard."

"I am hardly fluent enough in this dialect to present your case well."

"I would be grateful for whatever you attempt." What happened to chivalry? She did not believe in such sentiments, but his kind did. She was a damsel in distress and this gentleman should jump to help her, not stand in the garden looking like he wished he had never noticed her at the window above the guard.

He pondered her request. She felt her smile tighten into a beseeching grimace.

"This is not England, Miss Blair. If I am successful on your behalf you may not like the conditions they place on you in return for your freedom."

"I will force myself to accommodate any conditions, although I pray that you try to keep them from shipping me back to England at once. I came all this way and I really need—I want to visit the excavations at Pompeii before I leave. It is a dream of mine."

He thought it over an inordinate amount of time. His visible sigh communicated that his decision went against some better judgment. "I promised Alexia that I would see to your welfare, so I will do what I can. Finding the man whose order confined you may be difficult. Do you know his name? I would prefer not to ask around the court for the odious, stupid little man. He might hear the description, which would not help my mission, and it probably applies to far too many court functionaries in any case."

He had capitulated out of resignation to his sense of duty, not a genuine desire to assist her. She was too desperate to be particular about his motives. "His name is

Gentile Sansoni. Why do you look like that? Do you know him?"

"I know of him. Your self-defense fell on deaf ears, Miss Blair. Sansoni does not speak English or even Latin. And he is Neapolitan through and through, which is not good news."

Leave it to Phaedra Blair to come to the attention of Gentile Sansoni, a captain in the king's secret police. Of course, with her long red hair streaming down in the sun, undressed and uncovered, she had probably come to the attention of all of Naples.

Elliot had learned about Miss Blair's persecutor during his last visit to Naples three years ago. Sansoni's boat had floated in on a tide of blood in 1820, when a brief republican government in this land had been viciously defeated and the monarchy reinstated.

Sansoni had a reputation for arranging the unexpected disappearance of *Carbonari,* or constitutionalists, but he liked to abuse his unspecified authority in less political ways too. Sansoni was not the kind of man to be impressed by an English gentleman, and Elliot doubted he would take kindly to an attempt to circumvent his decision by appealing to his superiors.

Since Elliot could not deal with Miss Blair while she remained under house arrest, he accepted at once that he had to try to free her. He had only feigned hesitation in the garden to put her in his debt.

He had also yielded to the ignoble temptation to make this outspoken proponent of feminine independence beg for a man's assistance. Miss Blair managed to challenge a man merely by existing, and his instincts had reacted accordingly.

Duty called, however, and the next day he set about doing what he could for her. Sansoni would not be impressed by English gentlemen, but there was a chance he would at least listen to an English naval captain. The court of Naples still revered the memory of Nelson, and Elliot suspected that Sansoni would think of Nelson as a spiritual brother. The great English hero had once helped suppress another, earlier attempt at republican government here.

There were always British ships in Naples's port, and Elliot visited one whose captain he knew. Two days after seeing Miss Blair, he accompanied a superbly uniformed Captain Augustus Cornell through miles of palace corridors as they made their way to Gentile Sansoni's lair.

As appropriate for a court functionary who worked in the shadows, Sansoni was far in the back of the building and so far down that the stairs changed from fine marble to travertine as they descended. Despite his location, Sansoni had brought in enough opulent furniture to appear important. He had procured a space appropriately large for his ambitions but its low ceiling and lack of windows made it cavernous.

"I will do the talking," Cornell said. His soft, pale face wore the severe formality common to men of his military standing. "I have had some dealings with him, and one must be careful."

"Do you know the language?" Neapolitan was significantly different from the language spoken in Rome or Florence. Even with its heavy derivations from Latin, Elliot was at a disadvantage with it.

"Well enough, let us hope. You stay back here. I will act as go-between, physically and symbolically."

Elliot stayed near the door as commanded. Cornell paced down the length of the room and approached the little, swarthy man who sat at the big desk at the other end. Miss Blair's description of Sansoni had been apt. He did appear loathsome and odious, and right now very suspicious. His black eyebrows hovered low over the almond-shaped eagle eyes so common in this city.

Wine was offered, toasts made, and a conversation held. Eventually Cornell paced back to him.

"There is a complication," he said quietly. "This friend of Miss Blair's —Marsilio, the one who got the worst of it in that duel—is a distant relative of the king, but favored by the royal family because of his artistic abilities. He is also a young man to whom I think Sansoni there hopes to marry one of his own relatives, thus cementing his own position. That outcome is unlikely given Sansoni's poor blood, but Sansoni has made the young man's welfare his personal mission." He tipped his head closer and spoke more lowly yet. "I also believe that the king is none the wiser about that duel. I kept dropping your brother's title, and I suspect he only listens to me because he fears an English marquess could have ways to bring the matter directly to the king."

A marquess probably could, but it would take months. "Can you arrange Miss Blair's release?"

"I doubt it. The duel was not the whole of it. The king owns an art collection and one room is forbidden to women. It contains ancient images of a carnal nature. Miss Blair convinced young Marsilio to get her in. So criminal trespass and a taste for licentious art are among her crimes. Sansoni also says she is a common prostitute. While Naples is infamous for permitting such women their trade, her flaunting herself in places that the court frequents—"

"She is not a prostitute. I can vouch for that. She is odd, that is true. Eccentric. A free thinker, but essentially honest. Surely Sansoni knows of such people. Go explain that."

"This man's job is to break free thinkers, and he does so with relish. However, I will try again."

Once more Cornell walked down the chamber. The conversation was briefer this time. Sansoni's black eyes sought Elliot and gave him a sharp examination.

Cornell returned. "He spoke faster this time and I am not catching it all. However, he wants to know on what authority you and your family intrude on this matter. He demands to know if you are a male relative, or have other standing."

Elliot had absolutely no standing but it would not do to admit that. "Tell him she is a good friend of my family. Easterbrook receives her like a sister." That bald lie would never be disproved. Christian would have done the same under the circumstances. "Say that we endeavor to control her, but she unexpectedly made this journey to Naples to escape our influence. I have come to see to her welfare and can promise there will be no more trouble. And if he indicates that he wants a bribe, tell him I will pay it to get her back."

Cornell's discussions with Sansoni became animated this time. Sansoni's gestures flew in rapid succession. When Cornell walked back with his report, he appeared a little concerned.

"There has, I fear, been a misunderstanding. Now fixing it will create unknown complications. I blame my lack of total fluency in the language for this unfortunate turn in the negotiations," he said.

"He appears much calmer and more amenable, though. What is the misunderstanding?"

Cornell's face flushed. "I think he somehow has concluded you are Miss Blair's fiancé, and that she came here to escape an arranged marriage that your family accepted due to her very large dowry. He thinks that you followed to retrieve her."

"That is one hell of a misunderstanding. How did you manage it?"

"I am not sure. The words for family, sister, money, and escape—they must have gotten all mixed up and implied more than I intended." Cornell turned with a sigh, to go and rectify his error.

Elliot caught his arm, stopping him. "Is he prepared to release her if we let the confusion stand?"

"Yes, but—"

"Are you sure that is what he thinks?"

"I am not secure in my understanding of his misinterpretation, but—"

"Then we will not disabuse him."

"I am not sure that is honorable."

"You have told no untruths. You are not sure that he misunderstood." Elliot clamped his hand on Cornell's shoulder. "We will accept this as a gift from Providence and let it stand. This is not a man who is received by the

English community here. If he misunderstood, he will never be the wiser."

Cornell allowed himself to be swayed. "If you are determined, so be it. Come with me. He wants your spoken word that you will control Miss Blair while she remains in this kingdom. She must be under your constant authority, and you will be held responsible for any other trouble that she creates. Are you prepared to so swear?"

Elliot nodded. He walked down the cavern with Captain Cornell and took custody of Miss Blair from the odious, loathsome Gentile Sansoni.

CHAPTER
THREE

P haedra rose from her writing table in response to Signora Cirillo's call. If the woman wanted more money so soon . . .

A wonderful sight awaited her when she opened the door to her chambers. Signora Cirillo was not alone. Lord Elliot stood beside her.

Phaedra kept her composure even though she wanted to shout for joy. If he was here, it only meant one thing.

"Lord Elliot, please enter. *Grazie, signora.*"

Signora Cirillo raised her eyebrows over her dark cat eyes at this dismissal. Phaedra shooed her away.

"You bring good news I hope, Lord Elliot," Phaedra said when they were alone.

"Your house arrest is over, Miss Blair. We have Captain Cornell of the *Euryalus* to thank. He spoke with Sansoni on our behalf."

"Thank God for the Royal Navy." She ran to the window and threw open the shutters. The guard outside was gone. "I must take a turn along the bay this evening. I cannot believe—" She skipped back to Lord Elliot and gave him an embrace. "I am so grateful to you."

He smiled kindly when she released him. He seemed to understand her excitement and forgive her exuberance. If his gaze had warmed a little from her impulsive embrace, well, he was a man after all.

He appeared quite magnificent right now in his perfectly tailored, brown frock coat and high boots. His smile did much to soften the severity of the Rothwell face. Unlike his older brothers, Lord Elliot was reputed to smile often, and it appeared that was true.

He looked around her sitting room. His gaze lit upon her writing desk. "I have interrupted your letter, I fear."

"An interruption I most welcomed. I was writing to Alexia and pouring out my story of woe, on the chance I could at least throw my letter down to you when you returned here."

"Why not complete the letter at once and let her know all is well? I will take it to Cornell. He sails in two days for Portsmouth, and will post it to London from there."

"What a splendid idea, if you will not think me rude to jot a few more lines."

"Not at all, Miss Blair. Not at all."

She sat down and quickly added a paragraph telling Alexia that all had been resolved happily, thanks to Alexia's new brother-in-law Lord Elliot. She folded, addressed, and sealed the paper, and stood with it in her hand. Lord Elliot gently plucked it from her fingers. He tucked it into his frock coat.

He resumed his perusal of the sitting room and its

views. "You came to the door yourself, Miss Blair. Where is your abigail?"

"I have no abigail, Lord Elliot. No servants. Not even in London."

"Is that due to another philosophical belief?"

"It is a practical decision. An uncle left me a respectable income, but I would rather spend it in other ways."

"How sensible. However, your lack of a servant is inconvenient."

"Not at all." She turned on her toes and the drapes of her black gauze garment and long hair fanned out. "A dress like this does not require a maid to truss me, and my hair requires only a brush."

"I was not thinking of your dressing. I need to speak with you about this development, and with no maid in this apartment . . ."

He worried for her reputation should she be with a man alone. How charming.

"Lord Elliot, it is impossible for you to compromise me because I am above such stupid social rules. Besides, this is a business meeting of sorts, is it not? Our privacy is not only allowed in such situations, but also necessary." She doubted he would accept her reasoning, logical though it was. Men like him never did.

To her amazement he capitulated immediately. "You are correct. Therefore we shall proceed. Will you not sit? This could take some time."

He appeared very serious all of a sudden. Serious and stern and . . . hard. His gesture toward the divan carried more command than his polite request implied.

The temptation to remain standing nipped at her. She sat, but only because he had just procured her freedom.

He settled into a chair that faced her. He gave her a good look, as if sizing her up. He might have never seen her before and now tried to interpret the peculiar image she presented.

She could not shake the sense that, in a manner of speaking, she had never seen him before either. There was none of his quiet amusement now, just a long, examining, invasive gaze that made her uneasy. A very feminine response rumbled deeply in her essence.

That was the damndest thing about handsome men. Their beauty left one at a disadvantage when they directed attention at you. This man was very handsome. He was also very masculine in most ways, and subtly so in the worst ones. Right now he seemed to be deliberately trying to unsettle her. He did not do it for carnal reasons, she was sure. Yet his aura projected that lure too, and her blood reacted to it.

Protecting, possessing, conquering—they were all facets of the same primitive instinct, weren't they? A man could not follow one inclination without arousing the others in himself, and a woman was easily vanquished if she did not take care. She wondered which ancient part of the male character motivated him now.

"Alexia did ask me to look in on you, Miss Blair. That was no lie. However, I had other reasons to call and they must now be addressed."

"Since we only met once, at Alexia's wedding, and very briefly, I cannot imagine what your reasons might be."

"I think that you can."

Now he was annoying her. "I assure you I cannot."

His tone indicated that he found her annoying in turn. "Miss Blair, it has come to my attention that you are now a partner in Merris Langton's publishing house. That you inherited your father's interest in the business."

"That is not information that has been given out, Lord Elliot. With men assuming a woman cannot succeed in business, and with many believing it unnatural for a woman to even try, I chose to keep that quiet so prejudice would not affect the business itself."

"Do you intend to be active in it?"

"I will have a hand in choosing the titles published, but I expect Mr. Langton will continue to oversee the practical matters. I would like to know who informed you of this. If my solicitor has been indiscreet—"

"Your solicitor is blameless." His attention left her. His eyes assumed a brooding darkness. The distraction hinted at the brilliant mind inside this elegant man about town, and the intellectual absorption that had led him to pen a celebrated historical tome before he turned twenty-three.

"Miss Blair, I regret that I bring you some bad news. Merris Langton passed away from his illness after you left London. He was buried a few days before I sailed myself."

She had feared Mr. Langton would not recover, but hearing of his death was surprising anyway. "That is bad news indeed, Lord Elliot. I thank you for informing me. I did not know him well, but a man's passing is always sad. I had counted on him helping me maintain that publishing house, but it appears I will be left to do it on my own."

"Is it all yours now?"

"My father founded the press and subsidized it all along. His share was his to bequeath, but Mr. Langton's became my father's if Mr. Langton died. So, yes, I do believe it is all mine now."

His distraction disappeared. The sternness returned. Coldly. "Prior to Langton's illness, he approached my brother. He spoke of your father's memoirs being published. He offered to omit several paragraphs in the manuscript that touched on my family if a significant sum was paid to him."

"He did? That is terrible! I am shocked by this betrayal of my father's principles, and sincerely apologize for my partner."

She rose and began pacing, agitated by this revelation. Lord Elliot politely stood too, but she ignored him while she tried to take in the implications of Mr. Langton's foolish scheme. This might be all it took to bring that shaky press down.

She knew too well its precarious finances, and as a partner she was responsible for the unpaid debts. She had counted on her father's memoirs to pull them through. If Mr. Langton had compromised the integrity of that publication, the world might dismiss the book entirely.

"This is all Harriette Wilson's fault," she said, her dismay edging into anger. "She set a disgraceful precedent in asking her lovers to pay to have their names removed. I wrote to her about it, mind you. Harriette, I wrote, it is wrong to take money to expunge memoirs. It is just a pretty form of blackmail. She only thought of her purse, of course. Well, that is the result of the dependent life she chose and the foolish extravagance that she practiced." She strode more purposefully. "Mr. Langton no doubt approached others too. I cannot believe he would impugn the ethics of our publishing house in this way."

"Miss Blair, please spare me the theatrical outrage. My family was prepared to pay Langton. I sought you out to say that we will now gladly pay you instead."

Theatrical outrage? She paused her pacing and faced him squarely. "Lord Elliot, I hope that I misunderstand you. Are you suggesting that I would accept this money to edit the memoirs to your liking?"

"It is our hope that you will."

She advanced on him until she was close enough to see the thoughts reflected in his eyes. "Good heavens, you think that I knew Mr. Langton was doing this, don't you? You believe I was an accomplice to it."

He did not respond. He just looked back, visibly skeptical of her astonishment.

Furious about his assumptions, affronted by the insult, she turned away. "Lord Elliot, my father's memoirs are going to be published as soon as I return to England. Every sentence of them. It was his last wish, commanded of me while he was on his deathbed. I would never pick and choose which of his words the world should read. I am sincerely grateful for your aid with Mr. Sansoni, but it would be best if we ended this conversation. If I had a servant I would have you shown out. As it is, you will have to find your own way."

To make her dismissal of him complete, she strode to her bedchamber and closed the door.

She had not collected herself before the door to her chamber reopened. Lord Elliot calmly followed her in and closed it behind him.

"My visit is not over, and our business is not completed, Miss Blair."

"How dare—this is my *bedchamber,* sir."

He crossed his arms and assumed that irritating, masculine pose of command. "Normally that might check me, but you are above stupid social rules like the one that says I should not intrude here. Remember?"

She did not consider that particular social rule so stupid. It existed for a very good reason. A primitive one. This was her most private space, her sanctuary. The air began altering while he glanced at the wardrobe where her garments were stored and the dressing table that held her private items. His gaze swept over the bed slowly, then returned to her.

His thoughts were not as masked as he thought. She noted the subtle changes in his expression, the way the hardness that he wore rearranged itself ever so slightly. A man could not be near a bed with a woman and not start wondering. It was just a curse of nature that they bore.

It irritated her that she wondered too. The manner in which he had just insulted her should provide the best armor against the intimacy threading through this chamber. The brief silence grew heavy and full of a magnetic excitement that stirred her.

An image blinked in her mind, of Lord Elliot looking down at her, his face mere inches from hers, his dark hair mussed by reasons besides fashion and his thoughts completely unmasked. She saw his naked shoulders and felt the pressure of his body and the firm hold of his embrace on her skin. She felt . . .

She forced the image from her head, but acknowledgment flashed in his eyes. He knew her mind had wandered there, just as she knew his had.

He unfolded his arms. She thought he might reach for her. She wondered if he would insult her further now. There were men who misunderstood her and proposed things in ignorance, but Lord Elliot was not stupid. It would be deliberately and cruelly offensive if he attempted to act on the sensual awareness whispering between them.

He turned his attention from her, diluting the intimacy but not completely vanquishing it. Her pride was spared even if her primitive self simmered with discontent.

"Is the manuscript here?" he asked. "Did you bring it with you?"

"Of course not. Why would I do that?"

He eyed the wardrobe. "Do you swear? If not I will have to search for it."

"I swear, and don't you dare search. You have no right to be here at all."

"Actually, I do, but we will discuss that later."

What was that supposed to mean? "I left it in London, in a very secure place. It contains my father's memories, his last words. I would never be careless with it."

"Have you read it?"

"Of course."

"Then you know what he wrote about my family. I want you to tell me about that now. His exact words, as well as you can remember."

He was not requesting to know, but demanding. His dominating high-handedness was making her gratitude for his help dim fast.

"Lord Elliot, your family's name, and that of Easterbrook, is never mentioned in that manuscript."

That surprised him. His sternness cracked long enough for her to glimpse the amiable, helpful man who had first entered her apartment. It did not last. The brooding distraction took over and the sharp mind assessed what she had said.

"Miss Blair, Merris Langton approached my brother and described a specific accusation against my father. Is there anything in that manuscript that in your opinion could be interpreted as relating to my parents?"

She wished he had not phrased his question quite that way. "There is one part that might be so interpreted, I suppose."

"Please describe it."

"I would rather not."

"I insist. You will tell me now."

His voice, his stance, and his expression said he would brook no argument. She had never before in her life been so pointedly ordered to do something by a man.

Perhaps it would be best if he and his family were warned. The passage they discussed had been one of several in the memoirs to give her pause.

"My father describes a private dinner party several years before my mother died. They entertained a young diplomat just back from the Cape Colony. My father wanted to learn the true conditions there. This young man drank rather freely and turned morose. While in his cups he confided something regarding an event in a British regiment in the colony."

The mention of the Cape Colony had garnered his attention too well. She inwardly grimaced. She had always hoped that rumor was untrue, but—

"Go on, Miss Blair."

"He said that while he was there, a British officer died. It was reported as from a fever but in fact he had been shot. He was found dead after going on patrol. There were suspicions regarding another officer who had accompanied him, but no evidence. Rather than impugn that other officer, a false cause of death was reported."

He masked his reaction very well now. She looked upon a face carved of stone. His silence turned terrible, however, quaking with the anger leaking out of him.

"Miss Blair, if you associated that man's story with my family, you must know the scurrilous rumor about my father, and how he is said to have had my mother's lover posted in the Cape Colony. A place where that officer died of fever."

She swallowed hard. "I may have heard something to that effect once."

"If you did, many did. Neither Langton nor you had any difficulty adding up the references and drawing a conclusion. If you publish that section the insinuation will stand that my father paid another officer to kill my mother's lover. The lack of names in the memoirs will not spare my father's reputation, and he cannot defend himself from the grave."

"I am not convinced—"

"Damn it, that is exactly what will happen and you know it. I demand that you remove that portion of the memoirs."

"Lord Elliot, I am sympathetic to your distress. Truly, I am. However, my father charged me with seeing his memoirs published, and it is my duty to do so. I have thought long and hard about this. If I remove every sentence that might be construed as dangerous or unflattering to this person or that, there will be little left."

He strode to her and looked down hard. "You will not publish this lie."

His determination was palpable. He did not require expressions of anger or verbal threats to emphasize the power he would use against her. It was just there, surrounding her, tinged by the sexual awareness that had never left this chamber, creating a mood that held all the edges of that dark instinct.

"If it is a lie, I will consider omitting it," she said. "If you can obtain proof that man died of fever, or if my parents' guest recants, in this one case I will do it. For Alexia, however, not for you or Easterbrook."

That checked him. A slow smile formed. "For Alexia? How convenient for you. Now you can retreat without giving me a victory."

He understood her rather too well. She did not care for the evidence of that.

He looked down much more kindly. Their closeness, born of his fury, became inappropriate suddenly. As his anger ebbed that other tension tightened again.

He did not retreat the way he should. The way her raised eyebrows demanded. Instead he lifted a strand of her hair and looked at it while he gently wove it between his fingers.

"Did your father include the name of either of these men, Miss Blair? The young diplomat at the dinner party or the officer who was suspected?"

He did not touch her as such, but his toying with her hair implied things she should not allow to stand. Their isolation in this bedchamber, even their confrontation, had demolished the most protective formalities. The subtle tingling he created on her scalp was delicious, cajoling her to speculate about other physical excitements.

Conquering, possessing, protecting—she did not doubt that he was prepared to be ruthless and toy with more than hair if he thought it would achieve what he wanted. Nor was she confident she could defeat the challenge should it come.

"The young diplomat they invited to dinner was Jonathan Merriweather."

He looked in her eyes, suspicious again. "Merriweather is now an assistant to the British envoy here in Naples."

"How convenient for you."

His hand wound in her hair more firmly. The subtle play became controlling. "Did you journey here to speak to him? Is that why you are in Naples? Do you intend to annotate those memoirs and fill in the names and facts that your father discreetly omitted? The book will sell all the better then, and I daresay your press could use the income."

She purposefully took hold of the hair he held and pried his fingers off. Her indignation helped her ignore the sensation of his warm hand beneath hers, and the way his eyes reflected his awareness of her touch.

"I expect my father's memoirs to be popular without annotations, but I thank you for the suggestion. I am not here for that purpose, however."

That was a bald lie, but she felt no compunction about misleading this man. Her main interest in filling in the memoirs' gaps did not bear on his family in any way.

"Lord Elliot, I have come to visit the excavations and ruins to the south. I need to prepare to leave this city at once and continue my journey as I originally planned. Therefore, I must ask you, once more, to leave."

"Your tour will have to be delayed a few days more. I cannot allow you to go just yet."

She laughed. The man's presumptions had become ridiculous. "What you would allow is of no interest to me."

"It is of essential interest to you. I warned that freeing you might entail conditions, and you promised to accommodate them."

"You said nothing about conditions when you arrived."

"Your warm embrace distracted me."

She peered at him distrustfully. "What are these conditions?"

He slowly looked down her flowing locks, which meant he looked down most of her body. She thought she detected a possessive interest, as if he had just received a gift and judged its value.

"Gentile Sansoni would only release you if you entered my custody. I had to accept total responsibility for you and promise to regulate your behavior."

Hot anger flared in her head. No wonder Lord Elliot was preening with arrogance and command all of a sudden today. "That is intolerable. I have never answered to a man. To do so would make my mother turn in her grave. I refuse to agree to this."

"Would you prefer to take your chances with Sansoni? It can be arranged."

The threat left her speechless.

Lord Elliot did not exactly laugh as he strode to the door, but he did not hide his amusement at her dilemma either.

"We will journey on to Pompeii together, Miss Blair, after I speak with Merriweather. Until then, you are not to leave these chambers without my escort. Oh, and there will be no Marsilios or Pietros visiting you either. I'll be damned if you will provoke more duels while you are under my authority. I swore an oath to control you, and I expect your cooperation and obedience."

Authority? Control? *Obedience?* She was so stunned that he was gone before she found the voice to curse him.

CHAPTER
FOUR

Miss Blair's willingness to compromise on the memoirs improved Elliot's mood. He would obtain the necessary denial from Merriweather, pack Miss Blair off on the next ship sailing west, and turn his attention to more interesting matters.

Merriweather would undoubtedly cooperate. He better than anyone knew that Drury's story about that officer's death was false. Furthermore, his diplomatic career would be harmed if the whole world read that he had been indiscreet while in his cups. He would become an ally in efforts to have Miss Blair remove the incriminating paragraphs.

Elliot discovered within the hour that the matter would not be settled as quickly as he hoped. A clerk at the British legation in the Palazzo Calabritto informed him that Merriweather had gone to Cyprus on a mission, and was not expected back for a fortnight at least.

Elliot returned to his hotel and rearranged some of his plans. As afternoon cooled into evening he rode in a hired carriage to the Spanish Quarter to once more call on Phaedra Blair.

Her blue eyes blazed on seeing him at her door. "What do you want now, Lord Elliot?"

"You said that you wished to stroll along the bay this evening. I am here to escort you."

"I do not require your escort."

"You either stroll with me or not at all. It would be a pity if you did not enjoy your freedom now that you have it."

She pursed her lips. Debate reflected in her eyes. "Very well, let us go now."

She stepped forward in anticipation of him stepping aside.

"You forgot your hat, Miss Blair. The sun has not set and your lovely complexion will still be in danger. I am sure that you would like to avoid more of those tiny sun spots on your nose, charming though they are."

Her hand flew to her nose. For an instant feminine vanity conquered her pose of indifference to such silly concerns.

"You mix false flattery with criticism most adroitly, sir."

"The flattery was not false. The spots are adorably girlish, but you still need a hat. I will wait while you put one on. You do own a hat, don't you?"

"Of course." Exasperated, she turned on her heel and aimed for her bedchamber. "Do not follow me this time."

"I would never enter a lady's bedchamber twice in one day. Like four dances at a ball, it might be misunderstood."

"I misunderstand little about men, Lord Elliot. They are the most transparent of creatures."

He expected they were, for her. She was not inexperienced. She had known where his thoughts wandered earlier today when he saw her standing next to that bed. Her unbound hair made her appear like a woman prepared for an afternoon of pleasure.

She had not reacted with shock or modest embarrassment. There had been no virtuous indignation. Instead she just watched him while the sensual possibilities teased them both. Her expression frankly acknowledged the pull and its possibilities.

He had never experienced anything quite like it before. She managed to taunt and reject without saying a word. *You want me and I may want you but it will not happen now. It may not happen ever. I haven't decided yet.* She had to know that her manner would raise the devil in a man.

She returned wearing a straw hat that was far more attractive than he expected. Its diagonally angled brim and silk flowers in white and blue enhanced her eyes and fair complexion. Her long, streaming hair, her lack of paint, and those tiny spots gave her a fresh, country appearance.

Her garments marred the image. Black, lightweight, undecorated fabric swathed her from neck to toe. A sash bound her midriff but otherwise little of her shape could be seen in the voluminous, loose drapery.

The dress provoked more speculation than she probably anticipated. It hinted at what she had told him earlier. No maid "trussed" her. She wore no corset or stays and the general forms indicated that the body so free beneath the fabric was worth imagining. High breasts, he decided, of indeterminate but admirable size, and hips feminine enough to make her waist appear quite small. Some sleight of hand on a few hooks and all would be revealed.

"Alexia made it," she said, seeing his admiration of the hat. "I believe she hopes to reform me. As for my dress that you are eyeing so critically, do not expect me to change it. It was not my decision that forces you to accompany an unfashionable woman in public."

"The appeal of the dress is growing on me. I insist you cover your hair but I will not demand that you give up all the symbols with which you challenge the world."

She raised her chin and sailed through the doorway. "If you are wise you will not demand anything at all."

Noise, drama, feathered bonnets, and colorful parasols.

Princely wealth and abhorrent poverty and the glint of soldiers' armor.

London's fashionable hour was a pale imitation to what took place in southern climates in the evening. The causeway along the Bay of Naples had filled with the city's population. Aristocrats in fashionable dresses and coats strolled in packs between poor people loitering near the water. Tradesmen and their wives promenaded with their children.

The evening social hour, enjoyed near the bay or in church piazzas, served important purposes in the city, as seen by the way girls of marriageable age were turned out for display. Their young, dark beauty glowed between sober-faced parents who critically assessed the men who looked twice.

All of Naples was an opera and Phaedra Blair did not appear nearly as odd as she might have intended. Her hat made her at least half presentable, although Elliot noticed the attention she garnered with her flowing hair. He imagined the reaction when she came here her first evening, walking alone, her red locks flaming among a sea of black and brown. London had more patience with the kind of eccentricity that she displayed in her appearance.

"Did you speak with Mr. Merriweather?"

They were the first words she had spoken since leaving her apartment. Elliot had not forced conversation in the carriage. He did not mind the lack of it. He spent a good deal of his time in silence with his own mind as his only company. He enjoyed society up to a point, but only if hours of quiet balanced those of noise and talk.

"He is away on a mission and not expected back for a fortnight at best."

He wondered if she knew that already. He was not convinced Miss Blair was so innocent in her purposes in visiting this city. If she wanted to see the ruins, another time of year would make more sense. Embarking when her journey would overlap the heat of Naples's summer, when her press was in trouble, her partner ill, and those memoirs awaited preparation . . . He still suspected that quizzing Merriweather had been among her intentions here.

"I hope that you do not expect me to delay a fortnight or more before going to Pompeii."

"I have decided we will visit the ruins while I await his return."

That appeased her. She almost appeared relieved. Perhaps she really had come only as a tourist.

"Last spring Alexia told me that you are writing a new book, Lord Elliot. Is your visit to Pompeii connected to that?"

"I am going to see the new excavations and learn what has been discovered in the last few years. I will be talking to the archaeologists and researching some matters for my book."

"Alexia said it is to be a book about everyday matters, the way people lived. How unusual. Normally history books describe the wars and politics and the deeds of great men. Even your last one did."

"I am aware that this book may be criticized for lack of importance. The subject interests me, however, and I can afford to indulge myself."

"If you think I am criticizing, you misunderstand. I believe your book will be very popular no matter what the scholars say. It should sell very well."

"I am not sure that my publisher agrees."

"Then perhaps you should find another one. I would be honored to publish it if you can bear the thought of conducting business with a woman."

He laughed at her shrewd expression. That press might survive after all if Miss Blair displayed such talent in flattering authors into throwing in with her.

Her mood had improved since they began their walk. Perhaps the softening light of the low sun and the cooling breeze were the reasons. More likely Miss Blair had decided that anger would interfere with enjoying her new freedom.

Joy sparkled in her eyes as she marched along observing the passing crowds, the boats, and the gulls. She smiled his way often with a warmth that might be misinterpreted as flirting. He did not miss the way men looked at her. The novelty of her red hair was enough to draw attention, but Miss Blair would do so in any case.

She did not miss those looks either. She did not invite or discourage them. She took neither satisfaction nor insult either, from what Elliot could tell. She merely walked on, those black, swaying drapes revealing more than they were supposed to, confident in her difference.

She subtly projected an aura, however. It bore the same challenge that he had felt in her chamber, only now it spoke to every man who looked too long. *You want me, but I have decided it will not happen.*

She stopped to purchase a little bouquet of flowers from a girl selling posies from a box. He tried to pay for them but she waved his coin away and paid herself. She continued on, holding the fragrant blooms to her nose.

"Lord Elliot, I would like to make a proposition."

Not the one he wanted. His body tightened anyway. Her words had been chosen to tease. That only angered him because it worked.

He shouldn't, but . . . "I have seen the result of the terms you offer men in your propositions, Miss Blair, and I must decline."

Her expression fell. "What is that supposed to mean?"

"Oh, did I misunderstand? My apologies."

"What did you *mean*?"

He shrugged. "I thought you were going to offer to make me one of your friends. One of those bees who buzz around the queen."

Her white skin flushed. Her anger carried a good dose of dismay.

"What do you know of my friends?"

"You may scorn polite society, but it is aware of you. Everyone knows about the daughter of Artemis Blair, and how, like her mother, she considers herself above all those stupid social rules."

"Your rudeness astonishes me." Anger won out, and she stopped flustering. "You are so typical in misunderstanding my friendships, which is why I would never consider having one with such as you."

Oh, she would consider it. She already had. Negotiations had begun earlier today. "If I have been rude, I must apologize."

Her expression relaxed.

"Although—"

Her eyebrows shot up.

"—if you are above stupid social rules, is it even possible for me to be rude, Miss Blair? Within the context of your beliefs, I mean. The word 'rude' is all about those rules, is it not? In the days ahead you will have to help me see where your subjugation to the rules begins and ends, so I do not misunderstand again."

Again that knowing confidence, that challenge, saturated her. "You can be certain that I will, Lord Elliot."

Their walk had taken them to the Riviera di Chiaia and the great villas that overlooked the bay. Miss Blair admired their beauty while she buried her thoughts behind a passive mask.

"Lord Elliot, it is convenient that you speak of the days ahead, and that you have expressed your disapproval and scorn of me. As it happens my proposition has to do with both those attitudes."

"I neither disapprove nor hold scorn. I merely decided we should have a right understanding on one small point." The most important one.

"That you so badly misunderstand both my friendships with others and my interest in you indicates that we will not rub well together. Nor can you want the burden of a mere tourist as your companion. I will only be in your way, and your studies will only delay my plans. I propose that we separate once we leave Naples."

"That is not possible."

"Gentile Sansoni will never know."

"His reach extends beyond this city. Also, I gave my sworn word and that is one of the stupid social rules that I take very seriously."

"Sir—"

"No, Miss Blair. The morning after next we will depart together. We will sail down to Positano first, then to Amalfi and journey back up by land."

"I want to go to Pompeii immediately."

"The delay will be brief. I promised to visit a friend in Positano and he expects me sooner rather than later. If you are here as a tourist you should welcome a few days visiting the coastline south of here. It is spectacular."

She did not appear to welcome it at all. He anticipated seeing that strained annoyance in her eyes for the next several weeks.

They turned to retrace their paths. He almost stumbled over a young child who had been trailing them. Big black eyes looked up in the wordless hope one saw among the most impoverished of the city's children. This one did not beg outright but her frail, little body and ragged dress made the plea for her, poignantly.

He fished in his waistcoat pocket. By the time the coin emerged two more children had appeared by her side. More were coming, drawn by instinct to the Englishman who did not know better than to indulge the child beggars of Naples.

He found more coin. Miss Blair did not seem frightened by the crush of anxious poverty the way most women did. She tried talking to the first little girl while her hand dove somewhere amidst the drapery at her hip.

They waded together through a little lake of black eyes and sun-baked bodies, handing out coin until all they had was gone.

They returned to the carriage without further arguments. She only spoke one more time before he left her at her apartment.

"We leave in the morning, the day after tomorrow, you say? Then I suppose I have no choice but to prepare accordingly."

Her apparent submission did not fool him. He left to make his own preparations.

Phaedra retrieved the cameo from the shawl. She wrapped it in a handkerchief and pinned the little bundle inside the pocket deep in the skirts of her dress. Then she draped the shawl itself over her head and tied it beneath her chin.

She checked her valise, itemizing again the garments and items that she had stuffed inside it. She prided herself on an absence of feminine vanity but it still irritated her that she would be reduced to so little clothing for the next week.

It was all Lord Elliot's fault. Everyone knew that an oath sworn under duress did not count, and one sworn to save a woman from an uncertain fate qualified as duress to her mind. His insistence on keeping his word vexed her. Just her luck that the only person available to help her out of her dilemma had been a man with outmoded notions of strict honor.

She would not allow him to force them both to be victims of his narrow-mindedness. He did not want her company any more than she wanted his. There would be nothing but trouble between them.

One of those men who buzz around the queen. The man was incapable of understanding the honest and sincere friendships she had enjoyed with a few, rare, like-minded men. It would shock him to learn that some men could rise above the primitive urges of possession and dominance that had caused so much grief in history and in women's lives. There were actually men for whom sensuality did not evoke the need to also take and conquer and require submission.

Well, it was not her responsibility to explain it. Doing so would be a fruitless endeavor and would require that she spend more time with him.

She left a note and some money on her portmanteau, to ensure Signora Cirillo understood she would soon return for it. Then she slipped out of her apartment and into the dark corridor. She felt her way to the stairs.

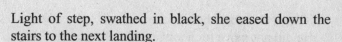

Light of step, swathed in black, she eased down the stairs to the next landing.

She felt her way blindly through the dark to the next set of stairs.

Suddenly the shadows took on forms of bannister and doors and walls, as if someone had opened shutters to the moonlight.

"Pietro is not waiting at the crossroad the way you think, Miss Blair."

Her heart fell at the calm, quiet voice behind her. She pivoted.

Lord Elliot stood a yard behind her at an open door that gave in to the apartment directly beneath her own. He was naked to the waist and barefoot, as if he had been sleeping and thrown on trousers to investigate a disturbance. Dim lamplight from his chambers washed him in a golden glow.

His presence heralded the destruction of her plan of escape. Despite the exasperation building fast, she could not help appreciating the body exposed to her gaze. He had a fine form, broad shouldered and lean. His body possessed the youthful tautness that blessed men for so long in life if they remained active. The dim light emphasized the hard muscles of his chest and stomach and arms.

He took two strides, relieved her of the valise, grabbed her arm, and pushed her into his room. He closed the door.

"What are you doing here?" she asked. The lamplight really flattered the hard chest and alluring skin so close to her face. If his interference had not disheartened her she might enjoy looking at his beauty.

"I took chambers here."

He did not move for a long count. She glanced at his face and found him watching her.

He had noticed her looking at his body. A low arousal hummed in her blood. His eyes reflected the same reaction, only with cool consent, as if he controlled it in both himself and her.

Yes, this man would be nothing but trouble.

"Do not move. Do not attempt to leave." He strode to the writing desk, picked up his discarded shirt, and drew it on.

She did not watch. Not really. But out of the corner of her eye she saw the way his limbs moved and his torso stretched. That image from the afternoon invaded her head again, more vividly this time, of his face above her and those shoulders and that chest under her caress . . .

She could see evidence of his inhabitation out of the corner of her eye too. The lamp stood on a writing table in this sitting room. A pile of papers did too. She noticed the ink stains of his fingers. He had been writing, not sleeping. She pictured him there, stripped to the cool night air, intent on his prose.

Dressed, barely, and looking too rakish and romantic for safety in that loose shirt, he faced her.

"Lord Elliot, did you move yourself here to spy on me?"

"I left the spying to Signora Cirillo. I moved here to stop you from slipping away in the dead of night."

He had guessed her plan. That discouraged her. "Involving that harpy in my private affairs was inexcusable."

"It appears it was necessary. She relished her mission and performed with initiative. I merely asked her to inform me if you disobeyed and left the hostel. Instead, she followed you and intercepted that letter to your friend." His expression turned critical. "That you tried to arrange this midnight assignation with a man is intolerable. Even worse, what if your Pietro had not waited at the crossroad? You would have been out there in the night, in this city of all cities, unprotected—"

"Do not scold me. Do not dare. If he had not come I would have found a fast way to hire a carriage or a wagon or a donkey if need be, and I would be gone." The full implications of this sorry episode had lined up in her mind. She resented every one of them.

"It appears that I have traded one gaoler for another," she said.

He lifted her valise. "Call it what you will." He swung his arm to the door, inviting her to lead the way.

Simmering with anger, she trudged back up the stairs to her apartment. To her horror he did not drop the valise inside the doorway, but carried it into her bedchamber. She did not follow. An intuitive caution, a very womanly one, kept her in the sitting room.

"Come here, Miss Blair."

His command caused a rumbling in her that she did not recognize or like. The anger it contained was understandable, but it also held other pulses and throbs that dismayed her. She hated when men tried to dictate to her, when they presumed to be her master, and yet . . .

She peered into the bedchamber. He stood there in dishabille, his white shirt open at the collar, his hair mussed and his expression set with resolve. He noticed her and that wordless acknowledgment passed between them. Tingles of thrills and danger scurried through her.

He walked over and pulled her into the room. His hold on her arm, so firm and confident, so full of assumptions regarding his right to do as he pleased, stunned her. Never in her life had a man treated her like this. She tried to collect herself and form the words to put him in his place, but . . .

He untied the knot of the shawl beneath her chin. It took far too long. It brought him much too close. Surely he was not such a rogue as to—she should stop him and do it herself. She should—

He slid the shawl off her head and shoulders. It fell in a long, slow caress. His gaze followed the edge slipping over her body until it hung from his hand.

Only moonlight from the open window lit the chamber, but she did not have to see his face clearly to know his thoughts. They were just there in the room, in the air, as they had been in the afternoon.

A new reaction startled her. Another one that she had never experienced before. She was afraid. Not of him, and not of being forced. Of herself, and of the peculiar, shocking way her body responded to how he played her master.

He gestured to the bed. "Remove your dress and lie down."

That almost snapped her back to her senses. Almost. An inexplicable excitement twinged low and scandalous at the order, however. Dear heavens—

"You go too far." Did she actually speak it? Had her mind finally dredged up some common sense and come to her rescue?

"You leave me no choice. I cannot risk your stealing away again."

"You have my word I will not."

"A woman who expects me to break my word to Sansoni will not keep hers to me. Now cooperate unless you want me to force you to obey."

She reached behind her back and released her dress's hooks. It only took a minute to drop it off and lay it on a chair. The light was not so dim as to cloak her. She actually wished she wore stupid stays. She suspected he could see more than he should beneath her simple chemise.

She approached the bed and climbed onto it, trying not to expose too much, excited because she suspected that she did. She lay on her back and looked up at him. Silence hung in the air for a long pause.

"What are your intentions, Lord Elliot?"

He laughed again. Quietly. Darkly. "This is not a good moment to provoke and tease, Miss Blair."

Suddenly he was bending over her. Hovering. Her heart began racing. His shirt billowed near her face. His scent assaulted her. His size dominated her. A terrible, wonderful anticipation titillated her. Her breasts grew sensitive and—

He took her left arm and moved it near the iron bars of the headboard.

"What are you doing?"

He threaded the shawl between the bars. "Making sure that you do not leave. I do not need much sleep but I cannot stay awake for two nights."

"This is excessive. Ignoble. I demand that you—"

"This is necessary. It is either this or I sleep beside you. Would you prefer that?"

She stared up at him. He paused in making the knots and looked down. Her heart rose to her throat.

"Would you?" he repeated. It was a frank, sincere question. An invitation to allow the sensual pull to have its way.

She swallowed. "Of course not."

Even in the dim light, she saw his smile. He returned his attention to the knots.

Finally he moved away and straightened. She yanked at the bond. There was no slack in the knots. She turned on her side and pried at the thick wad with her other hand.

"Feel free to try and untie them. You will not be able to. You can sit. You can move. You can even stand. You can use the chamber pot. But you cannot get away. Better to use the time sleeping."

A note in his tone made her stop trying. She rolled onto her back and looked up at him. Her helplessness and his control shouted silently between them. Her mind screamed rebellious insults, but her body experienced a delicious warmth and anticipation. It appalled her that this subjugation provoked desire, and a very erotic desire at that.

He knew, damn him. She could tell that he did.

"You look very beautiful there, Miss Blair. Very lovely, and vulnerable, and, dare I add, . . . submissive?"

"You bastard."

That quiet laugh again. Then he was gone, leaving her to argue with herself for the rest of the night over just how vulnerable and submissive he had made her.

CHAPTER FIVE

Phaedra held the cameo up in the morning light flooding through her sitting room window. It had become a talisman the last two days while she crossed swords with a man too confident in his rights to control her.

You should have warned me, Mother.

Perhaps Artemis had not known and could not warn. Maybe she had so isolated herself from men like Elliot Rothwell that she never battled them.

She pictured her mother, so beautiful it made one's breath catch. So sweet of face that people never guessed the brilliant mind until she opened her mouth or leveled that perceptive gaze at them. She had indeed been a queen around whom many bees buzzed. Scholars and artists and men who admired her intelligence were among the friends who loved her and hoped for more. Their home had been full of the famous and the striving.

Surely one of those men had tried to conquer. Certainly the famous Artemis Blair had experienced the primitive thrill of meeting her match in wits and power.

She should have warned her daughter that such a man might come.

Phaedra looked out the window. Down below Lord Elliot directed Signora Cirillo's servants as they hoisted portmanteaus onto the coach that would take them to the harbor. Her eyes narrowed on her enemy's head.

At least he had not tied her down last night. She had promised five different ways not to leave. He had only relented when she swore, *swore,* it on her mother's grave. He had made her plead like a supplicant to the lord.

Her mother was probably turning in that grave now. Artemis Blair had never submitted to a man, even symbolically. She had never married, not even her lifelong lover, not even when she found herself with child by Richard Drury. She had never given up her freedom, her independence, and her right to love and bed whomever she chose, even when she discovered she only wanted to love and bed one man after all.

The cameo warmed in Phaedra's hand. She gazed at it. No, not only one man. There had been another.

It had been a shock to read about that in her father's memoirs. Just remembering his words made her a little sick. She had always thought her parents shared a perfect love, unfettered by obligation and laws, a true meeting of the souls that would last for eternity. Their friendship proved to the world that there was another, better way.

It had been thus between them for years, but another man had finally interfered.

This interloper was charming but at the heart of a scheme that is both brilliant and nefarious. That was what her father wrote. She remembered the words exactly. She had memorized them prior to sailing from England. *He lured Artemis into an affair, used her most dishonorably in ways that would destroy her reputation, and ultimately his actions led to her death. He sold her lies as surely as those fraudulent antiquities that he flogs. It is only a matter of time before he is exposed, however, because the objects are out there, visible, just like the one he sold to her, and eventually someone will reveal their suspect provenance and his thieving seductions will undo him.*

Her fingers closed tightly on the cameo. An antiquity of suspect provenance. A gem added late to a will, said to come from Pompeii. Phaedra was quite certain this was the object her father referred to, and her only link to the man he described.

His actions ultimately led to her death. She had not been able to get those words out of her mind. They chanted at night while her dreams saw images of her mother those last weeks, too sober, too distracted. She had not even noticed at the time, because there were always smiles for her at least. But her mother's decline had come too fast and her death had been a shock.

Phaedra looked down again. Lord Elliot was gazing up at her. How long had he been watching her from the street?

Maybe her mother had issued no warnings because she had not known herself. Maybe the interloper had been a man like this one below, who could thrill with his mere attention and who tempted one to forget every belief, every principle, that anchored one's life.

She could forgive her mother for neglecting this

lesson. She could forgive Artemis anything, even leaving the world too soon. But if a man had indeed used her dishonorably, if his actions had led to her death, that was different. The daughter of Artemis Blair would never forgive *him*. If she learned that was true, she would see that man fall.

She reached for her shawl and draped it over her hair. Lord Elliot would be an inconvenience, but she would not allow his company to interfere with the real reason she had come to Italy.

Elliot returned to his apartment to retrieve the valise stuffed with his papers. He passed Miss Blair on the steps.

"I will wait in the carriage." Her crisp tone carried the chill that she always showed in his presence now.

She would never forgive him for tying her to that bed, and not only because of the humiliation and lack of trust. They both knew it had excited her and she hated him for that and all it implied. They also both knew that if he had not done it she would have slipped away during the night in order to avoid all that it implied.

She had been adamant that it not happen again last night. Her promises had been so heartfelt, her reassurances not to flee so genuine, that he had relented.

It meant that he could sleep himself. The first night he had lain abed, restless and hungry, desire carving through him like a ragged-edged knife. Picturing her up there in that thin chemise, bound to the headboard, her hair glistening like copper silk and her body too visible—*What are your intentions, Lord Elliot?*

Hell.

He retrieved his valise and a long package and joined her in the carriage. Her straight back and distant, blank gaze said she accepted his company because she had no choice. She would not ease their time together with pleasantries.

The boat he had hired waited near the Castel Nuovo. An hour later they were sailing along the land that rimmed the bay.

Miss Blair stationed herself at mid-deck, holding on to the rail. She watched the passing coastline and the growing size of Mount Vesuvius in its background. The breeze pushed the shawl off her hair and her pale, unusual beauty caught the eyes of the crew. Elliot ambled closer so there could be no misunderstanding regarding his protection of her.

He held out the package that he had brought.

"What is that?" she asked.

"A gift."

She smiled kindly, but firmly. "I do not accept gifts from gentlemen, Lord Elliot."

"You do not exchange gifts for favors, which is admirable. However, since I have not enjoyed the favors you are still free to accept the gift. If I seduce you, you can give it back."

He came damned close to saying "when," not "if."

Still hesitant, but curious, she took the package and peeled off the paper wrapping at one end.

"A parasol?" She stripped off the rest of the paper. She laughed. "Black. Totally black. How . . . sweet."

"I thought it would match."

"This is to save me from more tiny spots?"

"It is to save you from illness. The sun here is very hot and it is midsummer. When we go inland you will be glad for the shade."

She popped open the parasol and poised it over her head. "You know the country well. Have you been here before?"

"Twice. First on my grand tour, and again several years ago." He pointed to the coast. "That is Herculaneum there. The same eruption of Vesuvius that buried Pompeii in ashes buried Herculaneum in lava."

She squinted at the rocky site dotted with the colors of visitors' dresses and coats. "I had intended to visit Herculaneum too, but Signore Sansoni—I will miss much on this visit now."

"Why not dally and see it after we return from this little journey?"

"I cannot afford the time. I need to return home. I have a publishing house to run."

And a special book to print. If he did not receive satisfaction when he finally spoke to Merriweather, Miss Blair would not be sailing home for a good while.

"I also do not think I will enjoy spending time in Naples when we have completed this little journey," she said. "No doubt you will think that your word to Sansoni still stands then, and I will be stuck with you underfoot."

He admired the impressive view of Vesuvius's high cone while they passed close enough to Herculaneum to see some workers at the dig. Copper hair fluttered near his arm. "Miss Blair, I wonder if it is not so much having me underfoot that you dislike, but *not* having me under your foot."

Her deep sigh spoke her thoughts. *Heaven give me patience with this unenlightened, predictable man.*

"I suspect it is hopeless to explain this, but I will try in the interests of peace. I do not think either partner in a friendship, a marriage, or a love affair should be under the other's foot. My view is only extraordinary because the foot in question so often wears a boot, and everyone assumes it is natural for it to be planted on a feminine back. I believe that men and women can stand side by side, neither owning the other. My mother's life proved this is possible, and my own thus far proves it as well. Nor did we invent this belief. It is well known and has been espoused by people who are greatly admired."

"I know all about your belief, Miss Blair. I am not ignorant of the philosophy. It even sounds right and rational. The only problem is that it neglects to account for several things."

"Indeed? What things?"

"Human nature. Human history. The tendency of the bad to make victims of the weak, and the need of the weak for protection. Venture alone into the hill towns of the Campania or the back streets of Marseilles or Istanbul, walk into London's rookeries, and see what happens to a woman alone and unprotected."

"The lords of old gave their serfs protection. That does not mean it was right to demand their bondage in return."

He laughed. "Lords. Serfs. What a black view you have of women's lives. It need not be that way."

"But it can be," she said. "*You* know it can. The law makes it so."

Her emphasis on *you* was so subtle that he wondered

if he imagined it. She poked at an old sore very gently but he felt the pain anyway. A dark anger coiled in him.

She kept her attention on the coast. Her slight flush indicated that she knew she had crossed a line. He controlled his reaction, but predatory speculations slid into his head. He judged what it would take to be lord of this woman, to make her kneel.

"My apologies, Lord Elliot. I should not—"

"You compound your impertinence, Miss Blair. Better to have let your insinuation float away on the breeze." Only she hadn't, and he wondered about the secure way she had said it. "You were referring to the rumors about my mother, weren't you?"

She debated her response while she glanced at him carefully several times. "I will admit that her retreat to the country her last years has been interpreted as your father's doing."

He knew the lurid story whispered in drawing rooms high and low. That his mother had taken a lover and his father had punished her by sending the man to die in a distant colony, and then imprisoning her at their country estate.

Was it true? He and his brothers had concluded the lover had been real, but not the imprisonment part. His own father had sworn to him that he did not do what people said. And yet his mother's exile encouraged the gossip, until she herself even believed it.

He saw her in the library, her dark head bent to books and papers, lost in the world of her mind. Almost totally lost to her sons. As the youngest he spent the most time with her there. She would emerge from her concentration sometimes to guide him through the shelves, picking books for him to read, or commenting on his own pages.

A few times, however, the bond had been closer, like the day she had received a letter that left her weeping. It contained news about an army officer's death.

He did this. To punish me for loving someone else.

It had been an illicit love. She had been an adulteress. Her sorrow moved him anyway, but he had seen that her accusation was the dark fantasy of an unhappy soul.

He felt Miss Blair beside him. Even his anger could not kill the way he responded to her sensual lure. Her father's damned memoirs insinuated that a reclusive woman had been the only one who understood just how ruthless the Rothwell blood could make a man. His own certainty that it was untrue would not carry any weight when his father's name was impugned.

"They knew each other," Miss Blair said. "Our mothers."

"My mother was familiar with Artemis Blair's essays, but she never spoke of a friendship." But then, she had rarely spoken about anything.

"I do not believe they ever met. They corresponded. They were both writers, after all. Their interests were similar. Your mother sent mine a poem once. It was among her papers on her death. A beautiful poem that reflected an intelligent and sensitive soul."

He fixed his gaze on the approaching coastal town of Sorrento. It infuriated him that his mother had shared her writing with Artemis Blair and not her own children.

"Did your mother encourage her in her adultery?" His words sounded hoarse and harsh to his ears. "Did she preach her belief in free love in her letters?" He pictured the radical, renowned Artemis Blair turning his mother's head in ways that would result in so much grief.

"I believe they corresponded about literature and such. My mother only mentioned her once, upon news of her passing."

"What did she say?" It came out more a snarl than a question.

"She said, *He should have let her go, but of course, being a man, he could not.*"

That only made thunder rumble through the clouds in his mind. He wanted to say of course a man cannot allow the mother of his children to leave on a romantic whim. Of course his father had refused her that freedom.

Only she had found a way to leave anyway, in her own manner.

Out of the corner of his eye he noticed a crew member taking too long with some rigging. The man dallied at his chore while he feasted his eyes on the beauty of Phaedra Blair.

The storm in his head howled. Lightning flashed. He narrowed his eyes and spoke four words. The man hurried away.

Miss Blair noticed. "What did you say to him?"

"Nothing significant. A simple Neapolitan phrase that requests privacy." He did not bother explaining that the words roughly translated to *move on or die*.

A snapping wind helped them make good time. The landscape became increasingly dramatic as they angled across the bay to the Sorrento peninsula. High hills hugged the coast, dropping down to the sea in steep, green drops. Small beaches held some boats, and houses hugged the cliff, hanging like so many white and pastel cubes above the water.

They rounded the tip of the small peninsula, passed the isle of Capri, and sailed into the Bay of Salerno. Steeper, perilous, inaccessible hills loomed above them. The scenery awed Phaedra. Lord Elliot had been correct. It would have been a pity to miss this.

"What is happening up there?" She pointed to some activity halfway up the cliff side.

"The king is building a road to Amalfi. They are carving it right into the hillside."

She noted how the road would be above the fishing villages. "Either way, one must climb up or down."

"At least people will not have to rely on boats or donkeys. And the prospects from up there will be spectacular." He pointed ahead of them, down the coast. "Positano is right beyond that promontory. You can already see the old Norman watchtower on it. There are many of them on this coast, built to protect the medieval Norman kingdom that used to be here from the Saracen threat."

She walked to the bow of the boat so she could see better as the tower came into view. The old, angular stone tower rose several levels high, medieval in its construction and isolated on its finger of land. Small windows punctuated it like those on an ancient castle. It appeared a foreign and northern intrusion on this sun-washed land.

"Those high windows face due east and west," she

said. "There is nothing between that one and the sea's horizon, and nothing between the other and the peak of the high hill. Will we be here several days?"

"I expect so."

She had lost track of the calendar while she was a guest of Sansoni. Now she worked it out. "The summer solstice approaches. I wonder if the tower will be used in some ritual."

"This is a Catholic land. Such superstitions were suppressed thousands of years ago."

Although Lord Elliot responded, she could tell he was not truly with her. A silence claimed him that had little to do with sounds. It existed internally, as if his life spirit had retreated to secret chambers of his soul.

She regretted making even the vaguest reference to his mother's situation. It had slid out in her pique at his arrogance in assuming he was right and she was amusingly wrong. She should have known not to engage in an argument about how she thought and lived. When it came to such things this man was as foreign to her as the fishermen in these picturesque villages.

They passed very close to the tower, cutting close as the wind billowed their sails. It appeared deserted.

"Who is this friend we will be visiting?" she asked. "Since we will arrive soon, perhaps I should know his name."

"Matthias Greenwood. He was one of my tutors at university."

She swallowed her surprise. She knew Greenwood. She had tried in vain to locate his home in Naples. "Will he not mind that you have brought more baggage than he expects?"

"He will be delighted to have the company of the daughter of Artemis Blair. He stepped into her circle on occasion, I believe."

"Yes, he did. I met him several times, the last at my mother's funeral." Matthias Greenwood was one of many scholars who had come to honor the woman who confounded the world.

He was also someone who might shed some light on the "other" man. She had thought this delay in going to Pompeii would be a nuisance. Instead Lord Elliot was helping her check one thing off her list of things to accomplish in this land.

"He admired her. He said if she had been a man, she would have been recognized as one of the best experts on ancient Roman letters in England." Lord Elliot still spoke in a distracted tone, as if only half his mind paid attention.

Phaedra looked upon the town of Positano with more optimism, and not only because her mission might be furthered there. She did not conform to stupid social rules, but most of the world did. She had wondered how she would be received when she arrived with Lord Elliot. Traveling with him implied things she did not countenance and would not like to have assumed.

Mr. Greenwood would probably know better than to assume anything at all.

She sensed her companion looking at her, and turned her head. He had returned to the world, most thoroughly.

"He often entertains a mixed entourage," he said. "There may be other guests visiting him. You will behave yourself, won't you?"

She trusted he did not expect her to play the docile mistress in some vain attempt to become a woman these guests could tolerate.

Even if she wanted to create that deception, she would not begin to know how.

CHAPTER SIX

Positano lay on its own little cove that was cluttered with boats. The pastel buildings of the town hovered above the sea, stacked one above the other on the precipitous slope of the mountain. The town dropped steeply right to the shore.

Phaedra took in the view of towering cliff, endless sapphire water, and deep green foliage. She had never seen anything so physically dramatic in her life.

"Which house belongs to Mr. Greenwood?" she asked.

Lord Elliot moved close and extended his arm so her sight could follow it. "That one up there, with the columns."

Those columns supported a long, covered veranda on the topmost house. It rose a little distance above the town itself. Its breadth created a crown on the village cascading beneath it.

"Are we supposed to fly up there, or will he be dropping a basket down for us?"

One of their crew had wandered off. He now returned with the answer. Two boys followed him with donkeys.

Phaedra allowed the boys to help her onto the back of her animal. Lord Elliot merely swung his leg to get astride his. He dwarfed the animal, and his boots scraped the ground. The crew tied their portmanteaus and valises on two more donkeys.

She laughed at the picture they made. "What a retinue you have, Lord Elliot. You will make an impressive procession through the town. Perhaps I will get out my sketchbook, to preserve for the world how finely you sit on that great steed of yours."

He kicked his donkey forward to take the lead, swatting her animal's rump as he passed. "Tend to your own pretty seat, Miss Blair. Be careful you do not fall off or you will not stop rolling until you are in the bay."

She understood his meaning at once. Their donkeys paced up lanes so steep that they had been paved in deep, shallow steps. She thought she really might fall into the sea. The animals were sure-footed, but her perch, sitting sidesaddle, left her clinging on for her life.

They created a small spectacle. Villagers peered out their doorways and windows, curious about the foreigners heading to the villa atop the town. Children gathered behind them, making a true procession. Two girls walked alongside her for a while, poking with curiosity at the red ends of her hair hanging beneath the shawl's bottom edge. A few women made little curtsies as Lord Elliot passed, knowing from his bearing and manner that he had been born to the blood.

She relaxed as she adapted to the donkey's gait. She

dared not look back, but she allowed herself to notice the houses, handsome in their rustic stone construction. Simple balconies and tiled roofs helped create a jumble of forms and color. A few larger ones sported colorful majolica tiles around the main doors. They all appeared very ancient, like the tower. Stucco covered most of them, often worked in decorative flourishes and moldings. Some houses were white but many bore tints of red and pink.

Sounds of community life rang around her as people called to one another through open windows and down market streets. Somewhere a man lazily sang an aria from a Rossini opera, accompanying whatever labor he performed.

The lanes leveled as they approached the villa. It was as if someone had removed a chunk of the hillside so the big house could be built.

A man appeared inside the arched open loggia whose roof was supported by the columns. He stood tall, straight, and slim, with a shock of white hair and an aquiline nose. A jaw of uncompromising squareness gave way to a cleft chin. Phaedra had only met Matthias Greenwood a few times, but his appearance was so distinctive that one did not forget it.

He waved a greeting, then stepped out and walked toward them.

"Rothwell! What a relief you are finally here. My company is badly in need of your wit."

They greeted each other. Elliot introduced Phaedra.

"I have already had the honor, Rothwell. I am happy to see you again, Miss Blair, and under less trying circumstances than the last time. Your mother was much esteemed by inferior scholars like myself, and generous to us. I was grateful for the introductions her reception afforded me."

Servants appeared and Matthias rattled off instructions regarding the baggage. "Come inside and refresh yourselves. My other guests take their siestas but they will join us soon."

She walked up the stone path and followed Matthias into the loggia. She glanced through its arches and her breath caught.

The view was unreal, a prospect that begged for a paintbrush and canvas. If gazing up this hill was impressive, looking down left one in awe. The town's roofs and ribbons of lane spilled straight down. The drop was so steep one marveled that anything had been built here. The endless sea, the low sky, the embrace of the promontory—it all created a vast, dreamlike panorama from a precarious hold on the world, one that was thrilling and romantic, drenched in beauty but tinged with danger.

"It is a wonder that you do not simply live in this loggia and ignore whether the rest of your home falls to ruin, Mr. Greenwood."

"I almost do, Miss Blair. Here and on the other terraces and balconies. I go to the parish church even though I am not a Catholic, and light candles for the soul of the distant relative whose legacy allows me to live in paradise."

A woman greeted them when they entered the airy, marble-floored drawing room. She was an elegant, olive-skinned native of the country. She possessed a lovely, soulful face permanently touched with a melancholic expression. Her name was Signora Roviale, and the manner in which she came forward and saw to their comfort indicated that this was her home. Matthias Greenwood did not live in paradise alone.

Another guest ambled in soon after a servant brought some wine. Phaedra recognized him too. He had not been at her mother's funeral, but he had called at their home once or twice when she was a girl. He was so handsome in a golden, fine-boned, noble way that she had almost developed a *tendre* the first time she saw him.

"See who is here to celebrate your visit, Rothwell," Matthias said. "I wrote and told him you would come down from Naples, and he and his wife traveled from Rome just for you. Miss Blair, allow me to introduce Mr. Randall Whitmarsh, gentleman, scholar, and another refugee from England."

Mr. Whitmarsh had adopted Continental fashion and manners, reflecting his long years abroad. He muttered *bellissima* as he bent to kiss her hand, and fussed just enough to prove he had left reserve back in England when he adopted Rome as his main home.

"It is a joy to meet the daughter of the indomitable Artemis Blair," he said, bestowing a charming, admiring smile.

Phaedra was not above enjoying a handsome man's attention. She noticed that Lord Elliot kept glancing askance at Mr. Whitmarsh's long hold of her hand.

"I learned recently of Richard Drury's passing," Mr. Whitmarsh said, patting her hand. "I see that you are still in mourning, but it was perhaps healthy to come abroad so your grief is assuaged."

"My choice in fashion made ordering a mourning wardrobe unnecessary, but my father would not have wanted that anyway. He specifically forbade me to mourn when I last saw him."

She extricated her hand from the gentle grasp of Mr. Whitmarsh. "I did not anticipate that I would meet so many who knew my mother in remote Positano, of all places."

"We three are all members of the Society of the Dilettanti, Miss Blair. As a woman your mother could not join, but we all eventually called to pay her homage," Mr. Whitmarsh said. "Considering her expertise in Roman letters, it is not so surprising that you meet those who knew her if you visit the lands of the ancient empire."

"Are you also a member of the society, Lord Elliot?"

"I joined after my grand tour."

She had been merely eighteen when her mother died, and not yet admitted into those salons and dinners where Artemis entertained scholars and artists. Yet, here in front of her were members of her mother's circle, even if they had merely stepped inside the outer edge on occasion.

She would have to find out if either of these men had noticed or heard on which man Artemis had settled her late affections.

She was relieved that she and Signora Roviale would not be the only women in this house party. Soon Mrs. Whitmarsh came down from her chamber.

Phaedra knew at once that Mrs. Whitmarsh was not

as open-minded as her husband. A little, pale bird of a woman, she did not speak much, but she possessed a face so malleable that one knew her thoughts. Upon realizing Phaedra and Lord Elliot had arrived together, Mrs. Whitmarsh smiled thinly, glanced to Signora Roviale with subtle scorn, and retreated into silent, re-signed disapproval of the company of fallen women.

While they dined alfresco in the long loggia that evening, Lord Elliot graciously drew Mrs. Whitmarsh into conversation that she would enjoy and talked about London society. Phaedra allowed the gentlemen to re-gale her with advice about the ancient wonders she should not miss.

"You must go to Paestum," Matthias exhorted. "Rothwell, I command that you take her there. I do not understand all these English visitors who tromp through bakeries and brothels in Pompeii, when nearby are some of the finest Greek temples in the world that they ig-nore."

"If Miss Blair desires it, we will visit the temples," Lord Elliot said.

Matthias appeared very much the university don at the moment. White hair disheveled, jaw chiseling the air, and aquiline nose poised high, he intoned his lesson as if she were the student that the universities had never allowed a woman to be.

"That is why I am here, Miss Blair. Rothwell and Whitmarsh admire the Romans, but my focus is more ancient. This land was a colony of the Greeks when Rome was still a small town with five cattle. When you see Paestum you will understand the superior Greek mind."

"If it does not require extending my visit long, perhaps I will take your advice."

After dinner Signora Roviale led the women away
from the loggia, leaving the men to discuss and debate
antiquity. Phaedra did not relish forcing conversation
with critical Mrs. Whitmarsh. She begged off any further social obligations, claiming fatigue.

A servant brought her to the chamber she would use.
Square and white, with the same marble floors seen
throughout the villa, it had long windows that gave out
on a shallow balcony that stretched above the loggia. A
servant had already unpacked her garments into the
dark wood wardrobe. Water waited at the washstand in a
ceramic jug painted with red flowers and blue leaves.
Similar colors decorated the tiles around the fireplace
and the sill of one window.

She opened her doors to the breeze coming off the
sea and the final glow of twilight. Sounds drifted up
from the loggia, of Matthias intoning and Elliot laughing and long rumbles of conversation. She wondered if
her mother had ever really been accepted into those
male discussions. When the Dilettanti paid homage,
was it always that of men to a woman, with all that implied?

Chairs scraped and farewells flew. Silence slid over
the villa. She rose to undress for bed. She began to unhook her dress when the smallest sound outside her
door caught her attention. A slice of golden light
streaked across the balcony and into the night. She went
over and peered out.

Lord Elliot stood at the other end in shirtsleeves and

waistcoat. She was sure that she had made no noise, but he looked in her direction as if she had.

"I wondered if Matthias had put you in that chamber," he said.

She stepped onto the terra-cotta tiles of the balcony. The light came from another set of doors beside hers. Two rooms shared this terrace.

"It appears our host misunderstood," she said.

"Possibly. However if I have to share a balcony, I prefer it be with you rather than Mrs. Whitmarsh."

She ventured out a bit farther but stayed on her side of the space. Standing near the stone balustrade one could see down on the water, sparkling now with a million tiny reflections of stars.

"Mr. Whitmarsh said the Dilettanti paid homage to my mother. I am glad to hear her abilities were recognized."

"An honest man had to admit to her brilliance. Of course, there were those who were less honest and discounted it."

"Of course. Did you ever meet her?"

"I was still at university when she passed away. I had heard of her, and I had seen her in town, but I did not have the stature to call on her."

"What did you think of her?"

He turned and rested his hips against the balustrade and gazed through the night at her. She wished he did not look so handsome and appealing. She wished the light would burn out so his face was obscured.

"I was raised in a household of men and my father did not comprehend women well. So learning about your mother was a revelation. There was much discussion about her among schoolboys. Some fell in love with her, others thought her unnatural, but mostly she made one question the order of things. As for me, I thought she was beautiful, interesting, intelligent, and probably dangerous."

"I expect she *was* dangerous. If the world were filled with Artemis Blairs, men could not remain as they are. They would all have to question the order of things as you did."

"That was my thinking, but I was a boy then and did not appreciate the real danger. I had to meet her daughter to understand that part of it."

It was her turn to laugh. "I am hardly dangerous to you."

"You misunderstand, just as I did. The danger does not come from you."

No, it didn't. That was apparent out here in the night. A power flowed from him, carrying those masculine impulses. That did not surprise or frighten her. The way her own feminine instincts reacted did, however.

"Do not blame me for your worst inclinations, Lord Elliot."

"They do not strike me as even among the bad, let alone the worst, lovely Phaedra. Instead they seem natural and inevitable and even necessary."

His quiet, sure voice cast out velvet ropes to encircle her. Her heart rose to her throat and her pulse raced. He had not moved. He stood not one inch closer, but it felt as if he had reached out and slid his hand down her whole body.

"I want to take you." His leisurely, calm tone stirred her blood much like the breeze teased her hair. "I want you helpless to the pleasure and begging for me. I want you naked and trembling and stripped of your—"

"Enough, sir. If that is how you think of women—"

"Only you, dear lady. You throw down a gauntlet to every man you see. Do not be surprised if one picks it up."

"How dare—"

"Oh, I would dare. I am halfway to daring right now. You know that, but here you are. If you did not want me to dare, you would never have stepped out that door."

She opened her mouth to deny it but no words came out.

With a vague smile, he pushed away from the balustrade. Her heart jumped and her legs felt weak.

"This danger you incite in me—it excites you." He walked toward the light and his chamber. "Who is doing the buzzing now, Miss Blair?"

"An odd name to give a daughter. Phaedra," Matthias mused aloud. He and Elliot drank coffee early the next morning in the loggia. Down below them Positano was coming to life with the dawn.

"I doubt there is another woman with the name in England, considering the reference," Matthias added. "Just like Artemis Blair to decide the source did not matter and to actually prize its uniqueness."

Since in ancient mythology Phaedra had an affair with her stepson, it *was* an odd choice. Elliot doubted that Miss Blair and her mother's beliefs in free love went that far.

"I suspect it was a matter of the sound. It is a lovely name," he said.

"I could have thought of five or six better ones. No, her carelessness on this first motherly duty suggests she was indifferent to that part of her life."

"You spoke well of her when I was your student, and Miss Blair idolizes her memory. Let us not say things now that she might overhear."

"She is still abed and will not overhear my allusions to her mother's lack of feminine impulses, but your admonishment is well taken."

She *was* still abed, sleeping soundly. Elliot had walked over and peered in before coming down. Her doors were still open, like a repudiation of his last words to her. *See, you are not dangerous to me at all. Your honor and the law protect me from the worst, and my own self-possession will deal with the rest.*

He had seen copper hair flowing over pillows and creamy skin twisted in a sheet. One lovely, tapered, naked leg stretched atop the mound of bedclothes. The temptation to go in, to just watch her, prodded him, as did his annoyance that she slept so damned deeply. He certainly hadn't.

He was thinking about her too much. Wondering too frequently. Wanting too often. He trusted that the company of others and the call of his work would dilute her presence and return his mental state to something more normal.

"You are living like a king here, Greenwood," he said, to distract himself from images of Phaedra so ethereally erotic in her repose. "The improvements since my last visit are impressive."

Matthias beamed. "I assume you refer to the building, and not my mistress, although I am hard pressed to say which pleases me more. Getting the stone in was hell, but worth it. You should join me, Rothwell. Buy an old villa and see how far your English money goes on this coast."

"It goes far because it is so inaccessible one must sail miles to get to a town a stone's throw behind this hill. I need city life more often than twice a year, but if you are happy in your isolation I am glad for you."

"Not isolated at all. I always have company. They come to me from England and Rome and Naples and even Pompeii. I entertained the superintendent of the site last month. He does not mind riding a donkey over that hill behind us."

"I would appreciate a letter of introduction," Elliot said. "I would like to see everything new that they have excavated the last few years, not merely the things on the tourist map."

Matthias arched an eyebrow. "Want to see the frescoes revealing the delights of the night, do you? They will not allow Miss Blair in, no matter what letters I write."

"I will be researching other things. Before I go, I would like some time to discuss the direction I am taking with you."

"Let us decide now that tomorrow morning we will lock ourselves in my study and go to it. I miss being the tutor sometimes. Then I remember how dim-witted most of my students were, and I dismiss the nostalgia."

"Playing tutor and student will be useful. It will clarify my thoughts. Oh, and I am obliged as a gentleman to say that I believe you misunderstand my friendship with Miss Blair."

"Do I? That is a damned pity."

The lady in question joined them then, looking like a beautiful Celtic witch in her black flowing dress and unbound hair. Matthias sat her down at the table. He poured her coffee and made a fuss that revealed the stimulation he found in her company.

"I hope you slept well in my humble home, Miss Blair."

"It is anything but humble, and I slept very well. The sound and breeze of the sea is most soothing." She turned in her chair to look down on the town. "What are they doing down there? That big red thing by the water?"

"Ah, that would be the wagon for the procession. They must be painting it. Three days hence is the feast of San Giovanni. St. John the Baptist. It is a major holy day in these parts. No boats will put out to sea that morning."

"There will be a procession?"

"A procession, a mass, a festival—among other rituals they collect walnuts in the hills to press for oil."

"It is interesting that it coincides with the solstice," she said. "It may be another example of Christians taking over a pagan festival."

"Miss Blair is achieving a reputation in mythological studies that rivals her mother's in Roman letters," Elliot said. "She published a book on the subject that is well regarded."

"How commendable." Matthias managed to dismiss the achievement even as he admired it. "This common date is a coincidence. The sun god was not even a major figure in Greek and Roman mythology. Apollo is associated with him, but the sun himself, Helios, plays a minor role. Perhaps that is because there is so much sun in these lands that there was no need to appease its god."

"There is sun aplenty in Egypt and their sun god still reigned supreme," Elliot said. "I think Miss Blair is correct about the feast of San Giovanni."

"Possibly," Matthias said. "And the symbolism of the walnuts would be?"

Phaedra laughed. "I will think of one before I depart, Mr. Greenwood, since you are willing to be pliable in your opinions."

"For a beautiful woman, I can be too pliable, Miss Blair. It is my great failing." He gazed out of the loggia. A man approached on a path from the north. "Here is Whitmarsh, back from his dawn hike. I promised to show him a new treasure I found. Would you like to see my humble but prized collection of artifacts, Miss Blair?"

"Most certainly, Mr. Greenwood."

She took his offered hand to rise. Whitmarsh fell into line as they filed into the house.

Elliot was curious to see if Phaedra could maintain the pose of indifference toward him that she had adopted this morning. Not a blush. No fluster at all. She acknowledged his presence boldly and blankly. Her manner only provoked the darker side of the desire that plagued him.

That side was saying that he should have seduced her on the balcony last night like he had wanted to. The argument was making more sense by the minute.

CHAPTER SEVEN

It is a modest collection." Matthias beamed with pride despite his words. "I keep it here to imitate the example of a Renaissance *studiolo*. This is my retreat within my home, full of my favorite things."

His *studiolo* was a large cube of a room, frescoed with ancient-looking urns and foliage on the plaster walls. In addition to a large writing desk strewn with books and papers, it contained bits of artifacts. The capital of a Corinthian column perched on the desk's corner. An ancient portrait bust looked down from the top of a high bookcase. Glass cases on legs, such as one saw in bookshops in England, held other bits and pieces of antiquity.

Phaedra strolled along them, peering in. Randall Whitmarsh accompanied her, pointing out the coins bearing the likenesses of Julius Caesar and Tiberius, and the little flat glass bottles.

"Here is the great find," Matthias announced. He opened a drawer, lifted out a cloth-wrapped bundle, and began unwinding the material.

A little bronze statuette emerged, of a nude goddess in a relaxed stance.

"Some boys were diving in the cove and there she was at the bottom in the sand. She must have been there for fifteen hundred years. She is Greek, I am sure. Classical period. Probably part of a hold of Greek loot on its way to feed the collectors of imperial Rome."

Whitmarsh lifted the statue. "No doubt a ship went down offshore here. There is probably more where it sank, if it could be found."

"The water gets dangerously deep fast," Matthias said. "If there is more it will not be found until the tides do their work. I have carefully removed the barnacles that grew on her, and she polished up wonderfully."

Elliot took the statue in his hands. "It is beautiful. Do you intend to sell it?"

"I have not decided. If so, Whitmarsh here could flog it for me in Rome. Eh, Whitmarsh?"

"Or I could flog it in London," Elliot said. "You would get a better price there, wouldn't you?"

Matthias smiled with a tutor's indulgence. He slid the statue out of Elliot's hands. "And taint your blood with trade? I could not allow it."

"There is no trade if I merely refer a collector to you. Easterbrook might even be interested."

The men began debating its time of creation and its value. Phaedra wandered away to finish her little tour of the glass cases.

Matthias's collection was very eclectic, like that of a schoolboy who brought home bits and pieces of the world that fascinated him. One case contained pottery shards of little value but fascinating, primitive decoration. Swirls and geometric shapes crowded the reddish surfaces. A fine, intact Greek drinking cup held pride of place in another case, displaying the god Dionysus in a ship in its round, shallow interior.

She moved on past old daggers and bits of incised Roman armor, to a case holding other metal objects. This case was locked, and she saw why. Strewn inside were gold and silver and enameled items, some classical but others from later times, when the Normans and the Saracens were in this land. Tiny images of Roman gods vied with dense interplays of lines and arabesques for her attention.

The whole case glittered. Purse clasps and ear bobs and strands of glass beads.

"I have decided that I will keep my little goddess," Matthias announced. "Where should she go, Miss Blair?"

Phaedra made suggestions for spots to display the little bronze nude, but her thoughts remained on her host's varied collection. She wondered if he knew anything about old cameos.

That afternoon Mr. Whitmarsh decided he wanted to go fishing so the gentlemen walked down the hill to hire a boat after the town's siesta. That left Phaedra with Signora Roviale and Mrs. Whitmarsh.

The ladies sat in the drawing room and tried not to bore one another. When Mrs. Whitmarsh excused herself to go write a letter, Signora Roviale broached the one subject she thought she had in common with her remaining guest.

"He is an impressive man, your Lord Elliot. I am not so fond of all of Signore Greenwood's English friends. They are too often pale and very dull in their reserve, and their wives and mistresses without color and depth too. But Lord Elliot is both handsome and interesting. *Un uomo magnifico.*"

"Lord Elliot is brother-in-law of a good friend of mine, and escorts me at her request. I am not his mistress, however."

"Veramente?" She gave Phaedra a cool examination. "Perhaps, if you wore more attractive garments . . . Matthias says you are not in mourning and here black is more common among old women . . . and your hair, my woman could dress it so you do not look like a child, or a *puttana.*"

"Puttana" was a word Gentile Sansoni had used during his interrogation. It meant whore. Since Signora Roviale was not married to Matthias she was drawing a very fine line.

"I choose my dress and hairstyle for good reasons, *signora.* It means I am not encumbered by servants and hours of preparation before I start my busy day."

"Ahhh, *capisco.* I understand." She gestured expressively, her hand making a wide arc that included them both, and the house. "But your day is empty now, not busy, no? We have nothing to do while these Englishmen fish like peasants. I offer the loan of my servant, so you will remain, how do you say, not *encumbered.*"

"I am quite content, thank you. As for filling my empty day, I will go to my chamber and read, if you will excuse me."

"You can read another time. I think you are a woman who already does so too much." She rose and beckoned Phaedra to follow. "You may be content in your dress, but Signora Whitmarsh is not a happy guest. She thinks you are a witch trying to enchant her husband, and you are so unusual she does not know how to compete. She is mad to think it, but I can see her suspicions on her long face. We will make you presentable and ordinary for dinner tonight so she does not sit there like a dark cloud."

Rebelling at being coerced but unable to form an excuse to thwart her hostess's plan, Phaedra stood. Signora Roviale linked her arm through Phaedra's and firmly led her up the stairs.

Elliot stripped off the shirt now damp from sea spray. He handed it to the servant to wash, then groomed himself for dinner. The fishing excursion had been good sport, made more jovial by the wineskins that Matthias had thrown into the boat.

He stepped out on the balcony and listened. No sounds came from Phaedra's chamber. Assuming that she had already gone below, he made his way to the drawing room. The whole party had assembled, except the one woman he looked forward to seeing.

He wondered if she had used his absence to slip away. He cursed his negligence. The relaxing combination of sun and sea, the low arousal that would not cease, had made him forget the reason she was with him in the first place.

He spoke with Whitmarsh and Greenwood. With

each passing minute his suspicions about Phaedra's escape increased. He was about to ask Signora Roviale about Miss Blair's activities today when Whitmarsh suddenly stopped talking and stared past Greenwood's shoulder. The expression on Whitmarsh's face made Elliot look in that direction too.

Greenwood turned his head. "Oh, my. Is that our Miss Blair?"

Apparently it was, but this Miss Blair did not look much like the one Elliot knew. The black robes were gone, replaced by an azure dinner dress with ivory lace and short gigot sleeves. Its satin sash hugged her midriff and its neck and shoulders revealed a lot of white, dewy skin. The elegant, firm swells of her breasts rose above the décolleté.

Her hair had been dressed too. No longer streaming free, it formed a style thick with coils and braiding that appeared very fashionable. She sported a bit of paint on her face, or maybe the attention aimed at her merely caused her to blush.

"She is even more beautiful than her mother," Whitmarsh muttered. "If she can look like this, one wonders why she hides herself in that nun's habit."

Elliot knew why. The reason filled the drawing room. Silence fell as men eyed her and women assessed her. He walked through the stunned party to spare her from being a spectacle any longer.

"You look very beautiful tonight, Miss Blair. Let us find you some wine."

She fell in step with him while he led her toward the servant with the glasses. The party returned to its conversations.

"Signora Roviale did this to me. It is her dress," she said. "The woman is implacable. There was no way out."

He handed her a glass of wine. "You were kind to indulge her." He tried like the devil not to let his gaze linger on the white expanse above the dress. He wanted to lick and nibble the creamy skin all along the azure edge.

"It took *hours*. I had forgotten that part. And these stays—well, you can imagine how my poor body did not like *that*."

Not really. He could imagine her in chemise and stockings, before the stays, however, and after, before the pretty dress was donned.

"I expect with practice it all gets easier."

"There will be no practice. As soon as dinner is finished this experiment will be over. I merely pray that I do not faint first. I cannot wait to be relieved of this torture. It is unbearably hot, for one thing. The Arabs wear flowing clothes in hot climates for a reason, I have discovered. Furthermore—"

Suddenly in mid-sentence her harangue halted. She flushed furiously, as if she saw in his eyes what unfolded in his imagination, of the dress dropping and the stays loosening and her body emerging. The dress gave a better view of that body than her black robes and he pictured her naked very clearly now.

Whitmarsh approached, oozing charm. Greenwood kept an eye on Miss Blair while he spoke with others. Miss Blair took a deep breath and sallied forth to dazzle with her brilliance as well as her beauty.

When the dinner party broke up, Phaedra fully intended to escape at once to her chamber to shed her uncomfortable garments. She changed her mind when she saw Matthias Greenwood walking toward his *studiolo.* On an impulse she followed him, catching up as he opened the door.

"Mr. Greenwood, I wonder if I can speak privately with you," she said.

"Certainly, Miss Blair. Please join me. My attention will be yours alone in here."

She accepted his welcome and his offer of a chair beside his desk. Perched there under his tutorial scrutiny, she felt a bit like a student petitioning a don.

"Mr. Greenwood, at home I have been speaking with people who knew my mother. I have some questions about events at the end of her life. You knew her too, and your name came up several times. There are others who have suggested you may be able to help me."

"Others?"

"Friends of hers. Women who have helped me piece together who attended my mother's salons and such."

"I will aid in any way I can, but I was not a close friend. My duties at university meant that I saw her infrequently."

"I understand. However, it is your relative distance that may have enabled you to see more clearly than her closest intimates did."

He appeared skeptical, but willing. "What information do you seek?"

"You may find my questions a little bold."

He laughed. "I would be disappointed if they were not. If you are searching the world for answers I hope the questions are not the middling sort."

His good humor made it easier. She decided to start with the boldest question of all. "Did you ever suspect that my mother had a new lover the last years of her life?"

For all his demands for boldness, the question embarrassed him a little. The chiseled angles of his face softened into something approaching chagrin. "I had no real cause to think that. However . . . well, Drury was ever-present when I first met your mother, and much less present the last year or so."

"Do you know who the other man was?"

His eyes warmed with sympathy. His small smile was that of an uncle for a favored niece. "I do not even know there was one. Are you so certain there was?"

"My father thought there was."

"Men can be wrong about such things. Passion cools, distance grows—he could have misunderstood."

She knew that was possible. Matthias was not the only one who had said as much. Several of her mother's friends had suggested the same explanation. She rather hoped that was the answer herself.

"Was there anyone whom you considered a likely possibility?"

He shook his head. "Is it so important to know the name, or even if the suspicion is correct?"

"If it had been a normal affair, I would say not."

He waited patiently for her to continue, neither encouraging nor discouraging further revelations with his comforting demeanor. She understood why Elliot liked this man. There was something to Matthias Greenwood that inspired confidences and trust. He possessed a solid openness that refused even slight dissembling.

"My mother bequeathed me a cameo," she said. "Her will said it came from Pompeii. She intended it to provide me with some security, and I always assumed it would as well. However, before my father died he claimed it was a fraud, sold to her by this other lover."

A frown formed. Concern entered his eyes. "Are you dependent on the value of this cameo?"

"My financial situation has become more complicated of late. I might need to sell it. However, if it is a fake—"

"It will be worth a mere fraction of what she thought and probably what she paid. Nor can you sell it at all unless you know for certain, unless you want to risk being a party to fraud yourself."

"Exactly."

"I see your dilemma. I am dismayed that your legacy is in question. If an admirer took such ruthless advantage of Artemis, the scoundrel should be hung. She was nothing but generous to all whom she met, but—well, perhaps too trusting and too slow to see that there were those who would use her."

He glanced an apology for this mild criticism.

"She did perhaps trust to a fault, Mr. Greenwood. And her generosity means that she left little besides that cameo. I suppose I could keep it as a memento, but if it symbolizes the theft of both her affection and her funds it will have no sentimental value for me."

"I would ask to see the cameo in an attempt to lay your concerns to rest, but I regret that I cannot claim expertise in such things. We could show it to Whitmarsh, of course. He is better schooled in gems than I am. However, it would make more sense to ask the experts at Pompeii—" His frown cleared. He chuckled. "Which is why you are in Italy, isn't it? Of course. I see."

"Do you think they will be able to give me a secure answer there?"

"As secure as is possible. As you may already know, opinions can vary. I will write to the superindendent, however, to smooth the road for you. He has been involved in the excavations for twenty years, and can speak to your item's provenance as well as its visible signs of antiquity."

"I appreciate your willingness to help me. I wonder if I can impose on your kindness a bit more. I fear that it means asking for speculations that you may not want to make."

"I am not too good to gossip, Miss Blair. Up to a point."

She suspected she would broach that point, and perhaps step over it. "If in fact this cameo, real or fake, was given or sold to my mother by a man during the last years of her life, can you think of any man in her circle who would have had access to such things?"

His hawk eyes turned hooded and his sharp gaze looked inward. He pondered her question at length. She thought she saw him picking through memories of salons and dinner parties long ago, examining faces and recalling conversations.

"I do not have a name for you," he finally said.

Disappointment stabbed, but not very deeply. It would have been nice to have the whole mystery explained today, but she had not really expected that to happen.

"However, perhaps . . ." The hawk gaze flashed inward for another moment. "You see, I am remembering a gem said to come from a cache in Pompeii, only it was not owned by your mother. I recall its availability being discussed during one of those salons that she liked to hold. It could be the same one you now own, or a different one."

"Do you remember what was said?"

"Not much. I had no interest in it. I cannot even place this conversation in time very well."

She looked over her shoulder to the glass cases. "I would have thought you would be very interested."

"Not in this. I realized at once that its provenance was shaky. Anything removed from Pompeii is stolen property. There can be no documentation of its discovery there because that would reveal it as stolen." He shrugged. "There are those who do not care about such niceties, and others very quick to believe whatever tales are spun, of course. Thus do bad dealers make their fortunes."

"Do you remember how this cameo was available? Was someone selling it?"

He tapped his fingers on the desk and thought hard. "It was so long ago . . . I do not want to impugn . . ."

"You will impugn no one. Nor will I. I will make no accusations unless I am certain of all the facts. There will be no gossip, no slander or libel. I merely want to know in which direction I should perhaps go."

"I do not remember the particulars at all. However, there were several dealers who fluttered around Artemis

Blair. Two were often present those last years. One, Horace Needly, has a solid reputation but, of course, one never knows when it comes to trade. The other I had less faith in, mostly because he avoided conversations with scholars like myself. That made one wonder if his own expertise could stand scrutiny."

"What was his name?"

"Thornton. Nigel Thornton. Personable fellow. Successful too, as I recall, but his rarities were of a middling sort."

"I thank you for both names. I will see what I can learn when I return to England. You have been a great help and I am grateful." She rose to go. He smiled warmly, clearly pleased to have been of service.

"Mr. Greenwood, forgive me, but—wasn't there at least one other dealer in her circle then? Mr. Whitmarsh. You said the other day that he flogs antiquities in Rome and—"

"That was good-humored jabbing among friends, Miss Blair. Since he came to Italy he has been known to pass along an item or two that fell into his lap and that he no longer wanted for himself. Nothing more. I have done it too. It is hardly dealing." He spoke indulgently while he escorted her to the door. "Nor did he engage in such trade while in England, not even in a minor way. It would not do, would it? He is a gentleman, after all."

"Hurry. I cannot wait any longer. Faster." A deep groan followed Miss Blair's exhortations. "Oh, yes. Finally, *yes.*"

Elliot stood outside on the balcony with his back

rested against the building's wall. He laughed to himself at the moans coming through the door beside his. Phaedra being relieved and released of stays and satin sounded much like a woman being relieved and released in other ways.

He could hear her dismissing the servant, then muttering. "What hell. Never again. Women are mad to dress thus."

Vague sounds of her moving in the chamber seeped out. He walked a few paces down the balcony and resumed his pose right outside her door.

"Did you survive, Miss Blair? Or were you permanently deformed?"

She stuck her head out, looking for him. She startled when she saw him so close. "You find this amusing, don't you?"

"Not at all." His laugh made a liar of him.

She frowned furiously. "Stay there. I want to talk to you about something." Her head ducked inside.

A few minutes later she emerged, swathed in black. Her hair had not been taken down yet so she was not completely back to the Phaedra of old.

"How much longer do you intend to keep me here?" she asked.

Her words alluded to everything that had occurred since the day he entered that garden in Naples. They contained all of her resentments.

"A few days. Longer if you like. You must admit it is restful here."

"I did not sail from England in order to rest."

"We can leave in three days, if you want. However, I

thought that you appreciated the company of those who knew your mother."

She moved to the balustrade and looked out on the black sea. He watched her back and saw the naked body despite the drapery hiding it.

"I confess that I am enjoying this visit more than I expected, except for *la signora*'s impositions today. This detour, while inconvenient, has proven fortuitous. I should have considered that it would be useful to—that meeting people from my mother's circle was not only possible but more probable if I accompanied you."

Why she might find it *useful* would be intriguing if the night were not so quiet and cool, and the moonlight did not make her so lovely.

"Has Mr. Greenwood lived here long?" she asked.

"He bought the property perhaps six, seven years ago. He only took permanent residence four years ago. The last time I visited, the building was quite rustic still."

"I expect that he knows all the experts on antiquity, from Milan to Sicily."

"Most likely. It is not so large a group and they naturally seek each other out."

"So he was a university don who bought this villa, made improvements, and moved his life here. He must come from a wealthy family."

His hunger was impatient with her small talk but he would indulge her for a while. He pushed away from the wall and joined her at the balustrade.

"He lived frugally when at Cambridge. A relative bequeathed some money, however. This villa probably cost less than a small house in London. Property does not have the same value here." He admired the intricate workings of her hairstyle. It would take a long time to release this part of the night's finery. Too long. He would leave it be.

Aside from one glance she did not react to his proximity. "He spoke as if he visits the excavations often and knows the archaeologists there."

"I expect so. Why are you so curious about him?" Matthias was old enough to be her father, and Whitmarsh almost so, but their admiration of her beauty tonight had provoked a few jealous suspicions that probably were not warranted. They pricked now again, irrational but sharp, spiking his desire with the thorns of possessiveness.

"In my father's memoirs there are some pages that created questions for me about my mother's last years. I asked Matthias about them, and am wondering how much weight to give his answers."

Is that what she dwelled on when she grew serious and her vision turned inward? She had ventured out here despite last night's warning, but not to tease and challenge. She sought information that would be *useful*.

Christian had suggested those memoirs might contain revelations the daughter would not like to read. Her admission of that was probably significant, but right now he did not care. He wanted her and here she was with him in the glorious night, a woman who believed in free love and who was not fettered by stupid social rules.

The moonlight made her white skin almost translucent. The black robe rose to her neck, but he saw the top swells of her breasts in his head. "Sometimes it is wise to allow the questions to go unanswered."

She faced him, oblivious to how close she was to being ravished. "I do not think you believe that. Or, rather, I do not think you can follow your own advice. I saw your face when we spoke of the references to your father in the memoirs. You do not want them published, but you want to know if they are true."

Her stance and words threw down another gauntlet. He would not pick it up tonight, but deal with the others already on the ground between them. There would be time enough for this one later.

"I already know that they are not true. But you speak of such serious matters, Miss Blair. You will have to forgive me if I defer the argument you seek for another time. One when the moonlight and night and your beauty do not turn my thoughts to other things."

Her face fell in surprise. She did not move while she gazed at him hard. Whatever she saw caused sparks of alarm in her eyes.

She pivoted toward her door. "Then I will leave you with those thoughts, whatever they may be."

He caught her arm. "Not this time, Phaedra."

He turned her into his embrace. He cupped her face with his hand and kissed the mouth that had been taunting him for days.

What was he—how dare he just—

His kiss obliterated her shocked reaction to the way he swept her back to him. A different shock took over, at the way her heart leapt when he took control of her.

The kiss alone did that. Firm and hard and determined, his kiss contained his warnings from last night. *I want you begging. The danger excites you.*

It did excite her. The way his hold dominated her sent treacherous thrills down her body. Parts of her began begging at once, wanting more, hoping he would not stop.

Her mind raced. Thoughts formed and disappeared in rapid succession.

He had not even asked. Did he think—

Kisses down her neck blotted out the words. A dizzy, sensual fog obscured the rest.

This was a mistake. But, oh—

The warmth of his mouth entered her blood until she tingled wherever it flowed. Her breasts grew heavy and firm and could feel him through the fabric of her dress. The contact excited her more and she instinctively pressed harder for more stimulation.

He kissed her mouth again. Not so hard this time. Luring and leading instead, but just as demanding, just as confident that she would grant whatever he wanted.

The way he *took* thrilled her even though she should rebel. She saw the danger but she could not stop because it *was* exciting. Her body hurdled toward abandon and her mind escaped her grasp.

A caress. Not seeking, not searching, not requesting at all. Firm and sure, his hands moved down her back and hips and bottom, claiming her body as if she wore nothing, making her ache with anticipation of more.

His tongue entered, swept. Erotic shivers trembled in her vulva. His hands moved over her more boldly. She did not care that she capitulated to an enemy and gave ground she might never regain. Titillations itched and buzzed and throbbed, making sensible thought impossible.

I want you begging. Oh, yes, very possibly. Already her breasts were so sensitive that she thought she would go mad.

As if he heard her silent pleas, his caress smoothed up her hip and stomach and stroked beneath her breasts. Anticipation had her reeling, kissing him back, urging with her mouth and tongue and embrace.

His palm slowly swept up over her breast. An intense thrill of pleasure shook through her. His other hand pressed her back firmly, steadying her wobbly stance, moving down slowly as he released the hooks of her dress.

She should not—this should not—

A devastating kiss split apart the objection forming in her head. Deliberate strokes on her nipple scattered the pieces into the night air.

He stepped back a pace, separating their entwined bodies. The moon's glow washed them both and the golden light from her chamber limned his edges. He did not give her time to compose herself, to collect the broken threads of her rationality. He reached for the edge of her dress and began sliding the black gauze down her body.

No man had undressed her before. Never. She did not permit it. Now the gesture entranced her. Immobilized her. The slow descent of the fabric seemed the most erotic caress of the night. She could only stare at his face in the cool light, sensing more than seeing the leashed desire that charged the air with male power.

The sleeves slid down her arms and the bodice sagged at her hips. He reached for the shoulders of her chemise. Her breath caught. Her breasts tightened even more in expectation of another slow and delicious unveiling.

Instead he stunned her anew, throwing her off the fragile grasp on sense that was forming. He did not unveil carefully. He yanked the chemise down her arms. It was not an impatient or even passionate move, but one that asserted the rights of the conqueror.

Rebellion stirred in her soul but it could find no anchor in the rushing tide of pleasure submerging her. The way he gazed at her nakedness absorbed her attention so much she did not move to free her arms from the chemise that still restrained them.

It is just a game, this dance of dominance and submission. It will mean nothing. I will cede nothing in truth.

But—

Fingertips stroked. Palms glossed. She looked down as his fine male hands moved over her breasts, teasing and arousing so perfectly. Sweet madness filled her head and she drifted in luscious, building pleasure. Her last hold on control frayed quickly. She wanted it to break. She wanted him to vanquish the tiny last bit of resistance trying to ruin her bliss.

His arm embraced her again, arching her back. He kissed down her neck and chest in a hot trail that left her gasping. His teeth and mouth played at her nipple, torturing her with sensations that trickled low and deep and had her body begging and low moans sighing.

She tried to release one arm, to embrace him and hold him to her, to steady herself and feel him.

"No," he muttered. "Stay like that."

The sensual storm in her head wanted to obey. The pleasure was too exquisite to stop. Her body hungered for more, for completion, for the relieving fullness. Stopping now was impossible, unnatural.

And yet—

She peered through her oblivion with one eye of rational sense. Despite a pleasure so intense that it almost pained her, she noted her subtle bondage, and his assumptions since that first kiss.

Somehow the slave shed her chains. Already aching with regret and frustration, she found her voice.

"You must stop now. I want you to stop."

He stilled. For a few horrible moments he did not move. Then he straightened and looked down at her.

His arm pulled her closer, tighter. His other hand cupped her face as he had for the first kiss. His fingertips pressed, not hurting but not gently either.

"And if I do not stop?"

Since most of her wished he would not, it was not truly a threat. But his assumption that she would capitulate if he continued, that she was weak to his power, gave her back some spine.

"You will," she said.

"You trust my honor so much?"

"I trust your pride. A woman importuned will never *beg*."

He released her and stepped away. Everything in his aura and face said he might grab her again still.

She quickly pulled up her dress to cover herself. She

strode to her door. Her heart pounded and her body still responded to the danger with shocking excitement.

"I will not stop the next time, Phaedra."

She stepped over her threshold before she replied. "I do not think there will be a next time."

"There will be."

She grasped the edge of the doors and began to close them. "If so, it will not be a seduction. I will choose to let it happen before the first kiss, or there will be no kiss at all."

CHAPTER
EIGHT

He was still out there. She wanted to open her door to the cool night air, but she dared not. He would misunderstand.

Would he be so bold as to enter anyway? She sat on her bed, her arms wrapping her knees, half-dreading and half-hoping the door would swing wide and he would be there.

She did not feel as composed as she had acted when she closed the doors. Her arousal would not die. Her body remained sensitive to the air.

She did not know when she made the choice to stop him. It had been instinctive. Intuition had interfered.

I want you begging.

There could be no friendship with this man. He wanted her weak and besotted so he could influence her. He had sought her out in Naples for a reason, after all. One of her friends could not, would not, demand she excise those passages from the memoirs. But a man who vanquished and ravished, a lover who seduced, would not hesitate to use the power that passion gave him.

All of which was a damned pity, because she really wanted him.

She had never desired a man quite this way before. There was nothing comfortable about it. Nothing safe. This was not the attraction she had experienced with her friends, no meeting of the minds that happened to allow for other intimacies as well.

Instead his sensual sorcery provoked chaos and mystery and breath-choking awe. He knew it too. He knew his mere presence cast a spell.

Her arousal slowly calmed to a low inner hum, the same physical buzz that she had endured for days now. Silence finally settled on the balcony and in the chamber next door. She unwound her body and lay down, curled up on her side, still watching the doors.

Is this what had happened to Artemis? After years of comfortable friendship with Richard Drury had some man come along who did not play by Artemis's rules?

It had been such a shock to learn that her mother had been unfaithful to her father. Believing in free love did not mean one had to reject belief in lifelong, perfect love too. As a girl she had concluded that the two eventually went together, that free love made it easier to recognize one's soul mate when he arrived.

She pictured her mother. Beautiful, vivacious, self-confident. More trusting than her daughter would grow to be, however. Less practical too. Over the years Artemis had surrounded herself with a moat of people who accepted the way she lived her life. Her circle understood about Richard and his place in her world.

Maybe late in the fascinating drama that was Artemis Blair's life, a man had come along determined to cross the moat and assail her walls. She might have been defenseless through sheer lack of practice in dealing with such old-fashioned men.

Like her daughter had just been out on the balcony.

Phaedra hugged a pillow. She was beginning to understand now what had occurred with that late love affair that had undone her mother.

A seducer had arrived who had lured the primitive female that survives in every woman's soul. He had taken and conquered. He had influenced and weakened and eventually he had betrayed.

If he had initially pretended he was of like mind to the other men who surrounded her, Artemis would not have stood a chance.

The bitch.

Elliot's frustration heaped other insults on Phaedra while he finished his breakfast in the loggia the next morning. Considering the hell his body had given him all night he was beyond being a gentleman in his thoughts.

He wanted to take satisfaction in the discomfort she had experienced in that hot, closed room while he let the balcony's breeze cool him. Only every time he had glanced to her door a part of him had prayed it would open and she would fly into his arms.

The door had never budged, of course. The self-contained, independent, thorn-in-his-side Phaedra Blair would never hand him such a victory.

Eventually the door became a repudiation. An accusation. An infuriating declaration of self-control. *You dared seduce instead of petition? You foolishly sought to master me, of all women?*

He poured some coffee. Her erotic moans still sang in his head. He still felt her embrace and aggressive, deep kisses. The memories began making him hard again.

It had been good. Incredible. Where the hell had she found the sense to speak at all, let alone the strength to stop the torrent sweeping them away?

The faintest rustle and footstep disturbed the peace of the loggia. He did not need to look to the doorway to know who had arrived.

In the few moments it took Phaedra to walk to the table, he leashed the worst anger from the night's hot vigil. The last vestige spoke in his head as he greeted her, though. *You will not refuse me the next time, because you do not really want to.*

His calm welcome put her at ease. Her careful posture relaxed. She sat at the table and he poured her coffee. She sipped.

"Thank you for being so civilized," she said.

He could not believe that she was actually broaching the subject. He set his elbow on the table and rested his chin in his hand. Some very uncivilized, sexual images formed in his head.

"Are you referring to allowing you to retreat last night, or to pouring your coffee this morning?"

A servant intruded, carrying a platter of eggs and rashers. Matthias may have adopted Positano as home but he still offered a proper English breakfast to his guests.

Phaedra slowly spooned little bits of eggs onto her

plate. Her actions absorbed most of her attention. "I suppose I was referring to both."

"Well, Marsilio or Pietro might have created a spectacle last night, arguing and accusing until the household was woken. English gentlemen, however, are taught just to suffer."

Her lips pursed. She kept her eyes on her plate while she broke a roll. "I apologize for any suffering. It was not my intention. Perhaps, since you are being an English gentleman, I should not speak of it beyond saying that."

"That might be wise."

She slowly ate her breakfast.

He should leave, but of course he could not.

She set down her fork and dabbed at her mouth with her handkerchief. "Lord Elliot, if you intend for us to stay here a few more days then we need to come to an understanding about that balcony."

She was incredible. *Amazing*. She had to know that his impulse was to pick her up, throw her over his shoulder, carry her into the trees, and finish what they had begun. Yet here she was, negotiating lord knew what when a long night had made him less than amenable to compromise.

"How so, Miss Blair?"

"We do share it. It isn't fair that I should be denied its use, or feel that stepping outside my door might cause you to interpret it to mean other than it does."

"I promise that I will not misinterpret your joining me on the balcony in the middle of the night."

The implications of his promise received a thorough scrutiny. She was smart enough to see the holes. "Can we at least agree that I am entitled to leave my door open to the air, without fearing that you will walk in?"

"No."

"I can see that I was too optimistic about your character."

"On that we can agree. I did warn you."

"Lord Elliot, I—"

"I insist that you address me as Elliot in private conversation now, Phaedra. You do not mind the informality, do you? We can set that stupid social rule aside. After all, I have kissed your naked breast and you have moaned for me while I pleasured you."

Her mouth gaped. He felt like smiling for the first time all morning. She retreated into a manner of prim hauteur. "I would prefer if we avoided each other's company as much as possible, *Elliot.*"

"That will be easy this morning. Greenwood and I will be sequestered in his study until past midday."

She rose to her feet. "I think that I will take a long walk and avoid all of this party for several hours." She turned to leave.

"Phaedra."

She paused and looked over her shoulder.

"Phaedra, I require your promise that you will not attempt to leave and that come dinner you will still be here."

She arched an eyebrow. "Because of your oath to Signore Sansoni?"

"That too."

Her expression said she understood the other reasons. "And if I will not give my word?"

"I can tie you to the bed again. Would you like that?"

Her face reddened. She dismissed his insinuation with a quick turn of her head.

"Do I have your word?"

"Yes, you have my word, although it is unnecessary and ridiculous. I would not begin to know how to get off this rock, let alone how to travel to the interior."

Chin high, she floated away, her black sails billowing behind her.

Phaedra returned to her chamber and unpacked her baggage.

How had he guessed her plan? She did not think of herself as a predictable woman, but Lord Elliot seemed to know her thoughts before she had even formed them.

She set the empty valise aside. Preparing to flee had been an impulse born of a night of honest reflection about the way he affected her. She was in grave danger of making a fool of herself, of melting into a puddle just because a man provoked physical desire. Avoiding the challenge completely had seemed a good idea at dawn.

She sat down and put on her low boots. She walked out on the balcony and looked down on the town. Voices floated up from the loggia beneath her. Other guests were breaking their fast.

She took a deep breath and called forth the woman her mother had taught her to be.

Deciding to flee had been cowardly. She had come to this land to find answers about her mother, and some of them might be right here in this house. It made much more sense to stay and pursue the suspicions simmering beneath her fears and vulnerabilities regarding Lord Elliot.

Matthias Greenwood had disappeared into his *studiolo* with Lord Elliot when Phaedra returned to the loggia. Randall Whitmarsh sat at the table with his wife, however. Phaedra joined them and hoped Mrs. Whitmarsh would soon excuse herself. The interview with Matthias had gone so well last night that she was eager to discover if Mr. Whitmarsh could add to the information.

Unfortunately Mr. Whitmarsh left first, heading off for his long morning walk.

"You looked very lovely last night," Mrs. Whitmarsh said.

"Thank you."

"One wonders why . . ." Her gaze slid down Phaedra's current ensemble.

Phaedra did not bother with explanations. Mrs. Whitmarsh was not a woman who would comprehend the mixture of practicality and orneriness that had given birth to this eccentricity.

"What I mean is, your mother did not adopt such outward symbols of her unique views."

Phaedra's attention sharpened. "Did you spend much time with her?"

"Before we made our home in Rome my husband often attended her dinners. Unlike other wives, I agreed to join him. He was fascinated by her. I thought it best to make sure she never became fascinated by him."

Phaedra did not think it likely that Artemis would find Mr. Whitmarsh fascinating. But then before she read the memoirs, she would not have guessed Artemis had ever considered another man besides Richard Drury.

"Were you successful in thwarting a liaison between them? Or did my mother favor your husband in that way?"

Mrs. Whitmarsh did not show surprise at the bold question. "I believe I was successful. Of course, until very late in her life she had eyes only for Mr. Drury."

"You imply that her eyes found another man eventually. Do not mince words for the sake of delicacy. I am her daughter, and like her I think it is silly that people do not speak frankly about such matters."

Mrs. Whitmarsh shrugged. "One saw a coolness between your parents the last year or so. My husband did not notice, but I did. There were men who wanted her, you see. Not as a wife, of course."

The judgmental, confident tone of the last sentence rankled Phaedra. She rallied to her mother's defense even though Artemis needed no excuses. "If you did not see my mother moving her affection to another man the coolness might have only been the result of time passing, and two lovers becoming familiar and comfortable."

"Miss Blair, my husband and I dined often with your mother over the years. Usually Mr. Drury was present. The familiarity and comfort you describe between them was palpable from the start. No one had to tell me on my first visit that they were lovers and that you were Mr. Drury's child. The last year, however, he was not in attendance so much. There was an awkwardness when he was. You may think me dim-witted compared to yourself, but when I perceive that all is not right between a man and a woman, I am rarely wrong."

Yes, Mrs. Whitmarsh, who so carefully guarded her possession of her husband, would become astute in this one area of human nature. Was she also perceptive? Had she seen everything? A woman guarding a treasure would be most likely to notice if the pirate she feared had aimed for another ship.

"Who was the man who became the new object of my mother's attentions?"

"Is this a contest, where I must give a name in order for you to respect my judgment?"

"It is a sincere question, from a daughter who wonders about her mother's last years."

Mrs. Whitmarsh's defensive pique melted. "I do not know. I am only sure—almost sure—it was not my husband. For months she sparkled like she was young again, but then . . ."

"Then?"

"It was as if someone had snuffed out a lamp. She was melancholy the last times we called on her. Perhaps whoever it was had disappointed her."

Phaedra had seen that melancholy. She had not understood its reasons or depths, but the description was apt. A light had gone out.

"You are not alone in wondering if she had a new lover," Phaedra said. "Names have even been suggested to me. Mr. Needly, for example. And Mr. Thornton."

"Needly? Well, I suppose that would make some sense. He was not dissimilar to Mr. Drury. Of the same mold. His erudition on Roman art would give them common ground. Although if asked I would say they did not rub well together. He could be a very arrogant man."

Mrs. Whitmarsh warmed to the gossip. She enjoyed the topic more than Phaedra liked seeing. "Sometimes attraction can create storms, I suppose."

"Indeed it can. Now the other, Thornton . . ." She thought it over. "He was a bit young for her. Enigmatic too. But he was around quite a lot. One could not miss him. A handsome man, dramatically so. He had presence, but . . ."

"But?"

"It is difficult to explain. He was impressive. Startlingly so. But also somewhat . . . vague. My husband used that word to describe him once, and I thought it apt. Yes, he was vague in so many ways."

Phaedra tucked the description away in her mind. When she returned to England she would have to seek out arrogant Mr. Needly and vague Mr. Thornton, and also pointedly ask a few of her mother's intimate friends if Artemis favored either of these two men.

"I liked her," Mrs. Whitmarsh said. "I did not approve of her life, and she knew it. She accepted my views, however. She never allowed her other guests to make me feel unwelcome. She was very gracious."

"She was accustomed to your views, I daresay. They are the normal ones, after all. Whenever she walked out the door of her home, she was the odd one. Would that the world had been as gracious with contrary views as she proved to be, and as accepting of her company as she was of yours."

Mrs. Whitmarsh blushed. Her rising color told Phaedra more than she wanted to know. The Whitmarshes had never returned those invitations to dinners. Artemis Blair had not been included in *their* circle and *their* parties.

These morning confidences suddenly seemed traitorous to her mother's memory. Phaedra suspected that they echoed Mrs. Whitmarsh's gossip with her normal friends, in drawing rooms that had never opened for the bluestocking whose life defied the rules.

They also gave her a taste of the gossip about herself. She knew that there were women who laughed and speculated and clucked their tongues, just as there were men who misunderstood her freedom. Such people were easier to ignore if she did not actually suffer their company, however.

She had hoped Mrs. Whitmarsh could give the identity of the man who had usurped Richard Drury's place. Evidently she could not, but her perceptions were not without usefulness.

Phaedra excused herself. She walked out of the loggia and approached the steep road leading down to the town.

Positano became a women's town with the dawn. Able-bodied men had left on their fishing boats long before Phaedra entered the center of activity.

It took a long time to inch her way down the dense warren of old, narrow streets. Even with their stepped construction they proved treacherous. She wished she had brought her parasol to use as a walking stick, and to protect her from the sun, which was getting fierce as it hung over the high hill's peak.

Women and children stared as she strolled through the market street. She admired the lemons and leafy produce, the joints of lamb and beef. At the corner of the market some men sat on chairs outside a tavern. They eyed her with curiosity and suspicion.

The youngest one, a dark-haired man dressed in a fashionable brown frock coat, owned a heavy cane that he had propped against his seat. The others appeared old and wizened. She assumed that they had forgone the rigors of fishing many years ago.

She found the other main streets by following the flow of bodies. Her presence created a small spectacle, much as her ride on the donkey behind Lord Elliot had. Heads appeared at windows and bold stares followed her progress.

The streets led her to a little piazza hard against the hillside. Water trickled out of the mouth of a sculpted lion's head. It had been set in a small wall built flush with the hill's rock. Women sat on stone benches in the shade of some trees, waiting their turns to hold their jugs under the lion's mouth.

Phaedra found a spot on a bench to rest in the cooler air. Dark eyes glanced askance at her. A young woman whispered into a boy's ear and he ran down a lane. Women dawdled after they used the fountain, chatting in an expressive melody of conversations, keeping an eye on the newcomer among them.

Soon another woman walked down the lane toward them. Her black skirt swayed with her long strides. She did not look like the other women.

For one thing, she was blonde. Her dark golden hair formed a roll at her nape, visible beneath the deep brim of her black straw hat. She was not as fair as Phaedra but the rich bronze so common in this land had only tinted her skin.

Phaedra wondered if this was another foreigner who, like Matthias, had come to live here. As the woman drew near, however, her almond eyes, high cheekbones, and heart-shaped face revealed she was a native even if her coloring initially confused the matter.

She sat down on Phaedra's bench. She called a few greetings to her friends. Phaedra tried to translate them but the words came in a torrent and the accents in Positano were even different from those of Naples.

The woman turned and gave Phaedra a good look. The conversations around them dimmed.

"English?"

Phaedra nodded.

"They guessed as much, and sent young Paolo for me. My cousin Julia and I are the only women here who speak it. You have met Julia. She is your hostess in the villa. Are you a widow?" The conversation came in respectable English although the cadence and pronunciation reflected some labor.

"No, I am not a widow."

The woman's gaze swept over Phaedra's long hair. "I did not think so." She looked down the lane to their right and smiled slyly. "Ah, here comes Signore Tarpetta. Ignore him. He likes to act like a *padrone,* but his authority and power are all in his head."

The lame man who had sat at the end of the market street limped forward with his cane, exuding self-importance. Two of the old men accompanied him. The three took positions across the piazza.

"My name is Carmelita Messina. I am not a widow either, in case you were wondering from my black garments."

"My name is Phaedra Blair, and I am happy to meet someone who speaks English so well. I have tried with your language, but . . ."

Carmelita waved her hand, dismissing the apology. "I learned some English in Naples. I lived there for several years with Julia and her late husband." Carmelita gestured with her chin at Signore Tarpetta, who watched them closely despite his conversation with the old men. "He does not like when people from the villa come down here. He fears such as you will corrupt his little kingdom."

"Do they come down often?"

"We are merely colorful peasants to most of them. We are the little people in the corners of sentimental paintings."

"Not even Signore Greenwood mingles among you?"

"Sometimes. He visited frequently last year. One time when he went back, he brought Julia with him." She shot Tarpetta a look of scorn. "He hoped to marry her. He makes much of how he would not have her now, but we all know he would crawl if she did this." She snapped her fingers.

Their conversation had attracted an audience, and a giggle twittered from the women who had moved closer.

Carmelita again eyed Phaedra. "I wear black to mourn the *Carbonari* who died when the king killed the republic. If you are not a widow, what do you mourn?"

"I mourn my father, but not with my clothing. The black does not show soiling so fast."

Carmelita translated for their audience. Heads nodded.

"You do not dress your hair, or wear a veil. I would ask if you are a *puttana,* but I do not think you are because the mistresses who come with the men who visit up there are always fashionable. Perhaps you do it to thumb your nose at men like our Tarpetta?"

"Perhaps I do." She looked to the bay several hundred yards below them. "Do visitors come often to Mr. Greenwood? Do special boats arrive just for the villa?"

"There are often visitors, and some come often. He has many friends, Signore Greenwood does. He is not one of us but many here grow fat from the money he spends."

"Like the family of the boys who found the little ancient statue?"

"I did not hear about this statue. The families must want to keep it a secret so if there is more it is theirs alone. He likes the old things, Signore Greenwood does."

Carmelita again noted the men watching them. "They do not like that you sit here so long, so I hope that you will sit longer still. Tell us about your life in England, Phaedra Blair. No one is taking their water home because they hope to hear some stories from you."

She had taken to translating everything they said, and women smiled and giggled when she relayed her overture.

A girl no more than eighteen ventured closer. She cautiously reached out and stroked Phaedra's red hair.

Phaedra did not mind the familiarity but another person did. A male voice barked. Across the piazza one of the old men stepped forward. He scowled and gestured for the girl to come to him.

Head bowed and eyes fearful, the girl hurried to him. He grabbed her arm and pushed her up the lane, taking her away.

"He is the father to her husband," Carmelita said. "He will tell the family how she befriended a foreigner's mistress from the villa."

Phaedra did not want to think about the girl's fate if the tale angered her husband. The cautious expressions suddenly in the eyes of the other women at the fountain saddened her.

"I do not want to cause trouble for any of you." She began to get up.

Carmelita's firm hand caught her arm. "There is no change without trouble. These women are ignorant of the world outside this coast, and my tales of Naples grow old. Tell us about your home, and how you came to be a woman who ventures out alone in a foreign land, looking like a mourning whore who fears no man's hand."

Phaedra stayed an hour at the fountain, enjoying the feminine company. She told Carmelita and the others about her life, and how she lived alone and free in London. As the time passed the torrent of foreign words began to make some sense to her. She even comprehended a few of the questions sent her way before they were translated.

Across the piazza Signore Tarpetta watched. Someone brought him a chair so he could sit and rest his leg. The happy party of women did not care that he disapproved. He might think of himself as a *padrone,* but it was obvious to Phaedra that the women obeyed another power, and her name was Carmelita Messina.

Eventually the women drifted away, carrying their water and chatting excitedly with one another.

"Their men will return in the boats soon. They must cook the midday meal," Carmelita explained.

Phaedra stood. "I thank you for joining us, so I could meet the women. I am going to walk down to that tower before I return to the villa."

"I will come with you or you may not find the footpath that takes you there. If Tarpetta follows, pretend he is not there. He will be a fool to do so with that leg but such a man often proves he is stupid."

He proved it today once more. Phaedra thought he had declined to follow until she and Carmelita were on the promontory's footpath. Then she spied him limping onto the docks so he could keep an eye on them.

"How did he hurt his leg?" she asked.

Carmelita stepped through the portal, into the tower. "He was a soldier and among the ones who came for Julia's husband at our house in Naples. He betrayed us. We fought them, although it was hopeless. I hit him with a heavy iron pan, here." She pointed to her knee. "Better if I had aimed for his head."

"So now he follows you everywhere?"

"He is following you, not me. But he hates me,

because I was the one who made sure Signore Greenwood met Julia. She had nothing after her husband was executed as the republic fell."

"If he is jealous he should hate Greenwood, not you."

Carmelita led the way up winding stone stairs. "He dares not hate Greenwood. Like so many others, he grows fat from the Englishman's money."

They climbed up to the top of the tower where there was a square room. Small windows pierced each wall. One faced the sea and another gave a clear view of the mountainside.

"That one was where they stood watching the sea for Arabs or pirates who might attack the port," Carmelita explained. "Now, this eastern one here—they watched for something else, no? An army coming over the hill, or trouble in the town."

Phaedra looked out the western window. The view of the sea was endless, and miles of the coast on either side were visible. She moved to the eastern one. The sun hovered directly over the peak of the mountain.

This tower had been built for military reasons. During the dawns at midsummer, however, the sun might first appear directly in line with this window.

There was not much to explore in the guard's room. The stone walls rose up and curved to form a ceiling, much like the old Norman churches back home. Aside from a blanket on the floor, it was empty and surprisingly clean.

Carmelita toed at the blanket and revealed the straw under it. "Lovers come here," she said. "Down through the ages, this tower has had night visitors."

When she and Carmelita emerged outside again, the straight, staunch figure of Signore Tarpetta could still be seen on the dock.

"How does he grow fat from Mr. Greenwood?"

"I do not know. He lives well, though, and other than a poor pension from the army he has no living. They know each other. One can tell from the way they acknowledge each other on the rare times you see them meet. Greenwood is probably paying him to see we do not interfere with his important friends, or maybe just to stay away from Julia." She shrugged. "Now, let us find you a donkey boy. Even I will not walk all the way up to that villa."

As they walked down the promontory, Lord Elliot appeared on the docks. Suddenly Signore Tarpetta's arm and two men's eyes were aimed at the promontory path.

Lord Elliot strode back down the dock and aimed north to intercept them.

"Who is that?" Carmelita asked. "Has your lover come for you?"

"He is not my lover." Phaedra felt her face warming.

Carmelita laughed. "But he would like it, no? And he is so handsome you are tempted, I think. But see how stern he stands there, waiting for you. You had best watch your step with this one, Phaedra Blair."

Phaedra introduced Carmelita once they reached Lord Elliot. He responded graciously but he could not hide his displeasure.

"You had us all worried, Miss Blair. It is not advised to walk into the town alone." Lord Elliot's tone edged near a scold.

"I doubt any harm will befall people who visit this town."

Lord Elliot looked at Carmelita. "You have my gratitude that you offered Miss Blair your assistance and company."

"I do not need either assistance or company," Phaedra said. "I am glad to have made a friend, however, and I hope to see you again, Carmelita."

Still tight with pique, Lord Elliot walked over to some donkey boys to hire their mounts.

"I will leave you now so that you can deal with this man," Carmelita said. "If you need to borrow an iron pan, let me know."

CHAPTER
NINE

I will write the letter to the superintendent this morning," Matthias said. "Although the letters of introduction that you brought from England should suffice. I am
perhaps vain in thinking mine will ease your access to
the work sites more quickly."

"You know him personally. I will be glad to have
your letter."

Elliot managed to keep half his mind on these preparations for his visit to Pompeii. The other half kept seeing the balcony hanging over the top of this loggia.

Last night Phaedra had left her doors open.

Had she done it as a dare? A statement of indifference? He only knew for certain that it had not been an
invitation.

He smoked a long cigar out there during the night,
looking at the dark beyond her open shutters, unable to
resist the excruciating tease her proximity created. The
only sounds from within had been the soft sighs of a
contented woman sleeping too damnably well.

He had finally retreated to his own chamber in an

attempt to thwart the ruthless impulses that she goaded. When sleep finally relieved him it had been deep and long and lasted past dawn. He had woken to discover Phaedra missing.

She had left the villa again. He had *told* her not to. After searching for her yesterday he had laid down a few laws. She had wasted no time disobeying them.

"If you would like, Miss Blair can remain here while you go to Pompeii," Matthias said casually. Too casually, as if he comprehended what distracted his old student.

"She is determined to go herself."

"She does not require your company to do that. It is apparent she vexes you. I could escort her, separately, to spare you the inconvenience. As for that business you told me about Sansoni, I am sure that he would accept my proxy authority should he even become aware of the switch."

"I am sure he would not. I gave my sworn word. I am stuck with her for the duration."

His word to Sansoni did not really have much to do with his refusal of Matthias's solution. Nor, at this particular moment, did the need to control Phaedra's plans for that memoir affect his decision. Not directly, at least, although it was all of one cloth. His *vexation* with Miss Blair had taken on other colors and shadows. He wanted to control much more than when and how she published a book.

"Since you are determined to keep her with you, allow me to suggest some inns that might be suitable for a respectable woman." Matthias launched into a town by town litany of tourist facilities.

Toward the end of the recommendations Elliot's attention was diverted to the hillside. Whitmarsh was hiking up from the town, his fair face flushed from the exertion.

"Too steep even for you, eh, Whitmarsh?" Matthias called. "No wonder you are so late returning from your morning exercise."

Whitmarsh bent over, grasping his knees while he caught his breath. He waved Matthias into silence while he heaved. "Trouble . . . the town . . . tower . . ." Frustrated by his lungs' refusal to work, he pointed down the hill.

Elliot and Matthias went to him. Elliot peered down. The town was alive with a lot of activity. He focused on the tower. A large group had collected at the promontory path.

Whitmarsh took several deep breaths, collecting himself. "That hill can kill you if you start out at a run."

"Which is why you should not run," Matthias said. "Why did you?"

Whitmarsh pointed again. "Miss Blair is down there, in that tower. They want to arrest her."

She was going to be the death of him.

Elliot ran up to his chamber to fetch his pistol so that his exasperated reaction might not become a literal truth. He emerged to find Whitmarsh checking his own firearm.

"One wonders what she did," Matthias mused as they headed down the hillside.

Elliot could only imagine.

"As best I can tell, they think she is a witch or some-thing," Whitmarsh said between deep inhales. He had not entirely recovered from his climb and descending carried its own strains.

"Hell," Elliot muttered.

"Our duty is clear, gentlemen," Matthias intoned. "We must not allow them to arrest her. What with that Sansoni fellow looking to make trouble the way you said, Rothwell, and the primitive notions of religion and justice in these parts, if they take hold of her, matters could get out of control."

Elliot's deep exhale had little to do with the rapid way they aimed down to the bay and tower. If Phaedra had not been so deliberately willful and had stayed in the villa, three men would not now be marching into trouble.

His anger proved a poor defense against the other re-action weighing like lead in his chest. This was not London, but an isolated hill town in a foreign land. Phaedra's attire and behavior made her vulnerable. There was nothing comical about an accusation of witchcraft in this place. She was in real danger.

They reached the low lanes and cut through the pi-azza in front of the church of Santa Maria. Freshly painted and decorated wagons stood there, waiting for the morrow and the procession for the feast of San Giovanni.

Matthias led the way around the bay. A crowd of men blocked the path on the promontory. Not only the old and infirm formed this little mob. Some of the fisher-men had decided the drama at the tower was more inter-esting than casting their nets in the sea.

Emotions ran high among the men. Guttural curses rang. Dark eyes flamed. Hands gestured everywhere. A well-dressed man stood in the center, his weight propped on a thick cane, exhorting his friends on.

Matthias cocked his head, listening, collecting evidence.

"She was seen at the window at dawn," he muttered. "Praying to the rising sun, or something like that. Tarpetta, that lame fellow there, also watched her in the town yesterday, trying to corrupt the women. As far as I can make out, he is accusing her of sorcery, prostitution, and heresy."

"Heresy?" Whitmarsh asked.

"Let us make our way to the front of this crowd," Elliot said. "Whitmarsh, we should keep our weapons out of sight for now."

With military postures they bumped their way through the men. Their presence did nothing to calm the situation.

A scene fit for an opera waited on the promontory. The men had massed at the town's end because their way to the tower was blocked by a large group of women. The females were equally agitated and spoiling for a fight. Every one of them had taken off her kerchief or veil and let down her hair.

Carmelita Messina stood at the rear of the women, positioned as the last line of defense. Blonde hair streaming and black dress flying, she looked like a priestess to Phaedra Blair's religion.

She held a large, shallow iron pan in her hand. She occasionally brandished her weapon in the direction of Tarpetta, who did not take the taunts with grace.

A lone man stood between the men and the women. The town priest held up his arms, one in each direction, as if he alone kept the two waves of anger from crashing against each other.

"It is certainly colorful," Whitmarsh said dryly.

Unfortunately, it was also potentially dangerous. Elliot peered up at the tower. At the same time Phaedra peered out a high window. She noticed him. He tried to communicate reassurance.

"Let us see if we can sort this out peaceably, Greenwood," Elliot said. He stepped boldly between the factions. With Matthias at his side, he approached the priest.

Greenwood chatted with the *padre* while the men's anger warmed their ears. The news was not good.

"The sorcery charge is due to the ritual with the sun, on this of all days. It is the solstice, give or take a day," Matthias reported. "The charge of prostitution is a general one. Her appearance, her presence alone in the town, etc., etc. Regrettably, the ladies' support has only confirmed her corrupting influence in the minds of the men. There were, I gather, some odd conversations in the bedrooms of this town last night."

"And the heresy?" Elliot asked.

"Miss Blair tried to explain the business with the sun in more detail than was wise. A dissertation on the commonalities among world religions was probably not in her best interests."

Elliot imagined an accusation being relayed by the women to Carmelita and translated up to Phaedra. He pictured the lengthy explanation coming back through the chain, paragraph by long paragraph, stripped of any sense as it passed through each link until it arrived at the men. The wonder was the charge was heresy and not lunacy.

The priest was an elderly man, white-haired and soft-faced. The town's abandon of order distressed him. He spoke to Matthias and joined his hands in an expression of prayer, rocking them to and fro to emphasize his pleading.

Elliot understood the priest well enough. "Tell him I am not leaving Miss Blair to the whims of a mob."

"He is correct that our presence here in the middle is only inflaming matters, Rothwell," Matthias said. "The men think we usurp their power and the women, well, they do not think good of any man at the moment."

The last part was true. The women eyed him as the enemy. They threw out seething challenges that were undoubtedly rude insults. If he got past them, Carmelita of the Iron Pan waited.

He retreated, and pulled Matthias aside once they had squeezed past the men again. "I need to get to that tower to speak with her."

"That tower was built for defense. There are only two ways to approach it. This spit of land and the sea."

"Then I have to get there by sea."

Phaedra peeked around the edge of the window. The stalemate below continued. Whenever the men seemed to lose interest in their siege, Signore Tarpetta urged them on.

Elliot and Mr. Greenwood and Mr. Whitmarsh had left. They probably expected this little conflagration to burn itself out. With the priest urging reason she would have expected it to as well. Unfortunately, she suspected this was not really about the odd Englishwoman in the tower this morning.

The lines were drawn about other things. Ancient practices and recent events fed this fire. She worried that the women would pay dearly in the days ahead for this orgy of rebellion, even if she herself was spared.

She hoped Carmelita would not pay with her own freedom. She admired the blonde woman waving her iron pan. Carmelita announced she was not defenseless with the gesture. She also made sure that Tarpetta remembered his own crimes and why she would not allow the town to yield to his power.

This was all his fault. He had seen her walking in the town at earliest dawn. He must have followed again, and watched her at the tower's high eastern window when the sun crested the mountaintop.

The sun had moved a lot since then but the confrontation below refused to end.

She hurried over to the western window. Carmelita had called up a warning earlier to watch for an attack by sea. One boat had ventured nearby to assess that approach an hour ago, but she had thrown down loose stones from the building and discouraged them.

Another one approached now. It did not come from Positano's docks. Instead it aimed from the west, as if visitors from Capri were coming to see the Norman tower.

Three men stood in the bow of the boat while servants from the villa rowed. Elliot, Whitmarsh, and Greenwood had come to the rescue.

They brought their craft as close to the tower as possible. Mr. Whitmarsh waved. Mr. Greenwood called up to her. Elliot almost smiled, but his mouth never got past a hard, straight line.

"Now you see what I meant, Rothwell. If one could enter the tower easily from the sea, it would have been worthless to its purpose," Greenwood said.

"It was a splendid day to row out, in any case," Whitmarsh said. "It appears no one guessed we would double back. The docks remain empty." He gazed up at her. "That window appears much farther up when one is this close. We brought some provisions, Miss Blair, but I doubt our plan to get them to you will work."

A roar of shouts poured in the tower from the other side. Phaedra ran over and looked out. The men had moved much closer to the priest. The women huddled closer together.

She returned to the sea window.

Elliot bent and lifted a long rope and hook. "Stand back, Miss Blair. Move well into the tower. If I can get the hook in, secure it as best you can."

"Lord Elliot, I do not think you will be able to—"

His glare silenced her. She moved to the other side of the tower.

Three times she heard the hard noise of metal hitting stone, then the heavy splash of the hook landing in the water. It did not appear their plan would work.

Suddenly the big iron hook appeared at the window. It hung in the air for a long moment, then began falling. One of its three hooks caught the sill of the window and held.

She ran over, unhooked its point, and moved it

through the window until it bit deeply into the stones of the wall.

She looked out. All three men pulled on the rope to test its security. Satisfied, Lord Elliot jumped out of the boat and onto the strip of beach. Whitmarsh handed him two big baskets.

"Send up the food first," she requested. "I have not had anything to eat today."

"No doubt you thought the sun god could not be kept waiting." Elliot worked on the basket's handle. "When I was a disobedient child, I was sent to my chamber without supper. Perhaps a little hunger is in order for you today too."

She gave the rope a little yank. "Let us not be hasty. And let us keep our sense of humor."

The basket resisted for one irritating moment, then he released his hold. She pulled the rope hand over hand until she could grab the basket handle.

She examined its contents, and threw the rope back down. "This is quite a feast. Wine and ham and bread and figs."

"I hope you enjoy it. If the townsmen have their way you will eat only pasta with lard for the next ten years, assuming they do not hang you at once." He grabbed the rope's end and began on the other basket. "A blanket and other necessities are in here."

A roar sounded from the other side of the tower. He looked up. "What is happening?"

She hurried to her other window, then returned to report. "If I am going to enjoy my feast, I fear I will have to eat quickly. Signore Tarpetta is ordering the priest to stand aside."

"Pull this up quickly, then send the rope back down."

The noise pouring in the other window made her raise the basket as quickly as possible. As soon as she had it free she sent the rope down and ran once more to the eastern window.

The priest was gone. The front line of the men stood nose to nose with that of the women. The flanks of the women's army already had frayed. It would be a rout.

She returned to the sea window. Greenwood gestured to the coast. "We will put in right there and get to the battle lines in minutes," he said to Elliot.

"Matters are becoming dire on the promontory," she called down.

"Keep heart, dear lady," Whitmarsh called back. "Greenwood has some influence in the town, and Rothwell is armed. You will be safe."

If they planned to enter the melee about to break, she could not count on their victory. She doubted her English buccaneers would shoot and slash to save her, and they would be outnumbered otherwise.

Elliot surveyed the tower wall. He eyed the tiny strip of sand beneath his boots at its base and the large boulders positioned to discourage boats. "It is a good forty feet. I cannot risk your falling if I have you climb down. If the water were deeper . . ." Still calculating and muttering, he raised his hands, grasped the rope, and began climbing.

"What ho, Rothwell. Be sure you are not the one who falls," Greenwood said.

Screams flew up from the promontory, chilling her. She did not go to see what had happened. She could not take her eyes off Elliot hanging above the sea, growing larger as he inched his way up the rope, his body and face tense from his exertions.

She could tell the battle on the promontory was not going well for the women, which meant it was not going well for her. She stuck her head out the window and told Lord Elliot what was happening.

He cursed and found new strength. An odd sound came up the stairs. It sounded like a metal pan landing on something soft. Carmelita's voice called on the saints to help her and the sound repeated. A man howled.

"They have breached the tower, Lord Elliot." Phaedra pawed through the baskets. "I don't suppose you included a weapon with the food or blankets so I could make a last stand?"

"Do you know how to use weapons?" his close, strangled voice asked. She looked up to see him at the window. His arms hung over the deep sill and his fingers clutched its inner edge.

She grabbed for him. "I could use one if I had to." She pulled at shoulders and breeches. He grabbed any part of her body that felt secure.

He finally fell into the tower. He sprang to his feet with the grace of a cat that had tumbled. Outside Greenwood called for his servants to row hard around the promontory's tip.

Elliot withdrew a pistol from under his battered coat. "Whitmarsh regaled me on the way here with tales of rough justice in the hill towns of this country. It would be foolish for us to make light of your danger. Stay here. Do not follow me. If it sounds to be going badly, take your chances with that rope and the sea."

Elliot did not descend the stairs quietly. He allowed all of his annoyance to sound in his heavy step. His approach silenced the men below.

He rounded the final angle to find Carmelita Messina on the bottom step, iron pan at the ready. Four men menaced her but their attention now focused on him, not her.

Carmelita looked over her shoulder and noticed his pistol. He could not tell if she was relieved or annoyed.

An equally heavy but uneven step sounded outside the portal. Signore Tarpetta appeared beneath its curve. He too saw the pistol. He drew himself into military erectness.

"You interfere," he said.

"Miss Blair is under my authority and also my protection."

He looked down his nose with disdain. "You do not authority your women well."

Elliot could not argue with that, no matter how awkward the syntax of the criticism. "I do the protecting part much better." He aimed the pistol directly at Tarpetta. "Tell everyone to go home."

"She has broken our laws."

"She has broken no laws," Carmelita said. "She has only offended the private laws of a man who thinks himself a little king."

"See the trouble she has caused? She has bewitched the women and performed pagan rites. We do not permit such crimes in Positano."

"Hear him!" Carmelita said with a harsh laugh. "He even speaks like a king. The 'we' is him alone."

Elliot was in no mood to argue. He waved the pistol. "Everyone out of this tower. Signorina Messina, please translate what I say."

Tarpetta backed out of the tower. The men and Carmelita followed. Elliot brought up the rear. As he stepped out, a sound on the stairs made him glance back. One strand of red hair hung along the turn of the staircase wall.

The women were gone. He faced the remnants of the battle, twenty men who had not had enough.

His pistol impressed them. As he spoke and Carmelita translated, Greenwood's boat reached the back of the promontory and Greenwood climbed up the bank.

"I am Lord Elliot Rothwell, brother of the Marquess of Easterbrook," he said. "I was given responsibility for Miss Blair by officials in your king's court. If any of you harm her, you will answer to me. She is neither sorcerer nor heretic nor whore. There is no evidence to support those accusations and you have my word as a gentleman that your suspicions are false."

Carmelita rattled off a very long translation. From the gist he picked up and from the expressions on the men's faces, he suspected she emphasized the *lord, marquess,* and *court* parts.

Matthias arrived as she finished. Tarpetta, recognizing his forces had lost most of their resolve, limped toward him. The two men held a private conversation.

Tarpetta walked away. The other men decided that retreating with their leader would be a good idea.

Greenwood came to the tower.

"You have my gratitude, Greenwood, for whatever you said to him."

"You misunderstand. We are not victorious," Greenwood said. "They are going to send some men to Naples to get advice and also to request aid from the army."

Carmelita threw up her arms in exasperation. "Imbeciles."

Tarpetta was returning to the town, but ten of his men had stopped at the end of the promontory.

"What are they doing?" Elliot asked.

"Posting a guard," Greenwood said. "With your pistol at the ready they will not try to enter that tower, but they will not let her leave until they get word from Naples. I expect there will be a boat or two keeping an eye on the tower from the sea tonight as well."

Elliot bit back a curse. Phaedra's sanctuary had just become a prison.

"We will watch them while they watch her, to make sure there is no violation of this truce," Carmelita said.

"Do not martyr the women in your zeal to defeat that man," Elliot said to her. "I thank you for your help, but I fear the cost to your friends will be high enough already. Leave this to me now."

Carmelita Messina paid him as much heed as Phaedra Blair did. "We will watch. There are some of us, widows and such, who do not live with a hand strangling us. I will depend on your pistol keeping the peace, and on Signore Greenwood using all his influence with *that man* to end this nonsense before dawn."

She walked away, gathering her hair into a knot as she did.

"She speaks as if you can resolve this if you choose," Elliot said to Matthias.

"She is mistaken in my influence here. However, I will try to reason with Tarpetta once he has becalmed himself, although I barely know the man."

"See if he can be bribed."

Matthias grinned. "How much is she worth to you?"

Elliot tucked his pistol away and walked to the portal. "At the moment, I'm tempted to pay him to take her off my hands."

CHAPTER TEN

Phaedra watched from the window while Elliot and Matthias spoke. She could not hear them but their serious faces indicated they were laying plans.

A small group of men formed a circle at the end of the promontory. Another four approached a fishing boat at the docks, boarded, and launched it.

Matthias walked away. The tower resonated with the sound of boots coming up the stone steps.

Elliot entered the chamber. The activity below still occupied her attention but she snuck a glance at him. His expression revealed concern and annoyance. She found the worry charming, even flattering. She hoped the anger would pass quickly.

"You are safe for now." He set the pistol on the floor in a corner so there could be no accident with it. He plucked a wineskin from a basket and held it high. A stream of water flowed into his open mouth.

Her eyes locked on the pure flow. Her throat tightened. She had not drunk anything since before dawn.

He noticed her interest. He strolled over. "Tip your head back."

She obeyed and opened her mouth. A cool, slow stream relieved her thirst.

She wiped water from her lips with her hand. "I was afraid those skins only held wine."

"The other one does. If we are careful with it, this should hold us long enough."

Long enough? She looked out the window again. She realized the implication of those men stationed at the end of the promontory. "I cannot leave, can I? What has happened?"

He explained about the men going to Naples. Memories of the odious Sansoni loomed in her head. In the silence that followed his explanation, the air grew heavy with the possible danger waiting and the full weight of that already experienced.

He looked over her head to the town below. A profound distraction appeared to claim him, as if his mind worked hard at something remote.

"You disobeyed me," he said, proving that his thoughts had everything to do with her. "You came down the stairs."

"I was not seen by them. With you between me and the danger . . . it was a small disobedience."

"You disobeyed even coming to this tower. I told you to remain at the villa."

"I did not expect to be seen at this tower."

"Except you were. A pagan ritual, no less. In this land of all lands."

"There was no ritual. No prayers to the sun god. Tarpetta simply saw me at the window as the sun rose. I was not raising my arms in prayer. I was shielding my eyes from the bright light so I could assess the sun's exact position."

"I do not care *what* you were doing. You were careless with your safety and reputation. The result was a battle between the men and women of this town and your current imprisonment in this tower." His temper stretched more taut with every word. "Do not even think of speaking now about your holy independence either. I just scaled a tower wall and threatened to kill men with whom I have no argument. I may yet have to kill some, all because of your damned willfulness."

"I merely made a dawn visit to a tower. Are you suggesting I should have anticipated all of this?" She gestured to the promontory below and to the drama that had unfolded. "If I had thought anyone would know or care, I would not have done it. I admit it appears very stupid now, but at the time it did not."

It was not much of an apology but it seemed to take the darkest edge off his anger. His attention and gaze lowered to her so sharply that it underlined how close he stood. "Did you accomplish what you came for?"

He *would* have to ask. "Yes, if proving a negative can be called an accomplishment." She pointed to the high hill. "Matthias was correct. The sun does not rise directly over that peak when you watch from this window, or in direct line with where we now stand. It first shows to the right, the south, a bit."

She braced herself for mockery, or more anger that her little experiment had caused so much trouble and not even proven her theory.

Instead he ruminated over the evidence. "These

things are not exact. The precise day of the solstice floats, and we are still charting how subtle changes accumulate over time in astronomy. Five centuries ago the sun may well have crested that peak on midsummer's morn."

She thought it very kind of him to make excuses and not call her a fool. A more explicit apology was in order. "I did not seek to create all this trouble, and am sorry that I did. I am not surprised that you are a little angry."

"I am plenty angry, Phaedra. However, I am more concerned for your safety. Until I have secured that, you are to do as I say, especially if I have further cause to pick up that pistol."

He strode to the western window. He frowned at what he saw. She walked over and peeked out. A boat with the three men sat at anchor fifty yards away from the tower. The sun had begun its decline into the sea, but hours remained until dark.

"Your prison is complete," Elliot said. "We must wait, and trust in Matthias to negotiate your release before more trouble arrives from Naples. Unfortunately, Tarpetta appears to be the power at hand and Matthias barely knows him."

Phaedra knelt by the baskets and removed their contents. She lined the wineskins and fruit and packages of food against the wall. "Carmelita thinks they know each other better than they admit."

Elliot rested his shoulder against the wall and watched her deal with the baskets. "It would be useful if you are correct, but Matthias has no reason to lie to me."

She was glad to find a crockery cup below the food.

She did not want to drink from a streaming wineskin all day, colorful though the experience had been.

"How well do you know Matthias?" she asked. Greenwood might hold her fate in his hands, but that was not all that provoked the question.

Elliot moved away from the sun streaking through the window, into the cool shadows where she arranged their provisions. He sat on the floor with his back against the stones and reached for one of the figs.

"I revered him while at university. He is a respected scholar with two volumes to his credit. He encouraged my studies and guided me in the research methods used to chart new paths. His interest flattered me, especially since he harbored no predatory motivations like some other tutors." He bit into the fig, then gestured to the rest of the food. "You should eat something. If three days hence we must swim for our lives, you do not want to be too weak."

She chose some bread and cheese. "You do not appear to revere him now, and there is none of the tutor in his manner toward you."

"Well, I am no longer a student, and I have a volume of my own now."

"It appears more than a friendship built on those old roles, is what I meant."

He did not appear inclined to satisfy her curiosity. He took his time eating the fig. She retreated into her own meal.

"My father was not a warm man." He spoke casually, as if fifteen minutes had not passed since her last comment. "Imagine a man like my brother Hayden, but with none of the qualities that compromise Hayden's sternness. I felt fortunate as a boy that his attention was absorbed by my brothers and he ignored me. Matthias Greenwood, in turn, chose to focus his attention on me. He valued what I valued, was quick with praise and slow with expressions of disappointment. There was something of the father in his interest, I suppose."

She did not miss his expression when he described his father. She knew all about the last Marquess of Easterbrook's reputation. He had no doubt been the sort of parent it was impossible to please, and perhaps as hard with his sons as he was said to have been in other areas of life.

It was not Elliot's studied blandness that had arrested her attention, however. Rather another emotion flickered in his eyes.

He had insisted that Richard Drury's memoirs insinuated lies about the last marquess, but he could not be positive that they were lies. Sitting here with him, watching him, she just knew that he wondered if his father might have had that officer killed. Would that small suspicion become more real, take on substance and be unavoidable, if that insinuation appeared in print?

Some scientists believed that criminal behavior was inherited, much like some diseases could be. To learn that one's legacy included the capacity to ruthlessly plan a murder could be as bad as discovering one's blood was tainted by insanity.

"Matthias Greenwood has no children," she said. "You are his intellectual heir and part of his professional legacy. If there was something of the father in him, perhaps there was something of the son in you."

He shrugged. "You may be correct. He may see me that way, even within the friendship we have now."

She suspected Greenwood did see it that way, but she thought Elliot did as well. Their manners toward each other reminded her of the comfortable friendship and masculine love revealed by fathers and their grown sons when a close relationship has matured.

If so, Matthias Greenwood was an important person to Elliot.

Of course he was. Elliot was here, wasn't he? He had come to Positano to discuss his new research even though the student had surpassed the teacher as a historian.

Eating this humble meal on this stone floor removed them from the world. His frank description of his father had nudged open a door to an intimacy more appealing than that created by physical pleasure. This reminded her of the mood she enjoyed with her friends.

"Why are you so curious about Greenwood, Phaedra?"

She examined the relaxed familiarity they shared and debated her response. "I am very interested in him."

"Hell, he is old enough to be your father."

She almost laughed at his exasperated tone, but the hot annoyance in his eyes checked her. He was jealous. She found that hopelessly old-fashioned and presumptuous, but adorably so. She wanted to giggle, not scold.

"You misunderstand, Elliot. He knew my mother, and has been kind enough to try to answer some questions I have about a few things."

"What things?"

"My mother may have had a secret lover her last years."

He frowned. "Richard Drury—"

"Not at the end. There was another."

"And Matthias knew who it was? He lived in Cambridge then, and although he visited London sometimes . . ."

"He is a perceptive man. He was not surprised when I suggested there may have been another man in my mother's life. This lover also dealt in antiquities, and Matthias was able to tell me the names of some men in her circle who did. Many of her close friends put me off with denials. I suspect they did not want the world's image of Artemis Blair to be changed. But he was honest with me and I am grateful to him."

He puzzled over what she said, and appeared both curious and skeptical. "Why would you ask for names, Phaedra? Perhaps there was no lover at all if her friends denied it."

"I think there was, because of something my father wrote in his memoirs. This man, whoever he was, was a criminal."

His expression darkened. "Another reference without a name? Another bit of gossip that will destroy a reputation?" He was on his feet in an instant. He strode away, stared at the wall, then turned to face her. "Better if you burned it, or locked it away forever."

"That might spare your family, but it will not spare my mother's last lover."

"Why not?"

She wrapped the cheese in its damp cloth. "Because even if the memoirs are not published, I will annotate this part to my satisfaction, and I will deal with this man in my own way."

His mood did not lighten, his frown did not cease, but cautious curiosity showed in his eyes. "You speak calmly, but with bitter resolve. What did your father write about this man that you feel you must now identify him?"

She scrambled to stand. She brushed off the black gauze of her skirts. "He wrote that this man seduced her, then betrayed her in a most dishonorable way that led to her death. I need to discover if it is true."

"It is ambiguous at best."

"Not so ambiguous. There was more. I am not completely mad in thinking I can identify this man. Only half so."

She strolled to the center of the chamber and looked around. "If we might be here for days, we should domesticate this place." She upturned a basket. "It might serve as a stool if you can remove the handle."

He fetched the knife sent up with the food. He set the basket on the windowsill's stones and set to sawing. "You should not put too much stock in what your father wrote about your mother. He was a lover spurned and that can cloud a man's judgment."

She picked up the blanket that covered the straw and checked its cleanliness. She eyed some metal hooks set into the stone vault above. "My father understood what he had and did not have with my mother. He did not write with bitterness, but as a man who had seen the woman he loved misused."

Elliot sawed away, but his expression of resolve was not for the basket handle. "Tread carefully as you annotate his words on this, Phaedra. Do not accuse the wrong man or impugn a good one."

"If he is a good man, he has nothing to fear from me or from the memoirs. No good man does."

The basket handle gave way just then. It broke under the pressure he put on the knife. A harsh crack sounded off the stone vaults, as if Elliot's temper had snapped at her last sentence.

They spent the next hours more pleasantly, speaking of friendlier things. Phaedra's friend Alexia had recently married Elliot's brother Hayden, and they speculated on that match and what had and had not brought it about. The gossip lightened the mood wrought by their first conversation.

Elliot continued to mull it over, however. He had not missed her tone or her expression when she spoke of the lover who had betrayed her mother.

Phaedra was no curious tourist the way she had claimed. She was a woman on a mission. For some reason it had led her to Naples. It was why her humor had improved about his delay in taking her to Pompeii. Her investigation may have even been at the bottom of her friendships with Marsilio and Pietro.

For all he knew her every act, her every word, since that day he stood in the garden, had been part of her plan to learn about her mother's last months and the man whom she blamed for her mother's decline and death.

She gave instructions about arranging their humble abode while they chatted. At her request he managed to tie the rope to one of the vault's hooks and secure its end to the stone floor with its metal hooks. She draped the old blanket over it to create a private corner into which she placed the chamber pot that Matthias's servants had sensibly added to one of the baskets.

Dusk was settling when all was done. With the new blanket on the straw and the upturned basket for a stool, Phaedra had created a rustic but serviceable home. For one person.

A low-ceiling space existed below this highest tower chamber. He expected he would be making do there unless he could charm an invitation out of the queen to share her sanctuary.

"You have a talent for domestic organization, Phaedra. Is that the result of making do without servants?"

"I think that I learned to do it well because my mother did it so poorly. That proved useful because I needed the skills when I was sent off to fend for myself."

She carried the wineskin and the cup to the window facing the town. After a few errant splashes she filled the cup from the skin's arching stream and offered it to him.

He joined her at the window and drank. Beyond the long shadow of the tower Tarpetta's men had made a camp at the base of the promontory. From the distant sounds of their laughter they appeared relaxed and in good spirits.

"Why did you begin fending for yourself?"

She appeared very lovely in the gathering silvery light of dusk that entered this window. Behind them the opposite opening allowed in the flaming colors of the sun's final glory. Those rays illuminated the back of her hair, turning her locks into blazes that contrasted with the cool translucence of her white skin as she looked west.

"My mother believed that women learn dependency from their parents. We are taught to fear independence and then lured into rejecting it even when it is attainable. Therefore, when I received a legacy from her brother, she encouraged me to leave her house and live on my own before I grew complacent in my adult dependency on *her*." She paused while she calmly stretched to see the ground closer to the tower. Another little camp stood there, populated by five old women and Carmelita Messina.

"I was sixteen," she added, still distracted by the scene below.

Her attention on the camps ensured that she did not see his reaction. "You were a child." He tried to keep condemnation out of his tone. Phaedra would not like criticism of her mother, and he had no desire to argue with her now.

She still watched the promontory. "Yes, I was a child. However, there are many girls sent into marriage at that age. I suspect that is a more startling fate. They are too young for their parents' plans, and I was too young for mine as well. She did not remove herself from my life, so it was not a rejection of her duties to me. She helped me hire a housekeeper so I did not live alone the first years. I visited her often and we saw each other almost as much as when I lived under her roof."

She made it sound almost normal and sensible. He

could not accommodate the image of Phaedra at sixteen in her own household, with no protection or supervision except that provided by a paid woman. His cousin Caroline who had come out this season was so childish that one wanted to lock her away for another ten years.

Of course Phaedra Blair had probably not been so childish at that age, nor so innocent of the world. Artemis had raised her daughter to walk alone and make her own way. Still, it angered him to picture it. The woman should not have used her own child as an experiment to prove that her radical ideas had merit.

"At the time I did not mind, and it has all worked out as my mother expected. Once a woman tastes such freedom she will never relinquish it. However, when she died—I felt some anger then. I rather wish she had waited so I could have spent those last two years with her. She did not anticipate that her time was so short, of course."

"I cannot imagine the independence you describe. Even as a man I do not live such a singular life."

"It matters not if you still reside in Easterbrook's great house. As a man you are by your gender free."

"I do not speak of the law or of customs or finances, but of living. I am not alone or unfettered by others. There are my brothers ever-present in my life, and other relatives with claims on me. I am theirs and they are mine. Even if my brothers and I grow to hate each other, the burdens of life are shared."

Her expression turned wistful, beautifully so. "I would have liked to have a sister or brother. That would have been nice, especially now."

Now that she was all alone was what she meant. She

had chosen a path that would leave her forever alone too, unless like her mother she had an illegitimate child. He realized that she understood what she sacrificed. She did not discount its value. She had weighed it all, if not at sixteen then when she matured. He did not think the cost worth the prize, but he had to admire her bravery.

She appeared a little sad. He felt bad for forcing her to face her loneliness. "I expect your friendships help to replace the family you do not have."

Impish lights danced in her eyes. Her humor and spirit surfaced out of the depths of her thoughts. "In a way, but not family as you described yours. Some are like sisters and brothers, a few have even been like the most benign of husbands, but the bonds are not permanent. As I grow older I may wonder if I have been blessed with more independence than any person would want."

Which meant she wondered already.

The oblique reference to her lovers subtly altered the mood between them. He could not stand so close to her in this light and not think about making love to her. Images and inclinations had prodded since he walked up the stairs hours ago. That low stimulation boiled higher with her words. He thought he saw a challenge in the way she regarded him.

Suddenly the desire bound them as starkly as it ever had. She made no effort to thwart its power. Soon his teeth were on edge. Never in his life had he met a woman who so boldly acknowledged the sensual excitement that can exist before a kiss or touch.

With any other woman he would act, just as he had with her in the past. He had not forgotten her parting words that last night on the balcony, however. If she were good to her threat right now he might not muster the honor to allow her to deny him.

She provoked the worst of his blood, a current that flowed from his father. He wanted to reach for her and embrace and caress and devour. The temptation to use pleasure to coerce her to submit to her own hunger, and to him, threatened to overpower what was left of his good sense.

He walked away from her. He picked up the pistol and one of the blankets and kept going, down the stairs. The alternative was to risk behaving like the worst scoundrel, or else becoming one of those pitiable bees, buzzing and begging for the queen's favor.

Phaedra watched the sun dip into the sea. Purple and orange lights continued to color the water in silken streaks while dark slowly closed in. Down in the boat the men waved at her and called up friendly greetings. They appeared to have a few wineskins of their own and had grown more amiable as a result.

She found the one big candle sent with the provisions and lit it. She set it in a corner where the night breeze would not blow it out. She heard Elliot moving about down below, perhaps trying to find some comfort on the floor with that sole blanket beneath him.

Her body had not entirely calmed since he left, nor had her thoughts strayed far from their last minutes together. Hot pulses continued to gently throb, coaxing her attention. Usually she only had to contend with that when Elliot was near, but it appeared her body knew he was close enough and would not give her relief. Her breasts remained tight and full, their tips reacting to every movement she made when the fabric of her dress brushed them.

Their last conversation had disarmed her. She could not think of him except kindly right now. He had understood more than she did herself. He had not gloated either, but instead expressed true concern for the less perfect side of the life she lived.

She had lied a little to spare Artemis this man's censure, but from his reactions that may have been unnecessary. The truth was that Artemis had been correct in her beliefs but not always so in her methods. Being cut loose at sixteen had been devastating and frightening, much more than she admitted to him. It had felt like her mother had thrown her overboard into the ocean and simply expected her to figure out how to swim.

She had forgiven her mother that miscalculation years ago, but she doubted others would if they knew about that tenuous year so fraught with big mistakes. The truth would be one more proof to the world that Artemis Blair had not been a good mother, or even a normal woman.

Elliot no longer made sounds down below, but she could swear she heard his breathing. Nor was he asleep so early. She just knew that too. She paced quietly, trying to relieve the way her body tormented her. She tried to reconcile how the desire was not only physical now, but also a yearning to explore the closeness she had felt with him today as they shared danger and confidences.

She laid her hands on her breasts. The stimulations collected, increased, and flowed down her body. She closed her eyes to try to tame them, and heard her mother's lessons about desire.

Carnal pleasure is as much a woman's need as a man's. Do not deny your desires, but beware whom you choose as a partner. Most men are conquerors at heart. Seek out the enlightened few who have risen above this primitive curse. If you choose to take your pleasure with a conqueror, make sure you cede only your body and only temporarily. And never, ever succumb to the delusion that you can change such a man.

Phaedra pictured the man down below. He had left even though this chamber had all but howled with the way they wanted each other. He might be one of the conquerors, but he was not stupid. He would understand that she ceded nothing except what she chose. She would make sure that part was clear.

CHAPTER
ELEVEN

Elliot settled in for a night with nought but his thoughts for company. With any luck he would soon cease picturing the woman above stairs.

He forced his mind inward to the world of the histories he wrote. He did not need his papers to journey there. The notes and preliminary drafts existed as records, not as reminders. All the information lived in his head, accessible at any time. He had spent many a party escaping to that world for spells of relief if the conversation bored him.

His brothers, Christian and Hayden, possessed similar secret chambers in their heads. When they ventured inside theirs they closed the doors behind them and lost hold on reality. Only he had been blessed with the ability to slip in and out at will, as if the door remained forever ajar. His connection to the real world always remained within reach.

Right now that was less a boon than normal. The world wanting to intrude consisted of physical frustration that refused to quiet itself. Speculations regarding

the movements above poked at him. His bad blood calculated the cost to honor and pride of taking first and
rectifying later.

Somehow he managed to keep most of that just outside the door, not completely interfering. He turned his
concentration to synthesizing the information on funer-
ary practices gleaned from the old Roman histories.

"Elliot."

He opened his eyes. Every part of him snapped alert.
She might have stood a few feet from him, he heard her
so clearly. The stones of walls and stairs had carried her
voice down. She had not even had to raise her tone.

She did not speak again. She just assumed he had
heard. Or maybe she knew he would come to her even if
she only spoke the summons in her head.

She might merely need help with the candle. Or perhaps she saw some movement from one of her windows
and anticipated trouble from their gaolers. He could just
call up and ask, but he wouldn't, even though walking
away again would be nigh impossible.

Trusting that Phaedra was too smart to play with fire,
he climbed the staircase.

Vague lights and dark shadows danced across the
stones of the upper chamber's walls and vault. The
hanging blanket sliced away a corner with its dark drop.
The lone, big candle smoked gently, its fat flame adding
golden glows amidst the moonlight's cool ones.

All the dim illuminations gathered and intensified in
one place. A pale statue absorbed them to enhance its
sensual display of fiery copper and white porcelain.

Phaedra knelt on the straw pallet, sitting back on her

heels. She faced the stairs and him. He stopped when he saw her, momentarily awed by her beauty and boldness.

She was naked. Her tresses streamed over bare skin. They looked like strips of silken drapery that parted to display glimpses of creamy shoulders, soft arms, round breasts, and curving hips.

She let him look a good while, acknowledging with her gaze the way the storm gathered in him, admitting with her eyes that she was with him in the desire.

She parted her hair and pushed it to her back, exposing her body completely. Her breasts rose high and full, their dark pink tips erect and tight.

"We can share pleasure tonight, if you want," she said.

He shed his coat and walked over to her. "If I want? I have wanted to have you since the first time I saw you."

She relaxed her body and stretched her naked beauty at his feet. She watched while he stripped off his shirt. "It will not be quite like that. We will have each other."

"Whatever you wish. I am beyond caring about the terms of this surrender." He was beyond caring about anything except the desire getting tauter and more compelling by the instant. He dropped to his knees beside her.

"It is no surrender, Elliot. It is a truce. One night when we enjoy our friendship." She reached up to help release the buttons on his trousers.

Her hands made his arousal savage. He gazed down at her naked body, so vulnerable and welcoming. Images entered his head and urges fired his blood. If she thought this was about friendship, she did not know men very well.

"Certainly, Phaedra. Of course."

He did not mean it. Her soul knew that but she did not care at the moment.

He looked sensual and beautiful. Even kneeling he was tall. His naked torso and shoulders towered above the straw pallet and her, making her feel small and . . . vulnerable. That sensation was a new one. She had never experienced it before meeting this man. It was not unpleasant. She allowed herself pleasure in its effect because she knew he represented no real danger.

The light turned his skin to bronze and drew dark lines along the edges of his muscles. There was nothing soft to see. Not in his body and not in his face. Passion turned the Rothwell features hard even in this most amiable son. His dark hair, mussed and free from the day's adventures, left loose locks skimming his brow and face. His eyes became black crystals when she reached to help him undress.

His own hands fell away, leaving her to do it. He just looked down, perhaps daring her to go on, testing to see if she would retreat from boldness.

She took her time while their gazes remained locked. Wonderful sensations enlivened her body. The titillation was more intense because she knew what was coming. Anticipation pulled between them so wonderfully that it became one of the best pleasures that she had ever experienced.

Her service done, she trailed her palm up his

stomach, savoring the touch of his skin and that masculine combination of soft surface and hard support. She loved the way desire intensified all the senses, even the intuitive one that told her how much he liked that touch and how the rest of reality was disappearing for him too.

When she could reach no further she glossed down again. Her hand hit the loose lower garments. With slow caresses she coaxed them down, freeing him until the fabric puddled at his knees. Her fingertips learned his body inch by inch. She slid and pressed them over the hard swells of his hips and thighs. She feathered up the length of his erection to its tip and circled softly, then caressed more aggressively.

He tried to contain what it did to him, but she could see the sensual fury taking control. It made all of him harder. His face and gaze, his entire body, became more taut.

"You are in danger of being ravished without courtesy or ceremony, Phaedra."

She assessed the threat, and her body's physical arousal. "I do not mind. I am more than ready myself."

He joined her on the blanket and kicked off his clothes. He settled his naked body over hers, resting on forearms that flanked her shoulders.

A kiss. A deep, intimate one so slow and luring that an odd, sweet longing conquered her impatience. She parted her legs so he nestled closer, instinctively inviting him to join her now so that maybe the entire night would be so touching.

He looked down at her. "You are a very generous woman."

"Not generous. If a woman is honest in these pleasures, she gains too."

"That is an admirable, democratic view. Only you
are not being honest and you invite me to be a bad lover
because of it."

"I acknowledged my carnal condition most honestly." So honestly that this delay maddened her. She
shifted her hips a bit to encourage him.

His response was slight, subtle, and devastating. He
pressed, but not enough. She felt him down there, barely
touching her, a horrible, wonderful tease.

He pressed kisses to her neck and shoulders. "You
said you were more than ready," he said between admin-
istering hot excitements. "That was not true, but perhaps you spoke in ignorance."

Indignation spiked through her preoccupation with
the marvelous tingles in her blood. "I am *not* ignorant. I
would think that is obvious."

He shifted his upper body so he could caress her. He
watched his fingertips trail lightly around the base and
swell of her breast, much as her own had recently
moved over his hip and thighs. "A woman more than
ready is not so composed as you still are. You are not
nearly as ready as you can be. If you are not ignorant
you know that. But perhaps you fear the abandon."

He brushed her nipple. A deep tremble shuddered,
resonating from her jaw to her toes. Her body ached to
pull him inside her so she might escape the sensual torture, no matter how delicious it might be.

He touched her breast more purposefully, rubbing the
tip, deliberately making the shudder repeat with growing
intensity. She had begun this seduction confident and

bold. Now the tide of that alluring vulnerability washed away her secure hold on herself.

She could not resist the current. He seemed to sense her attempts to try. He moved off her body as if to announce that he, not she, would decide when she was ready. Stretched alongside her, his upper body rising on one taut arm, he caressed her with long, sure strokes, carrying the possessive touch to all her skin and limbs.

Her breasts ached for his hand to return. The other pleasure and arousals that he incited made it worse. Frustration had her halfway to madness. She could not even embrace him while he hovered like this. His position forced her to lie open and submissive to his gaze and wicked hand.

She could not embrace, but she could touch. Not all of him was out of reach. She sought his inner thigh with her right hand. She caressed upward and made sure she would not drown alone.

He responded as she hoped, the way her essence cried for. He caressed her breasts so fully, so perfectly, that insanity threatened to claim her. The unbearable pleasure got wonderfully worse and the hunger for more filled her awareness.

He lowered his head so he could use his mouth on her breast. A new sensation rang through the rest. One sweet and intense and so powerful it ripped her grasp from reality. She grabbed his shoulders in a fierce embrace so she would not be adrift alone. The vaguest perceptions entered the dark, focused place her mind had become. Sounds echoed the pleas in her thoughts and the needs wracking her. Hard holds and violent kisses pulled her deeper into pure sensation.

A new touch. One welcomed and feared and so necessary that she thought she would faint with relief. Her
consciousness screamed. She parted her legs more so he
would not stop. Profound shivers collected there and
spread, increasing the torture until she wanted to beg for
relief.

Then he was with her again, nestled between her
thighs the way this had started, pressing slightly in that
infuriating, incomplete way. He kissed her with savage
command while he entered her, swallowing her groan of
relief.

Hard thrusts, deep and full, took her to fulfillment.
The exquisite explosion of pleasure drenched her with
peace and perfect sensation. She floated in it, awed by
the violence of the climax and the physicality of the
ecstasy.

She emerged from the holy darkness slowly. Her
arms felt the shoulders she embraced and her legs the
hips they circled. He remained hard and large in her.

She gazed through his damp locks at eyes still hot
and hard with sensual sternness.

"You seem well contented, Phaedra."

So well contented that she thought she could never
be ill contented again. "Most certainly so."

He moved slowly, creating a long stroke on flesh still
intensely alive with the aftermaths of her climax. "I do
not think I have ever met a woman so adept at taking her
pleasure." He placed a firm kiss on her lips. Deep inside
her the contentment became less so. New needs trembled subtly but distinctly.

He made it happen again. He gazed down, too
composed, too sure of what he was doing with these

slow, deep thrusts. "I do not think I have ever been so thoroughly had by a woman before."

"Do not blame me if you did not share the satisfaction. Normally, there is unity in such things."

"I doubt there has ever been unity with you. Your friends find their own pleasure while they service you in finding yours, but that is different."

She heard an insult in his quiet observations. If she were not so aware of the masculine power pouring out of him, if the shivers of new excitement were not preoccupying her, she might find the words to castigate him for his presumption.

Only, her body's contentment was dimming fast. Deep, resonating needs awoke, colored by confusion and teeth-gritting desperation.

Oblivion beckoned again, but remained tantalizingly out of reach. She remained too much in the world, too aware of the man taking too much time, too conscious that he did not lose sight of her either.

She shifted her hips to encourage more. Faster. He caressed with one hand to her right hip and pressed, stopping her. "You said we would have each other, and I want to have you slowly."

"It was very impolite of you to not be done with this when I was." She had not even been aware that a man could control matters to this extent.

She got the barest smile as a response. His hand left her hip. She thought he had capitulated. Instead he reached back and released her leg's hold on his hip.

He moved the other leg too. He pushed her thighs together beneath him. When he moved in her again the pleasure focused and spiraled so sharply that she gasped.

The sensations stunned her. Conquered her. She could not deny them and she surrendered to the abandon. But her first climax meant this was different. She never totally lost hold on the world. She heard her own cries. His aura saturated her. The vulnerability returned, more nuanced this time, still exciting but vaguely frightening.

He never lost control, never succumbed. Even when his thrusts quickened and increased in power, even when she was screaming at the moment of ecstasy, she sensed how he controlled the power to the end.

There was unity this time. She was not alone in the oblivion. If anything his presence grew more prevailing. The glorious relief split through her the way lightning claims a tree, but he remained tangible through it all.

In the aftermath, while her soul sought and collected the remnants of her self-possession, while she struggled to recompose a woman she recognized, misgivings slid into her thoughts. She felt him in her arms, his body covering hers. He was spent and contented and quiet, but starkly, awkwardly real.

She had never felt at a disadvantage in these things before. Beneath her sated bliss, she lazily examined this new situation. She tried to decide what it meant and how it had happened.

Surely this mysterious sense of selflessness would disappear when he left. It was only the night and the dark and the pleasure that caused it.

He rose up on his forearms, lifting his weight off her. His gaze invaded deeply, and so hotly and intensely that she wondered if he was trying to burn a brand on her mind. Then he rolled off her and stretched on his side along her body. He soon fell asleep with one arm across her.

He intended to stay here all night. She never permitted that with her friends, but she could hardly wake him and demand that he go back down to the blanket on the stones in the chamber below. Still . . .

She stared at the dim lights playing across the stones above her. His gaze had been warm and touching during that last long look, but it had also demanded she acknowledge the power of their joining. It had contained the deep intimacy still binding them, and refused to permit her to disentangle from its hold.

But there had been something else, something she had never seen in a man's eyes before, at least not when a man regarded her.

She had just gazed into the eyes of a conqueror.

She wondered what it was that he mistakenly thought he had won.

The door to his mind remained ajar. He heard her sigh and mumble in her sleep. Dawn was breaking and she would wake soon enough. For now he enjoyed the peace and her company and the cool air on his body while his mind finished sorting through other things.

A sound had woken him to the vaguest indications of the new day. Now he peered through the silver light while a form took shape. Another basket was in the room, a new one. It rested right at the top of the stairs. One of the old women had brought more provisions.

Phaedra slowly woke like a purring kitten. She

curled then stretched her naked elegance, and turned
away so he could admire the lovely line that dipped
down her side and up her hip.

She appeared very soft right now, and much younger
than her years. Stripped of her dark habit, free of the armor with which she faced the world, she struck him as
fragile. Last night had revealed this other side of her
spirit, in ways unspoken and undefined. Her passion had
been both worldly and ignorant, both confident and
frightened. He had sensed the weakness and softness
that she dared not allow the world to see. She lived a
symbolic life that did not permit such contradictions.

He wanted her again, because she was so beautiful
here in the morning and because the naked Phaedra,
both unclothed and unarmored, fascinated him. He
guessed he would continue wanting her for a long time.
He calculated time and place, night and day, while
memories of their embraces tempted him.

She came alert with a start, as if she heard his
thoughts. She fell onto her back. Through barely raised
lids she assessed where she was and who was with her.
The vaguest blush tinted her neck down to her pretty
breasts. Their tips tightened, and not because of the cool
ocean breeze.

Her embarrassment made her appear girlish and un-
sure. He wondered what thoughts caused the little frown
she directed at her body. She was not so bold now, when
darkness did not set events in another world.

He pulled on some garments so she would not have
to find her own way out of the place her choice had put
her. He handed her the black pile of her dress. She sat
up and drew it over her head.

He sat down beside her on the pallet. He wondered if she would speak of last night, and what he should say when he did. This was not a woman who expected either gratitude or apologies. She certainly would not be looking for an offer of either payment or support. She expected absolutely nothing from him, and would interpret any such overture badly.

"There is Alexia," he said. "Yesterday you spoke of being alone, but Alexia is a loyal friend." Her words had played in his head this morning as he lay with her. He wondered about her friendships as a girl, and if she had even had any. He guessed that not many mothers would allow their daughters to be friends with the daughter of Artemis Blair.

She stretched to peck a kiss on his cheek. At some point today he assumed the latent intimacy would cease and she would treat the night as history. Now, however, she let him know with the gesture that she thought his concern charming at least.

He took the opportunity to move his arm around her. Sitting like this on the straw bed, his back against the wall, a lovely woman's head on his shoulder and the sounds and scents of the sea blowing in the windows, would not be a bad way to spend the day.

"She made your brother promise to permit our friendship," she said. "When Alexia negotiated that marriage, she made him promise. I just assumed . . . I declined her wedding invitation and wrote to say it would only cause strife with her new husband. She wrote back and told me how it was." She inhaled deeply. Her voice grew small. "I wept when I read her letter. It was the most noble thing any friend has ever done for

me. That she thought about me at all at such a moment—
I still find it hard to believe your brother agreed to it. I
am not a woman most men want their wives to know.
A courtesan would be more welcome in Mayfair drawing rooms."

Elliot guessed that his brother's generosity had been
part of a larger scheme. Phaedra Blair was an easy con-
cession for Hayden to make in the negotiations to get
the woman he wanted.

It would not do to put it quite that way. "Hayden has
never been society's slave. He wants Alexia to be happy.
He knows that her friendship with you holds no danger
to her."

"If he believes that, love has made him stupid. I do
not resent the fathers and husbands who will not allow
me to be received, Elliot. If I were them and believed as
they do, I would make the same rules."

He looked down at her crown. Her hair appeared
more gold than red now in the crystalline morning light.
She did not want his pity for her solitary childhood. She
did not expect the world to change to accommodate
who she was. She merely wanted to be left alone to live
in her heresies as she chose.

Understanding that added a new warmth to the contentment he experienced right now. Unfortunately leaving her alone would be nigh impossible.

"Lord Elliot."

Carmelita's call did not come up the stone stairs. It
bellowed up the exterior of the tower. At least one of
them had intruded earlier and now they took efforts not
to do so again.

He got up and looked out the window. The five old

women milled around Carmelita, talking closely and still keeping guard.

"Lord Elliot, here comes Signore Greenwood." She gestured down the promontory, past the men waking to the new day at its end.

Greenwood was passing the docks, now filled with fishing boats. Noise in the town reminded Elliot why none had been put out to sea. Today was the feast of San Giovanni.

The men let Greenwood pass. He said something to them as he walked by. He noticed Elliot at the window and waved greetings. His smile and jaunty gait indicated that he had good news.

He bowed deeply to Carmelita and the old women, then peered up. "I am to be profusely thanked by you and Miss Blair, Rothwell. I have been so diplomatic, so brilliant, that I deserve a living in the foreign service."

"You convinced that fool to end this?" Carmelita asked.

"I forged a compromise. Enough of one that the services of you ladies will not be required in the future."

Carmelita explained things to the old women. She met some resistance there. A little argument ensued but Carmelita won the day. All of the women started walking back to the town.

"I will come up and explain," Matthias said. His head dipped below the portal's header.

Elliot turned back to Phaedra. She appeared much herself, composed and proud and unusual. Black gauze covered the body he had possessed just hours ago. She bent down and smoothed the blanket over the straw, eliminating the most obvious evidence of the night's events.

"I should have yielded to temptation and woken you earlier," he said. "Such a night should not end this abruptly."

Her small smile appeared nervous. "Abruptly or slowly, they always end anyway."

There was a lot he wanted to say in response to that, but Greenwood's boots were nearing the chamber.

Matthias's white hair and smiling face emerged and rose. He appeared very pleased with himself.

"I have brought you the key to your prison, Miss Blair. Unfortunately, for this to work as planned, you must leave Positano immediately."

CHAPTER
TWELVE

"I plied Tarpetta with wine for the better part of the night," Matthias said. "I convinced him that he did not want to risk the king's displeasure by creating an international spectacle involving the brother of an English marquess."

"One would hope that a rational argument would carry more weight than a threat," Phaedra said. It rankled her that Elliot would once more procure her freedom.

She should be grateful. After last night she should find it romantic to be saved by this man. That reaction blossomed in her, but her mind also calculated how much she would once more be in his debt. If this kept happening he might call the note in ways she did not want.

"We will take whatever argument succeeded," Elliot said.

His tone all but said, *Silence, woman. Leave it to men to settle this.*

Matthias offered an appeasing smile. "Miss Blair,

Tarpetta is a man much enamored of his own pride and sense of authority. The best argument turned out to be one that suggested his intended course of action would damage both."

"If it is the one that worked, so be it. I would have preferred some vindication but I will settle for safety and freedom."

"When you say she must leave at once, how quickly does that mean?" Elliot asked.

"We will return to the villa, retrieve your baggage, and send you off in a boat immediately." Matthias gestured to the baskets and blanket. "Leave this. I will send servants for it later."

Phaedra accepted their escort out of the tower. She gave the chamber a final look before she went down the stairs. It still appeared humble and domestic, but not nearly as charming as it had last night in the dusk and dark. Now it was what it was, a crude abode carved out of danger and fear, and an attempt to make a home so she would not feel so helpless.

She suspected the whole night had only been a feminine reaction to danger. She had never understood the appeal of the knight in shining armor before, but then she had never been the damsel in distress either.

Her mind sorted it out rationally. The bright light of day implied the romance of the night had been a dream to be remembered fondly, but nothing more. And yet, as she began walking down the stairs, Elliot took her hand in a gesture of both courtesy and command, to guide her and lead her forth from their tower of love.

Her heart twisted at the gentle way he escorted her. Her pulse raced at his touch. When they passed a thin slit in the stairwell wall the light lined his fine face so he looked much as he had last night. For a moment she was dazed, awed by the manner in which he could alter the air and space and invade her so thoroughly.

Midsummer's day greeted them outside, hot and sultry. The morning sea breeze had waned and the sun carved the town into bright lights and deep shadows. The promontory was empty of people. So were the docks.

"The feast is under way," Matthias said. "They are all in the church piazza."

"Let us bypass it," Elliot said. The small frown of concern marred his brow again. She sensed that he remained alert for trouble, like a cat carefully making its way through unknown territory.

"By all means, but you will miss the preparations for the procession. It is very colorful." Matthias guided them to a lane that would flank the piazza. "Your vigilance is admirable, Rothwell, but Miss Blair is quite safe now. Tarpetta understands it is in his interest to stand down."

There were no donkey boys to be seen so they began the long climb to the villa through empty lanes. Sounds from the piazza floated between silent houses. As they crossed a street that headed south, she saw a flash of black out of the corner of her eye. Not everyone in the town was at the church.

Climbing the hill was a strain. Phaedra's legs grew sore, then felt watery. The sun beat down relentlessly and sweat began to dampen the gauze of her dress. Elliot did not appear the least discomforted, but Matthias was not such a young man. His breathing became labored.

"I must slow, Mr. Greenwood. Would you be good enough to stay with me. Lord Elliot can forge ahead and begin preparations."

"Certainly, Miss Blair. You appear a little paler. Would you like to stop and rest? While haste is in order, we do not have a pistol at our backs."

"The sun is dazzling me more than I might like, but I am sure that if I walk more slowly I will be—."

"What in—"

Elliot's exasperated tone interrupted her. She released Matthias from her attention and he from hers. They both looked ahead to see what had arrested Elliot.

Five figures stood in the lane. Dressed in widow's black, veiled like Arabs or nuns, Carmelita's old women blocked their way.

"Just smile and walk on," Matthias said, beaming his most benevolent expression on them.

It might have worked if these women remained the only barrier. Unfortunately, others joined them. Phaedra recognized some of the women she had met at the well and others who had stood against the men. All of them peered down the lane most critically.

The object of their disapproval was none other than *i'uomo magnifico,* Lord Elliot Rothwell.

Carmelita pushed through the gathering throng. Her arms flew while she castigated the old women. Their response was as crisp and sharp as the daggers their eyes kept shooting at Elliot.

Matthias turned to find another path. "Oh, my," he muttered.

Phaedra glanced back. More women had bled onto the lane behind them.

Carmelita walked the twenty paces separating them from the old women. She grimaced with apology and resignation. "There is a little problem."

"Tarpetta and Greenwood have an understanding," Elliot said. "Explain that to them. These women who risked themselves to protect Miss Blair are now interfering with her timely escape."

Carmelita nodded in solemn agreement. "Except they still seek to protect her. They are now concerned for her honor." She leveled a knowing gaze at him. "They think you . . . they think . . . actually, they *know,* they don't think."

Phaedra felt her color rising. Elliot's face remained passive but it flushed a little too.

"They cannot *know* anything," Phaedra said.

"Phaedra Blair, your isolation in that tower with a man would alone compromise you in their eyes. However, Maria there brought up some water and bread at dawn and . . ." Carmelita spread her hands in a gesture that said all had been seen. "I told her that she should forget what she saw. The women of the town, however—each one sees you as a sister now. They have fought for you and will not let this seducer have his way without putting things right."

"*Seducer?* See here, I am not—"

Matthias's dramatic sigh interrupted. "Rothwell, dear boy, you have been disastrously indiscreet."

Phaedra stepped forward. "I do not need other women fighting this particular battle, Carmelita. I am a grown woman and I believe that—Good heavens, now what is the priest doing here?"

The hapless priest from yesterday's battle was being pushed toward them through the crowd.

"I believe this is what is called an untoward development," Elliot said dryly.

"Elliot, *do something*." Phaedra hissed the words in a tone approaching panic. The whole town appeared to surround them now. The bodies formed a slow-moving river aiming through the lanes. Elliot, Phaedra, Matthias, and the poor priest formed the flotsam from a wreck being borne along by the current.

"What do you recommend, Phaedra? As a gentleman I cannot refuse to marry a woman whom I have compromised."

"Oh, for heaven's sake. This is coercion, and refusing would not make you a scoundrel. Nor have you compromised me. You cannot think to actually go through with this?"

He did not know what he thought yet. He only knew that standing his ground here and now might be a dangerous mistake. The town was elated by the impending nuptials. Even Tarpetta's most staunch supporters grinned with delight. The general sentiment, from what Elliot could tell, was that the town thought this would be the finest Feast of San Giovanni in memory.

With each step Phaedra's eyes got wider. "Then *I* will refuse."

Matthias stuck his head close to hers. "Miss Blair, I have just spent hours convincing Signore Tarpetta that you are not, um, unvirtuous. If you refuse to marry a man with whom you were seen on, um, intimate terms, all my efforts might be for nought."

"I will not marry, least of all at the point of a sword."

Elliot had no desire to marry at the point of a sword either, but he did not find the looming church as alarming as Phaedra did. Although he had never found himself moved to propose to a woman, he was not opposed to marriage on principle like she was. Of course, his family history had shown that a bad union could create a life of hell, but that did not bear on this situation. Yet.

"Will this even be legal?" she demanded of Matthias. "We are not Catholic. This is not England. There will be no bans, no license. Are such unions even recognized at home? After all, a Catholic ceremony alone is not legitimate at home and—"

"I really do not know for certain. I am sure it can all be sorted out later."

"*Sorted out later?* What if the sorting is not to my liking? Talk to them. Tell them that—" Her response was interrupted by a shift in the crowd.

The lane suddenly spilled into the piazza. The bodies rearranged and loosened their hold, but still formed a thick wall. A new figure joined their little nucleus. Signore Tarpetta limped into place beside Elliot.

"This is a good ending," he said with pompous approval. "If she is *una sposa,* there will be a man's law for her. You can perhaps authority her better now."

Elliot bit back the curse that leapt to mind. Tarpetta's presence was no accident. No doubt the man had heard the old women's gossip and encouraged the town into playing out this farce.

Matthias pushed his way over to Tarpetta and muttered lowly. He did not appear to make much progress in whatever case he pled. He shifted back over to Elliot.

"I am going to see about the preparations for that boat, Rothwell. The absence of an English witness can only help a claim that this was not legitimate."

Elliot was already lining up that case in his head. Phaedra looked like a woman being led to the stake, not the altar. His sympathy for her desperation contained a dose of annoyance. She acted as if marriage to Lord Elliot Rothwell was a fate worse than death.

That it was a fate neither of them had chosen and that neither of them anticipated or wanted was beside the point. *He* was going to the slaughter to save their honor and her hide. She might at least pretend some grace about the situation.

Matthias bled away. The crowd parted and allowed the priest and his sacrificial lambs access to the church doors. Phaedra looked very pale.

The priest turned to face Elliot and the bride. An acolyte rushed out of the church with a shiny vestment that the priest donned. The priest spoke to the crowd.

"What is he saying?" Phaedra asked.

"As best I can tell, he is announcing that the wedding will take place here, then we will go into the church and sign the documents."

"Here?" She stared down at the ground, as if wondering where here actually was. For a moment he thought she would swoon. *"Now?"*

"I am afraid so." He took her hand. "Courage, little wife."

His tease brought some color back to her complexion. She looked like she wanted to hit him.

The priest began his prayers. The crowd hushed. Elliot realized that the first defense against the efficacy of this ceremony, that the vows would be in a language Phaedra did not understand, would not hold. The priest spoke in Latin and she would comprehend every word.

His mind raced in a quick debate. Their affirmations would be requested soon. He glanced over his shoulder at the throng listening with rapt attention. He wished that he knew something about canon law.

The priest warmed to his role in the pageant. He raised his voice and it rang over the heads in the piazza. Phaedra kept glancing around like a damsel waiting for the white charger that would carry her rescuer.

The priest spoke the vows and turned expectantly to the groom. Elliot looked at Phaedra, whose eyes pled with him to play the scoundrel.

A small cough from Tarpetta arrested his attention. It served as a reminder of yesterday's danger, and of those messengers headed to Naples.

Elliot turned back to Phaedra. He did not think this ceremony was legitimate, but it might be. If so, they would be bound forever.

He could do worse. So could she.

He spoke the words of consent.

It took Phaedra forever to say the words. They stuck in her throat, refusing to emerge. She might be sealing her fate in a way she had consciously avoided. She could be trading one prison for another.

She stared at Elliot, unable to hide her desperation.

He waited patiently, his gaze kind but his expression firm. She knew what he was mentally saying to her. The dark form of Signore Tarpetta hovered ten paces away, a physical reminder that while this all seemed like a strange dream full of buffoonery and farce, she still walked the edge of a precipice in this land.

The panic she had been swallowing boiled up. What if . . . He might . . . It could take years to . . .

She corralled her thoughts and imposed rationality on them. Of course this was not a legitimate wedding. Of course Elliot would help get that resolved correctly should there be any question. He did not want this any more than she did. A night of pleasure did not turn a man's head and make his brain a mass of porridge.

Her hesitation became awkward. A little buzz hummed through the crowd. The priest's eyebrows rose, two half moons aiming toward his balding pate.

Carmelita gave her a curious look, as if reappraising her worth.

Phaedra took a deep breath, and spoke the vows.

A cheer went up. Pandemonium broke. The festival of San Giovanni had begun on a high note.

The priest stepped back. He told the crowd to get the procession ready to start. He crooked his finger at the newlyweds and turned to enter the church.

"He wants us to sign the documents now," Elliot explained.

Phaedra tried to hold on to her hard-won calm. "At least we will get out of this sun. I have never been so warm in my life."

Elliot stepped closer to her. "You do look wan. I fear

the sun has made you sick. I hope you are not going to faint."

A special note sounded within his concern. She looked up at him, then at the priest waiting at the church door, then at the remnants of the crowd still milling nearby.

She pressed her hand to her cheek, then her forehead. "I am very light-headed. Nor do I have salts with me. The excitement and the heat—" She wobbled just a tad.

Elliot's arm instantly supported her. "Let me help you inside, my dear."

Carmelita stepped forward to accompany them and serve as witness on the documents. So did Signore Tarpetta.

"No," Elliot said to him. "You have been no friend to my wife." He looked at Carmelita. "Choose another. Anyone else."

It had begun as an act but Phaedra truly felt sick now. Elliot guided her into the cool darkness of the church. Carmelita and a fisherman came too. They shut the door on the noise from the piazza.

Through the dim light Phaedra spied the priest bending over a lectern. He busily scribbled on some parchment. A thick tome stood at the ready too.

She knew nothing about Catholic marriages, but she knew a thing or two about English law. Saying words was one thing. Signing documents was quite another. If she put down her name of her own free will she could be doomed.

She pressed her palm against Elliot's chest, making him stop. She did not have to fake sun illness now. The cool church air raised a sweat on her skin. Her blood drained from her head and extremities.

Elliot's face hovered closely, then quickly receded into blackness.

"Is she pretending?" Carmelita whispered.

"It does not appear so." Elliot gazed down at the body he held in his arms. He had swept her up as she fell, impressed by her ability to feign a faint worthy of the best actress. Now the deadweight he bore and Phaedra's ashen color indicated that it had been no act.

The priest rushed over, wringing his hands. Elliot spoke to him in Latin. "I am taking my wife back to the villa to recover. We will return this afternoon to sign the license and records."

It had not been a good two days for the priest. He waved them off with relief. Elliot aimed down the nave, not back to the front portal. "Show me another way out," he told Carmelita.

She hurried ahead, pointing him to a small door off the side aisle. He paused briefly to thank Carmelita for all her help, then strode down a deserted lane toward the sea.

Phaedra stirred in his arms. Her eyes opened. It took a few more strides for her to collect herself. Then she critically assessed her situation.

"Why are you carrying me?"

"You fainted."

"Put me down. I never faint."

He stopped and set her on her feet. "You did this time. Dead away."

She tested her steadiness. "Well, I have never fainted *before*."

"That is because you have never been forced to marry me before. The notion so horrified you that you could not contain your shock."

"You told me to faint. You all but commanded it."

"If you obey all my commands with such thorough precision, marriage to you might be tolerable." She seemed to have recovered. He offered his arm. "Hold on. The lane is steep."

She slid her arm through his and skipped to keep up with his strides. "We are not going to the villa."

"I am counting on Greenwood having the boat ready before that procession winds its way down there. With luck we will be launched before anyone is the wiser."

She picked up her pace at the promise of escape. When they emerged near the docks they could see Matthias waiting beside a fishing boat manned by four men.

He hailed them and ordered the crew to prepare to launch. "In you go. No time for ceremony and long farewells. Your baggage is on board."

Elliot handed Phaedra up. He paused for a farewell anyway. "You must come and visit England. You have been gone too long."

Matthias turned his face to the burning sun. "I am too acclimated to this land, Rothwell. England's damp holds no appeal. But, perhaps . . . who knows."

"I will write and tell you how I fare at Pompeii."

"My letter is among your papers. I slipped it in." While Elliot climbed on board, Greenwood addressed

Phaedra. "Whitmarsh sends his felicitations on your marriage."

"I am not married."

"Well . . ." His shrug underlined the ambiguity of that point. He bowed to take his leave.

"Mr. Greenwood," she said. "I may not chance to meet you again. Thank you for your hospitality and your help."

"It was my pleasure to have the daughter of Artemis Blair as a guest. You must write to me and tell me if you ever solve that little mystery we discussed."

The boat drifted away from the dock. They watched as Matthias grew smaller against the dramatic backdrop of Positano's spill of roofs and steep lanes.

Safe now, free from the danger that she dared not contemplate, Phaedra's heart filled with soul-drenching relief.

Elliot's arm slid around her waist. He moved and embraced her from behind. She succumbed to the security and protection offered by the intimate, human cloak he formed. She sank back against him, and ignored the way his strength lured her into relinquishing her own.

CHAPTER
THIRTEEN

Phaedra fell asleep in Elliot's arms. He moved her to a wooden bench away from the boat's railing. He directed the crew to secure a makeshift canvas awning over them, to protect her pale beauty from the high, hot sun.

Two hours passed with Phaedra absorbing his thoughts. The vows that they spoke in Positano may have been the last lines in a comic opera, but they complicated his intentions. He doubted she would accept the responsibility that he now felt for her. No matter what English law might decide, she would never agree that he had a right to protect her. She would deny any man the authority that exercising such obligations required.

As if his thoughts summoned her to battle, her eyes opened. Still nestled against him, she peered across the sea to the hazy line of the coastal hills on the eastern horizon.

She glanced to the sky and assessed the sun's position. "We are some ways from the shore. Should we not be in Amalfi by now?"

"I told them to take us down the coast to Paestum. You expressed an interest in seeing the temples there."

Her lashes hung low while she considered this change in plans. "You might have woken me and asked if a visit to Paestum suited me."

He had not asked because he did not want to give her any choice. When they reached Pompeii she would once more be consumed with whatever mission she pursued. He would be obligated to take up his own quest when they later returned to Naples. Soon they would be at odds again. He wanted to avoid those arguments for a day or so.

"Your illness at the church was real. You need to rest."

She nodded slightly, her hair rubbing his shoulder. He was pleased that she made no attempt to extricate herself from his embrace. The sleeping Phaedra was a lovely wonder. He had spent the last hours studying the details and nuances of her face, breathing in her feminine scent, and holding her soft body. But Phaedra alert and aware interested him far more.

"We are not truly married, of course." She spoke as if they had been talking about it for hours. In a silent manner, perhaps they had been.

"Actually, in the Kingdom of the Two Sicilies I think that we are."

"No documents were signed."

"This is a Catholic land. They see marriage as a sacrament, not a contract."

"We are not Catholic."

"That could make all the difference. I do not know

for certain, however. I think if it is legal here, it may be legal at home." He braced for her explosive denial.

Instead she expressed consternation in ways so subtle he would miss them if her face was not inches from his and her body not cradled in his arms.

"What this kingdom thinks is legal does not matter," she said. "We will soon return to England where better laws reign. What is important is that *we* both know we are not really married."

The boat turned. Its bow aimed southeast, toward the coast. He narrowed his eyes on the distant, tiny port that was their destination.

"Say it," she demanded.

"Say what?"

"Say that of course we both know that we are not really married."

He could say that to appease her, but he was not inclined to lie. Nor did the ambiguities disconcert him the way they should. He had never sought marriage, least of all to a woman like Phaedra Blair, but he had spoken the vows well aware that they might stick.

In the meantime there was a usefulness in being her husband in this land. He could protect her better and throw the special immunity of the family's aristocratic cloak around her. He could keep an eye on her too, day and night. And should they learn upon returning to England that the vows in Positano bound them—there was a certain usefulness in that too.

If they were truly married the decision to publish those memoirs would no longer be hers. He had never calculated such a drastic path to protecting the family name, but fate may have provided an unexpected solution to the problem that brought them together.

She would loathe the solution, of course. That was why he had told the crew of this boat to aim toward Paestum. He wanted to indulge his fascination as long as possible before discovering whether Phaedra Blair would spend the rest of her life making his existence on this earth a living hell.

"You are demanding that I say what we both *know* when I know nothing of the kind. Nor do you. You are really asking me to say that I will *act* like we both know we are not married."

"It would be a wise way to view it."

"I do not agree. I think that would be a criminal waste of a grand opportunity."

Peeved at his refusal, and perhaps at the teasing note that entered his voice, she pushed out of his embrace and stood. She faced him with her hands on her hips, the picture of a woman planning to scold until she swayed him to her point of view.

The dusky shade beneath the canvas sail gave her skin an ethereal shimmer. The breeze lifted tendrils of her hair until they danced around her body like a living halo. The thin gauze of her skirts blew back, revealing the forms of her legs and hips, reminding him of her naked body and how this day had begun.

"Allow me to explain all the reasons why we must ignore that wedding until we are back in England." She began itemizing the logic of it all, ticking off her reasons on her fingers.

He heard her voice like a distant chant. He was back in the tower, on his knees, gazing down at her naked body. Then he was taking her like he had last night, only this time it was an act of true possession decreed to a husband by law.

She paced in front of him, crossing back and forth along the edge of the shade. Her argument went on and on, insignificant words barely audible outside the door of the room where he had ravished her.

She stopped walking. Her hands went back to her hips.

"You are not even listening."

"I am. Your logic would do an Oxford don proud. Nor can I disagree with a single word. I merely do not care one way or the other right now."

She sighed deeply at the stupid man on the bench. "You do not think it is worth considering whether you might be tied for life to a woman you do not want?"

"I have considered it thoroughly already. As for not wanting the woman in question, that is where it gets complicated."

He pulled her onto his lap and kissed her. He forced the intimacy of the night back on her. He commanded her desire to join his, so that she would understand the only part of this untoward development that mattered to him right now.

The innkeeper's wife threw open the door of Phaedra's bedchamber with a flourish worthy of a queen's courtier. Down the passageway the innkeeper himself showed Elliot to another room. Their hosts had decided that the arrival of this particular *uomo magnifico* necessitated a little groveling.

Phaedra glanced down the passage just as Elliot glanced back. She suspected he measured the steps between their doors. Her calming arousal fluttered hard again for several uncomfortable moments. She stepped into her chamber and closed the door, seeking a sanctuary from how he affected her.

The last half hour on that boat had muddled her thoughts about the peculiar situation that she found herself in. His kisses had confused her mind, her body, and her heart. Minute by pleasurable minute he had slowly pried her hold from the moorings that kept her securely in a place she knew. She felt as if she had been towed into uncharted waters.

She was almost positive those vows would not stand scrutiny, but they promised to create terrible problems anyway. It would be sensible to assume there was no marriage. Unfortunately, Elliot appeared to think it would be useful to assume that there was.

She did not think it was only the prospect of an ongoing liaison that appealed to him. As her husband he could claim rights to other things. To know her thoughts and plans. To protect and possess. To interfere if he disagreed. No one in this land would accommodate her if her "husband" did not want her accommodated.

The woman opened the portmanteau. She lifted and shook the dresses, then hung them on hooks in the wardrobe. Her dark eyes scanned the array of black gauze and crepe. *"Mi dispiace."*

She thought they were mourning garments. Phaedra did not know the words to disabuse her of that notion. Nor had her explanations in Positano led to much good.

The woman left to get water. She returned, poured

some into the washing bowl, and offered to help Phaedra undress. "Your husband—*bello, elegante,*" she said, while she released the back hooks.

He is not my husband. The denial remained a silent objection. It did not matter what this innkeeper thought. Elliot was right about one thing. This journey would be easier if people thought they were married. She had already seen the difference. Instead of the subtle scorn that she normally endured in her life, on the boat and at this inn she had been treated with respect and deference.

Dusk began to gather by the time she was settled in. As the woman left, Elliot arrived at the door. His command of the southern language had improved over the last week, and he gave the innkeeper's wife some instructions.

"What did you tell her?"

"That we will dine alfresco. They have a lovely garden. I also told her to prepare baths for us afterward. Let us go down now. Except for that bit of bread and cheese on the boat, we have not eaten all day."

"I will join you soon. I would like a few minutes alone first."

The door closed. She inhaled the silence that fell with his departure. She waited for his presence to thin too, for the air to return to normal and for her isolation from him to be complete. It took longer than she expected.

She blamed last night for that. The intimacy had been too intense. He had indeed taken, and more than his pleasure. She had made very plain what she permitted and what she did not, but he deliberately pressed his advantage. She did not shrink from admitting that she had been helpless to stop it because he was the first man to have an advantage to press in the first place.

She looked around her chamber. She guessed it was the finest in the inn. It held wood furniture that appeared a country version of the elaborately carved pieces so common in Naples. Pale blue patterned drapery swathed the bed in simple luxury and a hooked rug spread flowers on the wood planked floors.

She looked forward to dining in the garden. The bath would be most welcome too. He had anticipated her needs and she could overlook the assumptions behind his plans if she wanted to. He was taking care of her the way men did with women, and any other woman would be delighted. To object would appear ungracious and perhaps even ungrateful.

The problem was that she knew how it would all turn out if she permitted those assumptions to continue unchecked. The danger was not in him so much as it was in herself. The world conspired to convince women to live the normal lives decreed by society. There had been many times when the choice to do it differently had seemed so hard, so lonely, that she had questioned her beliefs. Swimming against the current of the world's expectations could be exhausting. If a boat passed going downriver, it was very tempting to climb on board.

If the man offering to lift her up and protect her was handsome, wealthy, intelligent, and passionate, how easy to conclude one had been swimming in the wrong direction all along. It would probably be a long while before one realized one had totally forgotten how to swim at all.

She sat at the dressing table and brushed out her hair. She bound it into a thick roll at her nape for Elliot's sake, so he would not be embarrassed by her eccentricity if other guests also dined in the garden. She opened her portmanteau, found her hat, and pinned it on.

She gazed in the looking glass. This small compromise in her appearance had been easy to make. It really cost her nothing and she had done it fully aware of why she made the choice. Such small gestures did not redraw the outline of her character. The changes that could do that would not be so obvious, nor so clearly selected.

She thought of the man waiting in the garden. So handsome, so appealing. It was very tempting to play at marriage with him for a few days. A tired part of her soul yearned to let someone take care of her for a while. Perhaps she could just give up the fight for a week or two, and pick up her weapons again when she returned to England.

Her mother's memory intruded. One skeptical eyebrow arched on the internal vision of Artemis Blair's lovely face. Artemis had never demanded that her daughter follow her path. She had merely explained and described what one lost and what one gained if one claimed such freedom. She had also warned there could be no half measures, no respites of acceptability and respectability. The world did not permit a woman to find a place of compromise. The laws were written to make the decision to be a normal, acceptable woman an irrevocable one.

Phaedra finished her preparations. She would allow the strangers in this land to assume she and Elliot were married, but she could not afford to allow him to think it. Not even maybe married or temporarily so. If they played that game, she could only lose.

She grew more lovely as the sun set. Dusk's light gave her dramatic coloring a cool cast, softening her. Elliot permitted himself some poetic sentimentality while they finished their meal. The flowers in the garden formed a deep circle of blended jewels around the terrace where they sat.

They had spent the long supper talking about their visit to the temples of Paestum the next day. Now Phaedra grew quiet as night closed in. He sensed that she contemplated the following hours and those chambers upstairs. Her eyes reflected her awareness of the anticipation tightening between them. She tried to hide it for the first time, but she was not well practiced in that.

One by one the other guests left the terrace. The innkeeper brought out coffee, served it with elaborate deference, then retreated into the house.

"The sun is gone, Phaedra. The others have left. You can remove the hat now." He did not know if the hat had been a symbol of compromise or merely a precaution against a recurrence of sun sickness. Now its brim cast a deep shadow, obscuring her bold eyes. He wanted nothing hiding her desire from him.

"You sound as if you are giving me permission, Elliot. Or making a demand." All the same she unpinned the hat and set it on a nearby table. "Whatever you think about our situation, you must not treat me like a wife. I will not like that."

How would she know? She had never been one. She had not even grown up in a household with one.

He trusted his vague smile would be read as agreement so he could return to enjoying her company in the waning light. She gazed at him expectantly, waiting for a more official affirmation. She appeared determined to settle this now. He guessed they would not be leaving this terrace until she did.

"How should I treat you instead, Phaedra? Like a mistress? Like a brief flirtation?"

"Like a friend."

"We were friends last night. I look forward to treating you like that as often as you will allow it."

He was sure he saw a blush, despite the dimming light. "Not exactly like last night. That is part of my concern."

"You did not seem concerned at the time. However, I am willing to change. Tell me, how do your friends treat you?"

"With less . . . It need not, as you spoke of it last night, be a surrender or a victory for either one of us. It need not be a matter of submission and possession. And a man need not—one need not intrude on the other's spirit so much." She seemed oblivious to the implications of her last words.

He instinctively reacted to these references to her past lovers. Badly, despite her admission that there had been no spiritual intrusion with them.

Jealousy cracked through him. It was not an emotion that had claimed him much in the past. Both awed and repulsed by its dangerous power, he tried to push it back into the dungeon of his soul. No doubt among all the *need nots* that Phaedra had decided men had no right to feel about her, this topped the list.

He controlled its violent madness, but he could not leash it completely. His annoyance sharpened into anger. "I can see that you have contemplated what this need and need not be at length, Phaedra. You have given it far more attention than I have, and your philosophy is too sophisticated and calculating for me."

"I know that tone. Do not get rude and sardonic with me, sir. I knew you could never—it is possible to share pleasure and —"

"And what? Face the dawn indifferent to the body beside you? If a man seeks mere carnal relief he can buy a whore. I would say you are a generous woman to demand nothing more, except that I think you speak out of ignorance. You do not face the dawn with your friends at all, do you? I'll wager you send them away long before that so there can be no claims on you."

"I was not indifferent. But I was not owned either. Not bound by the false ties that passion can create. And I was not dominated in the act itself."

He did not want to hear about her with *other* men. "Your friends decided it was in their interests to hide their true thoughts and reactions from you, that was all."

Now she was angry too. Well, if they were going to have a row over whatever principles she thought he had violated last night, they might as well let hell fly.

"These are not fools or scoundrels we speak of, but good, honest men. They were not *like you,* that is all."

Her words came clipped and tight and cold. A wise man would retreat now.

Damned if he would.

"If they were men at all, they were enough like me. A man does not stop thinking like a man because he is with a woman who does not like the way men think. Your friends merely pretended not to think like men in order to have your favors. We men do things like that all the time."

"I think I would have noticed if they were dissembling."

"Perhaps you were too intent on taking your pleasure and on avoiding those inconvenient spiritual intrusions to notice."

Her expression fell in shock at this criticism of *her* behavior last night.

"I had hoped . . . I can see my mother was right. Most men are not enlightened enough to comprehend what I describe, and they cannot be changed." She picked up her hat and stood. "I regret that you cannot be one of my friends, Elliot. You are not suitable."

She marched through the garden to the inn's door. The queen had made her choice. This particular bee could buzz elsewhere.

Normally he would accept a woman's rejection with humor and grace. Normally it would not really matter to him except for a brief physical discomfort.

This woman's imperious renunciation mattered a good deal for reasons he was in no humor to examine. She had thrown down a gauntlet again, and he could not ignore it. The ground between them had changed a lot since the last time he had permitted her to walk away.

The man was impossible. How could someone so obviously intelligent also be so stupid? How dare he insinuate—no, not insinuate, but bluntly imply—no, not even imply, but outright accuse—that she was no better than a whore in her dealings with her friends?

She scolded and cursed him all the way to her chamber. He probably had no female friends. No doubt Lord Elliot Rothwell only had mistresses and the whores he seemed to know about suspiciously well.

She grabbed the latch of her chamber door. He was hopeless. Now she was stuck with him for days on end and he would just be there, intruding in that irritating way that did not take physical intimacy to experience, making her heart do stupid little jigs just by walking into a room. He made her breathless but she dared not yield to temptation again.

She threw open the door. Moist heat greeted her. A servant curtsied and started moving fast, lifting big pails from the cinders of a low fire in the hearth and spilling their hot water into a waiting metal tub.

Suddenly she felt every ache accumulated the last two days. Her body seemed to reek of last night's scents. The odor hung sultry and sweet near her nose, reminding her of the pleasure and the power of what she had just rejected. It would be good to wash the last few days out of her life.

The servant finished with the tub. She sent the girl away and did for herself as she had for years. She removed her dress and chemise and announced with each movement that she was no pampered possession that a man protected for his own selfish reasons. She was Phaedra Blair, free and self-sustaining, bound by no rules except those that she made for herself.

She audibly groaned when she lowered herself into the bath. The water's heat actually cooled her skin. Her body went limp in perfect relaxation. Tiny waves soothed away the tight anger that she had carried out of the garden.

She floated a long time, then sat up, unbound her hair, and washed it. She used the fragrant soap on her body and played with the foam. Lighthearted, cleansed, and confident, feeling more herself than she had in days, she stood in the tub and let the night breeze lick at the water dripping down her body.

The sensation captivated her. She dwelled in the pleasure of being truly cool for the first time in days. She considered scooping more water onto her body.

A click of the door latch destroyed her isolation. Another presence intruded, physically and spiritually. Deliberately. She stood immobile for a moment, awed by the change in the chamber and in herself, stunned by the excitement that aroused her body and so quickly compromised her mind's careful choices.

She reached for the towel lying on a stool beside the tub.

A bronzed male hand closed on it first.

CHAPTER FOURTEEN

He had assumed she would be done with the bath by the time he sought her in her chamber. He almost retreated after he opened the door. Not to preserve her modesty. They were beyond that.

The vision of her standing naked in the tub made his mouth dry. She appeared like a statue, still and calm. Time slowed while his gaze slowly followed the perfect curves of her back and hips and lingered on the charm of the dimple at the base of her spine. The erotic, soft roundness of her bottom dipped away to hidden shadows. Her squared shoulders reflected her pride even now, in this most private moment.

It was not his physical response that made him pause, but instead a reaction even more visceral than the ferocious desire he felt for her. *Mine.* The instinctive declaration sliced through him, ruthless and determined.

Desire was familiar but this proclamation was not. Like the jealousy in the garden, he fleetingly acknowledged its danger. He also instantly understood things that he had avoided comprehending before. His hunger for Phaedra exposed truths that he was not sure that he wanted to know.

He walked over to her. She had not moved during the long pause while he admired her body, but now she did. When he reached for the towel she did too, with desperate quickness, as if she were afraid.

Tiny crystals of water still shimmered on her bare shoulder and outstretched arm. Her pale fingers clutched the cloth beside his own hand's hold. They froze like that, the towel becoming ground she did not want to yield.

Mine. The declaration repeated unbidden, a testimony to the impulses Phaedra unleashed in both him and herself. It spoke with calm confidence now. She had not ordered him to leave. She had allowed him to enter and look at her. She had done nothing to dispel the mood of teasing sensuality pulsing like a silent, primitive beat in the chamber.

She had already surrendered even if she did not know it yet.

He released his hold on the towel. She snatched it up and draped it around her nakedness, clutching it closed in front of her. She stepped out of the tub and faced him.

Her bold gaze lingered on his face long enough to incite madness. He had never before understood men who wanted women so much that they acted irrationally, recklessly, but right now he did. She glanced to his shirt and rolled sleeves, to his trousers and bare feet.

"Your hair is damp. You already had your bath too,"

she observed. Her own damp hair hung in a chaotic tumble over one shoulder.

She glanced down to her tub. Dying soap foam still floated here and there. "I dallied too long in mine."

Long enough for her to be having this conversation wrapped in a towel that did not cover her very well. Moist now, it adhered to her curves, obscuring very little.

She turned away and reached for a bell pull. "The servants will want to remove this water tonight."

It only took two strides to stop her. His hand closed on hers before she touched the pull. He circled her body with his other arm and pressed a kiss on her shoulder. The scent of cool water and fragrant flowers filled his head.

She tried to stifle her sensual sigh and halt her subtle, welcoming flex. "I did not invite you here."

"No, you did not."

"I think that we should not—" Her voice trailed into a quiet gasp when he embraced her more fully and kissed the pleasure spots on her neck.

"You are trying to seduce me," she muttered.

"I am not *trying* anything." He pressed her closer and caressed down the towel now molded to her body, seeing with his hands what his gaze had just enjoyed.

She laughed softly. "This is very wrong of you."

"Probably so." Her hands still clasped the towel closed at her chest. He gently pried at them, coaxing her to let go.

She only clutched tighter. Her arousal was obvious, but he sensed a rebellion forming. He slid his hands under the towel in order to silence its voice.

She trembled beautifully but the voice still spoke. "I said you could not be one of my friends."

"I told you in Naples that I have no interest in being one." He once more coaxed her to release the towel. "You will let go of this now, because you want whatever this is, no matter what you call it."

"I call it the devil's dangerous temptation."

He kissed her neck again. She was small and fragile within his hold. "I am no danger. I want you tonight, that is all."

"I do not believe that is true." She did not say which part she doubted. Perhaps she thought both statements had been lies.

He did not force it. He kept her clenched fingers under his own, trusting she would release her futile hold on the towel.

Whatever arguments she privately held remained silent ones. Slowly a new softness entered her body. He knew for certain that she had agreed to give herself to him when the fingers beneath his hand loosened.

He slid the towel away so nothing inhibited his caress. Her skin felt cool and luxurious, but an inner fire flowed into his blood from wherever he touched. He cupped her breasts in his hands and played at her nipples until her deep breaths carried soft moans of pleasure. He buried his mouth in the crook of her neck so he could taste the rapid pulse of her need.

Mine.

She had been thinking too hard about something that required little reflection. She had made more of this liaison than it was or would ever be. She only took and gave pleasure, after all. Nothing more.

That rationalization was the last clear thought Phaedra had before she succumbed to Elliot's seduction. He quickly took her into a state of overwhelming sensation where one did not think at all.

She had been halfway there by the time he embraced her. The fires he incited kept burning away the good sense to which she tried to cling. Try as she might to pick through her fogging mind, she could not summon the sound reasons behind her renunciation of this man in the garden.

Now his hands moved over her, arousing, claiming. With every warm, slow stroke he promised she would again know the ecstasy that she had experienced last night. All her articulations of the danger and the cost became silly and insignificant.

She loved what his hands did to her. She rested against the hard strength of his body and felt every inch of each confident caress. She savored the rough firmness of his palms on her hips and stomach and the exquisite tease of his fingers on her thighs and breasts. His touch thrilled her in part because he knew what power he possessed.

There was freedom in choosing not to care what it did and did not mean. Mindless, thoughtless, exhilarating freedom. Capitulation came as a relief after trying to deny her carnal hunger. She embraced the abandon and left calculation and debate for another day.

With her surrender his handling became less one of seduction and more that of a man who took what was his by right. She did not care. She was past caring. The eroticism of submission bewitched more than shocked. She let his strength control her. She offered her body, pleading for more, too entranced by the trembles of pleasure to think what they meant.

His arms bound her in his embrace. She parted her eyelids and watched his fine masculine hands on her breasts, glossing slowly over their tips again and again, each soft flick shooting an intense arrow down her body. She arched her back, raising her breasts, crying for more and desperate for everything else. All her excitement, all her physical awareness, pooled low and deep, until she could not control how anticipation maddened her.

With one long caress his embrace changed. His hand sought the musky damp between her thighs and ensured that desire owned her.

She could barely stand. She could hardly breathe, and each short gasp carried an impatient cry. She tried to turn in his embrace so she could hold and touch him the way her body yearned to.

He would not let her. Instead he pried her grasp off his forearms and placed them on the top of the bed's footboard. Suddenly his support was gone. Her hands clutched the carved wooden edge.

She pictured what he saw as he stood behind her. The vulnerability of her nakedness and passive position assaulted her.

She looked over her shoulder. He was undressing. Already he had stripped off his shirt. She began to turn.

"No. Do not move. You are beautiful there."

Her heart beat heavily. Beautiful and accepting and waiting. Her excitement took on new colors, dark jewel tones of astonishing depth. A different arousal licked at her body, creating a sly, unbearable torture.

She closed her eyes to contain this new desire that felt so primitive. Its power frightened her. It contained too much of what made this man a challenge and a danger.

He shed his lower garments and stepped closer. A savage excitement shuddered through her, like a quake of wicked anticipation. He covered her without touching her. He dominated her without even trying.

She felt his firm palms on her, smoothing from her shoulders, along her arms, and slowly back again. "Do not turn your head. Stay like that so I can see your face."

His caress moved down her back and around to her breasts. Their tips were even more sensitive now. The slightest touch sent wonderful shocks through her.

She did not turn her face but she kept her eyes closed. There was some safety in the darkness. Some denial. She could not retreat to a private place of all pleasure and sensation, however. He was there, like the second time in the tower. He made sure she knew who did this.

She thought he would move to the bed but he kept her there, arousing her breasts with delicious effectiveness, pushing her toward an insanity born of infuriating need. He left her clinging to the footboard, trembling, her body waiting for more. Only when she was moaning again, only when she instinctively arched her back down and raised her hips in offering, only when she thought she would weep or scream, only then did he embrace her again.

One arm came around to support her and one hand cupped her breast. His other hand's fingers followed the cleft of her bottom to the pulsing heat deep between her thighs.

She had never experienced anything like it. She dug her fingers into the wood but every other reality was eclipsed by the pleasure tightening and becoming more focused and more necessary. She neither saw nor spoke nor heard but in her mind there were words, needful words, unstoppable mad incantations of demands and pleas.

He finally took her. There could be no denying how it was. He positioned her hips with a firm hold and entered hard. She reached for completion but he prolonged the heavenly agony, using his hands to arouse her even while he teased her with the promise of fulfillment.

He seemed to know when the most profound trembles began. The deepest pleasure throbbed into her blood and shivered throughout every part of her. She felt him hard then, thoroughly filling her, guiding and pushing her into the pulse until it merged with the beat of her heart and the breath of her life. He was with her all through it, refusing to leave, controlling her even when the trembling turned to a roar and burst through her in a torrent of bliss.

Then she was in his embrace again, surrounded by him, bound to him by their bodies and their sweat. His deep breaths sounded near her ear while the cries of her last crazed moments still echoed in the chamber. She felt his heart beating behind her, its rhythm matching the throbbing in her body.

Elliot watched strips of light begin forming through the slats of the shutters on the windows. Phaedra would wake soon to prepare for their visit to the temples.

He would much rather spend the day in this bed. He had already seen the collection of temples at this colonial outpost of the ancient Greeks. The remains served as illustrations to what the ancient texts told about the way the aesthetics and proportions of the temples developed over time. It was all there, from the heavy muscularity of the columns of Paestum's Basilica to the more elegant, later Temple of Hera.

He had seen those ruins before but Phaedra had not. She had hardly objected to their long night, not even when he reached for her the last time for a union so slow and relaxed that they conversed all through it. However he did not think that she anticipated continuing like that for days on end, much as he would like to.

They should probably settle a few things about this liaison, although he had no idea what those things should be. This was not a typical affair. Normally by now he would be requiring at least temporary fidelity. With any other woman this passion would have a name and some kind of understanding and arrangement.

Mistress. Lover. Beloved. She would reject any of those labels, nor did any of them actually fit. Still, he speculated about keeping her. He would enjoy dressing her in gowns that fit her beauty and providing the servants that she could not afford.

Wife. Out of the question, and guaranteed to provoke a row, even if it might actually be accurate.

Whore. Sinner. The world might see her that way, but no one who understood her mind could characterize her behavior so wrongly.

Friend.

He turned the word over in his head. It was the only caption she permitted for the men in her life. The night had made him amenable to compromise, so he tried the appellation on her in turn.

The primitive beast within had been fed and soothed, so it did not roar in anger now. It spoke, however, with a confidence far more firm than its first proclamations. He could not ignore that possessive impulse. It did not permit him to think of her as a friend. Friendship entailed less certainty, less need, and more freedom.

She rubbed her eyes. She opened them and glanced down the bed at the hills their bodies made under the sheet. She turned on her side and looked at him.

"We should leave for the ruins soon, if we are going to avoid the heat of midday," she said.

"We could go tomorrow."

She reached out to walk her fingers over his chest. "We should probably go while you have left me still able to walk."

Her playfulness pleased him to a ridiculous extent. So did the indication that she had not decided this liaison would end once they left this bed this morning. Not that he intended to allow that to happen anyway.

"We were quite mad last night," she said.

"In the best way."

"Do you think it is the sun that does this to the English when they travel? Our countrymen have a long tradition of acting very odd when they go abroad, of abandoning good English sense. We are so unused to all this sunlight, after all. We blunder forth ill equipped and inexperienced in handling its effects."

"I do not need the Mediterranean sun to want a woman, least of all you, Phaedra."

There was more truth in her observation than he cared to admit. He had abandoned much of his good sense with her. He was allowing desire to rule him, and its complications waited to ensnare him. It was not like him to let obligations and responsibilities wait while he indulged himself. His impulses with Phaedra were not the ones he normally felt toward women.

She smiled at his response, but her mind was working on something. Perhaps she sought her own caption for last night's bacchanal.

"You are probably correct. It is not the sun. It is being far from home, away from the histories and obligations that form us. One has another life and becomes a different person when one is far away. When foreigners visit London, they probably try different lives too."

"And they probably say it is the fog and rain that make them mad."

She laughed. She turned on her back and the sheet formed elegant folds over her breasts and stomach. The lower swell captured his attention.

"Do you not worry that you will get with child,

Phaedra? I have been careless in my impatience but in the future we should take steps."

Her hand sought that lower hill and rested there. "I do not think I would like those precautions. If I have a child I will raise her as my mother did me. I am a woman, after all, and having children is a natural thing for a woman."

Artemis Blair may have birthed and raised Phaedra, but she had been all but married to Richard Drury. Whatever was happening in this bed, it was not that. "I trust that you would not expect me to deny a child was mine."

Her laugh was too warm to be mocking. "You? No. I would never expect that of you even if I requested it. I would expect instead that you would be an intrusive nuisance. However, I have not been with child thus far, and do not think it likely that I will ever be so blessed."

So blessed. She did not fear a pregnancy at all. Her unexpected view on this matter reminded him that she did not live in the same world that he knew, or obey the same laws that governed other women's fears and hopes. *Mistress, wife, sinner, friend.* None of the words he had tried out on her would ever fit.

He moved atop her so he could feel her beneath him again. He savored the silken warmth of her skin all along his own. He looked down at sparkling eyes full of humor.

"I think that we should indulge our desire, Phaedra. We should allow ourselves to be as mad as our countrymen. Let us enjoy the freedom to live different lives under this foreign sun while we wind our way back to Naples."

He caressed the delicate curve of her cheek and jaw and felt her subtle nod beneath his touch.

He kissed her, with no intentions of pursuing the promise in that nod right now. It was, he realized, the first time that he had kissed her or any other woman with no expectations of more.

CHAPTER FIFTEEN

I am awed, Elliot. This last week has overwhelmed me, but by far this is the most impressive of the experiences."

"I trust it only surpasses the other towns and ancient sites that you have seen, and not every experience."

They exchanged the kind of intimate look that lovers share when they know each other very well. Oh, yes, she only spoke of the ancient sites. Paestum in all its isolated, ruined glory and Amalfi, so picturesque it appeared to be planned by an artist, only served as settings for other impressive experiences.

They had dallied in Amalfi's sea-swept charm longer than necessary before coming overland to Pompeii. Even that brief journey back north had been an exercise in holding the world at bay. Elliot arranged their travel so they would take three days when it could easily be done in one.

They had lodged in a small hamlet last night. They made love madly, desperately. Perhaps they both knew that a dream would end with the passing of the night.

She woke to the dawn suddenly sad and nostalgic. Pompeii beckoned, and with it came realities that they had been ignoring.

Did she imagine now that there was some sorrow in his conspiratorial lover's smile too? Certainly his eyes reflected more layers and depths than in the previous weeks' lighthearted fun.

He had come to Pompeii because of his new book, but she did not think that his research was the only reason for his moments of distraction today.

She toed at the deep rut that ran in a straight furrow through the packed earth of the street. "To think Roman chariot wheels rolled down this lane. I do not mind the dust so much because I know it is the same dust that blew two thousand years ago."

"Here is the bakery. It appears much as ours do, in many ways." He led her into the building. The deep niches for the ovens showed in the walls. She could picture the people who baked here, and the servants arriving to buy their families' loaves. She could also imagine their horror when nearby Vesuvius began spewing forth its great clouds of ash, and their anguish as it settled on the town, burying Pompeii and all its people.

Other tourists strolled along the excavated streets too. Most had guides, but she did not need one. She had Elliot Rothwell explaining it all to her.

They found themselves at the edge of the current excavations. Work had resumed with the end of the siesta. Rows of men moved baskets of dirt in a human chain, slowly unearthing antiquity. Others rolled handcarts of the dirt to a destination outside the city walls. The town was slowly being reclaimed, section by section.

"I expect that they record everything they find," she said. "That is the correct method, as I understand it."

"In the past they just dug for treasure, but now every potsherd and every brick is documented."

"When they just dug for treasure, were those items not recorded?"

"Kings keep good inventories of their property and the kings of Naples have long claimed Pompeii as theirs. The logs from the last century were not as scientific, but anything of value was noted down."

She strolled along the edges of the current dig. A little weight tapped her thigh like an indignant demand for attention. She had almost forgotten to bring the cameo with her this morning. She had only remembered it when Elliot had left her to secure the carriage.

That was what pleasure with this man had done to her. Now the cameo kept tapping her thigh from deep within the practical pocket of her dress. Tap, tap, tap. *Do not forget why you are really here.*

She suspected that Elliot also experienced prods, of a different sort. He had left England for reasons too. Once his research here in Pompeii was completed, how long would it be before he turned his attention to the other goal?

She wished that she could make that quick work for him. In Naples she had been indignant at his assumption that she should edit the memoirs. He had acted like his duty to his father was more important than her duty to her own. Now she hated that her duty might deepen the rift waiting to open between them.

The sun beat down. The quiet spells between them lengthened with the shadows.

They stopped strolling. Together they gazed out over the excavations.

She thought back on the last week. Their liaison would probably survive for a few more days. At least until they returned to Naples. It would not be the same, however. They could no longer play at having other lives and being free from those duties. She could no longer ignore who she was.

"You should probably seek out the superintendent," she said. "You have research to do here."

He did not answer right away. He just stood there, still able to affect her by being close by. His presence did not only excite her physically. The intimacy did not require the night to move her. It slid all through her now, heralding that their thoughts were completely affixed on the other. It caused the same poignancy that had gripped her heart at dawn.

"Yes, it is probably time." His hand closed on hers. "Come with me. I will introduce you. He probably knew of your mother's scholarship."

The workers did not object when Elliot guided Phaedra through the excavations. They stopped and looked, however. Elliot knew that all their attention was on the woman by his side. The hat did not hide her red hair or her beauty. Phaedra was distinctive even with her eccentric garb made more normal. At that dinner party, dressed fashionably, she had garnered every man's attention.

A dust-covered man approached them, but from his frock coat and hat it was obvious he did not dig himself.

His dark eyes quickly assessed the intruders. His smile indicated he had decided to welcome instead of scold.

"*Buongiorno, signore.* Madame." He made a little bow. "English?"

"Yes. I apologize for intruding. I am Lord Elliot Rothwell and this is—" He stumbled on the introduction made so often the last few days. It was one thing to call her his wife to humble innkeepers, and another to present her as such to gentlemen. "This is Miss Phaedra Blair. We are seeking Michele Arditi, the superintendent. He was not at the museum. I was told he visited the excavations today."

"I am Michele Arditi. I am pleased that you have honored us with your visit, Lord Elliot. Signore Greenwood sent word that your arrival was imminent a week ago, and I feared something had happened. I regret that I was not in Portici when you went there and that you were sent out of your way."

"The way was not far, and it is always a pleasure to see the villas of Portici."

Elliot had never met Arditi. The superintendent had been away from Pompeii when he had visited before. Arditi appeared an amiable man who possessed enough confidence in his station to be friendly but not deferential.

Arditi gestured broadly to the dig behind him. "There is much new to see. I regret that some of it is not appropriate for a lady, and the terrain can be dangerous as well." His long gaze took Phaedra in. "Signore Greenwood wrote that you would come too, and that you are the daughter of Artemis Blair."

"Yes."

"I know her translation of Pliny. Not, perhaps, as

finely nuanced as the best Italian translations, but for an Englishwoman her choices were impressive."

Phaedra took the faint praise graciously. "Perhaps I could see those discoveries that *are* appropriate for a woman. Then Lord Elliot can view the rest at his leisure while I retreat to one of the guesthouses outside the walls."

Arditi thought that an excellent idea. He personally conducted a tour of buildings recently unearthed.

They poked around the Temple of Fortuna and other ruins near the forum. They spent a good deal of time peering at the first evidence of *insulae,* or houses, on Via di Mercurio, a recent discovery generating much excitement among historians. Arditi then took them to the House of Pansa. He treated Phaedra to a long history of its reclamation while a small army of men carefully cleaned walls.

When they emerged from the house, he sent a worker off with a message.

"I have called for Nicola d'Apuzzo, the current architect and director of the excavation," he explained. "He will show you everything that you wish to see, Lord Elliot. You are welcome to remain until the site closes at dusk, and return as often as you wish in the days ahead. However, I feel obligated to say that I do not think that Miss Blair will find a guesthouse here suitable. May I suggest that I escort Miss Blair to Portici? You can call for her at the museum later. I will direct you to lodgings there that are much more appropriate for you both."

They agreed to Arditi's plan. The director arrived and Arditi handed Elliot over. He then offered his arm to Phaedra. Elliot watched them stroll away, noting how

Arditi revealed his admiration for the young woman in his custody. His flowery flatteries floated on the dust.

He inwardly laughed at the spike of jealousy he had felt while he watched Arditi fawn. It was time to learn to close the door again, or he would never remember a word he heard today. The question was whether he dared even leave it ajar anymore.

Portici was a collection of magnificent villas to the west of Vesuvius, all displaying the classical styles popular for the last century. It was as if one collected the great country houses of England and lined them up on a road leading to the sea.

When Michele Arditi offered to give Phaedra a tour of the museum, she did not decline. She bided her time while he waxed eloquent with stories about the discovery of this artifact and that.

He stretched out the tour as long as possible, but finally all was done. Elliot had not arrived at the museum and there was at least an hour until dusk began falling. Signore Arditi made a display of noting that, then offered her coffee in his office.

A proper woman would probably not accept, even if Signore Arditi played the gallant protector. She was not proper in the normal sense, however.

"Lord Elliot says that you are the superintendent, but I understand that you do not actually excavate," she said after he had settled her into his spacious office. Bits and pieces of ancient Pompeii dotted the shelves.

"The architects and directors manage the dig and do

the restoration work. I control the business of the site, and the museum in which we now sit."

"Have you been here a very long time?"

"Since 1807. I was appointed by Napoleon. When he was defeated and the monarchy restored, I was asked to continue." His tone let it be understood that the king knew a superior superintendent when he saw one. "The methods improved under the French. We were able to initiate important changes in how the excavation was conducted. With the return of the Bourbons, however— the last king did not support our work. Eight years ago we were down to eighteen excavators. But this king sees the benefits of reclaiming this city and doing it correctly. It is our history. Our patrimony."

He spoke at length on the subject. He lectured her on the correct methods and his important role in making Pompeii what it had become. All the while her hand rested on her dress, over the little weight in her pocket.

When his enthusiasm for the subject began to wane, she finally broached the subject she really wanted him to expound upon.

"Signore Arditi, I wonder if you would allow me to intrude on your expertise further. I have special need of it, and I doubt any man can accommodate me as well."

His eyebrows rose a fraction. His hands turned palms up in a gesture of humility. "If I can be of assistance, certainly, Miss Blair."

She dug the cameo out of her pocket. She placed it on his desk. "I was told this came from Pompeii. That it was from the ruins and that it is ancient. I think you would know if that is true."

The cameo arrested his attention. He stared at it for a

long count, then picked it up and carried it to the window. "Where did you get this?"

"I would rather not say."

He studied the cameo hard, frowning down at its little sculpted figures. "I regret to inform you that this is a forgery. A very good one. There are a number extant and we have never discovered who is making them. I suspect one of the restorers who worked here long ago. Whoever he is, he is very sly. He does not make many and they are sold privately for large sums. There are unscrupulous dealers who will take such things and place them without asking too many questions."

"You are sure it is a forgery?"

"As sure as a man can be."

That was not as sure as she would like. "May I ask how you know? So that I do not fall prey to unscrupulous dealers in the future."

"I *know.* It is my business to know. The relief would show more wear if it had been buried. It is too clean, too perfect. The setting as well—the gold should be marked and less even. However, I mostly know because I have overseen this site for twenty years. For the last fifteen we have owned all the land within the town walls in order to ensure the heritage is not dispersed. I make sure that every artifact is catalogued and accounted for. Nothing leaves Pompeii unless I personally bring it here to the museum or send it to Naples."

"Could it have been unearthed before you came? When the methods were less scientific?"

"It is an item of value. In the old days artifacts of clay, common items and broken ones, might get cast into the rubble, but not gems. If a worker stole such an item then he would hang. No, it is forgery. I am so sorry to have to tell you that."

She held out her hand for the cameo. He appeared almost reluctant to give it to her, but he placed it in her palm.

The museum had fallen quiet. Arditi looked out the window. "Ah, here comes Lord Elliot's carriage. I must remind him that only red wine cuts the dust in one's throat. In Pompeii, even the dirt is very special."

Elliot assumed Arditi knew of what he spoke. He lifted his goblet to cut some more dust while he and Phaedra dined in the guesthouse where they had taken lodgings in Portici.

A good number of English visitors were in residence with them. They dwelled in luxury while they visited the excavations and enjoyed the hospitality of the Neapolitan aristocrats who had fled the heat in Naples.

He had taken two rooms this time. Nor had he named her as his wife. He did not recognize any of the other guests but there was a good chance that some of his countrymen recognized either him or the unusual Phaedra Blair.

Then again maybe not. She had worn a blue dress to dinner. It was, she explained, her one normal garment. She had also put up her hair, into a style more fashionable than the simple roll that she wore in Paestum. Looking normal would probably be an effective disguise for Phaedra Blair. He suspected that had been her intention.

"Did you learn what you wanted?" she asked.

"Yes, but I will return tomorrow." And he had learned a lot. Eventually his concentration had turned to the discoveries and his mind had escaped into this other passion. His guide had helped by engaging him in a spirited discussion of the remains, asking his opinion and debating the ultimate source of some of the artifacts.

It had been good to immerse himself again in his studies. He had been away from them too long. He had been too distracted by Phaedra. That had never happened before, which spoke to the power of this unusual woman. Today, however, his other self had reawoken, stretched, and revitalized itself. He had left Pompeii more content than he had entered it, feeling more himself than he had in weeks.

"And you, Phaedra. I assume that you also learned what you wanted to know."

"What makes you think so?"

"You came here for a reason and fate offered you an opportunity to ask your questions of the man who can answer them best. I do not think you would pass up the chance."

"Yes, I asked my questions of him. I received my answers."

"Were they about another paragraph in the memoirs?"

Her expression fell as if his mention of the memoirs saddened her. It was, he realized, the first time they had been mentioned since that day in the tower.

"My mother left me a cameo. She said it came from Pompeii," she explained. "My father wrote that it was a fraud, sold to her by that other man. I needed to know, of course. It affects the value considerably."

"If it is a forgery, do you think that also lends credence to the rest of what he wrote about your mother's lover?"

"Yes."

"Then I hope for your sake that it is real."

"Unfortunately, Signore Arditi was very sure that it is not ancient. It is a forgery, and he is aware that cameos like it have been made and sold over the years."

She spooned at the ice that she had requested. Thoughts seemed to roll over in her head while the cold confection rolled in her mouth.

"Matthias gave me the name of two dealers who knew my mother. I am thinking that it is very likely that it would take a dealer to obtain these forgeries. There were others, you see. My father refers to a scheme of flogging frauds. Plural."

"It will be difficult to identify who it is, no matter what names you have."

"I will find a way. However, I was not thinking about that. It is Arditi himself who occupies me. I am not sure I believe him."

"You traveled to Pompeii to seek an expert's opinion. You received one from the best expert in the world. Now you do not believe him?"

"It disturbed him to see that cameo. He has excellent reason to lie. If items are being stolen, he is responsible. It is very much in his interests to claim none have gone missing in the last twenty years, at least."

She had sought evidence with determination, but now she was rejecting it. He did not know if it was because she needed the cameo to have value, or if she did not want to accept Artemis had been played for a fool. "Phaedra, I hope you will not be so foolish as to accuse Arditi of that."

"I do not care to accuse anyone. I seek the truth for my own purposes."

He wondered if she truly understood what her own purpose was. "What if your seeking reveals your suspicions? It does not take an accusation to slander a man's good name. Whispers alone can do it."

She gazed at the remains of her ice, melting rapidly into creamy pools. He hated that she looked for all the world like a wife who had been chastised and who now hid her thoughts.

One thought was not veiled. It moistened her eyes when she raised her gaze to him. *Not yet. We have time still. A little time before we talk about truths and whispers and a man's good name.*

Her sadness moved him. He regretted his words. He wished they could wait an eternity before again talking about such things.

"I apologize, Phaedra. Let us avoid old arguments and new ones while we can. The Italian sun may be making me free and mad, but I do not want to block its light sooner than necessary. Shall I tell you what it was that Arditi said you could not see today?"

She accepted the peace offering. A naughty smile obliterated her sorrow. "I can imagine. I have seen the restricted part of the royal collection, after all."

"I wonder if the collection in Naples can match the frescoes still on the walls in Pompeii. I found the creativity of these paintings most impressive. I do not think that a mere description can do them justice."

"See? That is why it is so unfair that women are excluded. We are not children. Men want to believe we will be shocked and scandalized, but we rarely are. Don't you agree I should have been allowed to go too?"

Hardly. He stood and offered his hand. "The injustice was appalling. Words would not do the frescoes justice, but perhaps a demonstration would satisfy your curiosity."

She did not hesitate. No one else would notice the anticipation in her eyes but he did. He always had. Her honest desire increased his own. In possessing her he became possessed.

He brought her to his chamber, not hers. It lacked the simplicity of their recent rooms in both size and furnishings. They moved inexorably back to his normal life even in the surfaces and materials that surrounded them.

He did not care about that or anything except his hunger for her. They had avoided an argument at dinner. It would come soon, however. So would disagreements about the desire itself—its future and meaning, his rights and her freedom. He still did not have a name for what they shared, and he did not expect her to accept any of the captions that he might choose.

He locked the door behind them. He lit the candelabras. Phaedra watched. Just her gaze made him harder. She appeared very self-possessed tonight, much as she had when he first visited her apartment in Naples. He was not the only one whose old self had reawoken.

That goaded the new impulses that she had revealed

in him. The ones that wanted to brand her and hold her and own her. She appeared too worldly and independent in her desire right now. That old challenge poured off her. *You want me, but this will only happen because I allow it.*

Which meant that someday, maybe soon, she would *not* allow it.

He was past being rational by the time he lit the last candle. She waited, ready to share pleasure. To give whatever she wanted to give of her body and soul, and to withhold whatever she so chose.

He found the notion of the withholding intolerable. That would all come soon enough.

Mine. Tonight at least. *For now, completely mine.*

Phaedra asked Elliot to help her unhook the blue dress. They had locked out the servants and this normal garment had the normal inconveniences.

She thought he would undress her further. Instead he left her and walked away. She glanced at him while she slipped off the dress and bent to roll down her hose. He shed his own clothes calmly.

It was different tonight. He was different. Not in a bad way. Just different. Perhaps his aura reflected his expectations. She had promised the unknown in agreeing to demonstrations of the erotic images at Pompeii. That might have been foolish, since she was not certain what those images had shown.

The difference distracted her. She watched him discard his shirt and strip off his garments. The heat of his arousal burned in his eyes, but other fires flamed deeply in them too. This man did not look drunk when he was aroused. Instead passion made him appear dangerous.

Dangerous enough tonight that she might be afraid if she did not know him so well. An intuitive fear fluttered anyway, that of weakness facing power. She recognized it for what it was. More ancient than the ruins that they visited, it survived from times unknown, when there were no cities and no civilization, when these acts they prepared for carried implications that still echoed.

He finished undressing first. She thought he would help her then. Instead he merely watched. She tried to be more deliberate in her purpose, but his gaze actually flustered her. She could not stop looking over to where he stood a good fifteen paces away, so confident in his naked power.

She finally peeled off her chemise. For the first time with him, her own nakedness made her feel shy. She faced him and waited for him to walk over and embrace her.

He looked longer. Not at her body, but in her eyes. His own were unfathomable, hot and hard, with too many facets for her to see them all. Yes, if she did not know him better, she might heed the flutters of caution. Instead they only became rapid tiny licks at her excitement.

"Get on the bed, Phaedra."

Her pride frowned at the command. Her body trembled. He was playing the master fairly blatantly tonight. Of course, that was how it would be in the frescoes he had seen. Still . . .

"I see that there will be no seduction or ceremony," she said, to try to lighten the mood.

He did not respond to that.

She climbed onto the bed. He came over and she waited for him to lie in her arms. She expected it would be fast and hard tonight. It would be one of those joinings where their pleasure verged on violence in its fury. She would not mind that. Anticipation already teased her without mercy. She already ached for him to fill her.

He did not lie with her. He did not even kiss her. He grasped her ankles and swung her body so she reclined sideways.

The movement surprised her.

"Is it more like a Roman couch this way?" she asked.

"I think we will wait on those demonstrations."

"I trust we will not wait too long."

It was a mistake to say that. She knew it at once. Dark humor looked back at her from within the heat and hardness. "Be careful what you demand. The frescoes showed men with whores."

"I will not misunderstand. I know that you do not see me that way." Nor had she referred to the demonstrations at all. She was impatient for him no matter how it would be. He had aroused and seduced her without so much as a caress.

"Would that I did see you that way. I would have more contentment in the weeks ahead, I think. I would never want to lock a whore away so no man can see her but me. I would never want to devour such a woman."

He gave voice to the difference that she sensed tonight. His frankness astonished her. It had always been there, his impulse to possess, but he usually defeated that demon.

He separated her legs and knelt between them. He

hovered tall, looking down, and watched his fingertips slowly gloss over her body. The gossamer caress shimmered through her in a sweet tremble that made her clench her teeth.

Again that feather of arousal, only now on her thigh. She closed her eyes to what it did to her, and to the evidence of how profoundly he could affect her with such a small touch.

Another light softness. Warmer now. He kissed her thigh near her knee, then higher on its inner flesh. He bent her knees so his mouth and hands had better purchase.

She looked down her body at how he made love to her. He treated her legs like something beautiful that he adored. Like precious possessions.

The pleasure awed her. Unhinged her. All of her reacted, but especially the hot vacancy so close to those kisses. She throbbed there in need and increasing frustration. She felt the damp seeping out of her, forming on the bedclothes.

He caressed to the very top of her thigh, then gently pressed his palm over her mound. She clenched her teeth to contain the wonderful relief. A groan snuck out anyway.

He kept his hand there, pressing against her vulva, causing a delicious agony. His breath and kisses still feathered at her thighs.

His hand moved, touching more specifically. Her breath caught at the intensity of the sensations he created.

He kissed closer. "You will not stop me."

She understood what he meant. She had heard of

such intimacies. She knew because her essence begged him to do it. He had not requested. His words had been a command.

She was beyond shock. Beyond judgment. She did not stop him. She did not want to. His caresses prepared her, then his tongue devastated her. She cried and thrashed in a search for relief. She screamed into the oblivion when the explosion came.

The bed moved. No, she did. He entered her, so hard and hot and complete that she wanted to say a prayer of thanks. She emerged from the mist to see him standing beside the bed. He held her thighs around his hips. His taut expression promised the fury still to come.

"Say that you are mine tonight, Phaedra."

She almost did. It was only a lover's petition, one born of the pleasure. Her promise would end with the dawn. It should not really mean anything.

Except that it did. The heat in his eyes and the firmness in his tone told her that he was serious. His kisses and touches had always aimed to control more than her body. The difference in him tonight now had a name.

He understood that she would not say it. He did not ask again. He claimed her anyway, and he made sure that she could see him while he did.

Phaedra read a book by the light of the candelabra beside Elliot's bed. She looked up from the pages to admire the man she waited for. He sat at a large desk that he had charmed out of the owner of this elegant guesthouse.

He did not appear to remember that she was in the

chamber. He flipped through sheaves of paper and jotted lengthy notes.

They had been in Portici a week. By day Elliot returned to Pompeii while she played the indolent mistress. His visits to the ancient city had revitalized the historian in him. He and Nicola d'Apuzzo had formed a friendship and twice now the director had joined them for dinner. Other long evenings were spent like this, with Elliot's mind pouring its thoughts onto paper.

He did not seem in any hurry to return to Naples. She wondered if that was because his research and writing were going so well. If her own time lacked such serious purpose, she did not mind too much. She could not ignore, however, that although she managed to occupy herself, her activities were merely ways to fill time while she waited as she did now.

His profile looked almost too perfect with its regular features, but undeniably masculine. This was no pretty, poetic face like those so favored in London society. His expression bore the subtle hardness that both concentration and passion emphasized. The eye she could see reflected depths that hinted at the intensity of his mind's deliberations, ones on which Phaedra Blair did not intrude.

He appeared slightly unkempt the way he always did when he had been at this awhile. His shirt gaped open and his hair was mussed from his unconscious habit of combing it back with his fingers. Inevitably a strand would rebel and fall over his brow in a thick arc, inviting that gesture again.

She had woken the first night in Portici to see him sitting at the washstand. He had removed the bowl to clear the surface and set out his pen and ink. She realized at once that he had entered a place of isolation and that her intrusion would not be welcome. It might not even be possible.

So she had waited, as she did now, for him to emerge and rejoin her. Dawn might come before he did.

She waited for other things, however, with both foreboding and impatience. Mostly she waited for one of them to speak the words that would send them back to Naples. His progress on his book was reason enough for him to delay. When such a current of inspiration comes to a writer he would be foolish to dam the river.

She was the one with no excuse to linger here. Except for him, of course. Waiting for him. Wallowing in the excitement and the pleasure, drinking her fill. The waiting itself was too reminiscent of the wifely existence that she had repudiated. The warmth of his body and the strength of his embrace always made her forget to care about that when the waiting ended.

She began to forget now. She recognized the few blinks that woke him to the rest of the world. His posture relaxed. He leaned back in the chair, the feather of his pen toying at his chin. One more thought, one more jot, and he laid the pen down.

His head turned. The thick strand fell rakishly over his brow. "You are awake." He rose and walked over to the bed.

She had been awake for over an hour. "Do not stop your writing on my account."

"I am finished for now."

"It is going well?"

"Surprisingly so. I did not expect to do more than

make some notes here, but instead I have written two chapters."

"The setting inspires you. Did you not anticipate that?"

"I anticipated that the setting's inspiration could not compete with the lady I desired. I had begun to wonder if I would ever be able to complete this book."

She weighed the flattery, and lack thereof, of his guileless comment. "Well, having desire satisfied does have a way of dulling the fascination. I was supposed to make you work harder to catch me, wasn't I?"

"I am grateful you did not. Do you wish that you had?"

Did she? That was not a game that she believed in playing. She would not want to keep him from his writing and his book. Yet she could not deny that this week they had become almost too comfortable together.

Say that you are mine tonight. And tomorrow night. And all the nights that we share a bed. Pleasure alone had not bred this contentment in him. She never said she was his, but he believed it. Nor was he wrong. Not really. She lived as his mistress here. As his kept woman. While they remained here, on the edge of their old lives, he enjoyed the possession he wanted.

Her place in this love affair now was to wait, for the touch that now skimmed along her face. For the attention of this handsome man, now finally and completely on her. For the excitement that had changed because of what she temporarily ceded to him.

The excitement began inside her now, and not on the surface. The source seemed to be in her chest somewhere, deep in her essence. It would spread from there to the physical places. It would merge with the unbearable sensations and insanity of need, but the source never quieted.

And sometimes when they lay like this, slowly kissing, while she waited for the erotic lessons that had occupied their recent nights, she would, as she did now, unaccountably want to weep.

She embraced him closely so his caresses would pause. She did not understand this emotion, this drenching nostalgia. Nor did it make sense that she wanted to savor something so piercingly painful.

Maybe the lessons themselves had done this to her. The secret frescoes of Pompeii depicted sensual novelties. As the student in Elliot's demonstrations she had been at a disadvantage. That sly pleasure of submission had returned too often, affecting all the pleasure now, and maybe other things. He did not press his advantage too much as the lord, but that did not make her less of a serf.

She held him tighter, as close as she could. Her nose pressed his shoulder and she deeply inhaled his scent. She knew, just *knew,* that she would remember this exact moment forever. Decades hence when he had long ago forgotten this summer passion, she would be able to live this exact minute again.

That notion brought peace to the odd little panic that sometimes fluttered in her chest now. Her emotions calmed. Her mouth sought his ear. "We cannot stay here forever."

He did not respond. She thought that perhaps her ragged whisper had been too low. Then his own embrace changed until his arms encircled her totally, firmly binding her body to his.

"We will return to Naples if you want," he said.

Did she want it? Not so much that she could say so. "It is just that I have seen what I came to see." And learned what she came to learn, such as it was. There were a few more questions to be asked in Naples, but the real answers, if any existed at all, were in England. "Have you?"

He looked down at her, his expression much like she had seen while he wrote at the table. "Naples is an unhealthy city in the summer. I would prefer to keep you here, away from all the dangers it holds."

"I have things to attend to in the city, just as you do."

His vague smile ruefully acknowledged that she had just broached what truly waited for them in Naples. She thought that she also detected a hint of the Rothwell steely glint in his eyes.

This step was inevitable, but he was not pleased that she had forced it. Perhaps he thought that if she remained here, belonging to him, she would forget who she was and what she had to do.

She waited for him to ask her to expunge the memoirs. There would never be a better time to request that. She was half tempted to offer it. Her promise to her father and the financial demands of the press seemed far away and insignificant when she looked into his eyes.

He asked nothing. Instead he kissed her. There was no request in that or in anything else he did with her that night.

CHAPTER SIXTEEN

Heat shimmered off Naples's buildings. The sun raised malodorous mists on the distant bay. July was not the best month to visit the jewel of the Mediterranean.

Phaedra held a scented handkerchief to her nose as the carriage rolled through Capodimonte. The coachman stopped the vehicle at an especially unsavory crossroad. He barked a guttural exchange with a man walking by. It began as a greeting, but she heard the tone turn more serious.

Elliot's gaze rose from his book to listen. His expression firmed with concern. He turned, opened the trapdoor, and joined the conversation.

"I hope it is not a revolution," she said.

Elliot turned back to her. "There has been a malaria outbreak. It is common in Naples in summer. You cannot return to the Spanish Quarter."

"Signora Cirillo's apartments are airy and—"

"We will go to the Palazzo Calabritto at once. The

clerks at the British legation there will know of healthier rooms to let."

He spoke in the confident, firm tone of a man who had set his course and knew it to be a sound one. It was not a tone that encouraged debate. It was also not a tone that she was accustomed to hearing. Although on occasion in bed she heard something similar, just quieter and more gentle, but carrying similar assumptions of control.

He had not really wanted to return to Naples so soon. She anticipated a scold about how her impatience had led them into peril from this disease. Instead he only waited a short while for her to argue and, when she did not, he returned to his book.

The Riviera de Chiaia seemed depopulated. Either the malaria or the heat kept strollers from the promenade and the park bordering the sea. Their coach turned and passed through the high, broad arch of the Palazzo Calabritto and came to a stop in its courtyard.

"I will wait here," she said. "My presence at your side will only delay you, and will be awkward anyway."

"It will not be awkward. I will not have you think that way." The scold had come, just not on the subject she expected. He caught himself. He continued more reasonably. "If I go in alone there is less chance of this turning into a social call, so I will not expect you to accompany me."

He did not intend to sound like a husband today, she was very sure. Nor did she believe he took for granted that he had the right to think like one. She suspected that this manner was his reaction to the ambiguities that entered their affair with their return to this city.

She would not remind him now that she was not a woman who accepted direction or needed coddling. It was natural, after all, to want to hold on to the sweet fantasy of a passion that bore no costs and in which there was no past or future. He might be gripping too tightly right now, but he would eventually let go.

She would too, soon. Right now the nostalgia squeezing her heart left her too weak to draw any lines or indulge in philosophical resentments.

He was gone longer than she expected. She did not mind. The high stone building kept the courtyard in shade and a breeze off the bay funneled through the arched entry.

His expression when he stepped back into the coach would be inscrutable to anyone else, but she had come to know this man very well. She noted the distraction floating beneath his smile and attention. She saw complex emotions in the depths of his eyes.

"Most of society has left the city. They have gone to their country villas or to the islands," he said. "I have been directed to apartments just vacated by a Spanish family. It should suit for the few days we will be here."

Few days. Yes, that was part of what she saw and heard in him today. A resigned resolve tightened his jaw, like a captain who must carry out orders even if he does not agree with them.

"Where are these apartments? Not outside the city, I hope."

"They are right here on the Chiaia. I was told they are chambers fit for a queen."

———

"I thought that you spoke metaphorically when you said it was fit for a queen."

Phaedra strolled along the bank of tall windows looking out to the bay. The long grand salon of the Villa Maresche provided magnificent prospects. "If it suited our last queen during her scandalous visit here, you should know that it is too grand for me."

"It was available, grand or not. This district is less crowded and the malaria has not affected it."

All that was true, but the clerk at the legation had provided other good addresses besides the one where Queen Caroline had lived during her visit to Naples when she was a princess.

Having Phaedra in this villa appealed to him, however. She had known little luxury in her life and he had not showered much on her the last weeks. He liked seeing her here, holding her own in this long chamber full of silk drapery, damask cushions, and gilded candelabras.

"There is a large garden in back, off the dining room," he said.

"A garden. So it is not so different from our recent lodgings."

Not so different from the inns where they dined alfresco in the dusk before making love on clean but simple linens. Still, different enough in ways that had nothing to do with silks and views. It waited between them, the ways how it would be different.

A paper in his frock coat pocket reminded him of those differences. A letter from Christian had come in the diplomatic pouch that arrived on a ship last week. The clerk at the legation who handed it over did not think it odd that Easterbrook had been allowed to make use of that courier service. A marquess has his privileges.

Elliot sensed the letter flat against his body. It included nothing of note. No news of significance and not even an allusion to the family mission that had brought Elliot to Naples. There was no real reason for Christian to have written at all, to judge from the contents.

Except he had written. It would be like Christian to guess how this was going and to decide a nudge might be in order. Christian had an uncanny ability to sense things that one did not want him to know.

Phaedra removed her hat and set it on an inlaid table. He took that to mean she had agreed to live here. She sat on a pale rose sofa. The hue of the fabric made the black of her dress look even darker. He wished they would be here long enough for him to cajole her into ordering some new dresses and gowns.

He needed to convince her that being the mistress of the son of a marquess had its advantages. She would never marry, and he would not either, so this affair could continue indefinitely. As long as they wanted each other. There was no logical reason for the weight that had lodged in his chest the last few days. No reason at all for the damnable sense of loss that cloaked them like a mist.

"Is he back in the city?" she asked. "Jonathan Merriweather. Has he returned from Cyprus?"

Her question came like a ruthless response to his thoughts. *Actually, Elliot, there are some reasons. For example, we have not yet decided which of us will repudiate a family obligation, a promise, and a duty.*

"I do not know why you refused to come in with me, since you knew every move I would make."

"I did not want my presence to keep you from your purpose there."

"I went for advice on finding chambers."

And he had, although the rest could not be avoided. The obligation to take up his duty had shadowed his contentment the last few days, and especially on the brief journey here from Portici. She knew it, of course. The spiritual intrusions did not only go one way.

"Yes, he is back in the city."

"Perhaps he will be amenable to your request."

"I am certain he will be. I have asked him to receive me tomorrow. We will have that nonsense out of the way soon enough."

There was understanding in the smile she gave him. A little sympathy too. Much had changed since they had left this city, but not his promise to protect the family name.

Bold lights, the ones that made him a fool, entered her eyes. "Tomorrow, you say. Whatever will we do with ourselves until then?"

The Palazzo Calabritto, designed by the architect Vanvitelli, was a massive building with three high stories and classical detailing. Built in the last century, it now served as the home of all things specifically British in Naples. Even the Church of England held its services here since the king permitted no non-Catholic churches to be built.

Merriweather was a very English-looking Englishman. Blond, tall, ruddy, and portly, he could be a portrait of a wealthy country squire approaching his middle years. He so contrasted with the people of Naples that he must have been visible from a mile away on the promenades.

He received Elliot in a study in the palazzo's private wing. They had met before, as all sons of the aristocracy eventually do in England. The coffee that he offered indicated that he thought this was a social call.

"I am told that you sought me out while I was in Cyprus," Merriweather said, once they sat on two sofas in the study. "I am sorry I was not here. The summers in Naples do not afford the best society but I could have been of some assistance. Are you visiting because of your historical interests?"

"That is one reason."

"I assume that you have been well received on those matters. If I can help in any way, however, let me know. Ah, here is the coffee. Tell me about your brother's wedding, and how Easterbrook fares."

"Easterbrook is much the same, and Hayden's wedding was a joy to the whole family."

Merriweather possessed a soft, malleable, pale face. As a diplomat he had learned to tame its expressions, but a hint of humor flexed through it anyway. Whether he reacted to Easterbrook's much the sameness or Hayden's quick, private wedding was not clear.

"I am here for my historical work, but I also am addressing a family matter. It is the latter on which you may be able to help me."

"Pray, tell me how and I will use my influence any way that I can."

"I believe that you had an acquaintance with Richard Drury, who passed away last winter."

Merriweather chuckled. "A passing acquaintance at best. He accrued influence in the Commons despite his radical politics, and insinuated himself into Foreign Ministry decisions."

"Before he died, Mr. Drury wrote his memoirs."

"Did he, now? That should be interesting to read." Merriweather's smile did not alter a whit, which was a good sign.

"I hear that they are lengthy and detailed. The publisher who holds them plans to print them unexpurgated, unless evidence is given that proves a passage to be wrong. Since the events are often private ones, such proof will be difficult for anyone to muster."

"I expect that could prove discomfiting for some people. Memoirs often do. I hope the book makes its way here. We like good gossip as much as the next person."

"Regrettably, Merriweather, as the memoirs now read, you are one of the people who will be the subject of that gossip."

"Me?" His face folded into hills and valleys of consternation. "I barely—"

"A dinner. A private one years ago with Drury and Artemis Blair, after you returned from the Cape Colony." The man appeared truly dismayed. "It appears that Drury's memory failed him. If you did not attend such a dinner, or spoke of little of interest when you did, an error was made."

Merriweather frowned harder, in confusion and denial. Then his face fell. After one hooded, sidelong glance at Elliot, he averted his eyes.

Silence stretched. Elliot waited. That weight in his

chest unaccountably got heavier. No, it was not a weight, but instead an emptiness, a void.

"My family—Easterbrook in particular—are concerned with the interpretations that might be made of the dinner conversation that Drury describes."

Merriweather snorted. "As well you might be."

That was not the response Elliot expected. Time slowed for a long moment while he absorbed the surprise. For all intents and purposes, Merriweather had not repudiated the memoirs. He had instead just confirmed them.

"What does Drury write about that dinner?" Merriweather asked.

Elliot reported what Phaedra had told him.

Merriweather shook his head. "Hell. I am named, you say? You are sure?"

"Yes. Only you, as I understand it. Not the officer who died, and not the one who was suspected. And not any member of my family. However . . ."

He looked very concerned now. Almost desperate. "If it is published that I was indiscreet—" He glanced around the room, taking inventory of the environment that was in jeopardy along with his reputation.

Elliot let the man weigh his dilemma. The facts of that conversation had been confirmed, but that only increased his determination that they must not come to light. As to whether the implications regarding his father were true—the possibility sickened him.

He tried to push that horrible speculation aside. Instead it lodged in his mind, a dark shadow with an accusing voice. *You knew. Of course you did. She told you, after all.*

"As I said, the publisher is prepared to remove that part of the memoir if you say that Drury's memory was faulty."

"Has Easterbrook paid the publisher for this generous option?"

"The publisher saw the fairness of it without being paid. If the memoirs are in error there is no reason for good people to be harmed."

Merriweather stood and walked to a tall window that looked down on the courtyard. He stayed there, not moving, for a long time.

Elliot tried to accommodate the shift that had just occurred in the room. He had come here a seeker of truth, but he now played the role of the devil. He had just dangled both ruin and salvation in front of Merriweather.

Merriweather would recant, of course. He would swear Drury's memory of the conversation was wrong, that there had been no misreported death in the Cape Colony. They would laugh and joke about old radicals and bad memories. Phaedra would be good to her word. The memoirs would be printed with no allusion to that sorry episode.

He should be delighted. Triumphant. Instead the air in this study felt chilled and stale like a tomb's. The truth was bigger than what had been said at that dinner. Merriweather's decision would not change the reality that shouted in each passing moment.

That officer had been shot. Someone had committed a crime.

His jaw felt tight. He could no longer deny the possibility that his father had done this.

He was astonished to admit how long he had been denying it, and how hard he had been lying to himself. He had always known his father could be ruthless. He knew because the potential survived in his brothers and, apparently, in himself.

After all, he was here, wasn't he? He was calmly waiting for a man to choose dishonor to save his career and livelihood. He was depending on this man to lose his soul. His father's blood was calculating how it would solve so many problems once Merriweather said the words. In particular, it would remove the need to deal with Phaedra and those memoirs. Who knew where that affair might lead then?

It was terribly easy to weigh it all and see Merriweather's lost honor as a small cost. He suspected he knew how Christian would tip the scales. Truth, like reality, was not an absolute for Christian.

"Who is the publisher?" Merriweather broke the silence, perhaps hoping the devil would be more convincing and add yet more weight to the side of sin.

Elliot went over to the window. If he was going to tempt a man with such a terrible choice, he should at least do it face-to-face.

"Drury's daughter, Phaedra Blair." He explained how the inheritance had come to her.

Merriweather closed his eyes. "Dear God. She was in this city earlier this summer."

"She still is. You can speak with her privately. There will be no need to commit your statement to paper."

"She called on me and I—"

Phaedra had said nothing about trying to see Merriweather. Not one damned word. She had all but denied it. "Did you receive her?"

"I—British citizens of all stripes think this is their home. They often make social calls that we cannot—I misunderstood."

He had cut Phaedra because she was not of the normal "stripe" that a diplomat bothered with. Not rich enough or titled enough or acceptable enough. Elliot felt a tad less sympathy for Merriweather and his moral dilemma. "When did she call?"

"A month ago, maybe more. I remember because—well, she is somewhat known in London and I was aware of her and her—"

"Her fascinating eccentricities?"

Merriweather smiled weakly. "This is hellish, Rothwell. No doubt you wonder why I deliberate so long."

"I think that I comprehend the decision that you debate. I am sorry that circumstances force you to have a witness. I will leave if you like. I also swear that no one will ever learn from me that there was a choice to be made."

He seemed grateful for the understanding. "It weighed on me, you see. That death. It seemed wrong to falsify the circumstances. I thought it an extraordinary step. Better to air it all, I said, and let the officer under suspicion clear his name totally. But I was new to my duties and had no real influence. The colonel did not want the taint on his regiment. There was no proof, there was some trouble abroad in the region . . ." He sighed. "It was a fresh event when I accepted that dinner invitation. Mr. Drury was a convivial fellow and Miss

Blair—the mother that is—she had a warmth that—I must have been tired from my voyage—"

"Your trust in them was not misplaced. Neither spoke of it."

"Except that Drury had to go and write his memoirs, didn't he?" He sighed. "I expect Easterbrook will have my head if I don't give you what you want, and be a useful patron if I do. He has more influence than people realize."

Merriweather had not even needed to hear a bribe to know he would win a payment.

"Easterbrook, for all his eccentricity, does not like the family name bantered about in idle gossip."

"Idle gossip, hell. I know the rumors about your father and that officer's exile to the Cape Colony."

Everyone knew that rumor. That was the problem. Elliot could not promise to stay his brother's hand if the scales of Merriweather's conscience tipped an inconvenient way.

He knew he should be trying to exert his own influence now, for his own sake as well as the family's. He should point out the ambiguities to Merriweather. The circumstances surrounding that death were suspicious, but no one really knew what had happened.

Merriweather laughed, bitterly. "When I was a boy my father used to warn that the day could come when honor had a terrible cost. I always thought he meant I might have to fight a duel. I never guessed I might have to fall on my own sword." He shook his head and sighed deeply several times. He turned and faced Elliot squarely. "I cannot reconcile myself to lying, much as I want to."

"You are resolved?"

"Yes, God help me. The officer died of a bullet wound to the chest, and there was cause to think his fellow officer was responsible. I did confide this to Drury at that dinner. I cannot now say I did not."

They exchanged a silent acknowledgment that of course he had a choice. He appeared contented with the one he had made, however, and Elliot understood why.

Elliot took his leave, but paused at the door. "The other officer—what was his name?"

"It might be best to let that dog lie, Rothwell."

"No doubt. I would still like to know his name."

"Wesley Ashcombe."

"What became of him?"

Merriweather hesitated. "He came into a good deal of money soon after. A legacy. He sold out his commission and bought land in Suffolk. I have thought once or twice to look into that legacy, but decided it would do nothing to aid my repose at night. If he escaped justice there is little to be done now to change that. As I said, you should let that dog lie."

•

"*Una maritata!* You have wounded me worse than Pietro's pistol with this marriage. I will die!"

Marsilio's shock rang through the garden. His handsome face became a mask of sorrow. His lids closed over his black eyes. His hand pressed his heart.

"I do not believe that it is legitimate. We are not Catholic, you see. However, we will not be able to resolve the matter until we return to England."

"England! You leave? *Cara,* I fought a duel for you. I

was so close to death that I hear the angels singing. Now you marry and leave? When?"

"Soon." Very soon, she suspected. But not too soon. "I wanted to see you before I departed, to make sure you had recovered from that duel."

Marsilio calmed himself after a long display of melodrama. At her encouragement he played out the great event. He strode and postured through the garden, showing her how it had all taken place.

He was a very handsome boy, dressed fashionably and with sartorial bits of flair and color to mark himself as an artist. He wore his dark, wavy hair longer than most men and sported a full mustache that did not add the years to his face that he hoped.

She fanned herself while he performed. When he got to the part about being shot he sat beside her again so she could sympathize.

"It is better," he reassured her. "But, at times, eh—" He twisted his torso and grimaced, to indicate he would carry the memory of her forever.

His smile warmed. His gaze swept her and lingered on her head. "Your hair. Why do you twist it and pin it now? Does he force this on you?"

"It is less hot this way."

His finger poked at the roll. "It is sad. Take it down, *cara*. I will help you."

She slapped his hand away. "No, Marsilio, you will not."

"Then you do it. Let it flow and fly again as free as your spirit. You will do it for me, no?"

"The hell she will."

Phaedra froze at the terse, masculine interruption.

Marsilio did too. His gaze slid right and left as he attempted to judge from where this unfriendly voice came.

Right behind him, as it happened. Poor Marsilio could not see Elliot standing ten feet away. Just as well, because Phaedra could. She trusted Elliot would look less dangerous before Marsilio turned around.

It was not to be. Elliot walked over to join them. Marsilio eased away, putting distance between him and her by slow fractions of inches.

Elliot smiled down. It was not a smile that improved the situation. Marsilio tried to look confident and innocent but failed miserably.

"Elliot, I am so glad you are finally returned. This is Marsilio. I told you about him, remember?"

His smile did not soften. The steely glints got colder. "I am always happy to meet one of your friends, my dear."

Marsilio misunderstood. He smiled with relief and began talking faster than his English could accommodate. "*Si,* an old *amico. Solomente un'amico, si?* Your *signora* is a dear friend and I come—have come to say *arrivederci* and hope someday to see her again so we can once more be such good friends." He shot to his feet. He bobbed a quick bow at Phaedra. "I will go now."

"I will see you out," Elliot said.

"*Grazie,* but I do not—"

"I insist."

It took some time for Elliot to return. She waited in the garden. If they were going to have a row perhaps the villa's servants might not hear them out here.

Finally Elliot rejoined her. She watched him walk down the broad stone path between crisply trimmed hedges. He was not all that much older than Marsilio, but in the ways that mattered there was no comparison between them to be made.

That hardness still played at his eyes and mouth.

"What did you say to him?" she asked.

"I told him that if I ever find him alone with you again that I will call him out and that he will not be so fortunate with the results of his second duel. How did he find you? We have only been back a day."

"I sent him a note this morning."

She had not seen Elliot truly angry for some time. He did not express it overtly, but the garden seemed to tremble around him.

"Is this your way of reminding me that you are free and independent, Phaedra? Because it only makes me wish that those vows are real so that I can make sure that I never have to tolerate your friends again."

"Vows ensure nothing of the kind, Elliot."

"The hell they don't." It was the response of a man who knew a man's power all too well. It erupted like both a declaration and a curse.

She waited while he controlled the primitive soul that had been unleashed.

"Why did you invite him here while I was gone?"

"I expected you to return sooner. I thought you would be here when he arrived, if he did come."

"Why did you invite him here at all? You must know that I could not want to meet him."

"He fought a duel because of me. It was a stupid duel, but I owed him the courtesy to acknowledge it, and to make sure he had recovered. Also, when I was in this city the last time, spurned and cut and ignored by my countrymen, he was a friend to me."

"A friend. Damnation, but I am coming to hate the word."

There was much she could say to soothe him, but this conversation only made it painfully clear that he would never be the kind of friend that she had secretly hoped. Elliot Rothwell was no Richard Drury.

The temptation to capitulate completely, to give him rights no matter what the cost, spilled out of her heart the way it did so often now. The power of the emotion frightened her.

She sensed anger loosening its hold on him. All the warmth of their intimacies entered his gaze. So did the perception that came from all of the intrusions she had carelessly allowed. Does that knowing ever go away once it is acquired? She was not sure whether she wanted to believe it did or did not.

"Marsilio will tell Sansoni that you are back," he said. The rational mind had gained control again, and it was calculating.

"I expect that he might."

"Sansoni will not be pleased to learn that Marsilio came here."

"Probably not."

He took her hand and pulled her to her feet and into his arms. "I was late returning because I visited the docks. I booked passage to England. I will remove you from this city soon."

Soon. But not too soon.

His kiss held remnants of the jealousy he had just

conquered. He commanded and took with his mouth and his hands. She felt her dress loosening, dropping. He stripped her naked in the quiet garden while bees buzzed and hovered around the riot of summer blooms.

He sat on the stone bench against the tree and pulled her into his lap. Kisses bit her neck and his tongue teased her breasts. His caresses stroked over her body. Every touch was intended to devastate.

He smoothed his fingertips over her nipples until she squirmed. "Take down your hair. You did not do it at the boy's request, but you will do it now for me."

She raised her arms and plucked at the pins. It was a small victory that she gave him. A little symbol of submission to salve his pride.

His touch titillated her the whole time, promising ecstasy, luring her into the familiar abandon. She relinquished control as she always did now. She let him position her on his lap so her bare legs circled him and hung down the back of the bench.

He arched her nakedness so he could kiss her body while they rocked together in rhythm to his thrusts. She clung onto what she could in the dappled shade under the tree, taking and giving everything that they still shared.

CHAPTER
SEVENTEEN

Rain came that night, and with it a respite from the terrible heat. Elliot woke to air cleansed and fresh, billowing the drapery at the window. The dawn light still held a silvery cast that muted the forms in his chamber.

He rose and pulled on a robe. He went to the writing table and flipped through some papers there. Last night in a fit of inspiration he had written for hours. Now he barely remembered what words he had used. He read several pages quickly, impressed that they were not half bad.

He looked to the bed. Phaedra had been here when he sat down to write. When had she left? He could not remember. That was not like him. He did not suffer from the curse of losing hold on the world when he retreated into his mind.

Except that last night he had. In doing so he had wasted one of the last truly free nights with Phaedra. He would make sure they found some privacy on the ship home, but the need for discretion would be clumsy and awkward. Here in Naples no one worried about such things.

He let himself onto the terrace and walked down to the door that opened to her apartment. Their proximity was much like that in Positano, only much larger and more luxurious.

No bedclothes covered Phaedra. She wore only a simple chemise that ended at her thighs. Her hair fanned around her, glistening in the soft light entering the room. A high pile of pillows propped up her body, as if she had fallen asleep unexpectedly. One arm lay stretched awkwardly where it had fallen when drowsiness claimed her. Palm up, her hand remained half-closed on something.

He moved closer. Light glinted in tiny sparks off the object in her hand. He gently pried it free of her grasp. A cameo. This was no doubt the one she spoke of her mother owning.

It was of good size, with impressive craftsmanship on the carved figures. An ancient gem of this quality would be very valuable. He carried it to the doorway to examine it more closely.

He sensed her attention on him. He looked over to see her watching him. She appeared so beautiful there, all shades of white and gold, surrounded by the luxurious silks and satins of those pillows. She awed him sometimes. Too often.

"You left," he said, referring to her absence from his chamber.

"No, you did," she said, reminding him of the distraction he had not controlled. "Alexia told me how your brother leaves the world that same way, so I understand how it can be with the Rothwell men."

He joined her on the bed. "I regret that I did."

"It is who you are. The sun might make you forget for a few days or a few weeks, but you would not be whole if you forsook that world forever because of me."

He did not care for the warning implied in her words. She was not talking about only him and his world and his wholeness.

He set the cameo on the valley between her breasts. "It is lovely."

"It is, isn't it? I would have it set as a brooch except for what it stands for."

"It is no less beautiful for being a forgery. The value is much reduced, but not the artistry."

"I do not care about its value."

He could see her face clearly now. She appeared tired and drawn. Perhaps she had not slept much last night either, as she reclaimed her own wholeness.

She picked up the cameo and gazed at it. "I faced the truth last night. I imagined it all too easily. The discreet sales, the promise of confidentiality, the glee of collectors obtaining rarities more cheaply if no one learned the source. It was a very clever scheme. If buyers were told the gems came from Pompeii they would want them all the more but be secretive because they were buying stolen goods."

"You do not know for certain there was a scheme."

"My father said there was. *The interloper was at the heart of a scheme that is both brilliant and nefarious.* That is how he tells it. He refers to a valuable item of suspect provenance, and others like it that will be discovered."

Her reference to those memoirs brought a shadow to his mood. Yesterday's meeting with Merriweather had been blissfully forgotten during the retreat into his work. There had been no terrible choices in his head for those hours. No hard truths and harping questions about the past. No ruthless calculations either.

"How convenient for a man selling such things to insinuate himself into my mother's confidence and her life, and selling her this was the least of it," Phaedra mused bitterly. "He only seduced her so he could meet the kind of people who would pay well for the forgeries that he sold. Her introduction would be like a license from the crown."

He wished he could demolish her interpretation with a few careful words. Her deductions were too good, too plausible.

"Why does it matter to you so much, darling?"

She sat abruptly, pulling her body away and looking down at him. She was angry. Furious. Not with him.

"My father said that man was responsible for her death. I think she learned what he was doing, how he was using her. I did not understand that before but last night I suddenly did. She believed there was more with him, you see. More than she had known with my father. That is the only explanation for what she did."

Her face tightened. Her eyes glistened. She glared down at the cameo like it was an object of loathing. With the light's growing strength he could see the signs of weeping on her face.

He doubly regretted escaping into his work. He did

not like to think of her in this chamber alone, scrutinizing the little she knew and coming to her sad conclusions.

She looked at him as if she expected an argument. As if she hoped for one.

"Phaedra, even if it was as you say, it is unbelievable that any of this had to do with your mother's death."

"It was the cause of her decline, surely, but perhaps— there were some signs she consumed something. The physician decided there were not enough indications to pursue it, but . . ."

"Is it not more likely that she passed naturally? She does not sound to me like a woman to despair over a love affair."

She rose up on her knees, trembling with emotion. Her eyes blazed and her teeth clenched. "You do not understand. That man seduced her into relinquishing *everything*. Not only my father but *herself*. And *me*. That is why she put me out of her house. So I would not see how weak he made her."

"You do not know that."

"I *know*. She forsook her own beliefs with this man and she did not want me to see it. None of her friends know his name either. I asked those in her closest circle and not one person could point me to this lover even though most everyone had guessed a lover existed. Even Matthias. Even Mrs. Whitmarsh."

Her hand closed on the cameo and made a tight fist. She all but shook it in his face. "She knew she had ceded too much to him. She did not want the world to see that Artemis Blair had allowed some man to make her his serf. To then learn it had all been a fraud so that he could use her to enrich himself—*of course* that would lead to despair."

Fury poured out of her. It was not directed at the unknown lover, he realized. Phaedra's anger was aimed at the mother who had preached a religion and converted a child, but who had then fallen from grace herself.

Did her mother's failure make those beliefs nothing better than utopian speculations that could not survive reality? If a night of reflection had led her to the brink of thinking so, it might only take—

His hard calculation caught him up short. Who was this man who so quickly assessed his advantage? It was as if someone or something had breathed life into a dormant part of him since he met Phaedra.

He had been so sure there was none of the old man in *him*. Unlike his brothers, he had been spared both of his parents' worst legacies. Only now he suspected that he might have gotten the worst of his father's blood. In the past he had never wanted anything badly enough to cause that blood to flow, that was all.

She betrayed nothing, darling. She merely met a man who reminded her that she was a woman. There is no sin in that and no betrayal of self. It is the most normal thing in the world.

He almost said it. If he could convince Phaedra that her mother's compromise was normal and inevitable it would be easier to convince Phaedra to compromise as well. And there were many compromises he wanted from her.

Too many.

He took the cameo out of her hand. He placed it on a table next to the bed, then pulled her down to him. They had spent the night apart in their separate worlds. Soon most of their lives would probably be spent the same way. For now he wanted to hold on to her in the place they had created together.

He embraced her, offering whatever comfort he could. She slowly calmed. Her anger flowed away, leaving an emotion-laden peace.

"Do not be hard on her, Phaedra. She chose a difficult path in life. You know that in ways no one else does. Maybe you are right and she stumbled toward the end. If she could not forgive herself that is a tragedy, but her daughter can be more generous."

She stilled so thoroughly that he could not feel her breathe. Then she pressed a kiss to his chest. She laid her face against his shoulder and molded her body alongside his.

"You can be very wise sometimes, Elliot. Perhaps you are right. If my mother was tempted to forsake all for a man, I should be more understanding. It is not as if I have been immune myself."

Gentile Sansoni called that afternoon. He sent up his card as if this were a social visit.

They received him in the salon. Phaedra thought he appeared less dangerous than the last time she had seen him.

Perhaps it was the setting that made the difference. This light and airy space bore no resemblance to that dark, cavernous room where he had interrogated her. His dark garments and hair and eyes formed a very small stain on the pales hues and gold of this chamber.

Elliot donned all of his English reserve for the meeting. He stood next to her chair tall and proud. He exuded aristocratic assumptions. Of the three of them, only Elliot did not look out of place.

To her surprise, Sansoni bowed in greeting. Then he shocked her further. He smiled.

"Felicitations on your marriage, *signora.* I learned that you were back in Naples with Lord Elliot, and I wanted to pay my respects before you left our kingdom."

"Elliot," she said. "He is speaking English surprisingly well for a man ignorant of our language."

"So he is."

Sansoni shrugged. "Ignorance can be convenient in many situations."

"I expect so," Elliot said. "Your good wishes are welcome, and your timing fortuitous. We embark for home tomorrow. But then you know that."

Sansoni angled his head in half-acknowledgment. "One hears things. I was not sure, however."

"Now you are."

"Si. Grazie." He fished in his black frock coat and retrieved some parchment. "An army officer with whom I am friendly happened to be in Positano recently. A friend had called him there regarding an incident. Something to do with a tower and a riot and a heretic."

"How colorful," Elliot said.

"Yes, we are a most colorful people. My friend returned with these documents. The priest in Positano was very concerned that you did not have them."

Phaedra eyed the parchments that she had assumed

she could forget. She scrutinized Sansoni's face to determine if he intended to get odious again.

Elliot held out his hand for the parchments. "Thank you. We will set all in order once we arrive in England. To do so here would require us to remain in Naples. For months, I expect."

Sansoni looked from the documents to Elliot then back again. "Months? You need only sign—"

"It will be more complicated. If we hope to be on that ship tomorrow, we would do better to let English churchmen take their time."

Sansoni was not a man to hand over an advantage, and he did so now with reluctance. Once Elliot had relieved him of the parchments the odious little man began to take his leave.

"Signore Sansoni, I wonder if I might have some private words with you," Phaedra said. "I expected Lord Elliot to have to translate for us as best he could, but since you have miraculously learned English that will not be necessary. I promise the conversation will be a brief one."

Sansoni's eyebrows rose in disapproval at her boldness, but he looked to Elliot for his agreement. Elliot did not display any displeasure. She guessed he would save that for later.

Elliot nodded and walked to the salon door. She accompanied him. "You may stay, of course," she whispered. "However, I do not think he is a danger."

"You have requested private words with him, Phaedra. I will leave you to have them."

She faced Sansoni after Elliot was gone. The man

clasped his hands behind his back and subjected her to his most critical stare.

"I assume that your husband has instructed you to apologize for all the trouble that you caused both here and in Positano."

"Lord Elliot does not instruct me in that way. Aside from Marsilio's wound, I have nothing to apologize for either. I want to ask you about something else entirely." She removed the cameo from her pocket and set it on a table near the windows.

Sansoni's eyebrows merged. He paced to the table and peered down at the cameo. "Ah, I understand your desire for privacy now. You do not want your husband to know you were duped into buying this forgery. I regret that I cannot help you on this matter. Nor have you given me any reason to spare you from Lord Elliot's wrath when he learns of your carelessness."

"You knew at once it was a forgery? How?"

"I have seen it before. Or rather, others like it. I know where they are made and how they are sold. I know the dealers who sell them as ancient to foreign dealers and to ignorant visitors like yourself. It has been going on for years."

"If you know so much, why don't you stop it?"

"The artisan who is at the heart of it has interesting information to offer me in trade for his freedom. It is worth my while to leave him and his network alone. Compared to protecting our monarch, what do I care if some foreigners buy false goods?"

"What is this man's name?"

He laughed. "*Signora,* I said he was useful to me. If

it is known he traffics in such things he will have to leave the kingdom and he will no longer be useful."

She picked up the cameo and looked at it. "Are there many of them?"

"You will not see the same cameo on the gowns of half of London's ladies. If there are too many, it would be suspicious, no? That is the normal downfall of such men. This one and his friends are smarter. A few cameos, a few pots—" He shrugged. "It is enough, but not too much. You understand?"

She understood. It would not do for forgers to let dozens of fakes into the art market too quickly. "Are they being made here in Naples?"

"I could not permit that. Our king is a lover of such things and would not like to know such activities occur under his nose."

In other words, the king did not know such activities occurred at all. Sansoni allowed the crimes to continue because it gave him a valuable informant. Or because he was being bribed.

"If they are not here, where are they?"

He sighed deeply. "*Signora,* you are too curious. Pretend it is real. No one in England will know."

"I am most curious because I am most vexed. I could confess my error to Lord Elliot, I suppose. He could ask his friends at the British legation to look into it. They could ask their friends at court about it. *They* could ask your superior—"

"*Basta. Capisco,*" he snarled. "The artisans are scattered in remote hill towns to the south. I do not seek them for my reasons, as I said. Give me the dealer's name and I will tell him to return your money."

"No. I think that I will keep it. I have actually grown very fond of it."

He rolled his eyes in exasperation. His hand flicked in a gesture that she guessed was very rude. "You are a madwoman. I will be at the ship to make sure you leave on it, and I will say a prayer of thanks when you do." He jerked a bow, and strode from the chamber.

Elliot strolled back in. "I see that you made him regret his visit. He was mumbling darkly the whole way out to the Chiaia."

"It appears that the interrogator does not care for being interrogated."

Elliot noticed the cameo in her hand. "You counted on him coming so you could ask him about that, didn't you? That was why you wrote to Marsilio."

"I expected Sansoni might know a thing or two about these forgeries. He seems to know everything else."

"Did you learn what you wanted?"

"He did not hand me the answers on a plate. He did not name names, either. I have learned all that I can here in Italy, and it is not enough." She tucked the cameo into her pocket. "And you, Elliot. Did you learn what you wanted yesterday when you met with Mr. Merriweather?"

His pause before responding acknowledged that they both had avoided speaking about that meeting. She hoped it was because he did not want to ruin their last days in Italy with any references to memoirs.

"I learned things I did not know about. I learned that you had tried to see him before the unfortunate incident with Marsilio."

He had deflected her real question. She feared that meant he had not learned what he wanted at all.

She had counted on him bringing Merriweather back to the villa so they could be done with that. Since he had not, and since he now avoided the topic, it appeared Merriweather had supported her father's description of that long-ago dinner.

Her disappointment immobilized her. She had suspected as much yesterday but she had still hoped. Last night, in the depths of her anger and dark honesty, she had known how it would be, however. Maybe Elliot's total retreat into his work was a way of avoiding the entire subject and its implications.

"Why did you want to see Merriweather, Phaedra?"

"For the same reason you did, Elliot."

"So I was right. You did intend to annotate and add names."

"No. I hoped to learn that passage was false. I sought an excuse to remove it, to spare Alexia. She is one of my dearest friends and more loyal than any other that I have known. If I could obtain the proof that my father was in error, then Alexia would not have to live with the gossip and the scandal."

He did not move. She wished he would. She wished he would embrace her in all the sweetness she had felt this morning. And if he asked her this one favor, she would—what?

She wished she had never seen those memoirs. She wished at least that her father had not extracted promises from her. She even half-wished, God help her, that she had not received the summons to his deathbed.

Every word is true. There is no slander or libel in it.

Promise you will change nothing. She had hoped he had been wrong and that one part might not be true. Then it could be excised from her promise and from the text itself.

It appeared not.

She could not bear the silence while Elliot stood there, gazing at nothing in particular, so close but also oddly distant. He looked so right here today. His demeanor and presence were more appropriate to this grand salon than the luxurious furnishings were.

"You are not going to ask it of me, are you?"

Her question did not surprise him at all. He knew what she meant. It was in the air, after all.

"If I do you will think that every kiss I gave you, and every touch, was a calculated step toward this moment."

His image blurred. Her eyes stung. "I might not. I might be glad to have an excuse not to hurt Alexia. I might weigh it all and decide it is not so significant. I might—"

He pulled her into his arms and silenced her with a gentle kiss. "You might do all those things, but you will never believe any of it. Hush now. Leave all this for another day. The voyage home is a long one and our duties do not claim us yet."

She let his kisses seduce her away from her sadness. She rested her head on his shoulder much as she had in the morning. Being supported like this, enclosed by his warmth and strength, was the best part of this affair. She felt no danger or worry in such moments, but only the most soothing peace.

Even this morning his embrace had salved the pain and calmed the confusion. The night had left her torn apart, feeling a fool for becoming her mother's acolyte, for sacrificing so much for empty beliefs. He could have pressed his advantage then in so many ways. Instead he had helped collect the pieces and put them back together.

He nuzzled her hair and placed a kiss on her crown. "What was the other reason you called on Merriweather? You said there was another besides the memoirs."

"I had hoped he could introduce me to some people in the English community here."

"He should have received you. He should not have left you to fend for yourself."

"As it turned out the inconvenience was a small one."

She kissed his cheek to encourage him to leave all this for another day too. She was too happy now to talk about any of it. He would be reminded soon enough why the daughter of Artemis Blair was not received and always fended for herself.

CHAPTER
EIGHTEEN

London in September was as empty as Naples in July. It was not a month when polite society crowded the shops on Oxford Street or filled the parks during the fashionable hour.

Easterbrook's house had not been closed, however. Elliot found it fully staffed when he arrived from Southampton. The servants explained that his aunt Henrietta and cousin Caroline had retreated to Easterbrook's country estate of Aylesbury, but that the marquess remained here in the city.

Elliot assumed that his brother was reveling in his isolation after having rid himself of the females. It might be days before he even saw Christian.

He reaccustomed himself to the house and to the services of a valet who anticipated every need. He had been gone long enough for his old life to feel unreal and foreign. He tried to find contentment within the spaces and routines known since childhood.

Instead his thoughts dwelled on Phaedra. There had been joy at the beginning of their voyage, but a mood akin to desperation at the end. The last week his desire had been hard and drenched with a fury. He could not get enough of her and he had thrown discretion to the winds as a result.

Despite their fevered pleasure, nothing had been settled. They never again spoke of Richard Drury's memoirs after that afternoon in Naples. Nor had he received any promises from her about the passion itself. No declarations of fidelity. No agreement to continue as lovers. Not even suggestions that they be friends.

He had left her alone in her solitary independence in her small, odd house near Aldgate. He had ridden off in the carriage not even certain that she wanted him to return.

He poured some brandy and carried it up to his apartment. He unpacked his papers and sat down at his desk in his sitting room.

He had begun closing the door of his mind to life's vagaries when a servant arrived, pushing it open again.

"The marquess requests that you join him for dinner this evening, sir."

He was tempted to decline. The conversation that his brother sought could not be avoided forever, but he had counted on Christian's own distractions, whatever they may be, to delay it.

"Tell him that I will be there."

"You said that you were coming down to dinner."

The voice shocked Elliot alert. It was very close to his ear. So was a face. Christian hovered, peering down at the papers on the desk.

Elliot fished for his pocket watch.

"Do not bother. It is well past ten." Christian reached over his shoulder and turned a page. "This really won't do, Elliot. It is bad enough that Hayden gets strange at times, but at least that new wife of his will probably cure him of it. If you have now taken to such eccentricity—" He glanced down sharply. "Why are you laughing?"

"I find it amusing for you to describe Hayden as strange or eccentric."

"You do not find his behavior with those mathematical studies strange? Last spring he sank into an unhealthy, hermetic existence, and it was not the first time either."

"He is no more strange than you are, and I doubt I will ever be half so."

"If you have not gotten strange then you have become rude. I expected you in the dining room. I even dressed."

Indeed he had, if his open collar and brushed long hair could be called dressed. Still, he did not wear a robe and his feet were not bare.

Christian strolled away. He threw himself into an upholstered reading chair and pointed to a nearby table. "I brought up a plate and some wine. I feared the voyage had taken a toll and you needed decent food. Instead I do not find you too wasted to attend on me, but too busy."

Elliot got up and brought the plate and glass back to his desk. "You are looking fit and healthy, Christian. Not so thin as when I left."

Christian stretched out his legs and crossed his

boots. "I have been engaging in athletics. Boxing and rowing and such. I fence three times a week. It is all a nuisance but there is no choice."

Elliot tasted some of the capon. Easterbrook's cook was a fine one and this fowl swam in a redolent sauce. It smelled heavenly compared to the meals at sea. "What compels you now when nothing did just months ago?"

Christian got up again and nosed around the book-shelves. He found the cigars and helped himself to one. "I expect to fight a duel soon. It is best to be in military form for that."

Christian appeared the image of bland contentment while he lit the cigar. He might have just announced that he was boxing and fencing to prepare for a night at the theater.

"Whom have you offended so much that he will be calling you out?"

"I expect to make the challenge, not pick up another man's gauntlet." He lazily waved his cigar. "Our young cousin Caroline is being wooed by Suttonly, whom Hayden has broken with for reasons I do not know. Need I say more?"

"Yes."

"Her first season went to her head. Aunt Henrietta only encouraged her. Now they allow Suttonly to con-tinue his addresses after Hayden tried to crush the bud-ding romance with his boot. Hayden has informed Aunt Hen that if Caroline marries Suttonly, the door to this house and her welcome in this family will be over." He took a deep puff. "Bold of our brother, since it is my house and my welcome. However, he subdued Aunt Hen so thoroughly that I did not care to point that out."

"Christian, I suspect that you have spoken to no human being since the family went down to Aylesbury. Your lengthy explication suggests that you are newly fascinated with your own voice."

"I am recounting the family news. You are too impatient."

"Could you get back to the duel?"

"Hayden warned Suttonly off. Caroline cried for days. Aunt Hen and Alexia took her down to the country to recover. And Suttonly has now left town. It is obvious what will happen."

The only thing obvious to Elliot was that Christian had not talked this much in the last eight months combined. "Pray, spell it out."

"*D.,* Viscount Suttonly will not cease his pursuit. It is a matter of pride now. He will convince her to elope. *U.,* Hayden will follow and catch them before they marry but the deed, as it were, will have been done. *E.,* Hayden will not move from his rejection of Suttonly. Aunt Hen will have the vapors, Caroline will be ruined; and *L.,* I will be calling Suttonly out."

"Why wouldn't Hayden be the one to call him out? Hayden is trustee and guardian."

"I could not permit that. If he got himself killed, Alexia would be left a widow with an unborn babe."

"Alexia is with child?"

"That is the other news." He relaxed into the chair again. He tapped some ash off his cigar. Quite suddenly he ceased being the companionable brother and became Easterbrook, very completely. "Now, we are done with that. Tell me about your journey."

Elliot ate more of the capon. He chewed a good long

while. He drank down the wine. Christian's lids lowered a bit more with each gastronomic delay.

"I found Miss Blair at the address that Alexia had provided."

"Did she have the memoirs with her?"

"No, but she does possess them. We were correct about that."

"What is this going to cost me?"

"Regrettably, she would not take our payment."

The companionable mirth that Christian had brought into the chamber disappeared. "How much did you offer?"

"I was not specific. She was insulted by the mere suggestion."

"Everyone is insulted by the mere suggestion. That is why you do not merely suggest. You name an amount. A big one. Then they do not have time to get insulted because they are so busy calculating what they can buy with the plunder."

"No amount would have moved her. She promised her father on his deathbed to publish his words. She will not be swayed from that duty now."

Christian dismissed Phaedra's duty with another flick of the ash. "Then we must do it another way. Where is the manuscript?"

"She did not have it with her, so I assume it is here in London somewhere."

"It should not be too hard to find. She owns little property. It must be in her home or else with a third party, a friend or her solicitor." He pondered the problem. "When does she intend to return home? How much time do we have?"

Elliot considered lying. "She is back. She sailed on the same ship that I did."

Christian's attention froze on the burning glow of his cigar. Then it shifted sharply to Elliot. It was the gaze of a hawk who sees the details on the ground far below very well.

He stood. "You did your best, I am sure. However, I will deal with this now."

Elliot stood as well. "No, you will not. You will stay away from her. You will do nothing to coerce her."

Christian examined him again. Searching. Wondering. Finally, knowing.

"Hell. She seduced you."

"No." And she hadn't. Not really. "It was not like that."

"However it was, whatever it was, she disarmed you. While you enjoyed the favors of this fair damsel, did you at least request the favor that you wanted most? A woman well pleasured can be very amenable to her lover's requests."

"Do not speak of her in that way, damn you."

"How should I speak of her? As your beloved? Your mistress?" He gestured violently toward the desk. "I'll wager she has not given you cause to think of her as your anything. That is why you lose yourself in that dead, long-ago world. The truths you unearth there are more secure than the ones you must face here."

They were not yelling, but their voices sliced the air and each other.

"If any of us knows why it happens, it would be you, Christian. Hell, you are spending your whole life there."

"Well, I am not there *now,* nor will I be until this is settled."

It was not intended as a threat but it might as well have been one. It did not help that with each angry statement the current Lord Easterbrook looked more like the last.

"She was not indifferent to our concerns about the family name," Elliot said, trying to make his tone more reasonable in order to encourage his brother's reason. "She was willing to compromise for us alone."

"For you alone, you mean."

Actually, it had been for Alexia. He explained what the memoirs said, and how their father was not named. He described his unsatisfactory meeting with Merriweather.

Christian listened, darkly interested. "Merriweather is a fool."

"Honor would not allow him to lie. It would be ignoble for you to hold it against him."

"Are you now Merriweather's protector as well as Miss Blair's? No, wait, you do not have that role in her life, do you? Her belief in free love means she is free of both the rights and expectations that would give a man."

Elliot waited for more reaction regarding Merriweather's suspicions and the implications they held for their father. Denial. Fury. Instead his brother remained coldly expressionless and suspiciously calm.

"Damnation. You know the truth," Elliot said, amazed. "You know if he did it."

"I know nothing of the kind."

"Then, you know how to find out."

"I do not want to find out. Nor will I need to defend

him if Miss Blair removes that passage. If she does not, and Merriweather holds firm, we will have more than society gossip to deal with."

"If it is not true there will be nothing to fear and everything to gain if it all comes out. I think we should do that—find out if it is true or not, so we know."

"I repeat, I do not want to find out."

"Christian, it *may not be true.*"

Christian walked to the door. "What a hopeful son you are. But then, you did not know him very well. As for Miss Blair, I will consider staying my hand out of respect for your sentiment. However, there are others with a keen interest in those memoirs. It is unlikely that she can bewitch all the men in all those families."

CHAPTER
NINETEEN

Phaedra stepped out of the hackney cab, clutching a thick package in her arms. She waved to the women she had sat with. She had learned long ago that with a little boldness one could find strangers with whom to share the hire of a conveyance. Her visit to the City had not taken long at all as a result.

She had delayed retrieving the manuscript for several days. She needed to rest after her voyage, of course. Then she needed to resettle herself and call on some old friends.

She had also waited for some old friends to call on her. Alexia, in particular. She hoped the absence of Alexia's letter or card meant a visit to the country and not a repudiation of their friendship due to the package that she now carried.

She could not blame Alexia if it was the latter. Not one bit.

Honesty was a virtue that she tried to practice, especially with herself. And so this morning she had faced the truth while she dressed. She had a duty that she did not want, but it was time to get on with it. Those letters that had waited for her on her return made that clear. The other one that arrived yesterday sounded the trumpet.

People besides Elliot wanted the memoirs destroyed and were willing to pay dearly for it. The anonymous letter yesterday had gone beyond offers of bribes. It had been a veiled threat, but clear enough to raise the hairs on her neck.

If she had not made that promise to her father she might give them all what they wanted. She would burn these pages and let the press go bankrupt. She almost did not care that she would be left penniless if it did.

She turned a corner onto her street and approached her door. She stopped and gave a few pence to Beggar Bess.

"Them cats know you are here," Bess said, cocking her head to the building behind her.

Phaedra did not hear the mewing the way Bess did. She saw the cats, one black and one white, at the wavy glass of the house next to her own, however. An old woman petted one and a little girl the other. Her neighbors had taken the cats when she left for Italy. It was supposed to be temporary, but little Sally's attachment meant it would now be permanent.

"A carriage came by earlier," Bess said. "Big one, from the sound of it. It didn't stop, just rolled past real slow. No one's been to your door before that one there."

Bess had taken this spot for her trade five years ago. Although blind, the old woman had realized that Phaedra's visitors had more money than most of the people who came to this street, and that proximity to Miss Blair's door could be profitable.

One of those visitors waited now. He lounged against the door. A large portfolio rested against his leg and he held open a little book in which he drew.

Harry Lawrence, a young artist whom she had befriended the past winter, awaited her return. She had clearly forgotten his letter that arrived yesterday saying he would come by. That other letter had obliterated her memory of it.

"My apologies," she said after their greeting. "My visit to the City took longer than I expected."

"I do not mind. I sketched the beggar and also the whore at the window across the way. An artist is never bored."

She settled him in her sitting room. She put the manuscript on a table beside the divan to wait until she finished playing the hostess. She and Harry spent the next hour looking at his drawings. She much preferred his sketchbook's expressive jotting to the careful studies he had made in preparation for a large painting that he intended to submit to the Royal Academy.

Another caller interrupted her explanation of why. She opened her door to find Elliot waiting.

Her heart rose at the sight of him. Joy paralyzed her. She could only gaze at him, stunned anew by how he stirred her. For a long count they just looked at each other.

He presented his card. "I hope that Miss Blair is at home today."

She took the card and examined it critically. "Well, perhaps she is, just for you." She held the door wide and pecked his cheek when he stepped over the threshold. He closed the door and embraced her in a less proper kiss.

"You did not write," he said. "I could not wait any longer."

She had not written because she did not know what to write. She only knew that she did not want their affair to die in sadness, and she feared it would if it continued here at home.

Her joy now, in his kiss and his warmth, in his mere existence near her, warned just how sad it might be. That could not diminish her happiness, however. It had only been four days but she had missed him badly. She had not realized how badly.

She guided him to her sitting room, feasting her eyes on his face. He stopped at the doorway. His smile firmed into a line less friendly.

She followed his veiled glare to where Harry still pored over his sketchbook.

"It appears Miss Blair is not home just for me," he muttered. "One of your friends, Phaedra?"

She was so happy that she actually found his jealousy flattering, even though it heralded all that would be wrong between them here in London. She introduced the two men. Harry, dear innocent that he could be sometimes, all but danced over his good fortune in meeting a member of the ton here in Phaedra's humble home.

Elliot was nothing if not gracious. He sat and pretended interest in the drawings. Phaedra sensed his impatience with a visit that was not going the way he intended.

"I believe that I will let you both toast my safe return," she announced. "I will return shortly with the necessary spirits."

She slipped away while Harry explained his artistic intentions regarding a large image of a general on horseback. She retreated to her kitchen, poured two good measures of brandy, and made her way back to the sitting room.

Harry was gone, along with every sketch and drawing. Elliot stood by the wall studying her Piranesi etching of a macabre prison. He came over to take the glasses. He placed one on the table beside her divan and sipped the other.

"Mr. Lawrence had to leave," he said.

"Abruptly, it appears."

"I have probably seen a man move faster, but I can't remember when."

"What did you say to him to make him depart in a run, Elliot?"

"I admired his prodigious talent and alluded to the possibility of purchasing his new painting for Easterbrook's art collection. Oh, yes, and I also told him to leave or die."

She swallowed a giggle as she pictured Harry's reaction. "That was very wrong of you."

"I do not feel the least bit contrite." He looked around the sitting room. His gaze lingered on the worn upholstery of the divan. The strewn venetian shawls could not entirely hide its thinning fabric.

"Was this your mother's home?"

"She let chambers in Piccadilly. I bought this house when I began my own life."

"When you were sixteen. The poor choice of neighborhood can be explained by your inexperience, but you live here still."

"It is my home. I know the people now. I am content here."

"There is a beggar outside your door and a woman exposing her breasts at the window across the way."

"They are both harmless and either one would risk her life to pull me out of a fire."

"I am hardly reassured by your mention of fire, considering the condition of the buildings on this street. I want you to allow me to find a better place for you."

She sat on the divan. Elliot no longer wore the friendly face of his arrival. The Rothwell sternness had claimed him. She knew why, but she wished they could have delayed this conversation for at least an hour or so.

"Did you come here to offer to keep me, Elliot?"

He sat beside her. "I came because I could not stay away."

"So the offer of a better home was an impulse?"

"I had not noticed how poor this street was when I left you here the other day. My thoughts were only on our parting and how I did not want it. Nor did I expect to find you entertaining another man so soon after—" His jaw squared. He drank more brandy.

"Elliot, men call on women all over London. In the best houses. Even in the houses of women being kept by another man. No doubt you have done so. A visit from a man does not mean a love affair is under way."

"Are you saying that artist was not the lover who awaited your return?" He tried to keep it from sounding like a demand for an explanation. He also tried to hide his relief at the possibility of that explanation. She thought both reactions very sweet.

"I am saying he is not now my lover, and I do not expect him to be anytime soon. Since you are not married, no other woman has ever given you more reassurance than that. I cannot imagine why you would need more from me."

His expression suggested he was not happy with the lack of definite denial. "I would still like to have you live elsewhere."

"I am not a courtesan, Elliot."

"I do not speak of keeping you. I want to see to your safety."

"First my safety, then my comfort, then my security. Call it what you will when it starts, it will end the same place." She placed her hand on his face. The sensation of his skin under her palm made her heady. "Do not make me regret the little support I accepted from you in Italy. You had to know I could not allow that to continue here. If you let a house for me, I become a whore no matter what philosophy I claim."

"At least then I will not find you alone with other men, Phaedra. I near thrashed your artist today." He took her caressing hand and kissed her palm. "I do not want you less because we have returned to London. It appears my desire was not caused by the southern sun after all, but I greatly regret losing the few rights that circumstances gave me there."

She understood what he meant. His kisses revived the excitement too fast, but more than pleasure had survived their return. She had been swimming in nostalgia for days as memories and feelings invaded her head and heart.

"I will not allow you to be my protector. I will not be your mistress. We cannot live together like we did in Italy. However, we could be friends, Elliot. We can continue our lives as we know them and still share that with each other."

His lips pressed her palm again. He closed his eyes. "If we do this, there can be no other man. I am not enlightened enough for that."

"If I ever want another, I will tell you. I am sure that you will give me the same courtesy. We will end that part of our friendship with dignity if the sun sets on it."

He kissed her. She sensed a debate in him, as if he weighed what he lost and what he received in such an arrangement. He gazed in her eyes too seriously.

A terrible fear shook her heart. He might refuse. He was considering doing so right now. She just knew that he was.

Pain sliced through her heart. It burned worse than grief. Sorrow poured out the gash it made. Sorrow and dread and panic and fear.

She kissed him hard. Desperately. She spoke to his desire with her own so he would remember why he wanted her.

He reacted hard, grabbing her in his arms and holding her head to a punishing kiss. It reminded her of the fevered embraces on the ship, full of demands unspoken. She felt anger within the pleasure but she did not care now. Her heart knew such relief, such incredible joy.

"Where is the bedroom?" he asked hoarsely.

"Come with me." She took his hand and led him up the stairs to her bedchamber.

He did not notice the poor furnishings up there. She did not give him time to. She released the tapes on her dress and let it drop to the floor.

He began reaching for her. She held him off with both hands on his chest. "Get on the bed," she said.

He showed surprise at the command, so like his own in Portici. She gave a little push. With a laugh he allowed himself to fall back on the bed.

"Should I worry for my virtue?" he asked.

"Most definitely." She climbed up and straddled his body with her knees. His fingertips played at the hem of her chemise. She gave his hand a little smack. "I am doing the ravishing here, sir."

"Then remove it yourself, Phaedra. Let your beauty ravish me."

She pulled it off and sat back, looking down at him. His smile charmed her. His eyes appeared very deep.

"You are a goddess, Phaedra. That is what I thought that night in the tower when I came up the stairs and saw you. I had never seen such a confident and beautiful woman in my life. I am sure that I never will again."

She tried to smile, but her mouth trembled. His words moved her. She bent down to kiss him, then began to undress him. "While my beauty ravishes you, I will ravish your beauty."

He kept trying to caress her while she worked at his buttons. It became a game where she fended off his wicked hands while she tried to finish the job. Finally amidst laughter and fumbles and a good deal of trouble with his boots, he lay naked beneath her.

She sat back on his thighs again. Their mirth drifted away, leaving a sweet peace in which their desire and spirits were joined. He reached for the ends of a strand of her hair. He wove it amidst his fingers, watching. Then his gaze returned to her face.

The mood still glowed with their joy, but the special knowing and intimacy that they shared was in his eyes.

"Do you even know how to ravish a man, Phaedra? For all of your boldness, I do not think that you do."

She felt her face warming. "I do know. But knowledge and experience are not the same thing. I expect that I can manage it, however." There were reasons she had never ravished a man before. Her past friendships had not been like this one.

He gently pulled at the strand of hair. Her head followed the invitation. She kissed him. She sensed his impulse to take over, to make the ravishment mutual at least. Instead he submitted to her mouth and tongue.

She kissed lower, to his neck and chest. Reactions stirred in her, new ones that fascinated her even while her own arousal purred. She had been an active participant before, but this was different. She began to understand how her pleasure gave him pleasure.

She caressed him fully while she kissed and licked. She savored the feel of his body and the signs of her effect on him. Her power entranced her. It seemed the most natural thing to kiss all of him, his hips and thighs and stomach, and even the erection that her hand encircled.

He touched her head ever so lightly. It was a gesture of encouragement and request. She used her mouth to thoroughly ravish him, as best she could figure out how.

He could not contain his own abandon. He relinquished control of himself in ways he never had before. When she again straddled him and took him into herself, she could see his surrender.

It was not the first time she had been on top of him, but it was different this time. She allowed him to caress her but her attention was on their joining. Her awareness filled with his hardness inside her and her body's demands and the movements of her hips as she absorbed him.

Even her release felt different, more powerful and hard. She insisted that he accept that it was time for him too. She never lost herself, not for an instant. She experienced every pleasure with the fullest alertness.

She collapsed on him much as he would on her. His arms wrapped her, holding her close. Their breaths merged in their exhaustion. She turned her face on his shoulder so his profile rose just beyond her nose.

His eyes were closed but he felt her attention. The vaguest smile formed. "You do not believe in half-measures, Phaedra."

She wondered if he was shocked that the experiment went so far. "Did you only want half-measures?"

"Hell no." He turned his head and looked at her. "I am selfish enough to be glad you had the knowledge, but I am also glad you did not have the experience before."

There was no way she could have had the experience before, nor many of the others she had allowed with this man. There was a difference between a friend and a lover.

"It is said that is not something that normal decent women do," she said.

"I suspect that many normal decent people lie about it."

"Have you ever done that with a normal decent woman?"

"Do you mean before today?"

He startled her. She might qualify as decent, but the normal part . . .

He chuckled. He tapped her nose with his finger. "You were so enthralled by your power that I hesitate to say this, but . . "

She waited.

"I too had the knowledge, but not the experience."

If the sun sets on it. He trailed his fingers down Phaedra's chest and along the silken valley between her breasts. *If.* He marveled at the way that word had affected him. Not when, but if. His joy had been complete. Boyish. Ridiculous. *Mine.*

He wondered what would happen if that twilight never came. It astonished him that he found contentment and not concern in the idea. Perhaps Phaedra's philosophy was correct and the very lack of legal binds helped desire to survive.

Only she did not believe that herself, at least not with him. She spoke of forever in one breath but the end in the next. She may have said *if,* but she did not expect any part of their friendship to survive the publication of that manuscript, least of all this part of it.

Would it? Could it? He did not know. He should not

see her duty as a betrayal. He did not even want her to compromise for his sake. This passion possessed a clarity that he did not want to obscure with such base negotiations.

Still, he owed his family his loyalty as surely as she owed her family hers. He even owed his father more than he wanted to admit.

Christian did not want to know. He had, perhaps, taken great pains to remain ignorant. Yet knowing the truth might be the only way to solve the dilemma.

"I must ask something of you," he said.

"I can deny you little, Elliot. If you must ask, I probably must give."

That was not true. She reserved much that she did not give, which was why he petitioned now for a half loaf at best. Which was why he would be riding across town to this poor street in order to receive what she did give. Perhaps with time he would accommodate himself to his total lack of rights, to what she did not give, but he doubted he would ever be free of wanting more.

"In Naples, Merriweather could not deny that the dinner your father describes took place. Nor that the conversation was held. However, he does not know that his suspicions are correct. If I find evidence he was wrong, or that the death in the Cape Colony did not touch on my family, will you delete that memory?"

She appeared to find the suggestion interesting. "Since I assumed it did touch on your family, as indeed I think my father did . . . My father charged me with seeing his true words were printed. If I know they are not true, or might cast untrue assumptions on someone—yes, Elliot, I could delete it." She smiled ruefully.

"Perhaps I should take out an advertisement in the *Times* offering that to others. You are not alone in trying to bribe me to play free with Richard Drury's memoirs. My letter basket below is full of threats and pleas. It is clear that my old partner tried his scheme on others, and that they have all learned who now owns both the memoirs and that press."

"If you were less honorable you would soon have the means to buy a better home all on your own. Easterbrook alone would settle a fortune on you."

He did not intend it to sound as if he reopened those negotiations, but if she expressed the slightest interest in the size of that fortune . . . A good argument could be made that she should be practical. He would not mind having this problem go away if she were.

"A fortune now? From Easterbrook alone! My goodness, I had no idea blackmail was so profitable." She made an exaggerated display of pondering and wavering. "How big a fortune?"

"Five thousand." The amount had been given to him this morning. It arrived on his breakfast tray on a piece of paper, written in his brother's neat hand. No words, no pound sign, just the numeral five and the requisite zeros.

He had understood it for the command it was, and also for a warning that Christian had not accepted that Phaedra should be left alone to decide her own course.

"That is a ridiculous amount. I fear Easterbrook is indeed half mad. Fortunately I will save him from such ruin because I will not accept it."

So there it was. Christian was wrong. A big bribe did

not sway everyone. Phaedra was not insulted but she also was not calculating what she could buy.

"If I received such a fortune, I would then have to live accordingly," she mused. "Think of the results. A new wardrobe, of course. All those stays and tapes and hooks. Then I would need servants to care for my luxuries and to dress me."

Evidently she had begun calculating after all. It was annoying that Christian was correct. "You would learn to love the luxuries." And he would love to see her have them. She deserved better than this house and the penny-pinching she must endure.

"Ah, but all those servants would be such a nuisance. It would be difficult to lay abed like this all afternoon and all night, only to rise briefly for a simple dinner that I cook myself."

"Are you asking me to stay for dinner? One that you cook yourself?" The idea called forth charming, domestic images. Almost as charming as the ones having to do with the night following dinner.

And she was the one who worried about becoming enslaved. If only she knew . . .

"Certainly. Are you hungry?"

He moved his hand slightly. Her breast firmed beneath it.

"I am always hungry when I am with you, Phaedra."

He dressed in the fading shadows of the chamber. He looked down on Phaedra's body, pale and lovely amidst the tumbled sheets. She lay on her stomach with her face half covered by the pillow she hugged. Her legs remained parted and her round bottom exposed, just as she had been when he took her the last time, a mere hour ago.

He could have stood there looking at her for hours. Since that would make him even more of a fool for her than he already was, he left her sleeping and went down to the chambers below.

The kitchen still held the remains of the dinner she had served on the plank table near the fireplace. Since they were both naked it would have been ridiculous to set out china in the dining room.

The sitting room, with its motley collection of furniture and art, showed more of dawn's light than the other rooms. He walked over to the divan, and the table beside it. The second glass of brandy still sat there untouched, right beside a good-sized package wrapped in paper.

He had noticed the package yesterday when he arrived. It was about the same dimensions of a ream of paper. Just the right size for a book manuscript.

He broke the seal of the wrapping. It fell away. He gazed down on the first page of Richard Drury's memoirs.

He assumed the memoirs were presented chronologically. If he wanted to find the offending pages it would not be difficult to dig them out.

Silence surrounded him in the house. Phaedra slept soundly above. The street outside barely gave signs of life. He could not resist touching the pages stacked so neatly. He ran his thumb up their edges, letting them fan down with a gentle *thwap*.

He doubted there was a copy. It had been very careless of Phaedra to leave this here.

It entered his mind that she wanted him to give in to temptation. If the manuscript, or even those pages, went missing she would be relieved of her promise to Richard Drury. She could not violate that promise herself, but she might not be sorry if she had no choice in the matter.

What if she saw it as a betrayal instead? Christian would think the end of his brother's love affair a small price to pay. Christian would also find a way to compensate Phaedra without her realizing it, if Elliot demanded it.

She would have some security then. She would not have to live so frugally. If she dressed fashionably and moved west, she might take her mother's place among the literati, not be the lovely but odd daughter of Artemis Blair who dwelled in London's fetid east neighborhood.

One small theft and her life would change for the better. His duty would be finished. No one would whisper that the last Lord Easterbrook had paid a man to kill his rival. His sons could go back to pretending that they did not know that maybe he had.

He did not miss how ruthlessly he weighed and calculated. His better half was not even surprised or shocked anymore. Nor could it offer much argument besides sentimental ones about trust and affection. That counted little in the world. He was not even sure it counted much with Phaedra.

He ran his thumb up the paper edges again.

Phaedra woke in late morning to find Elliot gone from her bed. His clothes had been removed too, so she assumed that either he had left or he had gone below.

She slid her hand to where he had last lain. She imagined she still felt him there, sated like she, no longer hungry although it had taken several meals to fill them both.

She slid her hand up the sheet to the pillow where his fine head had been. She touched something other than muslin and down. She rose up on her elbows, curious.

Her father's manuscript rested on the pillow, roughly wrapped in the brown paper. The seal of the wrapping had been broken but the pages stood in military precision forming their thick block.

Her breath caught. She had left this on the table when she came in with Harry, then forgotten about it. Of course Elliot had guessed what that paper covered. The size and shape all but screamed "manuscript."

He had risen early and checked. He had opened the package to be sure.

He had probably taken the pages he did not want her to publish.

Relief burst in her. Deep, grateful relief. It overwhelmed her until her eyes misted.

She sat up to fix the wrapping. She would not speak to him about it. Not now. Not yet. Maybe not ever. It was wrong of him to steal the pages, most wrong, but she would not upbraid him. Nor would she ever speak of the pain he had spared her. Perhaps now, maybe—

Her fingers halted on the package. She cocked her

head. A new page had been added to the manuscript.
She slid it from under the brown wrapping.

My darling,
    You must be more careful with this legacy. It
is the kind of treasure that might tempt the
ruthless. There are those who would gladly steal
it, as the letters that you received have proven.
    It is not safe for you to keep it in your house.
Take it to the reading room of the British
Museum. I will inform them that you will be
preparing a work for publication there. The
librarians will hold the pages for you between
your visits. Those who care will soon learn
where it securely resides and you and your home
will remain unmolested.
    I did not take the pages that I seek, so you do
not need to check. I feared losing our friendship
over such a breach of your trust.
Thank you for dinner. It was delicious.

                          Your grateful friend,
                                  Elliot

CHAPTER
TWENTY

Thank you for accompanying me," Phaedra said. "I do not expect the man to admit everything, and your perception of his reaction to my questions will be useful."

"Since you are determined to ask the questions I do not want you making the call alone," Elliot said. "Your description of your meeting with Needly tells me that these men are not taking your suspicions well, which is not surprising."

"Needly was not angry. He laughed at me. That is hardly dangerous."

There had been a good deal of scorn in Mr. Needly's laugh, however. Scorn for her and her mother. It had been a brief meeting in a spare office the day before. The first antiquities seller whom Matthias had named, Mr. Needly, was elderly and elegant and erudite and arrogant. He had made quick work of her questions about the cameo.

"A fraud," he said, his prim mouth pursing in distaste. *"I told her when she brought it to me, and she did*

*not care for my opinion despite seeking me out for one.
She argued with me. As if she had any expertise in such
things. The great Artemis Blair had been duped like a
country lass. That her daughter now quizzes me on the
same gem tells me she refused to see the truth, no doubt
because the truth made her a fool."*

"That the last one laughed does not mean that this
one will miss the insinuations of your questions," Elliot
said. "I know this is important to you, but I ask you to
be discreet."

They walked the streets together, aiming for an address that Phaedra had procured. Their destination was
not that far from the offices of Langton's publishing
house on Paternoster Row.

Elliot had not said one word about the activities of
that business when he arrived, nor had he expressed displeasure in meeting her there. She doubted that in leaving the manuscript intact three nights ago he had
reconciled himself to the memoirs' pending publication.
Probably he still believed he would produce enough
proof for her to give him what he wanted, the way she
had promised.

She hoped that he would. She wanted that blight removed from their happiness. The last few days had been
idyllic, even better than the weeks in Italy. The fun and
friendship that they now shared proved that the passion
could survive their return to England. She had been, she
realized, as happy as she ever had been. Even complet-
ing her investigations regarding her mother could not
dim her mood.

Thornton's bookstore occupied a small shop on a
small street near the British Museum. The grime of

years covered windowpanes that looked into a dark cavern of tomes.

"I made some inquiries," Elliot said. "His history is obscure. He is said to have an English father and an Italian mother, and to have studied in Bologna. It would be difficult to disprove that, and those who have met him say he appears educated."

"If he is half Italian, he might be in a position to have access to objects being made there," Phaedra said.

"You may have the correct man this time. Unlike Needly, this one's reputation is hardly unassailable. There have been some rumors."

They entered the shop. Silence and darkness entombed them. Shelves reached to the ceiling, all stuffed with old bindings. More remnants of estate libraries rose in stacks higher than Phaedra's head.

The shadows in the far corner shifted. A figure rose from behind a wall of books and walked their way. The proprietor came forth to greet them. Elliot reached back and opened the door again, so some light would be shed on the man in question.

Nigel Thornton was not the fusty old bookseller that these premises called for. He appeared not much older than thirty although his too-perfect features, his fashionable frock coat, and his dark hair might be hiding a few more years. Still, he was much younger than Phaedra had imagined.

She pictured him younger still, his beauty still fresh and his energy unleashed. As the last remnants of Artemis's own youth fell away, did she seek renewal in an affair with a much younger man?

He greeted them graciously but managed to convey

that they had interrupted important matters that he had put aside just for them.

His dark eyes sized up Elliot and reflected recognition. His gaze then flickered over Phaedra and vaguely communicated that she complicated the assessment.

"Lord Elliot, I am honored. You are, perhaps, seeking to fill a new library? We have the best editions of the Roman histories, and can arrange for new bindings if you prefer."

"I find Easterbrook's library adequate for now. It is the lady who seeks you out, and she is interested in a particular story, not a library full of them. I am a mere escort."

Thornton accepted that, but his lowered lids indicated disappointment that this would not be a profitable afternoon.

"Allow me to introduce Miss Phaedra Blair," Elliot said. "You knew her mother."

The light from the door illuminated Nigel Thornton's handsome face enough for Phaedra to see his reaction. It froze into careful passivity but the dark eyes beneath those lowered lids appeared to gleam more the longer he examined her face. And he examined it a long time, very carefully, with great interest.

"I knew your mother as a generous hostess on occasion, Miss Blair. I did not know her well enough to tell stories about her, however."

"I have heard differently, Mr. Thornton. I am told that you attended on her frequently, not occasionally, the last few years of her life."

He angled his head in a nod that neither agreed nor

disagreed, but implied the level of friendship was open to dispute.

"I am also told that years back you sold more than books, Mr. Thornton."

"Even now sometimes other items come my way."

Phaedra fished the cameo out of her pocket. She set it atop a stack of books directly in the flow of light from the door. It glowed there amidst the dark, dusty tomes, in all its expensive artistry.

His gaze lit on it. Recognition flashed. A peculiar aura poured off him, like a wave of sentiment had unexpectedly breached a seawall. He began to smile, but stopped the impulse before it got past a vague, sad line.

"Did you sell or give Artemis Blair that gem, Thornton?" Elliot asked.

"That is the story you seek? The story of that cameo?"

"Yes," Phaedra said.

"I regret that I cannot help you."

Yes, he could. She knew he could. "But you do recognize it."

He gently picked it up and peered closely. He ran his thumb over the tiny figures. "It was hers."

"I have been told by the best experts that it is a fake."

"I expect that it is, then. Still, it is well done and very beautiful."

Right now she did not care if it was beautiful. "Did my mother get that from you?"

"If I say that she did, I admit to fraud, don't I? If I say she did not, you have no reason to believe me."

"That is because it would not be the only fraud,"

Elliot said. "I am told there was the matter of some coins a few years back."

Thornton sighed. "Those coins came to me from a solid source. Nor did I sell them as secure in their authenticity. Such trade is fraught with peril, and collectors who hear what they want to hear. Which is why I prefer old books."

"Is that what happened with this cameo? Did my mother hear what she wanted to hear?"

"There is no way for me to know if she thought it authentic. It sounds that way, though."

He handed the cameo back to Phaedra. For an instant both their fingers rested on it, as if he hesitated to release his hold.

"If you decide to sell it, let me know."

"You would buy it? So you could sell it again?"

He turned away, to melt into his dark corner within his castle of books. "I would buy it because it is beautiful. And because it was hers."

"What do you think?" Phaedra asked. She and Elliot strolled through the British Museum while she turned the meeting with Thornton over in her mind.

"What do *you* think?"

"I think it was him. He all but admitted it. If I had not said I knew it was a fraud, he might have told me everything. That was a mistake. He could not satisfy me without saying he was a criminal. But his entire manner, the way he recognized it, his words, while circumspect, indicated he knew my mother owned it and thought it authentic."

She sensed a response in Elliot but it was a long while coming out.

"So, what do *you* think?" she prompted again.

"I think that you have your answer, but it is somewhat different from the one your father concluded."

"How so?"

"Nigel Thornton was no scoundrel taking advantage, stealing affection and plotting great frauds. He was in love with Artemis. I think he still is."

His observation astonished her. She wanted to disagree. It did not fit with the picture of the evil interloper that her father had painted in his memoirs. It robbed her of indignation and anger over her mother's affair. If the other man loved Artemis, it complicated everything.

Only she suspected Elliot might be right. When Thornton saw the cameo the whole mood in the shop altered. The memories and sentiments called forth by the gem had almost been tangible.

"If he loved her, I don't get to hate him, do I?"

"Which story do you prefer, Phaedra? That a man seduced your mother in order to use her connections, and involve her in crimes that would ruin her? That this late affair led her to take her own life? Or that your mother fell in love with a much younger man who out of ignorance sold or gave her an artifact without being secure in its authenticity? You will have to decide which way you think it went, but I do not believe that man back there deliberately misused your mother."

"I find it hard to believe that my father was so wrong about Thornton's character and motives."

"Your father had lost the love of his life, the center of his existence, to a much younger rival. He probably thought your mother had lost her wits along with her heart. It is unlikely he could see the situation with objective eyes."

He spoke as if he did not have any doubt how it had been. She might have found Nigel Thornton an enigma, but Elliot had left that shop remarkably secure in recognizing the signs of a man in love.

"If I sell him this cameo, he will probably flog it as an original antiquity again. You said there were questions about some of his dealings. If so, it is likely that he *did* take advantage of my mother."

He took her hand and drew her into a corner of the gallery. "Is it so important for you to believe that, Phaedra? Important to believe that she was wronged? You said in Naples that you could understand why she might have chosen this new lover. If the man loved her in turn, doesn't that make it easier to accept instead of harder?"

She did not know what to say to him. Her heart rebelled at this simple explanation that Elliot so easily embraced.

"I suspect that if one examined Thornton's dealings one would find ambiguities and allusions, not false claims," Elliot said. "As he said, collectors hear what they want to hear. I am sure he knows how to exploit that without crossing into fraud. As for that cameo, if you sell it to him I do not think he will sell it. I think that he will keep it as a memento of her until the day that he dies."

She pictured Nigel Thornton standing in that bookshop. She pictured him eight years younger, dazzling the aging Artemis with his confidence and handsome face. She saw again the way his eyes had lit with warmth when he saw the cameo and spoke of her mother.

Dear heavens, Elliot was probably right. It also explained why none of her mother's friends knew the new lover's name. Thornton had been so young that Artemis probably kept him a secret so the world would not think her doubly a fool.

"What an embarrassingly ordinary denouement to my great mystery," she muttered.

Elliot circled her shoulders with his arm and gave an encouraging squeeze. "Are you disappointed?"

Was she? Her anger about the lover had calmed in the last weeks, but her father's accusatory words still burned in her heart. Perhaps she had wanted to blame someone for her mother's death and her father had given her a way to do that. Maybe she had actually been angry with Artemis, for betraying the perfection that free love could be.

She released the last of the deep fury that she had carried to Naples. Nigel Thornton was probably no paragon of integrity, but he was not the calculating conqueror either. Artemis had probably been disappointed to learn the truth about the cameo, but it was unlikely that the episode had destroyed her.

She fingered the cameo in her pocket. Maybe she would just give it to Nigel Thornton, since he still held Artemis in his heart.

"You can return to your dissipated life, Christian. There will be no elopement. No flight and no duel. Caroline has accepted my authority on the matter."

Lord Hayden Rothwell spoke in the firm, confident tone of a man who expects the world to obey his command. Phaedra doubted that assumption was wrong very often.

He issued his proclamation from the other side of the table. The dinner party he and Alexia hosted was much smaller than Phaedra had expected. It consisted only of the three Rothwell brothers, Alexia, and herself.

When Alexia wrote and invited her, she had considered not accepting. Alexia and Hayden had returned from the country several days ago, and they probably knew about those memoirs. If so, she would not really be welcome. Now, however, she suspected that Alexia and Hayden did not know. Easterbrook did, however. His behavior toward her had been correct, even gracious, but she had caught him eyeing her several times the way a hawk watches a mouse.

"As a man, I doubt you fully understand the matter or have interpreted our cousin's humor correctly," Easterbrook said in response to Hayden's assurance. "I would be more at ease if your wife joined in, or even nodded in agreement with you."

Alexia's color rose at Easterbrook's request that she either support or compromise her husband's opinion.

It still amazed Phaedra that Alexia had fallen in love with Hayden. Alexia had married for the most practical of reasons, then lost her heart. Phaedra would never have expected such a development, especially with the man in question.

Lord Hayden was handsome, to be sure, but severe and cold. Unlike Elliot, his demeanor and character did not soften the Rothwell face. Alexia, however, insisted that the world did not know the true man.

"Christian, you must not sow seeds of discord between husband and wife," Elliot said. "If Alexia chooses to disagree with her husband, she will do so. Our hostess has never hesitated to speak her mind when she thought it necessary."

Alexia appeared grateful for Elliot's interference. Phaedra had noticed that they shared a friendly bond. All three brothers seemed to hold Alexia in high esteem.

That impressed her, and made her more comfortable at this dinner. Nor had she been treated as the outsider that she was, both to society and to this table. Alexia's invitation had begged her to come. The two of them had shared some quiet talk and news in the drawing room before coming down.

"Nonsense," Easterbrook said. "Hayden would not mind if his wife moved from her position of neutrality. He knows that women know women's minds better than we do. What say you, Alexia? Has Caroline been cowed or does she plot an intrigue?"

"No one can know another's mind, Lord Easterbrook," Phaedra said. "Nor do all women think the same way. Alexia is much too sensible to know the mind of a young girl bedazzled by a title."

She succeeded in drawing Easterbrook's attention from Alexia rather too well. He regarded her so directly that bodies shifted in their seats.

Elliot came to the rescue. "I think that it is not Caroline's mind that will matter, but Aunt Hen's. She may be more bedazzled than her daughter."

"Exactly," Alexia said. "It is Henrietta who must be reasoned with. We are making great progress there."

Hayden changed the subject. The men carried the conversation. Phaedra and Alexia held their own, silently, exchanging female looks that spoke volumes.

Elliot noticed, but did not react. He had been a little odd tonight. Ever since he met her coach outside he had appeared just . . . different. She found him looking at her in the same way he had that first time in her chambers in Naples, as if he were seeing her anew and measuring what he had.

Perhaps it was the party affecting him. She was thoroughly in his world tonight. Nor had she pretended to be other than she was, except for wearing her blue dress. There was no benefit in pretending to be meek and normal. And she would be damned before she allowed Easterbrook to either awe her or intimidate her.

The meal finished, Alexia invited her back to the drawing room. The door closed on the brothers and their port and cigars. Phaedra wondered if the men would be discussing Caroline's precarious hold on her virtue, or the pressing matter of Richard Drury's memoirs.

"I am so grateful that you agreed to attend," Alexia said, sitting right beside her on a settee. "It gave me an excuse to leave Hen down at Aylesbury, for one thing."

In other words, Hen did not approve of Phaedra Blair and would not sit at a table with her. "Then I am happy I came, if it provided relief from her company."

"Have you enjoyed it at all? I know Easterbrook can be—"

"I have enjoyed it tremendously." And she had. She found the brothers' bonds touching. She rather envied

Elliot, and understood all the more why blood usually won out in any competition for a person's loyalty.

"I am also joyed to see how you are completely one of them, Alexia. I had not seen you among them before like I have tonight. You have found another family as surely as if you had been born into it. I think each man at that table would lay down his life to protect you and your child."

Alexia blushed. "They are all doting, aren't they? It was very sweet how Elliot spoke to me when I saw him again today. Although I wonder if his visit to Italy was to his liking. He seems distracted by something, as if he would not mind being alone instead of among a party tonight."

The man in question entered the drawing room. He appeared not the least bit distracted right now, but instead serious and determined.

"Alexia, please forgive me, but I would like to speak with Miss Blair alone. Would you mind if I stole her away for a short while? It is a conversation that should not wait."

Alexia's eyebrows rose a fraction. She gave Phaedra a subtle glance. *I expect to be told what this is about.*

"Certainly, I do not mind. I will go to the library."

"Please do not inconvenience yourself. The others will be up shortly. Miss Blair, perhaps a turn in the garden would suit you. We can chat while we enjoy the fragrance of the late blooms."

Phaedra ignored how interesting Alexia found *that*. She accepted the invitation, wondering what topic required Elliot's extraordinary demand for privacy.

CHAPTER
TWENTY-ONE

The garden was intimate and as redolent of summer blooms as Elliot promised.

"Did your brothers order you to sally forth to battle me again, Elliot?"

"They were as astonished by my departure from the dining room as you were by my request." He led her over to an iron bench and bade her sit. He remained standing, however. "Although if I had walked out on them in anger I would have been justified. Christian was telling Hayden about the memoirs. I daresay they will discuss that matter a long while."

"Discuss me, you mean." She wondered if she would regret his demand for this privacy. If Lord Hayden were of the same mind as Easterbrook, she might have just forgone the last few minutes ever to be had with Alexia.

She could not see Elliot's expression in the dark, but she sensed his mind working. Calculating. Deciding.

"Phaedra, there has been an untoward development about our untoward development."

It took a moment for her to realize that he referred to the wedding in Positano. "Not too untoward, I trust."

"Remarkably untoward." He set his foot on the bench beside her and leaned over his knee so his face and voice were closer. "This morning my solicitor told me that the marriage is most likely valid and will be upheld as such in any challenge."

All thought and feeling disappeared while she absorbed the shock. Then a variety of emotions burst in her heart. They shouted and clashed. They created chaos with their unruliness. Her mind, however, achieved an astonishing clarity.

"No wonder you were looking at me so oddly during dinner. It is a miracle that you did not take to drink at this news."

He did not respond to that, which was gallant of him. She also understood why he wanted to speak out here in the dark. She doubted he could hide his dismay any more than she could.

"I do not see how I can be married when I did not choose to marry, when I did not sign a contract, and when it was a Catholic ceremony," she said.

"I spent the afternoon with a proctor who has argued similar cases and he explained it. A marriage that is legal in the country where it happens is binding here. That is well supported by the ecclesiastical courts. Nor must it be a priest of the English church that solemnizes the vows in such cases. He believes no challenge will stand, but he suggested that for certainty the ceremony be repeated here."

"Why would I repeat vows that I never thought I made?"

He turned his head and looked at the house. He gazed up at the windows overlooking the garden. He offered his hand. "Walk with me, Phaedra. I will tell you exactly what was told to me."

He tucked her arm under his and spoke quietly while they strolled up and down the garden path. Her heart pounded harder with each step and each word.

"That marriage does not fit into the neat categories of the law. Therefore its validity becomes a matter of interpretation in the courts. There are no secure predictions of how a judgment in our case will go," he said. "When the proctor suggested the vows be repeated, he was thinking of a challenge later, due to questions of inheritance or the legitimacy of children. That is what my solicitor meant when he spoke of it surviving a challenge as well. Both of them were so confident that the marriage would be judged valid that they only recommended another ceremony to avoid someone creating a scandal by trying to exploit the ambiguities later."

"The lawyers viewed all of it backward, Elliot, and their advice is flawed as a result. We do not want assurances it will stand. We want to make sure it does not."

"There is a presumption of validity in the court. If we claim it was not valid then we would bear the burden of proof."

The panic in her blood began to enter her head. "I think someone else should have to prove that it *is valid*."

"Phaedra, I learned more about the case law in this matter today than any man needs to know. Even in England the statutes are not always applied as clearly as one would expect. Some of the judgments that were cited astonished me. Marriages deemed valid despite no proper license, for example. The fact we did not sign that license in Positano is of little account, especially since our words alone create the validity in that country, under those laws." He drew her under the canopy of a tree. "It appears that you are stuck with me, darling."

She could not believe she was hearing this. The panic grew, threatening her composure.

He moved to embrace her. She broke free of his arms. "This is not an *untoward development,* Elliot. This is a *disaster.*"

She paced away, struggling to reclaim her rational sense. Surely he had heard wrong. There had to be a way to set this aside.

"You spoke of ambiguities. I would think there are enough to void this from the start. Which ones did your lawyers see as creating problems later?"

"Phaedra—"

"No. *No.* I never married for a reason, Elliot. I made a decision after thinking hard and long on the matter. I will not find myself now married by accident rather than choice. You must tell me if there is any way at all to undo this."

He crossed his arms. It emphasized his size compared to hers, and communicated his mood, which now thickened the air.

She hated when men took that pose. *Hated* it.

"I could divorce you. That is one way to undo it. You would have to give me cause, however, and I am not inclined to allow that."

Allow it? Heaven preserve her, he was sounding like a husband already.

"Divorce means a marriage occurred and I deny that

one did." Her racing thoughts collected around her last statement. "We must explain that we were not willing. We must explain that there was no consent."

"An entire town heard us make those vows. No one saw a sword at our necks when we did so."

"The situation was as bad as a sword at our necks. Once we describe it, that will be clear to the Church. If we explain that neither of us said those words willingly, that should be enough."

He looked down at her. She searched the shadows of his face for indications of his relief.

"I was not coerced, Phaedra. I did it to protect you, that is true. But I said the words fully accepting that they might bind me. I will not lie about that."

His calm acceptance of this marriage shocked her. "You cannot want this."

"I did not seek it but I am not so distraught as you are. After what we have shared, it is a small step."

"You will be distraught soon enough. You do not need a marriage to have whatever you can share with me. You gain nothing by this except responsibility for a woman who will never accept your rights to her."

No sooner had she said it than the truth sliced through her desperation. He did gain something. Something he and his family wanted very badly.

She gazed at his dark form in the heavy night shadows. A wife lost everything in a marriage. The law gave the husband her property, her voice, her children, even her separate selfhood.

Would he do it? Would he take such a rash step to get control of the press and the memoirs? She thought the gain very small compared to the cost.

He strode to her and pulled her into his arms. He kissed her hard, as if passion could obliterate the horrible suspicion that had entered her mind.

"It is not that," he said hoarsely. "If I did not take that manuscript when I left your bed last week, I would not sell myself for it now."

His kiss confused her more. She could not sort her thoughts because they came so fast and scattered. "Then why?"

"Because of this." He kissed her again, long and deep.

"You already have that," she whispered.

"I will not have it any longer if you petition the court to invalidate this marriage."

"If I choose to give it, you will. It is my decision—"

"It is no longer. If you claim your words were coerced, we cannot continue as we were. We cannot say such vows, share a bed, and then claim we are not married. The past alone may cause the marriage to be held valid if it becomes known. We were not discreet in Italy. To continue an affair here, to have any private contact, would ensure the judges dismiss your petition."

His tone, so clear and firm, so lacking true sympathy, sounded cruel. He described a terrible choice.

Helplessness and anger poured out of her heart. She barely contained what it did to her. She should not have to give him up for such a stupid reason.

She saw the choice too clearly, and it sickened her. To relinquish their friendship, to never feel his touch, to retreat from all intimacy—or to accept the legal shackles the law forged for women, and to submit in every way to the rule of another person.

She could name the ways. She had heard them enu-
merated by her mother for eighteen years.

"It need not go that way," she cried, violently rejecting both stark alternatives. "No one really knows what
happened in Italy. No one was actually with us. If we are
discreet here, no one will know either."

He grasped her upper arms in his two hands, as if he
sought to control a madwoman. "We will be under oath.
I will not lie. Nor will you."

"You cannot want this. You *cannot*. Think, Elliot.
The world will mock you if we are man and wife. I will
not be other than I am, not for you or your family.
Everyone will laugh and say you have the most odd
wife, with strange ideas and eccentric habits. They
will—"

"They will say I married a woman who is almost as
odd as my brother. Nor do I care what is said."

Her eyes burned. She covered them with her hands
and pressed hard, trying to hold the tears back. Her
heart weighed thick and heavy.

He released her arms and embraced her again. That
only made it worse. The warmth, the memories, moved
her so deeply that she lost the battle with her emotion
and wept. She experienced the grief that was waiting,
the loss if they parted, the nostalgia that would tear at
her heart.

She wanted desperately for that pain to convince her
to accept the alternative. She urged her emotion to say
marriage to this man would be good, not a prison.

He held her while the worst of it poured out, wrapping her closely with his arms. The warmth of his
mouth pressed her crown.

Her heart twisted and tightened and shattered. She would miss this most of all. This and the knowing that went deeper than any friendship.

His aura changed. It was as if the Rothwell sternness lost its grip. The night breeze bore it away.

She pressed her damp eyes against his shoulder. "This is not the way that any marriage should be made, least of all one for me. I must try to undo this, Elliot."

His palm came to rest on the back of her head. The gesture of comfort almost made her weep again.

"Will you help me, Elliot? I do not expect you to lie, but will you not fight it?"

"You are asking me to give you up completely, Phaedra. I do not know if I can."

"Not completely. Afterward we can be friends again. I do not want to think that we will forever be parted over this, Elliot."

"It will be a long while before I can touch you again, darling. The courts work slowly." He turned her head and kissed her cheek. "You are asking more than you will ever understand."

"You think so now, but you will see soon enough that I would never make a good wife. My character is too malformed to find contentment in that role." She attempted a smile, but it only made her mouth quiver. "I am saving you. You seek to be honorable and do the right thing, and that is good and noble of you. But once your desire has passed, you would hate this unsuitable match, and be miserable that it had been forced on you."

He touched her lips with his fingers. "This separation will be more unnatural than the marriage you describe. For many weeks I have thought of you as mine. Kiss me now, so I have one last taste of you."

Her heart rebelled at how he named this a last kiss. It screamed its anger as their mouths met. It wept with frustration while she clutched him in a frantic embrace.

He held her more firmly, as if bidding the storm to calm. Her spirit obeyed the silent command. The clouds scattered, the cool air flowed, and she was totally with him again one last time, in a place of warmth and light and freedom.

"Are you drunk?" Hayden asked the question while he closed the library door. He glanced at the decanter on the table and the glass in Elliot's hand.

"That is the last thing I need now. I did want some privacy, however."

"I will leave you to it then."

"Hell, it is your home. Your library and your spirits. I'll go."

"Stay." Hayden's smile made it a request. "I am glad you delayed your departure. It gives me the opportunity to speak with you alone about the revelations belatedly granted to me today."

Elliot remembered Hayden's face after dinner while Christian laid out the matter of the memoirs. Hayden's annoyance had not been directed at either Phaedra or Richard Drury, but at the two brothers who had neglected to confide in him earlier.

That annoyance snapped again, quietly. "Learning about those memoirs explains much. Chalgrove approached me last month, asking if Alexia had influence with Miss Blair and could she arrange a meeting. I was stupid enough to think he had developed a fascination. Now I think it more likely that he worries he is in those pages."

"I have not read it. I do not know if he is."

"Perhaps you will call on him and find out how much influence he requires."

"If I have failed to help this family, I can hardly help him."

"With one word to Miss Blair you can find out how worried he needs to be. He is an old friend who has had enough trouble of late. Do this for me and I will forget that you kept me ignorant of this intrigue."

"Christian decided you were not to know." It was a weak excuse from a man lacking strength at the moment. He possessed nothing inside him except a void in his chest that near suffocated him. His soul had been a blank since returning from the garden.

Phaedra thought she was the one making the choice out there, but he had been facing his own dark reckoning. He had not been the least shocked to learn of their situation today. Those lawyers had mapped out a path to ensure that his possession of the woman he wanted was complete and permanent.

If she had given the slightest indication that she welcomed this development, he would have pressed his advantage. His inclinations were not to help her set the vows aside. He wanted her bound to him forever so he would never wonder if a new friend might steal her away.

He had told himself all day that she would get used to it. Her opposition was philosophical and there was no practicality in her beliefs. Pleasure and luxury and kindness would soften her view quickly. He would not demand any changes at first and very few later.

A memory had plagued him, however. It still did, and the brandy was not helping. Not a memory of Phaedra. Not even one of his mother. He saw his father at the door of the library at Aylesbury, gazing in at the woman whose head was bent over her pen. His face had been as stern as ever and his posture uncompromising. He did not notice the boy on the floor by the bookshelves, so total was his attention on his wife.

Elliot understood that memory now, in ways he never had as a boy. The last Lord Easterbrook had been looking at his wife with the eyes of a man in love. Hopelessly in love. Tragically so.

He looked at his brother. Hayden expected him to hold a conversation about something else, when all that mattered was that kiss in the garden.

"Christian knew I would not countenance his methods," Hayden said. "Nor do I understand why he cares so much. Everyone knows father was no saint. If they want to wonder if he killed a man, let them."

Elliot had to smile at that. "It is said you are the most like him. Perhaps that has allowed you to reconcile yourself to what he was or might have been."

"Is that what people say? How interesting. I would have said it was you or Christian. You see, I would never do to Alexia what he did to our mother. Nor would I take vengeance on a rival after he was defeated."

"And you think that I might?"

"I do not know. I only am sure I would not."

Elliot was not nearly so sure that *he* would not. He

had been well schooled in desire recently, and the lessons had not all been good ones. The eyes he kept seeing in that memory made him uneasy because they looked too damned much like his own when he gazed in a looking glass these days.

Perhaps Phaedra sensed that. Maybe during one of those intrusions she had seen it in him, or maybe she feared it might be a legacy he had inherited.

"We do not know that he took vengeance," he said. He did not want to believe the Rothwell ruthlessness could go that far.

"It does not matter if he did or not. That two of his sons fear he did signifies more than the act itself, doesn't it?"

It was not the soldier in the Cape Colony who had been on Elliot's mind. "Mother was not blameless."

Hayden pondered that observation. "Even not knowing if he did it, you seek to justify it? No, she was not blameless. She was an adulteress. Worse, it was not a frivolous affair but one of the heart. He would not let her go, but he did not have to isolate her. The marriage was prison enough for her. He did not have to make a real one for her down at Aylesbury."

"He did not force her to stay there. He told me he did not."

"He may not have given any orders, but he made their marriage impossible to endure. He would not forgive her even if she wanted forgiveness. Maybe she chose to remain there. Sanctuary or prison, she was not with him at least."

"You seem to understand it better than anyone."

"Better than I want. It is a lesson in the dangers of

pride, I suppose. A cautionary tale in the way that it can transform a man's character, for ill as well as good."

Elliot did not think it had been pride that caused their father's harsh treatment of their mother. It had been an emotion much more basic than that.

Hayden eyed the amber drops at the bottom of his glass. "Elliot, I did not come upon you here by accident. Alexia is concerned. She commented on how red Miss Blair's mouth and eyes were when the two of you returned to the drawing room. I confess I did not notice." He poured more brandy for himself and settled into a chair. "She thinks that mouth had been soundly kissed."

Very soundly. They had kissed for what seemed an eternity. It still ended too soon. "No doubt she is shocked."

"Alexia accepts the restraints of propriety, but very little shocks her. Least of all when it involves Phaedra Blair. It was the red eyes that caused her concern and had her send me down to wheedle information out of you."

Elliot debated how much he was willing to have wheedled.

"I assume that you did not importune her in the garden," Hayden said.

"It is unlikely any man has importuned Phaedra Blair and lived to see the dawn."

Hayden chuckled. The sound made Elliot laugh too. His mood improved even if his chest still felt full and empty at the same time.

"Hell. I have created a disaster, Hayden. If Christian suddenly cares about tongues wagging he will have apoplexy when he learns about the diversion that I am about to give society."

"I assume that Miss Blair has a leading role?"

"And I have the other. Pour me more brandy and I will tell you the plot so that you can appreciate the moral lesson in the denouement. It is a tale of desire and passion, of seduction and fantasy and danger, of marriage and—"

"Marriage?"

"Oh, yes. Of marriage and repudiation and —"

Hayden was busy pouring and did not notice how the unfinished sentence hung in the air. The final words spoke in Elliot's head, however. The fullness in his chest got emptier.

Of marriage and repudiation and love.

CHAPTER
TWENTY-TWO

Phaedra set down her pencil and rubbed her eyes. Her father's manuscript needed more preparation than she expected. His penmanship had gotten worse toward the end, so bad that it was unlikely the typesetters would recognize the letters. She judged she had at least another week of work ahead of her.

She looked around the reading room of the British Museum. Other heads and backs bent over tomes at other tables. Most were men but a few were women. Her attention lit on the former, one by one.

Elliot was not here. Looking for him had become a habit. They could not meet privately but a public encounter held no danger. Should he work here while she did . . .

There need be no acknowledgment. No greeting or conversation. She would just like to see him again. She could take pleasure merely in having him in this chamber even if he sat far away and never turned his head.

She closed her eyes and saw him in her mind. She tasted that last kiss and inhaled his scent. His hand caressed down her body. She savored the memories, experiencing them by the moment.

How long would it be before they faded? She feared that they would, and with them the emotions that stirred her soul. She called up the memories too often because she worried they had begun to slip away.

"Phaedra, are you sleeping?"

She opened her eyes, startled. A smart, fashionable hat tilted over the table. A woman peered at her curiously, and had spoken in a whisper.

"Alexia, what are you doing here?"

"I was told that you spend your days here." She glanced around the chamber. Their whispers carried and others sent frowns their way.

"Let us go outside. I need to take some air," Phaedra said.

Alexia waited while she tied the manuscript. She carried it to the librarian, who set it away on a shelf.

They escaped the reading room and Montague House. "We can take a turn in Bedford Square," Phaedra suggested.

"So that is the infamous manuscript," Alexia said while they strolled toward the square.

Phaedra's heart sank. "They told you about it."

"There is little that Hayden and I do not share. Do not look so distressed, dear friend. I have not come to plead for your mercy. Easterbrook wants me to but I choose not to hear his insinuations about it."

"You were my first thought, Alexia. When I read it, I did not care so much about your husband and his brothers, but you—"

"That is sweet and I am grateful. However, I understand the loyalty one owes to family. If your father charged you with a duty you cannot pick and choose what part of that promise you will fulfill."

Phaedra's composure had remained unsteady since the dinner party. Now Alexia's generosity made it wobble again. Alexia glanced over and gave a reassuring smile.

"Who told you that I work on the manuscript in Montague House?"

Another glance. Another smile. A sympathetic one. "Not him. Viscount Suttonly has returned to London and Aunt Hen foolishly followed him with Caroline in tow. Hayden is furious, and laid down very strict rules. He charged Easterbrook with enforcing them."

"I cannot picture the marquess lecturing a girl on her virtue."

"He has not said a word on the subject, according to a very distraught Aunt Hen. Instead, every day he cleans his dueling pistols in the library, in full view of Caroline."

Phaedra laughed at the image of that. "I can see how Henrietta would be distraught. Marrying her daughter to a title is within reach, after all."

"I do not mind her return, actually. It allows me to stay in town as well. And she is a magnet for the best gossip. She told me you would be here, for example."

"Lord Elliot recommended I keep the manuscript with the museum's librarians. He was wiser than I. I am sure that someone was in my house last night, no doubt looking for it." She had heard nothing while she slept, but in the morning when she entered her sitting room it had seemed wrong somehow. Slightly altered, with the

venetian shawls tumbled differently and the book-
shelves too neat.

"It was not one of us," Alexia said. "There would
have been no reason for it. Easterbrook and Hayden
know where you leave those pages."

They took a turn around the Bedford Square's little
park. The homes surrounding it appeared modest but
comfortable. All of a type, they were the sort of homes
that successful writers, barristers, and foreign diplomats inhabited. Their neat facades lined up in uniform
design, the roofs not overly high. The houses fit the
small proportions of the square very nicely.

"Elliot intends to leave London soon." Alexia might
have been answering a query. Perhaps she had heard the
one playing on the tip of Phaedra's tongue.

They walked on another ten paces. "How much do
you know, Alexia?"

"Almost more than I want. I do not agree with your
philosophy, Phaedra. I have never pretended that I do.
Now I fear that we are about to see the wreckage that it
can cause. However, you never tried to convert me, and
I will not attempt to convert you." She aimed them into
the park. She took a seat on a stone bench. "Elliot had a
row with Easterbrook yesterday."

"A big row?"

"In Aunt Hen's words, *a royal row.*"

Phaedra sat beside her. "Did Henrietta hear the
row?"

"Henrietta would not miss overhearing a row for all
the world. I have convinced her that she misheard this
time, however. You see, she says this row was about a
marriage."

"No doubt she misunderstood." Phaedra studied a tendril of ivy snaking near her shoe.

"She said this argument was about the rights of a husband and the need for husbands to exercise those rights. In short, Easterbrook was telling Elliot that if anything resembling a marriage existed between him and you, that he should seize that publishing house that you inherited."

"If Elliot did not agree, that was very noble of him."

"What an odd response, Phaedra. I expected you to laugh at the very notion that there was something re- sembling a marriage between you and Elliot." She cocked her head quizzically. "Just how bad will this wreckage be?"

Phaedra wished Alexia would not use that word "wreckage." Although perhaps it was an apt one. The situation may have destroyed something valuable and might still cause more grief.

She told her friend the truth. Alexia's expression re- flected increased amazement.

"I agree those vows should not be valid," she said. "Hayden did not share everything after all. However, your story explains this little note."

She set her reticule on her lap, opened it, and plucked out a folded piece of paper. "He asked me to give this to you. I could not imagine why, since I noticed that they are all lawyers."

Phaedra read the three names penned on the paper. She recognized one. He had represented a countess seeking a separation from her husband. All the particu- lars had been in the newspapers. She guessed the details about her action would be published as well.

"I will not be able to afford men such as this."

"Hayden gave me that note and said to tell you he would settle with them. Now that I understand the circumstances, I am certain that he meant that he would pay the fees."

So Elliot's own brother would pay the expense of this petition. His other brother might want him to exercise his husbandly rights while they remained ambiguous, but Easterbrook would be glad to have the family rid of her as well in the end.

Perhaps Elliot had concluded the same thing. In the least Hayden's help probably also meant that Elliot would not contest her claims.

The twist of disappointment in her heart was a silly reaction. Hearts did not think clearly and make decisions. They indulged sentiment and did not anticipate the future. The wistful regret would not go away easily, but that did not mean she should let the traitorous emotion rule her.

She tucked the paper in her pocket and turned the conversation to topics that distracted her from thoughts of Elliot.

Mr. Pettigrew kept tapping his fingertips against his multiple chins. The habit had ceased impressing Phaedra as a thoughtful one. She was beginning to think the man daydreamed away the time.

"What say you, sir? Will my petition receive a fair hearing?"

Even her question took a fair time to penetrate.

Finally the thick fingers left the soft chin. His cocked, gray head straightened.

"This is a very interesting case, Miss Blair. Most interesting. I am fascinated by the potential ramifications and implications that a judgment in this will have."

"I am delighted to provide you with mental stimulation. However, I am seeking some reassurance that I am correct in my view of the matter."

His attention sharpened on her. Mr. Pettigrew was a short, stout man whose cravat appeared to strangle him. His blue eyes could turn most piercing when he let them. "If you set down this road, the journey will be lengthy. As for evidence, it would be best to procure sworn letters from others who were there and that alone will take months. Will the witnesses to that marriage ceremony say you were coerced?"

"The woman will. I also think the priest was aware that there was no true consent. I do not think he was comfortable conducting the ceremony."

"See, there is the trouble. Right there in your words. *True consent.* It all hinges on that. You gave consent, but it was, you say, not true consent. The court will not be friendly to such a claim. How many others would then say there was no *true consent*? And yet you tell a story that possibly supports the notion. Fascinating."

"Is it fascinating enough for you to represent me?" Pettigrew was not the first name on the list. She had already been refused by the other two.

He peered at her critically. "Are you certain that Lord Elliot will tell the same story as you? It will be essential that he not contest this. If he does, no court will set it aside. He is the son of a lord, after all."

"He has done nothing to enforce those vows. We do not live as man and wife. He has made no move to take my property."

"Ah, well, if he has left the property alone . . . Here is how this will unfold, Miss Blair. The court will be suspicious that this is an attempt to undo a marriage made in haste while abroad. Such impulsive marriages are not unheard of when our citizens are stimulated by contact with warmer climes and their more passionate people. Good sense often returns too late."

"You are not describing what transpired with us. The vows were spoken merely so I would not be subject to accusations of crimes I did not commit. It was a desperate bid to save me, that was all."

He accepted that without comment, but she detected a bit of skepticism slither over his bland expression.

"Then there is that matter of the night in the tower," he said. "You and Lord Elliot will be asked if there was sexual congress there. If there was, your entire case will be undermined." He paused and pursed his lips. "If such activity continued after you left Positano, wellll . . . And if there is any issue from the liaison, it will be hopeless."

She braced herself for the rejection that was coming. These were not the only three lawyers available. She would have to find other, less fastidious ones. Eventually one would see the rightness of her position.

"I think that you do not find my petition worth your while, sir."

"I am merely explaining the difficulties to you." His round face creased into a smile. His hand cut the air in a long, sweeping arc. The gesture encompassed his view of her. "Normally this would be futile. However, you are not normal, are you?"

"Excuse me?"

"Miss Blair, your antipathy to marriage is well known. Your mother's life is the stuff of legends and your own eccentricity and probable lack of fidelity is not something a lord's son would tie himself to willingly. If any other woman claimed she did not give her consent to marry Lord Elliot Rothwell, the court would make sport of her. You, however—" Again that hand moved. "Your behavior and beliefs will support your claim. The court will be inclined to free Lord Elliot of any obligations to you. Yes, I will take it on, and see that you have the best proctor argue your case. I expect he and I will dine off the notoriety of this petition for years."

The promise of notoriety did nothing to improve Phaedra's spirits. She left Pettigrew's chambers in the same sad daze with which she had entered. Since the day was fair she made her way to the British Museum on foot.

She tucked her hand into her pocket and rested it on the letter hidden there. Elliot had written two days ago, expressing concern about her safety in her house. Alexia had told him about the intruder that night.

The letter's tone was formal, almost distant. Did she fantasize that with those cool expressions of caution and care that he really was saying something else? *Give it up and come to me and you will never be in danger.*

Nothing of the kind had been written. No words of passion, no allusions to what they had shared. He could have been writing to an acquaintance not seen for five years.

Perhaps he did not want to risk a letter that gave lie to her claims about that marriage. Then again, maybe he already had begun to see her differently.

She could not blame him for that if it was true. She had chosen freedom over him, after all. He had convinced himself to accept the validity of those vows and no doubt had been insulted by her refusal to do the same. She did not think he would ever understand why she could not.

She was beginning to lose hold of why herself.

Just touching the letter gave her comfort. She had never felt alone in her life before, but she did now. She had never questioned that life in its essence either, but late at night, sick-hearted and lonely, she now did. She could not accommodate the misery this separation caused her. The pain just sat there in her soul, never easing.

She entered the reading room and retrieved the manuscript. She had come to hate this daily chore. She carried the pages like the weight they were. She dropped them on the table and glared at them.

The air behind her subtly moved. A presence intruded nearby. Her heart flipped. She closed her eyes and savored the joy that spread through her like rays of the sun breaking through dark clouds.

She turned to see Elliot depositing a bound volume and a folio of papers on the table in front of hers. He favored her with a smile, but it was the kind one gave an acquaintance, not a person one had slept beside.

"Miss Blair, what a pleasure to have this chance meeting. I did not know that you still labored here."

"I am almost finished with it all, Lord Elliot."

His gaze lit briefly on the manuscript that had brought them together. Then he gestured to his table. "I too am almost finished. I will not block the window's light if I sit here, will I? There are other tables if I will be intruding in any way."

"The sun is bright today. What light there is can be shared."

He said nothing more. He took his chair, opened his tome and his papers, and retreated into his mental exercises.

She sat with the manuscript in front of her. She kept her eyes on it and pretended to read. In truth she did not see her father's jottings at all even though Elliot did not block the light in the least.

She just felt him there, so close. She basked in his presence and the way it soothed her. She savored how her heart swelled with emotion. She marveled at how close to tears she was.

She had fallen in love with him. That was what all these emotions meant. The joy, the pain, the peace, and the confusion—they were the reactions of a woman who had lost her heart.

She did not know why that truth came to her now, here, during this hour of distant intimacy. She thought she had been in love before, but those brief excitements had been nothing like this. She had misunderstood so many things about herself, and about the bonds that she had formed in this most special of friendships.

She did not know how long she remained like that,

feeling his presence and marveling at the contentment it brought her heart. His rising from his chair jolted her out of her sweet daze. He walked to the shelves, removed another book, and walked back.

She had to watch him. She could not release him from her gaze. He appeared so handsome in his elegant dark coats and crisp cravat and collar. If his eyes still reflected his intellectual absorption and his hair appeared mussed, that made him all the more appealing. It was not only the body that made the man.

He noticed her attention and his own emerged from his thoughts. His progress through the reading room seemed to slow. He came forward with eyes locked on her own. Desire burned in his gaze, quietly and subtly, hidden to everyone but her.

She responded as she always had. Like she always would. She imagined being old and gray and chancing upon him in town one day after being apart for decades. If he looked at her like this then, she would be reminded in a blink how much she had always wanted him.

He did not sit this time. He came to her table, one scholar calmly curious about another's work. He stood a bit behind her and hovered over her shoulder. She felt him there so clearly, so warmly. She gritted her teeth to control the impulse to turn her head and kiss his chest.

"There are only a few pages left," he said.

"I may need to go through it all again. It could be some time before it is in fit form for the press." She looked up at him. "I expect that you will need to come here often now too, to verify the details of your book."

"Normally there is quite a lot of that at the end."

"Then we might find ourselves sharing the sunlight again, Lord Elliot."

"That is doubtful. I will be leaving London tomorrow for a week at least. You should be well done by the time I return."

His eyes remained warm. Knowing. She saw his affection even if no one else would. She also saw those glints of steel.

"Do not delay long at your task, Miss Blair. You have chosen your course in this and other things, and I am not interfering. However, it would be unwise for you to trust me to forever be convinced of such noble inclinations. I confess the scales in my conscience have been tipping of late."

His warning flustered her badly.

"I am expecting a final request regarding the content of this work," she said.

"Any requests will come in the next week if they come at all. After that make your decision. Either go forward or do not. But do not dally on the matter or I will question your resolve on this and other things. I am too aware, and too often reminded, that one word from me will settle everything regarding you very neatly in ways I would prefer."

He walked to his table, put down the book, and collected his papers. "It has been a pleasure enjoying your company today. Too great a pleasure. I have accomplished nothing for the last hour and a half except imagining you naked on this table, begging me to take you."

He glanced around the book-filled chamber, at the spectacled readers and sober-faced librarians. "Damn it,

Phaedra. I will never see this library quite the same again."

Elliot had intended to travel to Suffolk to visit Chalgrove as Hayden had requested, but he had put it off for a variety of reasons. As he rolled through the countryside in his carriage, he admitted the real reason had been Phaedra.

Seeking her out in the reading room had been a weak capitulation to the melancholy that plagued him. He had sworn he would not sit near her. He had not even planned to let her see him. Then as soon as she walked in the door he had buzzed over so he could drink in her mere presence like a sot too long sober.

Knowing he was ridiculous did not stop the urge to make a bigger fool of himself. Love was hell, that was all there was to it.

He stared out at the farms but really saw him with her in the years ahead. Visiting her in that little house. She probably would not even accept the normal sorts of gifts that a lover gave his beloved. Days would go by when he did not see her at all. No matter how long the affair lasted, no matter if they declared undying love, she would not truly be a part of his life.

The man in him rebelled at the notion. So did the besotted lover. She may have grown up learning that such a relationship was normal, but he could not reconcile his head or heart to it.

Worse, the suspicion had lodged in his mind that she could accept such a life because she truly did not want him in hers. Which raised the question of whether he had stupidly fallen in love with a woman who did not in turn love him.

They had never spoken of love. He had ignorance as his excuse, but she might have a very different reason.

The carriage aimed off the road onto a lane, and he turned his mind to the meeting ahead. This would be the more welcome of his duties while out of London, but he still did not look forward to it. He could not influence Phaedra where the memoirs were concerned, least of all for the Earl of Chalgrove.

Chalgrove's estate showed the evidence of a lord in residence. The fields appeared productive. The manor house looked well kept. Hayden said that his friend's finances were not in order, however. Inherited debts and losses during the recent bank crisis had Chalgrove placing his boots very carefully while he walked a precarious financial line.

He received Elliot in his study. It was a well appointed chamber. If some rare volumes had disappeared and a few walls had lost some paintings, no one would guess it.

Chalgrove was a big man with an athletic build. As a man-about-town in his younger years he was known as a Corinthian. He rarely came to town anymore, and had been notably absent through most of the last season.

They sat in the study, spirits in hand. Chalgrove's deep-set gray eyes barely reflected his concerns, but his presence bore the sobriety of a man with more responsibility than he desired.

"Your brother wrote to me. It was good of you to come," he said.

"I do not know if I can be of any help. I have not read the manuscript."

"The publisher has, however. That woman, Miss Blair." He rested his boots on a stool and relaxed with his drink. The boots showed bits of dried mud, as if the earl had been out in those fields today. "I was approached by Merris Langton prior to his death. Richard Drury, it seems, included my name in those memoirs incorrectly."

Elliot guessed that everyone named and not praised would insist Richard Drury made a mistake. "Was it a personal matter?"

"Political. Drury greatly exaggerated my relationships with certain radical factions while I was younger. It is nothing illegal or seditious even in his telling, and I was little more than a boy, but it would be embarrassing. I prefer the error not be indelibly put into print. You understand, I am sure."

"I regret that it is unlikely that I can help you. Miss Blair promised her father to publish it as it stands. You are in a long line of people who want changes and she is not entertaining the requests."

"Damnation." Chalgrove's dark eyebrows lowered over an angry glare. "The man just did it as revenge. That is all posthumously published memoirs are, usually. A chance to settle scores from the grave and suffer no ill effects from the effort."

"I have never heard your name linked to his. Did you even know him well enough to create a score to be settled?"

Chalgrove scowled over his glass while he drank a

good deal of the spirits. He set the empty glass on the floor and gave his guest a long, hard look.

"I barely knew him, but we had one conversation that did not go well. It was about eight years ago. I was young and in love and despite my expectations and birth the lady's family would not have me. No doubt her father comprehended the limitations of those expectations in ways I had not yet discovered."

He gestured to the chamber, the house, and all beyond it. His weary exasperation spoke to the financial burdens better than any verbal explanation.

"I had found myself included in Artemis Blair's circle on occasion. So I knew Drury, of course. At a dinner party one night he favored me with a lecture about my disappointment."

"Foolish of him. A man disappointed would not appreciate that."

"*This* man did not, I assure you. He treated me to a long, boring explanation of how I was better off, how marriage ruined love, how much preferable it was to love freely, etc."

"It was the philosophy that he lived."

"To hell with his philosophy. I became angry at how he pontificated on his superior and enlightened views. So I told him he was a poor example of what he preached since Artemis Blair had taken another lover." He vaguely grimaced, and shrugged. "As I said, I was very young."

"He would not have liked that thrown in his face, but you were not the only one who knew. I do not think it created the score—"

"*He* did not know yet. I was the one who made him

aware of it. I am certain of this. He was shocked. Angry. I thought he would call me out for suggesting such a thing. Soon after, however, it was clear how he stepped out of her life. Once his eyes were opened he had no trouble determining who the man was, I suppose. Or perhaps he just asked her."

"Did you know who it was?"

"I believe so. I had some dealings with the man, I think. He was a scoundrel. A thief. He was selling antiquities that were frauds. He liked to approach green young men like me with them."

Chalgrove's expression remained placid. If his eyes reflected any anger it remained inwardly directed. Elliot considered letting the topic die, but it sounded as if he and Phaedra had been too generous in interpreting Thornton's activities.

"You speak as if you bought some of these frauds."

"I have no proof that he knew they were frauds, although I think he did. In either case I will not slander him through gossip. I chose not to lay down information years ago, and to do so now—"

"Of course. Actually, I believe I know who it was. I merely sought confirmation."

Chalgrove thought it over. He stood. "Come with me. I will show you something."

He led the way out of the study, toward the front of the house. "I fancied myself a collector even while at university. Roman coins to start. A few fragments of the past later. It was that which attracted me to Miss Blair's circle, and led to my brief inclusion. So when offered a great prize privately, from someone who should know about such things and who had Miss Blair's friendship, I felt secure in paying a good deal of money."

He turned into a ballroom. Their boots echoed in the huge chamber. Covers shrouded the furniture and dust coated the wall sconces. The room had not been used in years.

"When my father became ill, he finally confided the estate's problems to me. I had been living like there was no end to the money, only to learn the end was in sight. So I began to sell the collection. It was then that I learned that the great prize was a fake."

"You are sure?"

"No fewer than four experts have told me. I kept looking for one who would disagree, to no avail."

"Did you confront the man?"

They moved into the gallery that ran along the side of the house. Chalgroves from centuries past peered down from their ornate frames. "I did. He insisted my experts were wrong. So I went to Miss Blair with my evidence. I do not believe she was complicit, but she did not accept outright that I was correct. Her reaction, her expression itself . . . She showed dismay, but remained protective of him. That is why I think he was the new lover."

Chalgrove stopped in front of a glass case. He pointed to the middle shelf. "There it is. Impressive, no? I tell myself that I was not too much a fool, but I keep it here to remind me that I was enough of one. I have been reassured that it is a very good fake, identifiable mostly because the casting used a more modern method that only a few archaeologists would recognize."

"Yes, it is very impressive."

"Found in the sea off Italy, he said. Hell, he knew just how to pluck at my vanity."

They stood side by side in front of the glass case. Chalgrove smiled ruefully at the evidence of his youthful mistake. A new void opened in Elliot's chest.

"I suggest that you talk to Miss Blair yourself, Chalgrove. Go up to town and ask Hayden's wife to arrange a meeting for you. Tell Miss Blair the story that you have just told me. I have cause to think she is most interested in the man who sold you this prize, and she may hear your request about those memoirs with an open mind."

"I would not want to name him, Rothwell. Not after all these years, not even in privacy to her."

"You will not have to. Just bring that with you."

He pointed to the case, and to the little bronze statue of a nude goddess that was just like the one he had recently seen in Matthias's study in Positano.

CHAPTER
TWENTY-THREE

Phaedra crossed her hands on her lap to hide the ink stains on her right glove. She had been to the printer today to discuss the production of her father's book. A careless gesture near some fresh pages had sullied her only pair of gloves that were not black.

Her hostess would not care if ink streaked her face. Alexia had never judged her by her appearance. Phaedra's impulse to appear more normal today had nothing to do with their friendship.

She was not sure why she had worn the blue dress and dug out these white kid gloves from her girlhood. Perhaps the setting of this visit had encouraged it. Alexia had written, asking her to call, and had even sent her carriage to facilitate the visit. If Alexia's husband was willing to tolerate Phaedra Blair's presence in his wife's life, it might be wise not to be too flamboyant in her lack of "normal" while in the man's house.

"I have a present for you," Alexia said after the conversation drifted into a pause.

Alexia had spent a lot of time asking Phaedra for

advice on her cousins in Oxfordshire and on Henrietta's reckless behavior regarding Caroline. Alexia had described at length some new decorating planned for the library in which they now sat. Alexia had taken her up to admire the new winter carriage ensemble recently purchased.

Alexia had filled almost two hours talking about everything except the things Phaedra desperately wanted to discuss. Unfortunately they were subjects that Phaedra did not know how to broach.

Alexia stood and retrieved a muslin-wrapped package from a corner table. She unveiled the prize and revealed a new hat.

"I thought that you could use two," she said.

Phaedra instinctively touched the one on her head. "This has been seeing an inordinate amount of wear recently. Did you make this new one too?"

"Of course. It gave me great pleasure."

Phaedra pulled off the soiled gloves so she would not ruin the hat. Alexia's designs always impressed her. They managed to appear fashionable while avoiding the worst excesses seen about town. In their restraint and perfect lines and proportions they stood out as superior.

"You are an artist, Alexia. Your husband does not mind that you still ply your needle?"

"Why would he mind?"

Phaedra could think of several reasons why. Alexia's skill at millinery was a little flag of independence waving in her husband's face. It always had been, even during Lord Hayden's peculiar courtship.

"I read your mother's pamphlet. The one on marriage," Alexia said. "It is in Easterbrook's library."

Phaedra looked up from the hat. "Why did you read it?"

"You never tried to convert me, so you never really explained your beliefs. I thought I would understand them if I read it. I thought that I would understand you better too."

"What did you think of it?"

Alexia gave that some thought. "I will admit there is a logic to her argument. The laws are bad and in need of reform, that is undeniable. But the rejection of marriage completely . . ."

Phaedra waited.

"Forgive me, Phaedra. I do not want to criticize. However, I felt it was written by a young woman who did not know much about life or marriage as it really is lived. I found it a lot like philosophers who expound on the meaning of life in ways that have nothing to do with the practical worries that occupy most lives."

Phaedra had to smile. Elliot had said something similar. "Artemis was young when she wrote that pamphlet. However, even after living more she did not forsake the essential points."

"Yes, young." Alexia repeated the word knowingly, as if that explained much if not everything. "Before you were born, certainly. Most likely before she had ever loved a man."

Alexia's calm observation stunned Phaedra. The impulse to defend her mother spiked but she respected Alexia too much to dismiss the comment as ignorant. It also poked at questions that had been plaguing her at night, when she tossed in her bed thinking about the costs of her own choices.

"Alexia, do you never question the power that you gave to Hayden when you married him? He has your future and your happiness in his hands."

Alexia found the question amusing. "And I have his future and his happiness in my hands, Phaedra."

"It is not the same. You are his possession. The law—"

"The law is about other things and other kinds of property. I am his, that is true, but he is mine too. Our love makes it so, but so do the vows we spoke. In this even the law is clear. I have lost nothing of myself in this union, dear friend. Nothing at all. I am now more than I was before I knew him, not less."

She spoke with a calm confidence that affected the mood between them. The unexpected intimacy moved Phaedra. She felt much as she had as a girl when she listened to her mother's lessons.

She took Alexia's hand in her own. "You cannot know that he will never use the power badly."

"I suppose it is possible to love and not know for certain. However, I *do* know. It is one of the few things in life of which I am completely sure." She squeezed Phaedra's hand. "Now, I must see you in my new creation. It could be that I need to make a few changes for it to be perfect."

Turning to feminine games did not end the intimacy but it did lighten the mood. Together they walked to a looking glass on the wall. Alexia removed Phaedra's hat and settled the new one on her crown.

"I thought to make a bonnet, but that would look odd if you do not dress your hair," Alexia said. She twitched at the large soft bow on the hat's crown. "The prussian blue looks even better than I hoped. It is a soft color with your complexion, don't you think?"

Phaedra gazed at her reflection. It was not an image that matched the one she had of herself. The hat made her appear paler, somehow. But also less young. She saw a woman approaching full maturity who was no longer an innocent. No longer a girl. No longer a daughter.

She stepped closer and peered harder, stripping away the memories of other reflections so she could see what was really there now, in front of her eyes.

"It is beautiful. You are beautiful."

The praise startled her out of her reverie. The reflection of the room had changed in the looking glass. Alexia no longer stood behind her. Elliot did.

He would have liked some warning. Perhaps Alexia feared he would refuse the assignation if she proposed it. Maybe she believed he and Phaedra could not claim it was accidental that way. Still, he had never expected to find Phaedra here when he responded to Alexia's note requesting that he call.

Phaedra had not even heard him enter the chamber. She had been engrossed in her reflection, studying it as if she did not know the face she viewed. Alexia had silenced his greeting with a finger to her lips, then walked away ignoring his scowl of displeasure.

Phaedra turned in surprise just as the library door quietly closed on Alexia's departure.

"Do not scold her," Elliot said. "She no doubt thinks she is helping."

"I was not thinking of scolding her." She carefully

lifted the new hat off and set it down on a chair. "I am glad to see you, Elliot. I thought you were out of town."

"I returned yesterday."

He was glad to see her too. Ridiculously glad. Elated like a boy. He did not care for the evidence that he had made no progress in conquering the hold that she had on him.

She sat on a divan. He dared not join her. He wanted her so badly his teeth were already on edge. If he got close enough to touch he would be lost. He remained standing a good fifteen feet away.

"It is convenient, this meeting," he said. "I was going to write to you. You will be approached by the Earl of Chalgrove. He wants to talk about the memoirs. I ask that you listen to him."

She did not object, but her expression reflected her impatience with all the requests she received about those memoirs.

"Your home has remained secure?" he asked.

"There have been no other intrusions. The printer now has the manuscript and he will keep it very safe for me."

"How long before—"

"A month, he says."

A little smile played at her lips. He did not think the pending publication amused her. She merely appeared happy, much as she had in the library that day while she looked at him.

She confounded him. How could a woman make him so proud and also so miserable and angry?

"I met with Pettigrew yesterday," he said, broaching the *how* without planning to.

She picked up some white gloves and fussed with them, smoothing them together into a neat pair. "It was good of you to do so."

"Yes, it was." Too much of his resentment sounded in his voice. He had left that meeting seething. "He intends to make a mockery of you, Phaedra. They will paint you as a woman that no rational man of good standing would ever want as a wife. They will use that to convince the court that the vows were not consensual, that I merely fell on my sword to save you."

She looked up from the gloves. "He will only speak one truth that the whole world already accepts, and another that you and I know to be accurate."

"You are very cool, Phaedra. Very confident in what you think is true. Damnation, but I almost told him to go to hell. I came within one breath of—"

She waited for the rest.

Of telling him we married willingly. Of claiming you as mine forever. Of lying if necessary, in order to end this separation and to avoid the life of half-measures you offer me.

"Phaedra, I want you to withdraw your petition. I will make any promises that you want to reassure you about this marriage."

"You would go to such extremes to save us all from the scandal this will create?"

"I don't give a damn about the scandal. Not for me at least. I do not want to see you endure it, however, and this will avoid that."

"I will survive it. I have always been somewhat scandalous. I think that I know the real reason, and it is shortsighted. I miss you too, Elliot. I miss the pleasure and your company. I count the days to when I can hold you again. It would be a mistake to act rashly to hasten that moment, however."

"Once again you assume you understand when you do not."

She was going to make him spell it out. Of course she was. She did not know where his head and heart had been the last weeks.

"I want this marriage to stand, Phaedra. I want us to repeat the vows so there is no mistaking its validity. I have been thinking about this and I find myself praying that your petition is denied. I do not want you married to me that way, but God help me, I find myself wanting that if it is the only way."

She rose and walked over to him. She looked like an angel in that blue dress, with her copper curls rippling down to her hips. But no angel had eyes like hers, that so frankly revealed desire.

He crossed his arms to thwart the impulse to grab her. She saw the movement for what it was and stopped far enough away.

"I am flattered, Elliot. However, it is our separation that makes you think that way. Once we are together again—"

"No, damn it. I am not speaking out of base hunger and lust. Even when I can have you again, it will not be enough. I love you, Phaedra, and being your good friend will not satisfy me. I cannot live that way."

He had not planned this ultimatum. His angry heart had spoken without consulting his brain. Now there it was suddenly, hanging like a sword between them.

"You tell me that you love me for the first time,

Elliot, then you list conditions." She appeared astonished and sad. So sad it made his heart clench.

"I was not allowed to speak of love before. I wanted things from you, remember? But that is behind us now if you have gone to press. I have wanted you more than anything else for a long time, and I must speak honestly so you understand why I cannot do it your way."

She stepped closer. Desire long denied tensed through his body, making all of him hard. "If we love each other, truly love each other, it should work any way we choose, Elliot. Is it not better to share free love, the way we have up until now?"

"We have not been sharing free love up until now, Phaedra. We have been sharing free pleasure. I miss that, but I have seen more clearly in its absence. It is not enough anymore. Nor is mere friendship. Not for me at least."

She reached out and gently touched his face. Her fingers felt like cool velvet, but they still seared his skin.

He clutched her hand and kissed her palm. He closed his eyes while he tried to control what she did to him. He had been living in hell since that dinner party. Now he endured its worst torture in touching her again. That, more than anything else, told him that he was right. He could not do it her way.

His hold on his sense frayed rapidly. He wanted to settle this argument the way they always had, by claiming her body and trying to brand his name on her soul.

He looked in her eyes. "I speak of love, but you do not, Phaedra. Perhaps I was wrong and you do not feel it. Maybe you fear it and what it does to a person, or maybe it was only desire on your part after all."

He did not want to hear that he was right. He did not need to face that truth today too. He released her and strode to the door.

"I do love you, Elliot. More than I can bear. I love you so much it pains me."

He stopped. He looked back. Emotion twisted her face and tears flooded her eyes.

"If you do, then you know that there is no such thing as free love, Phaedra. If there is truly love, one cannot remain truly free."

"One *can*. We *can*."

He shook his head. "The urge to possess is too strong and the tendency toward jealousy too human. To love with no requirements on the other, with no desire or hope of permanence, is not natural. I lost my freedom when I fell in love with you, darling. I am now bound by chains no matter what happens between us. I fear that I am enslaved for life, but I'll be damned before I submit to the constant torture of wondering if you are mine."

She looked like he had hit her. The impulse to walk back and take her in his arms, to accept whatever she offered, swept him like a tidal wave. He could probably find some simulacrum of happiness living the way she wanted.

He waited a long count for her to say something. Anything. Feeling so empty that he thought he would never breathe right again, he left the library.

Elliot was long gone before Phaedra fought through her confusion. Her shock left her trembling. She sat on the divan, dazed and disbelieving. The cold stream of reality began sliding through her, chilling her to her core.

She tried to accommodate what had just happened. In the space of a few minutes Elliot had declared his love, demanded marriage, and thrown her over.

Thrown her over.

His way or no way. That was the sum of it. Just like a man.

Her heart tried to offer her some armor. It found the breastplate of her beliefs and even dredged up the shield of anger.

It didn't work. Nothing did. The truth sliced her heart to shreds. He was gone. Totally gone. Even if she lost the petition and they found themselves actually married, he was leaving her life.

Her eyes stung so badly that she could not see. Her throat burned and tightened and she gasped for breath. A sob shook out of her, wracking her body. Then another and another, until she buried her face in her skirt.

Arms circled her shoulders and lifted them. A soft voice soothed endearments. She accepted the motherly warmth and the sisterly support, and cried out her misery into Alexia's shoulder.

CHAPTER TWENTY-FOUR

I will never forgive Hayden. Whoever expected him to
be so strict and capricious?"

Aunt Henrietta's vexation finally penetrated Elliot's
concentration. He had managed not to hear most of her
complaints. He turned the last page of his manuscript
and reluctantly gave her his attention.

She had refused to return to Aylesbury last month.
She had kept her daughter here with her as well.
Christian had cleaned those dueling pistols every
evening until Suttonly left town. Now mother and
daughter wore long faces that said there would be no
forgiveness.

"You do not need to stay here, Aunt Hen. Return to
your own home in Surrey. If he is a true suitor, he will
find you and Caroline there. Give your consent and all is
done."

"Leave this house? Easterbrook cannot manage
without me. He is indifferent to domestic matters and
his housekeeper and steward were robbing him every
day. It is my duty to be here."

With the end of the drama regarding Suttonly, Christian had reverted to his old ways. He rarely came to meals and spent his time in his own chambers. Normally Elliot would have disappeared too, leaving the house to Hen, but he dared not venture to the museum's reading room again.

If he saw Phaedra there he would abandon all sense. He would beg her to forgive him and agree to anything she wanted, no matter how miserable it made him. Then he would strip her and lay her down and lift her hips and put his mouth—

Hell.

Easterbrook's library had all the necessities. The book was as good as it was ever likely to be. It would have been done a week ago except for Aunt Hen's frequent intrusions.

"I expected Alexia to support me more," Hen fretted. "If any woman understands the importance of a good marriage, it is Alexia."

"Well, Hen, we could have Caroline try it Alexia's way. We can turn her out without a penny, make her become a governess, and hope that a man like my brother falls in love with her."

Hen could be a bit vacant and dreamy, but she was not stupid. She raised her eyebrows at the sarcasm. "What has affected your humor so badly? Of late you are beginning to sound like Easterbrook."

Many things were affecting his humor. Sleepless nights and distracting days. Hungers of the body and angers in the heart. Another meeting two days prior with Phaedra's lawyer had done nothing to improve matters.

Christian's fury that his own brother refused to seize Phaedra's publishing house while that marriage remained ambiguous had created a rift that might never be breached.

Mostly his humor turned dark because he had not seen Phaedra since that day in Alexia's library one month, two days, and twenty hours ago.

By now he should be conquering whatever hold she had on him. He was not a fool. He was not a poet either, damn it. It annoyed him that he had fallen so stupidly in love with the only woman in England who did *not* understand the benefits of a good marriage and who loathed the notion of any marriage at all.

He hoped his aunt would leave him to his stormy mood. She was the sort of woman who thought it was her duty to help one be happier. If she embarked on such efforts now he would want to strangle her.

Fortunately, a footman entered the library just as she began cajoling him to adopt a sunny outlook. The man carried a package that he placed right on top of Elliot's manuscript.

"Lord Easterbrook told me to bring this to you, sir."

A note from Christian accompanied the package. *Well done.*

As soon as Elliot touched the paper he knew what it was. His brother's two words were not those of praise but instead an expression of sardonic fury.

He peeled off the wrapping. Unbound pages faced him, awaiting a trip to a bindery. The first printed sheet held a lengthy title. *Memoirs of an M.P. during the Reigns of Kings George III and IV: Being the recollections of Richard Drury regarding events political and cultural in London and its environs, with considerable comments on persons both famous and infamous.*

He had been expecting it to be published any day now. Christian must have told the footmen to haunt the bookstores and grab the first copy off the press.

"What have you got there, Elliot? A book?"

"Yes. A rather dry political one." He picked up the stack of paper, his own manuscript along with Drury's book. "Please excuse me now. I must attend to a few things."

He left Henrietta in the library. He carried his pile to the morning room to find some privacy.

The pages were all cut. Christian had read it before sending it down. *Well done, you worthless, disloyal excuse for a son.*

Elliot turned the first page. Seeing this book angered him more than he expected. He had no right to the anger, none at all. He did not regret that he had not stopped her. He just resented profoundly that he had been forced to choose between bad actions for a good cause and good actions in a hopeless one.

He set aside the emotions evoked by this book and Phaedra's duty and his love. Those were for another time. Eventually they would be about a different life.

He began reading.

Phaedra penned some figures into the account book at the offices of Merris Langton, Publisher. She added up the results. The final sum heartened her. If things kept up like this the press might survive. The debts could be paid down enough to keep the bailiffs from the door at least.

Jenny came in, carrying another sheaf of papers. "Hatchard's is taking forty more, and Lindsell another twenty."

Phaedra took the orders. Some of these booksellers had been surprised to find themselves dealing with a woman, but the success of Richard Drury's memoirs made such sentiments insignificant. If they were also surprised to deal with Jenny, a female clerk, that had mattered even less.

"It is going very well, isn't it, Miss Blair?" Jenny said.

"Most well, Jenny. As people talk, there will be better sales in the days ahead. I think we will need to print more copies."

Jenny left and Phaedra returned to her accounts. She remembered her father lying in his bed, putting that manuscript into her hands, demanding the promise that had since caused so much trouble.

Had he known how it would be? Had he included the "considerable comments on persons famous and infamous" to ensure it would sell well, and she would be given more security? He had little else to bequeath her and that hundred a year from her uncle only went so far.

She could probably take some money for herself soon. If she chose the next book well, there could be a regular income from this business. She dipped her pen, wondering what she would buy with the first few pounds. Maybe a new divan—

A twinge below her heart caught the daydream up

short. No, not a divan. There might be other needs for the money soon.

The twinge twisted again. So did another sensation, that of a hand squeezing her heart.

She set down the pen. Now that the book was published, it was time to speak with Elliot. Today was as good a day as the next. Her heart beat heavily with both dread and excitement at the thought of doing so. It was not that she did not welcome seeing him. If anything she welcomed it too much, even if she did not expect the meeting to go very well.

She stood and steadied her courage with a deep breath. She swung her black cape around her body. She lifted a wrapped copy of her father's book, told Jenny she was leaving for the day, and set off on a long walk.

Elliot gazed out the windows of the morning room. The garden's trees were beginning to change colors and the last blooms hung their heads in response to the day's chill. A memory came to him, of velvet jewels surrounding an evening terrace near Paestum.

He glanced back at the table. Richard Drury's memoirs sat there in a neat stack of pages. It had taken him three hours to read the book.

It would cause a sensation, that was certain. Drury had an eye for the foibles of his fellow men. The observations in that book were incisive, clever, and too revealing.

He should write to Phaedra and congratulate her on the success of her publication. He should write about other things too. No, he would visit her.

A footman entered the room. "Sir, a woman has called."

Elliot gave him a tenth of his mind. "Take her to my aunt. I am not at home to visitors today."

"She was very explicit that she does not desire to visit with your aunt, but with you."

Elliot's full attention settled on the footman. "Her card?"

"No card, sir. I tried to put her off, but she was most insistent." He made a face. "She is dressed very oddly. She looks a bit like one of those reformers. Or, actually, more like a . . . a . . ."

"A witch?"

"Yes, sir. How did you know?"

He felt himself smiling. "Bring her here."

Elliot turned back to the windows, but he saw nothing in the garden now. He pictured Phaedra walking toward this room, her black habit flowing around her, her hair streaming freely.

She had come to him before he could go to her. He did not know her reasons for coming, nor did they matter. He closed his eyes and felt her presence in the house. He listened for the tap of her steps, astonished by the joy branching through him.

The footman left her inside the door of the morning room. Another person was already there.

A man stood by the window with his back to her. A man handsome enough to leave a woman speechless. A man confident enough to imply a right to an arrogance that he chose not to indulge. *Bello. Elegante.*

He turned. She saw the warmth in his smile and eyes and exhaled her relief.

"Phaedra. I am glad you are here. I was going to come to you. We might have passed on the street and not realized it."

She had not known what to expect. His welcome heartened her. His effect had not dulled one whit in the month apart. She found herself breathless.

Elliot invited her to sit at the breakfast table. He took the chair at an angle to hers.

She found her voice. She placed her package on the table. "I brought you a copy of my father's book."

"Thank you, but I have already read it." He pointed to the pages at the other end of the table.

She inhaled deeply to control her composure. And to absorb his presence and scent and reality. Seeing him here seemed too much like the dreams that had filled her head on so many nights. Only in those dreams he swept her into his arms and they tumbled into bed and—

There was a distance to him even if he was close enough to touch. His composure indicated that he had made good progress on ending whatever spell they had experienced together.

That disappointed her horribly. Her heart physically burned. But what did she expect?

He tapped the top of her package. "You have a success on your hands, Phaedra."

She wanted to press her lips to his hand. It had been a month. Forever. Her heart cried and laughed all at once.

"I noticed there was no mention of Chalgrove," he said.

"He convinced me that my father had exaggerated that part. He was the only person who so argued to my conviction."

He nodded. "You did some annotating when it came to your mother, however."

"Do you hate me for it? I know what he means to you."

"It is best if no one else is hoodwinked. I suspect those statues and cameos are still making their way to England. He probably found that ring of forgers when he visited after the war. The items he brought back sold easily, so he decided to move there and make it his life." He smiled ruefully. "I offered to become a party to his fraud myself, with that new statue he had."

"He did not accept the offer, Elliot. He did not allow you to be tainted with it." Matthias had allowed others to be tainted, however. He had misused Artemis badly, the one time she had allowed herself to fall romantically and irredeemably in love.

"Actually, I received a letter from him last week," Elliot said. "He must have written it soon after we left Positano. Among other things, he expressed an interest in having me find a home for the little goddess after all."

"I am sorry to hear that, Elliot. I had hoped he had scruples at least where you were concerned."

"Apparently not."

She pictured young Nigel Thornton longing in silence while the woman he loved was conquered by Matthias Greenwood. Thornton may have seen the cameo in Artemis's possession, but she had not received it from him.

"I might have never learned it was Matthias and not Thornton if you had not sent Chalgrove to me and ensured I would meet with him, Elliot."

His acknowledgment was a sad smile. "I wrote at once and warned Matthias that you knew. That it would all come out."

"So did I." For Elliot, she had done it. Not for Matthias.

He laughed quietly at that. "Well, he can leave Italy before your accusations in these memoirs make their way there."

"He may have company as he flees. I suspect Whitmarsh is involved. He would know that little bronze that Matthias showed us was cast wrong for an antique work. He pretended ignorance. Mr. Sansoni told me the forgeries are made in the hill towns down south. I think that was what Whitmarsh was doing on those morning hikes. Visiting the workshops. I am only sorry that Tarpetta will not need to flee too. I believe that he took bribes from Matthias to look the other way."

"If he did, Carmelita Messina will make sure all of Positano knows." Admiration showed in his eyes. "You have worked it all out, haven't you? Do you feel that you have avenged her now? Are you more content in your last memories of her?"

Was she? All of her memories of Artemis had changed in recent weeks. It was as if she had finally shed the last parts of her childhood and seen her mother more honestly.

She still revered her. She still respected her. But she

no longer felt an obligation to defend her for her errors in judgment. And like any person, Artemis had made some.

"I am more at peace about all of it, Elliot."

His hand closed over hers. "You annotated some parts, but you removed some others, darling."

She looked at that hand on hers. Darker, stronger, and so very masculine. She loved his hands. Everything about them. She especially loved the way they felt on her, with their firm but gentle holds and caresses. A woman could learn a lot about a man from his hands.

"Why did you not tell me that you were removing that passage about the Cape Colony death, Phaedra?"

"I decided very late, Elliot. The typesetters were well into the book." She described her impulsive run to the printer with her last-minute demand to make one more change. "I kept hoping you would bring me evidence that it was not true. The smallest shred would have been enough. Even with the way you left the last time I saw you, I was sure you would still try to learn the truth."

The proof had not come. Nor had he. She had been left to decide on her own, with no excuse or rationalization except the one that her heart gave her.

He gazed at her hand while he smoothed his thumb over its back. The subtle caress sent shivers up her arm. "I had no evidence to give you, Phaedra. I met the man. I sought him out even before I saw you at Alexia's house. I asked him about it. It is a hell of a thing, asking a man if your father paid him to kill someone."

"Did he deny it?"

"Of course."

"Then why not tell me, Elliot? I would have been relieved to have any reason at all to—"

"I did not believe him, Phaedra."

She did not know what to say to that. One word was all she would have needed. Just one, even if that man had lied. Elliot had decided he would not use the lie that way, however. He had been honest with her. More honest than she required.

"It might be best to decide that you do believe him, Elliot."

"I cannot lie to myself that much. Not anymore. However, I am understanding my brother Christian better. I am concluding that I do not want to know for certain. Soon I may agree with Hayden, and realize I do not even care what the truth is."

"Hayden's view is a good one. If it happened it was his sin and his choice, not his sons'."

"Blood is blood, and it stains indelibly." He shrugged aside the ambiguities, as if he did not want to contemplate them anymore. "Christian offered five thousand if you removed those pages. You should take it now. It would help stabilize your press."

Five thousand pounds. It would wipe out the debts and leave the business on sound footing. She wondered if Easterbrook had investigated just how much she needed before he had Elliot offer the bribe.

"I will not say that I am not tempted, Elliot." She was so tempted that she grimaced at what she was about to do. "I did not do it for money, however, and I will not take it."

"Then why did you do it?"

She swallowed hard. "I did it because Merriweather's

suspicions could be wrong. I did it because of Alexia's friendship." A fine burn stung her throat. "Mostly I did it because of you, Elliot. When I stood at the point of no return, it suddenly seemed a small compromise of my duty to my father."

She thought for a moment that he would kiss her. The impulse was in his eyes.

"I thank you with all my heart, Phaedra. You showed more generosity than I deserve. Your decision spared innocents the glare of scandal and my parents' names the worst whispers."

"I am content with my choice, Elliot. I made the right one, I am sure."

He looked around the morning room, at the windows and table.

He took her hand again. "Come with me. We need to talk, and the library will be more comfortable."

He sat beside her on the library sofa. Close enough to touch. She tried to compose her thoughts. They did need to talk, but now that it was time all of her rehearsed lines escaped her.

He did not look at her for a long while. He did not speak. When he again turned his face her way, however, his gaze was finally that of a lover long absent.

Immediately he stirred her in all the ways he ever had, only now the regrets and longings of a month intensified every sensation and emotion.

"It is hell to see you and not kiss you, Phaedra."

"I have not said that you can't kiss me."

His expression firmed. "As long as your petition

stands, I cannot. That has not changed. Nor have my intentions."

"Would you like me to leave, Elliot? Seeing you has brought the sun back into my life, but I do not want to anger you."

"I am not angry. I am glad that you are here, but I am more tempted than I expected to make quick work of your plans."

She wished he would lock the door and embrace her and do his worst. Instead he stood and paced away, scowling. He turned and crossed his arms.

She would have to tell him not to do that anymore.

"I have spent a month hammering away at those chains, Phaedra. To no avail. What must I say or do to convince you that we belong together?"

"Whatever you want to say, Elliot. I came here to listen. I came here to be convinced, if you still want me that way."

He strode over and pulled her up, into his arms. Finally, the embrace that she craved. At last the connection and reassurance that her heart sorely needed.

"I am no Richard Drury but I am not my father either. If you are afraid I might become like him, do not be." He spoke with determination, as if he had made a choice and now swore an oath.

"Every man has it in him, Elliot, but I do not fear that. If ever a man imprisoned me or bound me against my will, I would break free. However, you know this is not about your character. It was not *you* that I rejected."

"I know why you do not believe in marriage. I understand that. I will not expect you to be other than you are. I fell in love with Phaedra Blair and I will not want you

to change. I will not ask it and I certainly will not demand it." He glanced down at her bodice. "I do not care
if you continue to wear your black habits. You can keep
your press." He paused, then shrugged. "I will not interfere with your odd friends, so long as the men do not
want more."

She laid her palm against his face. The connection
felt so good and right. "It does not matter if they want
more. I never will. I told you that you do not need marriage for that."

He sighed audibly. Whether it was in relief at her
touch or frustration at her resistance, she did not know.

"I want this marriage, Phaedra. I need it to know you
are mine. I love you even more than I desire you. I want
you with me always. I want to return to a home where
you live. Do you never dream of such things too?"

He kissed her gently. The first kiss in too many
weeks. It went to her head like too much wine.

His words touched her heart. Not only the declarations of love, although that moved her to the point of
tears. He had been most honorable with her. He had
agreed to this petition even if he did not want it. He had
not pressed his advantage in the past because of those
vows, and she knew that he would not in the future either.

He had been fair and honest. He had made his
choices out of love. Selfless choices. So many . . .

"It is good to know that you still want the marriage
to stand, Elliot, because there is a good chance that my
petition will not be successful. There may have been another untoward development."

"Then retreat from this, love. Do not subject yourself

to it if your lawyer sees small chance of success. I promise that you will never regret—" He cocked his head and frowned. "What development?"

"My lawyer said that my petition certainly would not receive a successful judgment if there were any issue."

"There are many issues, so—" His frown deepened. Then it disappeared. "Do you mean issue from the marriage, as in children?"

She nodded.

"Is there? Will there be? Are you—"

"I am not certain yet. However, it appears that is a possibility."

"How possible?"

"More possible with every day. It has complicated many things, of course."

"And you did not tell me? Never mind. I do not care about that. Phaedra, this is one reason I said we could not do it your way. A child deserves better and sooner or later you would get with child. This complicates nothing. It simplifies everything."

His acceptance heartened her, but his judgment did not. "I did not have better and I did fine, Elliot. I am the woman I am because of how my mother educated me. Richard was still a father to me. Nor does a court's rejection mean that we must live together."

"Of course we will live together. We will find a house at once. I'll be damned if I am going to make morning calls on my own wife. You must give this up now. You surely see that you must."

Yes, she must. She saw it. She had seen it even before she recognized the signs that said she might be with child. Nor did the notion horrify her. In truth a giggle of happiness bubbled inside her when she thought of a home and a family with Elliot. A fear that she had destroyed the chance to make it a happy marriage had preyed on her.

It was not stubbornness or blind adherence to a belief that caused this last rebellion against accepting this accidental marriage. It was not even because she anticipated the world seeing her as defeated, or Elliot as entrapped.

The emotion making her heart race came from astonishment and wonder and surprise. Desire had opened her heart to love, then love had carried her further than she ever knew it was possible for a heart to go. Now she balanced on the very edge of her world.

The next step would leave her walking on nothing but the air of hope and trust and love. Here she was, Phaedra Blair, daughter of the famous Artemis, a woman who like her mother forged her own destiny, cowering like a child in front of a vast unknown.

It thrilled her. It also frightened her witless.

He sensed it. She could tell that he understood and sympathized.

"You are strong, Phaedra. Strong and proud and I love you for it. But what if our child is not strong like you? What if she feels the wounds when she is denied friends and hears the taunts that call her a bastard?" He held her head with both his hands and looked deeply into her eyes. "You overcame all that, but not every soul can. And you will be happy, Phaedra. I will make sure you are, no matter what that takes, because I love you more than I do my own pride."

She looked up at him. She had never seen so deeply

into a person's eyes as she did this man's. She had never been so certain that she saw the truth of a person's heart. *I do know. It is one of the few things in life of which I am completely sure.*

Yes, dear Alexia, my wise friend. One does know.

She touched his hand and pressed it closer to her cheek. "I agree, Elliot. It is how it should be. I am fortunate and relieved that you still welcome this. I believe that you love me enough for us to be happy. I trust you and I know that I love you enough for this friendship to last a lifetime."

For the child she would do it. For him too. Mostly, however, she would do it for herself, for the chance to love and be loved and to dwell in their bond of intimacy. She would do it so she could hold on to the one good thing of which she was certain.

Nor would she be alone out there while she walked on air. Elliot would be with her, helping her find her footing.

She did not say another word but he knew all the thoughts in her heart. His eyes said he did. So did the kiss that he gave her.

And if there was a tiny glint of triumph in his tender, warm look of joy, and a caress of possession along with the kiss, she did not mind.

He was a man, after all.

She felt her dress loosening. He laid her down on the sofa so their embrace was complete. It would be hard and fast this time. She was glad. They had been apart too long and her impatience matched his.

She held him close to her as pleasure and love carried her to their private world. She breathed his breath and groaned when he filled her. She cried out her love while their fever reached its zenith.

In the peace afterward, in a bliss so laden with quiet unity that her heart could not contain it, a word whispered.

Mine.

She did not fear the word at all. She understood that it meant sharing friendship and eternal love. It promised happiness and an end to loneliness. It heralded a new whole created by their joining together in mutual possession.

The word whispered again and again in secure contentment and with poignant gratitude.

Elliot did not speak it.

Her own heart did.

Mine.

ABOUT
THE AUTHOR

MADELINE HUNTER's first novel was published in 2000. Since then she has seen fifteen historical romances and one novella published, and her books have been translated into five languages. She is a five-time RITA finalist and won the long historical RITA in 2003. Twelve of her books have been on the *USA Today* bestseller list, and she has also had titles on the *New York Times* extended list. Madeline has a Ph.D. in art history, which she teaches at an eastern university. She currently lives in Pennsylvania with her husband and two sons. Readers can contact Madeline through her website www.madelinehunter.com.

If you loved LESSONS OF DESIRE,
read on for a sneak peek at the next
scintillating historical romance
by

Madeline Hunter

SECRETS

of

SURRENDER

Coming in June 2008

SECRETS OF SURRENDER

On sale in June 2008

CHAPTER
ONE

Miss Longworth walked beside him like a queen. Kyle admired how well she hid her humiliation. No one else saw the moistness in her eyes.

She almost broke once the doors closed behind them. Almost. One long pause in her steps, one deep inhale, and she walked on.

She refused to acknowledge him. Of course not. She was in a very vulnerable position now. They both knew she was at his mercy. The amount he had bid gave her good reason to worry.

Nine hundred and fifty pounds. How impulsively reckless. He had been an idiot. The alternative had been to allow that sordid auction to take its own course, however. Fat, pliable George would not have won, either.

Sir Maurice Fenwick had been determined to have her, and the way he examined the property for sale did not speak well of his intentions. Sir Maurice's dark excesses were infamous.

"I called for my carriage," he said. "Go up with the footman here and pack. He will carry your baggage down. Be quick about it."

Her posture straightened more, if that was possible. "I will not need to pack. Everything up there was ill-gotten, and I want no reminder of the man who gave it."

"You have more than paid for every garment and jewel. You would be a fool to leave them behind."

Her exquisite face remained calm and perfect, but the glint in her eyes dared him to make a horrible night worse.

"As you wish." He shrugged off his frock coat and placed it around her shoulders. He beckoned her to follow him.

"I am not going with you."

"Trust me, you are. Now, before Norbury thinks twice about allowing it."

She kept her gaze skewed to the side of his head. She might have been looking past an obstructing piece of furniture.

He admired her pride. Right now, however, it was ill timed and a nuisance. He wondered if she realized how perilous her position had been back there . . . and still was.

"I am sure you know that I did not agree to that spectacle, Mr. Bradwell."

"You didn't? Well, damnation. How disappointing."

"You sound amused. You have a peculiar sense of humor."

"And you have chosen a bad time and place for this conversation."

She refused to budge. "If I go with you, where will you be taking me?"

"Perhaps to a brothel, so you can earn back what I will be paying Lord Norbury. To be deprived of both the price and the prize doesn't seem fair, does it?"

Her attention abruptly shifted to his face. She tried to

make her gaze disdainful, but fear showed enough to make him regret his cruel response.

"Miss Longworth, we must leave now. You will be safe, I promise." He forced the matter by placing his arm behind her shoulders and physically moving her out of the reception hall.

He got her as far as the carriage door before she resisted. She stopped cold and stared into the dark, enclosed space. He forced himself to be patient.

Suddenly his frock coat hit him in the face. He pulled it away and saw her striding down the lane, into the night. Her pale hair and dress made her appear like a fading dream.

He should probably let her go. Except there was no place for her *to* go, especially in those flimsy slippers women wore to fancy dinners. The closest town or manor was miles away. If something happened to her—

He threw the coat into the carriage, called for the coachman to follow, and headed after her.

"Miss Longworth, I cannot allow you to go off on your own. It is dark, the way is dangerous, and it is cold." He barely raised his voice but she heard him well enough. Her head turned for a quick assessment of how close he was, then snapped left and right as she sought an escape.

"You are safe with me, I promise." He walked more quickly, but she did too. She angled toward the woods flanking the lane. "Forgive me my crude joke. Come back and get into the carriage."

She bolted, running for the woods. If she reached them he'd be searching for her for hours. The dense trees allowed little moonlight to penetrate their canopy.

He ran after her, closing fast. She ran harder when she heard his boots nearing. The scent of her fear came to him on the cold breeze.

She cried out when he caught her. She turned wild, fighting and scratching. Her fingers clawed his face.

He caught her hands, forced them behind her back, and held them there with his left hand. He imprisoned her body with his right arm and braced her against him.

She screamed in fury and indignation. The night swallowed the sounds. She squirmed and twisted like a madwoman. He held firmer.

"Stop it," he commanded. "I am not going to hurt you. I said that you are safe with me."

"You are lying! You are a rogue just like them!"

All the same she suddenly stilled. She gazed up at him. The moonlight showed her anger and anguish, but determination entered her eyes.

She pressed her body closer to his. He felt her breasts against his chest. The willing contact startled him. He reacted like any man would, instantly. His erection prodded her stomach.

Jesus.

"See. Just like them," she said. "I would be a fool to trust you."

He barely heard her. Her face was beautiful in the moonlight. Mesmerizing. A moment stretched while he forgot what had led to this crude embrace. He only noticed every place where they touched and the softness of the body he held. Thunder rolled in his head.

Her expression softened. A lovely astonishment widened her eyes. Her lips parted slightly. The fight completely left her and she became all pliant womanhood in his arms.

She stretched toward the kiss he wanted to give her, and the moonlight enhanced her perfection even more.

Suddenly it also revealed her bared teeth aiming up at his face.

He moved his head back just in time. She used the opportunity to try to break free again.

Cursing himself for being an idiot *again,* he bent down and rose with her slung over his shoulder. Her fists beat his back. She damned him to hell all the way to the carriage.

He dumped her into the carriage and settled across from her.

"Attack me again and I will turn you over my knee. I am no danger to you and I'll be damned if I will let you claw and bite me after I paid a fortune to save you from men who are."

Whether his threat subdued her or she just gave up, he could not tell. The carriage moved. She was no more than a dark form now, but he knew she watched him. He found the frock coat buried amidst his rolls of drawings and handed it to her. "Put this on so you are not cold."

She obeyed. Her fear and wariness filled the air for several silent miles.

"Nine hundred and fifty was a high amount to pay for nothing," she finally said.

"The alternative was to let a man pay a lot less for something, wasn't it?"

She seemed to shrink inside the frock coat. "Thank you." Her gratitude came on a small, trembling voice.

She was not weeping, although she had good cause to. Her pride, so admirable thirty minutes ago, now irritated him. The burning scratches on his face probably had something to do with that.

He wondered if she understood the consequences of this night. She had dodged a man's misuse, but she would not escape the ruin coming when the world learned of that party and that auction. And the world *would* learn about it, he had no doubt.

Perhaps now, in the calm after the storm, she was assessing the costs, just as he was assessing his own. Norbury had been angered by his interference. He had not liked his fun spoiled and his revenge made less complete. The Earl of Cottingford might be the benefactor, but his heir now held the purse strings and influence.

"I apologize for losing my head."

"It is understandable after your ordeal." It still impressed him, how well he had learned the lessons and syntax of polite discourse. They had become second nature, but sometimes the first nature still spoke in his head. *Damn right you should apologize.*

"I am so fortunate that you arrived. I am so glad there was one sober man there, who would be appalled at what Norbury was doing, and immune to his evil lures."

Oh, he had been appalled, but not nearly immune. He had paid a fortune, after all.

A few speculative images entered his head regarding what he would have been buying if he were not so damned decent. That embrace on the lane made the fleeting fantasy quite vivid.

He was glad for the dark so she could not see his thoughts. He could not see her face, either, which was for the best. She possessed the kind of beauty that left half a man's soul in perpetual astonishment. He did not like that kind of disadvantage.

"May I ask you some questions?" She sounded very composed again. Damnably so. The lady had been rescued, as was only her due. She would sleep contentedly tonight.

He would not. The costs of this chivalry, in money and other things, would be calculated over and over for days. Already the sum was growing in his head.

"You may ask anything you like."

"The amount of your bid was an odd one. A hundred would have been enough, I think."

"If I had bid a hundred, Sir Maurice would have bid two hundred, and by the time we were done the amount might have been much higher than I paid. Thousands, perhaps. I bid very high to shock the others into silence."

"If he would have bid thousands, why would he not bid one thousand?"

"It is one thing to jump from one hundred to two, then to four, and then on up. It is another to jump from seventy-five to a thousand. It would have had to be a thousand, of course. Nine hundred seventy-five would sound small and mean."

"Yes, I see what you mean. Bidding a thousand so soon or right away would give anyone pause. It is such an undeniably foolish amount."

So was nine hundred and fifty, especially if you barely had it. A year ago he could have covered it easily enough, although few men would not notice the depletion of their purses. A year hence he probably could too. Right now, however, paying Norbury would make somewhat shaky finances wobble all the more.

He hated that feeling of insecurity. He hated the caution and worry it bred. Miss Longworth had chosen a bad time to need rescuing. It had been the only thing to do, however. He wanted to believe he would have done the same for any woman.

Of course, she was not just any woman. She was Roselyn Longworth. She had been vulnerable to Norbury's seduction because she had been impoverished by her brother's criminal acts. He did not miss the irony that Timothy Longworth had, in a manner of speaking, just managed to take yet more money from Kyle Bradwell's pocket.

"You are aware, I think, that I will never be able to pay you back nine hundred and fifty pounds. Do you hope that I will agree to do so in other ways? Perhaps you expect me to feel an obligation and thus remove the question of importuning."

Is that what she thought had just happened out on the lane? He had not been thinking about repayment, or anything, much. Nor did he believe she had felt any obligation to respond as she had. And she had responded. Before she tried to bite him, of course.

"I have neither expectations nor delusions of enjoying your favors in that way or for those reasons, Miss Longworth." *My, how noble you are, Kyle lad. Such an elegant idiot, too.*

Those speculations kept having their way, however. The memory of that embrace remained fresh. He would probably indulge in a few dreams. Since he would pay dearly for them, he would not feel guilty.

"Perhaps instead you spoke of the brothel to make certain that I understood that tonight makes me fit for little else. I am all too aware of that. I know the high costs of what has occurred."

Yes, she probably did. Her poise had made him wonder, though. And the boy from the pits of Durham had resented her reclaimed composure even as he admired it. A woman ruined irredeemably should not be so cool. She should weep the way the women of his mining village wept over loss.

"Miss Longworth, your accounting will have nothing to do with me. Forgive me for teasing you so unkindly. My annoyance at my own costs got the better of me."

She angled forward, as if peering to see if he was sincere. The vague moonlight leaking into the middle of the carriage gave form to her features—her large eyes and full mouth and perfect face. Even this dim view of her beauty made his breath catch.

"You have been kind and gallant, Mr. Bradwell. If you want to scold and remind me of my compliance in my final fall, I suppose that I should show the grace to listen."

He did not scold. He did not speak much at all. She wished he would. Their brief conversation left her feeling less awkward. During the silences she could only sit there with her worry while his presence crowded her.

She could not really move farther away, either. A collection of large rolls of paper filled almost half the carriage. She wondered what they were.

An inner instinct remained alert for any movement from him. She knew she was at the mercy of this man's honor. He knew it, too, and that moment out on the lane had confused matters. There had been a second or two—no more, she was sure—when that embrace had been less than adversarial.

She put the memory of it out of her mind. She did not want to dwell on how quickly her stupidity lured her to misunderstand a man again. She did not want to remember how she had stirred more easily than a decent woman ought.

He had spoken of his own costs. She wondered what they would be. His name would be attached to the gossip about that dinner party and to her "purchase," but as a man it would not destroy his reputation. Among some people it might even make him more interesting.

Maybe he referred to the bid itself. It was a huge amount for anyone. Perhaps he did not actually have the money to make good on this odd debt.

If he did not pay up he would be destroyed in the circles that mattered. In most circles, she suspected. Even the ones around the pits of Durham.

That reference had been an interesting comment. She wondered what Norbury had meant by it. Mr. Bradwell's speech and manner did not mark him as that common.

"If you are not taking me to a brothel in London, where are we going?"

"I am taking you to your cousin. The county paper noted that she is in residence at her husband's property here in Kent."

This man continued to surprise her. Not only with this information, but also with his awareness of her cousin Alexia's movements.

"I had not realized that she had come down from town. I wish I had known. I might have escaped this morning and walked there."

"It is at least an hour by carriage. You could not have walked. Nor, I suspect, could you have escaped."

"Is she alone, do you know?"

"The paper mentioned the family coming down."

That probably meant that Irene was with her. She would at least see her sister before . . . Her eyes stung and she bit her lip so hard that she tasted blood. The thought of seeing Alexia and Irene undid her as nothing else had.

"I assume that Lord Hayden is with her." She heard her own voice break. Mr. Bradwell's form blurred. "I pray, let us not intrude."

"I can hardly keep you with me at an inn."

"I do not see why not. My reputation is already totally ruined."

"Mine is not."

"Of course. Yes, I see. I am sorry. I do not want to bring more scandal to you. It is just that Lord Hayden has already been too kind and I have been ungrateful in the past and now to show up at his door with this horrible, hopeless—"

A sob snuck out, strangling her words. Then another. She bit her lip again, hard. It did not help this time.

He took her hand in his and pressed a handkerchief into her palm. His firm, dry hold branded her skin and mind. Not hurtful like Norbury. Not weak or grasping, either. Just careful and strong, and a little rough. Like that embrace on the lane.

It felt like the touch of a friend. Her wariness left her then. She finally knew for certain that she was safe. Her composure left her, too. Her rescuer made no effort to console her. He understood that nothing would change what was going to happen.

Her composure had annoyed him. Now her weeping dismayed him. He resisted the impulse to gather her into her arms and offer comfort. He might frighten her. She still wondered about him. On the lane she had proven that he wanted her, which gave her good cause to suspect his motivations in making that bid.

She continued crying. He could not take it anymore. He shoved aside the plans and moved to the place beside her. He carefully embraced her, ready to move away fast if she wanted to be alone in her misery.

She didn't. She cried into his shoulder while he held her. He tried to ignore how aware he was of the feel of her fragile form in his arms. He bit back the false words of reassurance that wanted to spring from him. She would reject them outright, he guessed. He suspected that she would never again lie to herself about much of anything.

The carriage turned off the road. She realized that the journey was ending. She valiantly tried to swallow her tears.

He called to the coachman to slow down so she would have more time. And so he would, too.

Her composure returned before they reached the house. The embrace did not become awkward, however, and she made no attempt to break it. He held her until they rolled to a stop.

He climbed from the carriage and offered his hand.

She looked up at the house. The vertical forms of classical columns and long blocks on either side of the central temple facade could be seen.

"It is the middle of the night. The whole household will be abed," she said.

"There will be a servant by the door. Come now."

She placed her hand in his. He felt a subtle roughness that surprised him, but the touch was mostly soft and warm. She stepped down. One pause, one deep inhale, and she walked with him to the door. She left her hand in his like a frightened child.

A servant eventually responded to the knock.

"This is Miss Longworth, Lady Alexia's cousin," Kyle

explained. "Please ask Lord Hayden to receive us if he is in residence."

The servant ushered them to the library. Kyle took in the room's perfect proportions. His practiced eye noted that even the wooden Doric pilasters decorating the mahogany bookcases were true to the ancient system of measurements. Lord Hayden favored a pure classicism based on Greek rather than Roman models.

Miss Longworth refused to sit. She returned his frock coat, then paced the edges of the chamber, twisting his handkerchief in her hands.

"Will you stay while I explain, Mr. Bradwell? Please. Lord Hayden is a good man, but . . . I do not fear him, but after all the rest . . . he is not so stern as he appears, I think, but this story would strain the patience of a saint, and his love for my cousin may not spare me his worst reaction."

He had met Lord Hayden only once, and agreed the man appeared stern. However, he also knew what she meant by "all the rest," and how it indicated the man was not as hard as he looked. Or, as she suggested, Lord Hayden was so in love that he had put sternness aside in the case of his new wife's relatives.

Presumably "all the rest" would now include support of the relative in question today. Miss Longworth faced utter ruin, but Kyle assumed that Lord Hayden would make sure that she did not starve in her exile from family and decent society.

"I will remain until you have explained, if you wish."

Lord Hayden did not come down alone. His wife accompanied him. They arrived in dishabille, he in a dark blue brocade morning coat and she in a pale yellow undressing gown. A lace-edged cap covered most of her dark hair. Kyle had never met Lady Alexia but she appeared a kind woman of about Miss Longworth's age. Mid-twenties, he guessed. Right now her violet-gray eyes held noticeable worry for her cousin.

Lord Hayden appeared resigned, as if he expected nothing good if he was roused from his bed by a Longworth. His sharp gaze took in his visitors and did not miss the way Miss Longworth's attempted escape had soiled the skirt of her dress. His attention lingered on Kyle's face, no doubt assessing the scratches so obviously made by a woman.

The ladies embraced and Miss Longworth made introductions. Lord Hayden nodded a silent acknowledgment that the introductions had been unnecessary since he and Kyle had met before.

"Mr. Bradwell helped me to escape from a house party of Lord Norbury's," Miss Longworth announced.

Lord Hayden caught his wife's eye in a meaningful glance. It was the look of a man who knew about that love affair and had predicted the worst from the start.

"I fear," Miss Longworth added after an awkward pause, "I fear that something very scandalous happened at that house party that will be known to the world in a few days. Mr. Bradwell brought me here because there was nowhere else to go tonight, but come the morning I ask for transportation back to Oxfordshire."

"Exactly what happened?" Lord Hayden asked.

She told them. Bluntly. She spared herself not at all. She took full blame for her situation, which Kyle thought a bit hard. Her inclusion in a party of whores, her sale at the auction, her stupidity in misunderstanding Norbury's affection—it was all clear, specific, and honest. Ruthlessly so.

"So, I will return to Oxfordshire tomorrow," Miss Longworth concluded. "If I disappear completely and we cease any social connection, perhaps you will not be affected too much by the consequences of my behavior."

"Do not be so rash," Lady Alexia cried. "Surely it is not as bad as you say. Hayden, tell her she does not have to break with us completely. If we—"

"No, Alexia," Miss Longworth said. "I know how it

must be, and so do you. Do not force your husband to command it."

Lady Alexia looked close to tears. Miss Longworth held her poise. Kyle bowed to them both and eased away, to make his escape from this most private of family crises.

Miss Longworth looked in his eyes. "I am sorry that I did not trust you. I am very sorry for those scratches. Thank you for your kindness."

There was nothing to say in response, so he walked out of the library. He found Lord Hayden in his wake.

"Tell me, Bradwell— Was it as sordid as she says? Or is there some hope that perhaps . . ." He shrugged, unable to think of what "perhaps" might be.

"Do you really want the truth, Lord Hayden?"

The man hesitated. "Yes, I suppose that I do."

"He publicly declared her a common whore, and treated her like one, in front of a dozen men whom you see daily at your clubs. I am sincerely sorry for her, but this is one Longworth who your money and protection cannot save."

Lord Hayden's dark eyes flashed anger at the allusion, but his ire passed quickly. Weary acceptance took its place.

"You have my gratitude that you stepped forward to take care of her and give her protection, Bradwell. In a dining room full of gentlemen, only you acted liked one."

"Since I was the only man there who was *not* a gentleman, that should be the real scandal, don't you think?"

He walked out of the house and away from the sad notes being played inside it. The melody would turn into a dirge of mourning soon.

He strode through the cold night to the carriage. Miss Longworth's scent lingered on his frock coat, filling his head.